ZNB
PRESENTS
Year Two

Other Anthologies Edited by:

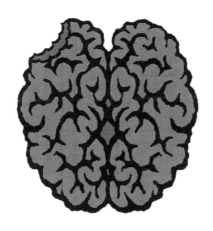

ZNB Presents
Year Two

Edited by

Joshua Palmatier

Zombies Need Brains LLC
www.zombiesneedbrains.com

COPYRIGHTS

Table of Contents

"Preserving Phylais"   1
by Daniel Roman

"The Tithonus Effect"   19
by Ty Lazar

"The *Blou Trein* Suborbirail"   37
by L.P. Melling

"I Heard the Bombs on Christmas Day"   53
by Nathan W. Toronto

"Phantom Sanction"   63
by Caias Ward

"As Big as the Ocean"   77
by Jonathan Robbins Leon

"The Silver Dame and the Box of Mystery"   85
by Marie Vibbert

"Ignore the Restless Dead"   99
by Rob Cornell

"Very Important to Us"   111
by Mike Jack Stoumbos

"Shadows Like Hunting Sharks"   127
by J.L. George

"The Key Turns Once, and Once Only"   145
by Brian Hugenbruch

"IfThenDo"   161
by Andrew Gudgel

"The Fallen"   175
by Alicia Cay

"Apart From That, Mrs. Lincoln..."   191
by Elektra Hammond

"Third Eye Peeled"   201
by Derrick Boden

"We Will All Remember Bread"   213
by Alma Alexander

"Palatable Potions"   223
by Melinda Brasher

"Nothing Happened Here"   237
by Louis Evans

"Scaling Up Business"   247
by Niall Spain

"Solstice"   267
by Brian Crenshaw

"Kremlin Necropolis"   281
by S.C. Butler

"Harrold of the Gods"   297
by Sam Robb

"Hungry Skins"   309
by Liam Hogan

"Sunset at the Western Front"   321
by Christine Lucas

About the Authors   335

About the Editor   340

About the Artists   341

Acknowledgments   343

SIGNATURE PAGE

Joshua Palmatier, editor: _____

Daniel Roman: _____

Ty Lazar: _____

L.P. Melling: _____

Nathan W. Toronto: _____

Caias Ward: _____

Jonathan Robbins Leon: _____

Marie Vibbert: _____

Rob Cornell: _____

Mike Jack Stoumbos: _____

J.L. George: _____

Brian Hugenbruch: _____

Andrew Gudgel: _____

Alicia Cay: _____

Elektra Hammond: _____

Derrick Boden: _____

Alma Alexander: _____

Melinda Brasher: _____

Louis Evans: _____

Niall Spain: _____

Brian Crenshaw: _____

S.C. Butler: _____

Sam Robb: _____

Liam Hogan: _____

Christine Lucas: _____

Kat D'Andrea, artist: _____

Ariel Guzman, artist: _____

Greg Uchrin, artist: _____

Justin Adams, cover artist: _____

c

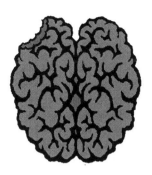

Preserving Phylais

Daniel Roman

From the moment the door hissed open, Elona knew there was a problem. No one would interrupt her while she was cloistered otherwise. Especially not at this hour.

"Acolyte, I'm sorry to disturb you…but we have a situation."

Her eyes slid open. The ethereal flicker of the glowlamps shimmered against the vines blanketing the shrine's altar. Leaves draped the squat metal table; their tendrils, a web of foliage which covered the rear wall. A hand-sized piece of gray steel sat nestled amongst the creepers. A reminder of where they came from…and where they were headed.

Uncrossing her legs, Elona rose and faced Security Chief Weylan. The glowlamp reflected off the hard contours of the woman's white exosuit, deepened the frown lines on her austere face.

"There's a Preserver at the gate," she said without preamble.

Elona swallowed past the lump in her throat and gave a small nod. It could have been little else. "Let us not keep them waiting."

Weylan led her through the steel hallways of the biocube and out onto the grounds of the compound. The triple moons were at zenith, bathing the square buildings within Menon Center in a pale light which gleamed off their reflective surfaces. This late, the only colonists about were the odd person checking on a generator or walking home from the bar cube. The night was damp, pregnant with moisture from that afternoon's rain. Elona breathed it in deeply, savoring the privilege of breathable air as

Chief Weylan keyed in the code for the compound's two-story gate. Unlike the doors in the biocubes, there was no hiss of compressed air as the gate swung open, only a soft mechanical whir.

Beyond, the Preserver awaited.

Vines thick around as a person's leg covered the dirt pathway, their broad, serrated leaves so numerous that the well-maintained road appeared completely overgrown. The leaves fluttered at the gate's movement. Directly in front of the entrance, a huge vine reared up before them. At its end was a single leaf, three times the width of a human's skull and twice as tall. It was serrated like the others, but unlike those smaller appendages, the leaf of the primary stem had two slashes of red, fibrous growth cutting diagonally across its face in a symmetrical pattern.

The large leaf rippled its edges. Elona stepped forward and dipped her head.

"Hello, Green One. Why have you come to us tonight?" She said the words; projected the thoughts.

The tip of the Preserver's leaf dipped forward until its point was directly in front of her face. Its edges flared and rolled inward, cupping the air.

Elona nodded, and took another step closer.

The Preserver's primary stem stretched out to meet her. She closed her eyes as the leaf pressed against her face, folding around the back of her head. Tiny hairs tickled her skin, eliciting calm to counteract the thrum of blood rushing through her veins. The membranous red parts of the leaf were hot against her eyelids.

A tingling sensation spread through her head as she inhaled the spores. The darkness behind her eyes brightened, becoming colors which gradually coalesced into shapes her mind could interpret.

...*A large biocube spanning a crack in the ground. Its thick glass, shimmering in the dry season sun. Vents protrude along its height, from its roof...*

...*The majesty of the sky, bright blue and filled with clouds. Slowly, the blue changes to ominous red. The clouds evaporate. The sky wheels, turning, until she looks down on the compound from above. Except it is...larger. Much larger. The plants around it are black and withered...*

...*The biocube explodes. As the flickers of its flames die out, the sky returns to blue and the plants grow hale...*

Elona gasped, her eyes snapping open as the Preserver's leaf unfolded, releasing her. Her chest rose and fell in ragged breaths. The leaf fluttered before her, waiting.

"Is there no other way?"

The leaf jerked once, sharply.

She was a long moment in answering. "I understand. This is a large sacrifice you ask of us…but if it is what's best for Phylais, we will see it done."

The Preserver's primary stem rolled toward her, undulating like a wave against the sand, and withdrew. The vines which covered the road slithered away from the compound, back toward the jungle where their roots dwelt.

"What did it say?" Chief Weylan asked.

Elona watched the receding tangle of the Preserver, debating if there was any way to soften the blow.

"We must shut down the geothermal reactor build."

Weylan sucked in a breath. "That's going to be a problem."

"I know."

"There has to be some compromise. Some way we can appease them, or repurpose whatever parts of it they find threatening. We've had people working on that project for a *decade*. Miko Pas…God, he's going to take it badly."

Elona shook her head. "They were quite clear. The reactor must be shut down, or they will destroy it. Left unchecked, it will eventually cause permanent damage to the planet's atmosphere. The Preservers will not risk that. Should our engineers come up with a way to retrofit it differently, perhaps I can present that idea to them. But in the meantime, construction must be halted."

She gave the security chief a rueful smile. "Foreman Pas will simply have to accept the Preservers' will…as we all do."

* * *

"Fucking plant-ass sons of bitches! Who do they think they are, to tell us how to live?"

Miko threw back his shot of tequila, grimacing as the liquor burned its way down his throat. The bar biocube buzzed with conversation, everyone at every table discussing the bad news the security chief had relayed that afternoon.

"I can't believe they're shutting down the reactor," Jantor agreed, once he'd downed his own drink. "The colony has been working on that project for so long."

Miko's eye twitched. "I wrote that blueprint fourteen years ago. The job should have taken a couple years, tops. But *nooo*. Because of all the limitations the plants keep putting on us, it's taken five times longer than projected. I've had to redesign more times than I can count…and for what? So the fucking plants can pull the plug at their whim? That shit is my life's work!" He pounded a fist against the table, sending stone mugs rattling.

"Could you imagine something like this happening on Old Earth?" Kafe asked as she settled back into her seat, distributing another round of drinks. "We would never have reached the stars."

"Damn right!" Jantor crowed.

"I have nightmares about the plants sometimes, you know. The creepy way they slither around. It's just not right." She shivered. "The thing I don't understand though, is why they chose now to shut the reactor down. Why let us waste all the time and resources?"

A frustrated sigh burst from Miko's lips. He threw back his head, shaking it slowly from side to side. "They're fucking with us," he said to the ceiling. "Want to make sure we know our place on this planet—always under them, right in range of getting teabagged by their leafy nads."

Jantor frowned. "Do plants...have nads?"

"Do I look like a plant-fucking acolyte to you?" Miko snapped. "It's an expression, and the point of it is that so long as the plants call the shots, we'll always be second class citizens on Phylais. I don't know about you, but I don't think my parents traveled eleven hundred years in stasis so that we could have our lives dictated to us in the new world by goddamn shrubs."

When the *Artania* crashed on Phylais—the only planet it had ever encountered with an actual livable atmosphere—the surviving colonists must have thought they'd discovered a new Garden of Eden. A place for humanity to start over. *If they could see us now*, Miko thought.

The next shot of tequila burned less, and the one he snatched out of Jantor's hand, even less than that. Miko rose on wobbly legs, fueled by alcohol and rage.

"They want to keep us in the *fucking Stone Age*," he bellowed. "They're afraid we might grow stronger than them and make Phylais ours...the way it's supposed to be!"

It wasn't until he heard his own voice echo back at him that he realized how quiet the room had gotten. The music was still playing, throbbing beats of bass and electronic arpeggios...but it was only a drone in the background. No other conversations. Jantor looked like he'd swallowed a fish. Kafe was studiously examining the table.

"*Or* the Preservers are simply doing their best to keep this world healthy and habitable."

Miko turned around. A woman stood behind him, short enough that she barely came up to his chest. Her dark skin and eyes were accentuated by the voluminous purple folds of the robe that covered her from neck to ankles. The hood was back, letting her mane of brown curls tumble down around her shoulders. The look in her eyes was hard...but also tinged by a glint of pity that made Miko's hands bunch into fists at his sides.

"Acolyte Elona. Wouldn't exshpect to see you in a place like thish." God, was he *slurring?* Those shots were hitting him like a ton of bricks.

"Foreman Pas," the acolyte said in her cool, unemotional voice. "I suggest you take a walk and get some air. It might help you see things more clearly."

Maybe it was the tequila making him bold, but in that moment he didn't give a fuck what kind of trouble he'd get himself into by picking a fight with the acolyte. He'd just found out he wasted a decade of his life. What else could she do to him?

"And I suggest *you* shtop bending over and doing whatever the plants tell you. How can we live like this?"

Her face hardened. There was a scrape of chairs moving—Chief Weylan was standing behind Elona now. When had she come into the cube?

"I think you've had enough, Miko." The security chief's tone made it clear it wasn't a suggestion.

Anger boiled in his chest. Why even bother? Everyone had already made up their minds to do whatever the plants wanted. They were content to be slaves to creatures that would have been lucky to be in their gardens back on Old Earth. Yet *he* was the one in the wrong.

Fine. Fuck 'em. If no one was going to do anything about it…he would do it himself.

Miko snorted, plucked one last shot off the table, and downed it in their faces. Then he shoved past Weylan and made for the door.

* * *

After how tense things had been at the colony the past week, Elona was grateful for an excuse to spend a day in the jungle. Demeter was the farthest-flung outpost on Phylais, deep in the wilderness to the west of Menon Center. It was dedicated primarily to wildlife research. So many species of animals, insects, and creatures that were some previously unimaginable melding of genes called the planet home that being stationed there was a biologist's dream. Many chose to spend long stretches at the outpost, watching the six-legged Zats forage through the undergrowth with their tuberous noses or documenting Scrambler migrations in the trees above.

Elona liked to think that, had she not taken the path of the acolyte, she might have been one of those biologists, losing herself in the bottomless well of ecological research that Phylais offered. But such was not her fate. She'd been identified by the aptitude tests at a young age for mental resilience—the most important trait one needed to interpret the messages of the Preservers accurately. Few individuals were strong enough to undergo the intensive training and meditations needed to be an acolyte. Currently, she was one of six on the planet, and the only one stationed at the central colony.

Normally, one of the others would have gone to Demeter to interpret for the researchers there, but given the stress she'd been under since the reactor announcement, Elona figured she could allow herself this small respite. After all, she *was* still working.

The platform where she stood beside Chief Weylan provided a clear view of the new observation tower that was being erected beside Demeter's walls. The construction crew buzzed about the metal frame, securing rivets and checking wiring. Three workers operated large suits with grasping claws, doing the majority of the heavy lifting. The tower was as tall as the understory, topped by a lookout equipped with windows that retracted into the walls for open-air observation. Its steepled roof was designed to defend against Phylais' persistent precipitation.

Yet the true marvel of the tower-raising wasn't the human construction effort, but the three Preservers which aided it. Vines wrapped around the four legs of the tower, steadying them as the Preservers pressed their might against the underside of the building. It leaned precariously to one side, and the vines wrapped tighter, preventing it from tipping over.

One of the mechs moved to help, grasping claws at the ready. Abruptly, the closest Preserver turned, its primary stem shooting toward the mech. The large leaf at its end fluttered, the red slashes catching sunlight as they rippled back and forth.

"Tell that mech to wait," Elona said. Security Chief Weylan tapped a button on her hand console and relayed the orders. The mech halted.

The Preserver's leaf withdrew, wrapping back around the support. It strained alongside its companions, pushing, pushing…

A resounding *thud* vibrated deep in Elona's stomach as the building's supports settled into the pilot holes which had been drilled in the planet's crust.

As the mechs moved to screw the supports into their housings, the Preservers set about reinforcing the structure. Vines tightened around the legs of the tower. At the base, yet more vines swept outward and anchored themselves amidst the thickest parts of the undergrowth. Anything secured to the tower would be detached from the primary stem, eventually becoming part of a new Preserver bound to the human outpost, learning from them as they learned from it.

A cheer went up from the construction crew as the mechs finished the last of their work and the red-slashed faces of the Preservers withdrew from the tower. It stood stable, a pillar of steel encased in lush greenery that shone in the afternoon sunlight.

This is what this world could look like if we live in harmony with the Preservers, Elona thought. *Who knows what marvels would be created with both species working together?*

After how hard things had been of late, it was nice to get a reminder of why it was all worth it. She nodded to Weylan, saw her optimism mirrored in the other woman's rare smile.

No sooner had they shared the moment than footsteps crunched on the soil behind them.

"Chief Weylan, comm message from Menon Center."

They turned as one. Demeter Outpost's communications officer stood below their platform, alarm written clearly on his face.

"What is it, Sam?" asked Weylan.

"One of the dropships took off without permission, ma'am. All attempts to hail it have gone unanswered." He swallowed nervously. "It's heading toward the Vats."

Elona's breath caught in her throat.

"*What?*" Weylan growled. "Who's flying it?"

"We don't know, ma'am. I've still got Veyni on the comm if you want to talk to her directly."

"Yes, I'll speak to her immediately." Weylan marched off the platform, heading for the biocube at the center of the outpost with a satellite dish on its roof.

Elona remained, frozen by indecision. Why would a dropship be headed toward the Vats? She could only guess...and none of her guesses were anything good. But if she alerted the Preservers, she might be putting other humans in danger. The guardians of Phylais were fiercely territorial when provoked.

She glanced back to where Preserver and human circled the newly-constructed tower. A symbol of their joint efforts to build something better than Old Earth. Something built on mutual trust.

"Green Ones," she shouted, "I need to speak with you."

* * *

The engines roared as the dropship shot over the jungle. The craft was designed for carrying small teams of scientists on short-range missions. It had no weapons, no real armor. Its sleek frame contained fuel for a four hundred kilometer round trip and barely enough room for eight people to cram inside.

Today, it carried only three...and a pair of half-kiloton fission mining charges.

Miko grimaced at the endless expanse of green below. For days he'd been dealing with a perpetual hangover—though not from booze. He'd been sober since he'd had that run-in with Acolyte Elona. No, this hangover was from dread and fury and the inescapable feeling that he was committing his life to one last gesture of fiery resistance. Because he sure as fuck wasn't going to get the freedom he longed for anyway.

Whatever happened after, well…he'd worry about it if he was still alive.

Kafe was behind the controls of the dropship, one hand on the orb of the steering holo and the other punching glowing buttons along the panel above her head. Jantor was checking over the mining charges, making sure they were rigged for maximum dramatic effect.

Miko hadn't been sure that either of them would come with him, had explained what it would mean. "Fuck it," Kafe had said. "We're just as fed up as you, boss. We put years into that reactor project, too. What's the point of anything we're doing here, if it can just be wiped away at the whim of the plants?"

He could have kissed her. Instead, he'd nodded and they'd started making their plan.

When a vastly connected network of plants ruled a planet, there weren't many things you could do to actually hurt them. As much as Miko hated to admit it, the acolytes did have one thing right: Phylais couldn't exist without the shrubs. They'd dug themselves into the planet's ecosystem too deeply, made the entire damn thing dependent on the oxygen they created. Miko wasn't fooling himself; he knew there was nothing he could do to actually get rid of them. But he could sure as shit make a statement.

The dropship zipped around the side of a mountain, revealing a broad stretch of land split by a river. The Vats. One of a handful of places on Phylais with the perfect habitat for young Preservers to grow, due to the river, the mountains regulating the rain, and the malleable soil. One of the few places where they could do some real damage and the plants would get the fucking message.

"Jantor, how are those charges looking?"

"All good, boss! I tweaked the detonators to be extra sensitive." The muscled worker grinned. "The fall should more than do the trick."

"Good…good." Miko took a few breaths, his eyes going out of focus as he gazed down at the field of small plants that spread to either side of the wetlands. He blinked hard to snap himself out of it. "Take us in, Kafe."

Her hand hesitated over the steering globe. She turned toward him. "Last chance to back out, boss. You sure about this?"

"Last chance to back out was two hours ago," he sneered.

Kafe hesitated a moment longer. Then she nodded, turned back around, and ran a hand over the steering holo.

The dropship cut hard to the left, forcing Miko to grab one of the overhead bars to keep from stumbling. Jantor howled with excitement, slapping the open doorway of the transport. As the ship tilted, the ground loomed up beyond the doorway. Delicate plants lined the river bank, green creepers with leaves that rippled in the wind.

Miko let go of the bar. "*Now!*"

Jantor was at his side, each of them with a shoulder to the mining charge. It was like pushing a boulder, the large circular metal casing hard and immovable. Miko gritted his teeth, straining…

The charge ground forward. Over the edge and out of sight.

"It's away," he screamed as he grabbed the bar again, Jantor following suit on the other side of the doorway. Kafe rolled her hand upward over the holo. The dropship climbed back toward the sky.

There was a flash and, a second later, a boom so deep that it rattled the entire ship, burrowing into Miko's guts like a jackhammer. The ship jolted.

"Hang on!" Kafe's voice was hardly audible over the roar. Miko clamped his teeth shut, closed his eyes.

Gradually, the roar receded.

He cautiously opened his eyes and looked out the door. A large swath of the river and vegetation below had become a smoking crater, fire spreading along the shore.

"Take that, you fucking plants!" he shouted, laughing. Jantor joined in, pumping his fist in the air. They still had one mining charge left, but the fact that they had gotten the one out without dying felt like an accomplishment. Like the first step, one that proved that just maybe, they actually *could* be the masters of this world and leave it a better place for their children. Miko sidled over to slap Kafe on the shoulder and congratulate her on her excellent flying. She was already dipping the ship into its next descent, a huge grin plastered on her face.

"We did it, Miko," she said. "We—"

An enormous vine rose in front of the ship, cutting across the viewport. Kafe screamed as it slapped against the glass. It was joined by a second, then a third. The ship went into a nosedive, pitching forward and to the side. Alarms flared to life along the consoles as more vines reached up from the jungle and snared them.

Get us stable, Miko tried to shout. But the ship was careening out of control and that meant he was, too. He caught hold of one of the seats only to have it torn from his grasp. Kafe scrambled about the cockpit, hands flying over controls as she tried to get them free. Jantor strained to hold on to the overhead bar with one hand and the mining charge with the other, to keep it from slamming into a different part of the ship and setting off its rigged trigger. His eyes turned, meeting Miko's, and the fear in them was undeniable. Jantor *never* looked afraid; he was a goddamn adrenaline junky.

Then the sight was ripped away as the ship jerked and Miko slid out the doorway.

He screamed as air whipped around him, sent his body spinning as he fell. The trees were much closer than he'd have thought; the plants had nearly dragged the dropship to the jungle. He scrabbled at the chestplate of his exosuit, trying to fire his emergency booster.

A burst of sulfur flooded his nostrils, heat at his back. His descent slowed, but not anywhere near enough.

When he hit the ground, all he heard was the crack of something breaking inside him. Miko choked on his scream as he flipped head over heels through the dirt, leaves slapping at his face.

At some point, he stopped rolling. Water lapped at his legs. He coughed, raising himself painfully on one shaky arm…just in time to see the dropship crash through the canopy. No, not crash—get *pulled* through it. The ship was covered in vines, a piece of metal and technology being reclaimed by a jungle that had never owned it in the first place. There was a loud crunch and the tiny, distant sound of screams as the ship vanished beneath the tree line.

And then a *BOOM.*

A wave of heat and debris exploded upward, vines and trees flying through the air on a plume of fire. The screeching of birds and shriek of animals. The force of the second mining charge swept the tiny plantlings around Miko to the ground, shoved against his battered face so hard that he flipped backward. The last thing he smelled was burning flesh and hair.

Then the river swallowed him, and there was only cool darkness.

* * *

Though Elona often found the darkness of the shrine comforting, tonight it was suffocating. Sweat beaded the small of her back as she sat before the altar. The shard of the *Artania*'s hull gleamed upon its bed of carefully tended vines. Her burden. All of it, her burden.

Security Chief Weylan's words echoed in her head as she sought desperately for stillness.

We found him. Fifteen broken bones, severe burns on his face…but he's alive. What are we going to do with him?

Elona sat until her knees ached, until her watch beeped to announce the triple moons were at zenith…and still, she was no closer to an answer. The Preservers had destroyed the dropship, had killed two people and critically injured a third. But what those people had done to the Vats…how many thousands of Preserver seedlings were killed? How many fully grown ones, when the dropship exploded?

Elona couldn't deny her own part in what had happened. The deaths of the Preservers lay at the feet of Miko and his companions, but the death of those crew members, the maiming of the foreman…those lay at hers. She'd alerted the Preservers to the threat. If she hadn't, the dropship might well have escaped. But what else was she supposed to do? It was her duty to be the bridge between human and Preserver. How could she have known the toll it would take? That she would trade the lives of one species for another?

Except she hadn't done that, had she? Both had died. The only survivor was Miko…and there was little doubt that his actions were going to bring the wrath of the Preservers down on the humans of Phylais. If she had only shown more compassion that night in the bar instead of shaming him, perhaps this all could have been avoided.

Elona squeezed her eyes shut. *Goddess…please help me find a way to keep the peace between these two peoples. Help me keep our colony safe.*

She didn't know if anyone heard her…but the act of praying helped. When she'd been training as a young acolyte, Elona had studied the religions of Old Earth. Of all of them, Wicca spoke the most to her, made the most sense given her task of connecting humans and the plant lifeforms of Phylais. Its creed, the Rede—*if it harm none, do as ye will*—was a perfect fit for the kind of dynamic that needed to be fostered between Preserver and human. She'd come to understand over the years that it was also how the Preservers operated. They fostered other life on Phylais, welcomed it to strengthen their planet's biodiversity, and only imposed restrictions if it became a danger to others.

After today's events, how could they not view humans as a danger? Wouldn't she, if she were them?

But not *all* humans were a threat. There had to be a way to convince them of that. To convey that these were the actions of a few misguided individuals and not indicative of an entire species. She had studied enough records to know how such a crime would have been handled on Old Earth—the guilty punished, the wronged given recourse. At least in theory.

Yet on Phylais, with the Preservers…would they accept such justice? And could she truly find it in herself to condemn yet another life? When she'd warned the Preservers, she hadn't known what would happen…but if she gave them Miko Pas, it would be for only one reason. She would be breaking the Rede again, this time knowingly.

Would it be enough to keep the peace? And even if it did, would she be able to live with herself afterward?

Elona sat with those questions for a long time, until finally, she sighed and rose. She wouldn't find the answers in this room…but she had a feeling where she would.

* * *

Miko woke to the sound of a door hissing open. He was lying in the medbay, his wrists strapped to the bed and an IV of some clear liquid hooked to his arm. The monitors beeped next to him, lines drifting across to show he was still alive. If it weren't for them, he might not have believed it.

Acolyte Elona drifted through the doorway in her deep purple robes. She turned to the guard standing beside it.

"Give us a few minutes of privacy, please," she said. The guard hesitated. "He is strapped to the bed and in critical condition. There is no danger."

With a grudging nod, the man shouldered his pulse rifle and left. The doctor—Ramirez—set down his datapad and followed. "I'll be right outside if you need me," he said on the way out.

Then Miko was alone with the acolyte. Her piercing brown stare bored into him as she walked over to his bedside and sat on the stool there to bring them closer to eye level.

"How are you feeling, Mister Pas?"

Miko's eye twitched. "Like absolute shit."

The ghost of a smile crossed the acolyte's lips. "I can imagine. You're lucky to be alive."

Lucky. He sure didn't feel that way. "Jantor and Kafe aren't."

"No. No they are not." The smiled faded, replaced by a look hard as carbon steel. "What were you *thinking*, going out there and bombing the Vats? You put the entire colony at risk."

There was that familiar flare of anger at being talked down to...but it hardly had a chance to be kindled before it was sputtering out. Miko was too damn exhausted. Haunted, by Jantor's booming laugh and Kafe's wry smile.

"I'm...sorry. I never meant..." His voice trailed off lamely. What could he even say?

"Never meant to destroy thousands of young Preservers? Never meant to put yourself and your friends in harm's way and try to start a war?" The acolyte shook her head. "It's too late for that."

Miko's sigh devolved into a wet cough. It felt like having his lungs raked by claws. "What's going to happen to me?"

"I don't know, Mister Pas. I have no idea what lies in store for any of us when the Preservers come—and they *will* come. Menon Center could be gone by this time tomorrow."

He swallowed. "They...can't hold the whole colony accountable. I was the one who did it, me and Jantor and Kafe." Mentioning them caused his throat to close up, but he forced the words out anyway. "There must be some other way."

The acolyte stared at him for a long moment. "I've thought long and hard about that...and there might be."

Something in her voice made a chill run down Miko's spine, but it was forgotten as another coughing fit overtook him. "Whatever it is, please do it," he gasped. "Promise me, acolyte. I never meant to endanger everyone, I was just...so damn *angry*. My parents went to space aboard the *Artania* because they wanted to start a new life somewhere. To give their children a chance to live on a planet that wasn't doomed by the choices of their grandparents' grandparents. Instead, we ended up here, and the plants dictate everything we can or can't do. I just wanted to live the life they wanted for me. Free."

Elona leaned close. "Did it ever occur to you that perhaps this *is* the life they wanted for you? That the dream you speak of is exactly what we have on Phylais—a planet where the fauna controls the world's well-being? Imagine how differently Old Earth might have turned out if the plants had been able to tell us what they needed in order to keep the ecosystem stable. What if the path to that new, unbridled life is simply *learning to listen* for a change, instead of doing whatever we wish simply because we can?"

They were silent for a long moment, the foreman and the acolyte, staring at one another.

"I...hadn't thought about it that way."

Slowly, Elona stood. "I know, Mister Pas." She hesitated...before laying a soothing hand on his shoulder. "I promise you. I will do everything I can to protect the colony."

"Thank you, acolyte," he murmured, the salt taste of tears on his lips. "Thank you."

* * *

The Preservers came at dawn.

Thousands of vines crawled out of the jungle, slithering across the road and surrounding the compound. It was impossible to tell how many primary stems there were among the mass of foliage which cut Menon Center off from the rest of Phylais...but Elona counted at least a hundred. It was the first time in the history of the colony that more than ten Preservers had come to them at once.

The message was clear. There was a problem. One way or another, it would be solved.

Four humans went out to parley with the rulers of Phylais: Security Chief Weylan, Elona, Miko Pas, and Doctor Ramirez. No one asked what the plan was or presumed to speak first. This was Elona's responsibility and everyone knew it.

The humans stopped just outside the gate, in the small patch of unclaimed land before the vines. Elona turned to the others. Miko was being half-carried by the security chief, one leg dragging uselessly behind him.

"On his knees."

Weylan dropped Miko as if she couldn't wait to be rid of him. The foreman groaned piteously as he collapsed to the dirt.

Doctor Ramirez's jaw tightened. "He shouldn't even be out of bed in his state. There's no need to be cruel."

Elona rounded on him, surprised by the fury in her own voice. "What *he* did was cruel. This is necessary."

A vein stood out along the doctor's cheek, but he said nothing else. The Preservers were watching. Bickering would only weaken their position. Thankfully the man had the good sense to realize it.

Elona took a deep breath, squared her shoulders, and walked ahead of the group. Five massive leaves fluttered up from the primary stems, like five cobras rearing upright and flaring their hoods. Each bore the telltale red slashes of a Preserver's communication appendage. They rippled, the edges of the leaves twitching and their pointed tips jutting forward. Even without inhaling the spores that would allow for a direct message to pass into her brain, the anger and accusation were apparent.

She made no attempt to hide the emotion from her voice—it was necessary to help the Preservers understand her better. "Green Ones...I am glad you have given us the chance to speak. First, I must apologize on behalf of my people for the horrible tragedy that occurred yesterday. The attack on the Vats...it was wrong, something that we deeply condemn."

The leaf of the largest Preserver flicked its tip away from her, then shot forward, stopping so close to her face they nearly touched. She did not flinch.

"This atrocity was committed by a small group of unstable humans," she continued, speaking directly to the leaf. "A group...sick-in-the-stem, as you say. They acted on their own, against the wishes of the colony. We ask your forgiveness for their actions and your mercy for those who had no part in it."

All around them, the vines rustled, inching forward. Yet the large leaf before her stayed perfectly, eerily still. Though she knew the red patches were not eyes, in that moment, it was hard not to feel like they were watching her. Weighing whether her answer was satisfactory.

Or perhaps waiting for what she had to say next; what she dreaded to say. Perhaps the Preserver could sense her conflict. Once the words left her mouth, she wouldn't be able to take them back.

"On our home world, we believed in holding the people accountable who committed the crime. Sixty-three years ago, when our ship crashed here, you welcomed us onto Phylais. Encouraged us to become a part of this world, to share it with you and strengthen both our peoples. We have done everything you asked of us. Now I'm asking *you*—do not blame our entire colony for the actions of the few, not when we have worked so hard to find a place of mutual benefit with each other."

She took the breath. Made the choice.

"We ask that you hold to our method of resolution now. If retribution must be taken, then we ask that it only be meted out to the one responsible for the crime." She swept a hand toward Miko, kneeling in the dirt, his dark eyes glittering in his burnt face. "This man is the only one of those who attacked you that survived. The one who caused the carnage."

Elona stared into the leaf, cold spreading through her chest.

"We offer him to you."

* * *

Miko knew he should have been outraged. The acolyte was giving him to the plants like a dog to be put down. He should have been snapping and biting and resisting. Cursing and screaming. It was what he would have done only a few days ago.

But maybe…it was better this way. What he deserved. Everything the acolyte said to the Preserver was true—he *had* caused all this pain, had gotten his friends killed. When he'd seen the jungle come alive and surround the compound that morning, he'd been filled with horror. Not for himself, but for everyone else that his actions had damned.

If the acolyte thought this would keep the colony from being destroyed, all the people who lived there from being killed, well…to Miko's mind that was a trade he'd make any day.

He pushed himself up higher on his knees, gritting his teeth at the throbbing in his hip and leg. And arm. And every other inch of his battered body. The skin on his face felt tight when he winced, hot from all the burns. He was a ruin anyway. Might as well be a ruin with a purpose.

The huge leaf in front of the acolyte turned toward him. There was a gasp somewhere behind, from the doctor maybe, but Miko felt oddly calm as the leg-thick stem slithered over to him so that the leaf was hanging just above his face. Looking down on him.

"Yeah, it was me," he said. "So if we're gonna do this, let's get on with it."

The leaf swayed in the breeze…then shot forward and slapped into his face, covering his mouth and nose. He gasped as it wrapped around the back of his head. There was something warm against his skin, tiny hairs tickling as it compressed his skull. An odd tingling sensation exploded through his sinuses, his throat.

He shivered violently…he…

…sways in the wind of the life-sphere, delighting as its cool tendrils trace his leaves and stems. He is one of the first growths, and the gentle nature of that wind is a prize hard won…

…Webbed feet, rising out of the water to touch dry soil. A head with beady eyes follows, covered in a slick coating of slime to keep it moist beyond the waves. For the first time, there are others…

...A jungle, filled with life. The six-stemmed-ones root through the undergrowth, their trunks plucking out morsels. The flitterers help the growth expand, strengthening the network. And in turn, they are sustained and strengthened as well...

...A fiery ball, streaking across the sky. A loud crash as it strikes hard ground. Many die, growth and mover alike. Yet others emerge from the hard gray shell of the fallen star-that-is-not-a-star. They wear strange white shells and make a vast array of complex sounds. They begin changing the jungle to their needs, building. Sometimes in ways that hinder the growth. Dangerous. Unless a connection can be made...

...A tower rises in the jungle, pushed by human and growth alike. Strengthened by the efforts of both...

...A blast of heat and flame. The pain of a thousand seedlings lances through the network of root and consciousness. Growth does not emit sound, but the not-sound is a scream that shakes every corner of the life-sphere...

...Another burst of fire. This time, there is a human among it, a human with a burned face and malice in its shroud. More dwellings, cutting down the growth. The growth floods over them in turn, swallowing them, returning life to the way it was before the humans. Repairing the damage will be the work of generations...

The shiver finished at the base of Miko's spine as the Preserver released its hold on his face. He collapsed onto his hands and vomited in the dirt, his mind torn in a thousand different directions. He took a deep breath and was surprised when it was only air and he could actually taste it. Doctor Ramirez was at his side, but Miko couldn't hear his words.

When he was able to look up again, the leaf was withdrawing. Another was detaching from the acolyte's face. She swayed slightly, eyes closed. "I understand," she murmured.

Slowly, the vines receded back into the jungle. The large communication leaves fluttered, their red streaks making them look like enormous butterflies as they blended back into the dense foliage.

Miko was still grappling for understanding when Elona came and stood over him.

"They let me live," he gasped.

"They did. And they...showed you things?"

He nodded. "Humans arriving on Phylais, I think? I...felt what the Preservers did when the mining charges detonated on the Vats." He shivered. "And I think they showed me what they would do if it happened again."

The acolyte's smile was grim. "They showed that to me as well, among other things." She paused. "We will never conquer this world the way we conquered Earth. If we are to remain on this planet, the only choice is to learn to live in a place where we will never be the dominant species. And perhaps that's not such a bad thing. Just look at what happened to Old Earth, because humans dictated everything."

The gentle voice of the jungle filled the silence between them. The call of its creatures, the quiet rustle of its plants, was her answer.

"So that's it then?" Miko asked. "They just…leave, and we go back to normal?"

"The colony is safe for now, as are you Mister Pas," said the acolyte. "Fortunately, the Preservers view life in a different way than we do. There is no justice, only survival. They will cull a sick being from their network… but only if there is no chance for it to heal. Which means they must have sensed something in you, that you could grow past this." She leaned close, her voice going strangely flat. "But make no mistake, *I* am the Preserver of this colony. If you put it in danger again…"

For a long moment they held each other's eyes. Finally, Miko shook his head and chuckled, then winced at the pain it caused. "I…understand. I don't think I could explain everything I just saw…but I know a second chance when I see one." He thought of Jantor and Kafe, his friends who would never get such a chance. "I won't waste it."

Elona smiled, obvious relief melting her stern expression. She straightened and sighed, her gaze drifting out to the jungle.

"I'm glad to hear it, Mister Pas. There's much work ahead if we're going to make a home for our people on Phylais. We'll need everyone working together to make it happen." She offered her hand. "That includes you."

Illustration by Greg Uchrin

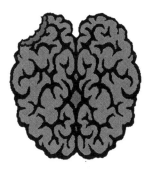

The Tithonus Effect

Ty Lazar

Articells, Year 40

My first time cheating on Leona was, like all nights, just another night.

I took a deep breath and shifted uselessly in my chair as the meeting hit the three-hour mark. For Jaladhi it might as well have been three minutes. She paced spryly at the head of the table, twirling a stylus around her thumb as she tore into my client's financials. She was young. Half my age, maybe less. Of course, these days you could never be sure. Her associate, a man of about bio-fifty, sat across from me wearing his best stern-lawyer face, his head clearly checked out. I looked around the room—he wasn't alone. At this rate Jaladhi would single-handedly win the takeover through force of will.

Four hours. Finally, battle-weary suits started making their exits, and soon it was down to the two of us: Jaladhi, leaning against the wall in her close-fitting skirt that revealed shapely hips, and me, hoping for something I shouldn't.

"We'll pick this up tomorrow," I said when the hypercaf started wearing off. I swiped the screenTat printed on my wrist; documents vanished from the table.

Jaladhi, who needed no hypercaf, flicked her stylus across her palm, clearing the remaining detritus. "If you like," she said, with more than a hint of cheek.

I opened the door, smiling a gracious smile that bordered on farce. "We'll be in touch."

She didn't say anything, but didn't leave either. Just flashed me the look—the same impish smile underlying predatory eyes that she'd been flashing me throughout the meeting. I didn't look away; I'd already resigned myself to the rest.

As we went down on the table, Jaladhi had to kick the door shut, since I didn't bother closing it.

* * *

It was during our fifth hook-up, the diffuse afternoon light lending the bedroom a sense of mismatched time and place, that I had to ask.

"Why me?"

She slid out of my arms and turned to look at me inquisitively.

"If you're trying to play me," I said, "I'm happy to keep playing. But that's all you'll get."

Her eyes and mouth opened wide and she touched her chest theatrically. "Oh, so I'm not good enough to win on merit? My only hope is to sleep with opposing counsel?"

I kept my face impassive. "Seriously. Why me? I'm sure you've got plenty of good-looking hot shots your own age to screw around with."

"How do you know how old I am? I could be your age."

"When you get to be my age, you'll know how I know. Besides, I've had Articells for a long time. I'm older than you probably realize."

"Maybe *I'm* older than *you* realize. Maybe I'm a rich old lady who offed herself for a hot young body."

"Maybe RenewaLife should be more selective about their customers."

"What a pity that would be for you."

I gave her the stop-being-a-brat look.

"You want to know why you?" She nuzzled up to me and kissed me for a good half-minute. "Because unlike all those good-looking, age-appropriate hot shots, you don't get attached."

Before I could say anything, she flung the covers over our heads and we went for another round.

* * *

For the most part I ran automatically. It was easier, and usually got me to where I would have ended up anyway. The night it all came crashing down was no exception. It started in a ritzy lounge near my office that reeked corporate, the same lounge I'd been wandering into after work for the better part of a decade. The same drink I always ordered sat neglected as Jaladhi and I stared at our screenTats and exchanged intermittent words, buried in the case. At one point my hand slipped under the table and began stroking her knee, mounting the pressure and contact as it migrated under her thigh. I peeked up from my screenTat—the corners of her lips curled into a smile, then snapped back down as she started talking about asset purchase agreements. Jaladhi was not automatic. She was still young, still caught up in the game. Maybe one day she would say to hell with it and flip the table, but today we were two big important lawyers duking it out over a big important acquisition, and that was it.

So it must have been something in my face, some reflexive flash of horror, that gave it away. No sooner had I spotted Leona waving at me from the bar, her eyes and smile both wide with surprise, than the smile vanished and the eyes became wider. She left her friends and bolted for the door.

I told Jaladhi we'd made a mistake, waved my wrist over the paypad, and ran after my wife.

Articells, Day 1

We were on the patio, sitting in the early-morning sun. Leona was vaping and playing fetch with the dog; I was drinking coffee and doing nothing in particular.

Matt appeared at the screen door, looking graver than usual. He leaned against the threshold and stared at his feet.

"How's it going, kiddo?" I said. "Ready for school?"

"I was talking to Alexa," he said. "She said that the five-year survival rate for acute myeloid leukemia for thirty-eight-year-olds is seventy-seven percent which means that when Mom is forty-three there's a twenty-three percent chance that—" He ran out of breath as the tears welled up.

Leona and I exchanged exasperated glances. He must have been eavesdropping last night. Or maybe we'd been too loud. In any case, the jig was up.

Leona slid her vape pen into the charging dock and went to him. She opened the screen and knelt down, stroked his cheek. "Matthew, look at me."

He didn't look. The dog padded over; Matt started petting him methodically.

"Sweetie, you can't believe everything you hear on the Internet," Leona said.

"Your mother's right," I said, kneeling next to her. "I promise you that your mom's chances are much better than seventy-seven percent."

"How do you know?" Matt asked, carefully tracing figure-eights on the dog's back. "Doctors and scientists said so, and you're not a doctor *or* a scientist. You're just a lawyer."

Ouch. But the tone was pleading, not accusatory. He wanted to believe me, he just needed to know he could.

"Because when those scientists came up with that number, they didn't consider your mom. And your mom is very stubborn. More stubborn than anybody I've ever met. And in my line of work that's saying something." She grinned sideways at me.

"I'm not done yet," she said. "Not even close. Especially as long as I have you and your father to look after."

Matt didn't look convinced. As always, my kid needed numbers.

"You're not the only one who's friends with Alexa," I said. "I know where that percentage comes from. It's from a study they did over ten years ago, and in the world of doctors and scientists, ten years is a very long time. Things have gotten a lot better."

Matt's face hinted at a smile.

"In fact, we have an appointment with Dr. Le this morning, and I hear he has something cool to show us that could really help your mom. Something the people who did that study could only have dreamed of."

"Really?" The smile was full-fledged now. "Can I join?"

The appointment was during school, but I'd already dangled the carrot. "How's that homework coming along?"

"I'll finish it now." He turned to go back inside, revivified. But he stopped short of the threshold. He turned back around and, for the first time, looked at his mother. "Is it because you vape? Because vaping causes cancer and leukemia is a kind of cancer."

Leona and I looked at each other again. Nothing like getting cross-examined by your six-year-old to wake you up in the morning. *I'll take this one*, her expression said.

"No, it's not because I vape," she said. "It was just bad luck. But you're absolutely right—these pods don't help." She pulled the mouthpiece from her vape pen and dropped it on the table. "Which is why I just had my last one. Starting right now, your mom is vape-free."

I'd been trying to get her to quit for years, and my kid manages it in a sentence. Fine by me. I clasped my wife's hand and locked eyes with her. I smiled solemnly. *Thank you.* She would beat this shit and come out of it even stronger.

I turned to Matt. "Go finish your homework. We're video-calling Dr. Le at nine-thirty sharp."

Articells, Year 40

I caught up with her a block away, waiting in the chilly darkness for the red hand to change into the walking man.

"Leona, wait."

She ignored me, keeping her eyes on the traffic light opposite the crosswalk. As soon as it turned yellow and the cars started slowing down, she stepped out into the street.

"Please."

I came around into her path, forcing her to stop. I was about to grasp her shoulders but somehow the thought made me nervous. She looked at me, her expression blank.

"She's a colleague," I said. "That's all."

She stared at me, her face unwavering, as if in a trance. I stared back at my wife of forty-nine years, hot blood pounding through me, waiting for an answer.

"OK," she said.

"I'm serious."

"I believe you."

I worked up the nerve to touch her arm. "Let's go back inside. I'm sure they're wondering what's going on."

"Actually, it's getting late. I'm gonna head home." She pulled her tablet from her bag—she never was one for screenTats—and scribbled something out, presumably to her friends. "But you can do what you like." She brushed past me into the street as the countdown timer hit zero.

I jogged up alongside her. The light turned green; cars honked at us. "I'll take you."

Once across, I ordered a ride and took us home.

* * *

The next morning, I found her leaning against the kitchen counter with her coat on, studying her tablet and powering through a piece of toast. I told the kitchen to make coffee and started scrolling through the financial news in the table, too tense for any of the headlines to register.

"Where are you off to, honey?" I asked.

"Work." She folded up her tablet and disappeared down the hall. It was Saturday, but running a legal aid clinic often meant weekends in the underbelly.

"Bye, Leo," I called. "You're a trooper."

I heard the door open and close.

I didn't see her again that day, only felt the rustling of the covers as she climbed into bed long after I'd turned in.

Sunday was a repeat of Saturday, but with fewer words exchanged.

When I woke up on Monday, her clothes and toothbrush were gone.

Articells, Year 11

"Stop here."

The car registered Leona's instruction and pulled into the station. I took over the wheel and parked on the farthest charging pad.

"You want anything?" she said.

I shook my head. She got out and headed into the convenience store as the car started charging.

My watch chimed. Christ. Another update. One of these days I'd have to do like Leona and let them install automatically. Her Articells had been policing her blood for over a decade without a hitch. The cancer they'd destroyed hadn't shown its face since. And according to Dr. Le it was thanks to the endless updates that in eleven years she'd barely aged four. She certainly looked just as good.

But still. These things were swimming inside me. The least I should do is skim the damned update notes…

v17.0.9:

 • *Fixes a minor bug from v17.0.8 affecting pluripotent stem cell induction in fibroblasts*

 • *Introduces a new enzymatic process for enhanced lysosomal function in arterial macrophages*

 • *Introduces two new enzymatic processes…*

It went on like that for a dozen more bullets. And that was just the summary. You'd think the people who had wiped out blood cancer and were making good headway on aging itself could write comprehensible English. Not that I was complaining. After climbing for years, my blood pressure had leveled off in week one, and recently had started to drop. My incipient bald spot was staying incipient. No doubt I would soon be reading about my new spider powers and x-ray vision.

I hit *Accept* as Leona ducked into the car.

She leaned back in her seat, exhaling at length. She was empty-handed.

"You didn't buy anything?"

"I did. But I threw them out."

I said nothing. It had been a stressful day for both of us. When the car finished charging, I told it to hit the road again.

We'd crossed into Pennsylvania before I broke the silence.

"I was thinking we could move back into the city," I said. "Find a nice condo downtown. Might beat staying holed up in the 'burbs in a big empty house, you know?"

I glanced over. She was staring out the windshield, with no indication that she'd heard me.

"Just something to think about."

She sighed. "Honey, I just drove eleven hours across five states to abandon my only child in the middle of New York City, where he'll spend the next four years partying and boozing and getting up to God-knows-what eight hundred miles away from me with people I've never met. Right now, the last thing I need is something to think about."

"You really think Matt's the partying type?"

"Like I said, I don't think anything right now." She slid her window down. "Just enjoy the trees, honey."

We drove on in silence. I slid my window down, letting the wind billow against my face, and enjoyed the trees.

* * *

I woke up to Leona prodding my ribs. "Honey."

It took a few seconds for the sleep to fade away. "How far along are we?" It was getting dark and the trees had thickened.

"Quick—look." I caught the sign she was pointing at just before it flicked by. *West Branch State Park - Exit 5 miles.* "I've heard it's beautiful. Let's camp there tonight."

"What?"

"Camping. Here. Tonight."

I rubbed my eyes. When had we last gone camping? Matt must have been in elementary school. "We've just spent two days on the road—don't you want to get home? Besides, we don't have any gear."

"We'll figure it out." She nestled up against me. "You have somewhere you need to be?"

Something flat and boxy pressed against my leg. I glanced down; a pack of disposable vapes sat below the lip of her pocket.

I shrugged and closed my eyes again, then wrapped my arm around her as she started singing orders to the car and into the wind.

Articells, Year 40

The call came at the office.

"Just so you know, Leona's staying with me."

Selene lived in our building. She was there that night.

"She says she needs some time," she continued, when I didn't say anything. "To think."

"Selene, please, put her on."

"It's Monday, dude. She's at work."

My head was swimming. "Right."

Silence on the other end. Then: "Look, I get it. I do. When my ex-husband and I decided to end it, we were still OK, for the most part. But we knew it was just…there was no way. We couldn't keep it up forever."

I stayed quiet, waiting for her to say more.

She sighed. "I'm not saying that's what you guys should do. Maybe you'll get through this. But whatever you decide, you can't stick your head in the sand and pretend the world hasn't changed. I have a couple of friends in an open marriage; I can introduce—"

I ended the call. On the wall screen a message from Jaladhi was waiting in my personal inbox; I deleted it unopened, took a gulp of hypercaf, pulled up a case file, and dove in.

* * *

I dive deep. The water is clear and bright and I can see for miles. Or a few yards. There are no fish or reefs or forms of any kind to lend perspective. Just blue.

Some unknowable distance above, the surface shimmers. It stretches in every direction, but never far, always swallowed by the water it tries to contain. I swim toward it. The shimmering intensifies; specks of light flicker like sparks. A shape appears on the other side, round and sharp against the blur. A face. I get closer and the face gets bigger, but I can't make out who it belongs to. Closer, until the face is all there is, and I'm inside of it. Back inside the blue.

The shimmering is gone.

* * *

It was evening when I came to. I didn't know whether I'd attended those afternoon meetings or dreamt them, and didn't care. I dragged myself to the breakroom and ingested a sandwich from the printer before plodding to the elevators.

In the car home I lay sprawled on the seat, feeling drained and vaguely sick. Leona wasn't answering. Probably blocked me. I tried Selene; she gave in the third time.

"Put her on," I said.

"Seriously, you have to leave this alone for a while."

"Selene, for Christ's sake, put her on."

"No."

"Fine. I'm coming over."

"Do *not* come o—"

I swiped off my screenTat.

I was crossing the plaza that fronted my building, racing through scenarios in my head, when the lobby doors opened and Leona came out. She walked briskly in my direction, hands buried in her coat, breath visible in the frigid air.

She didn't stop.

"Leo," I said, catching her by the crook of the elbow.

She wrenched herself free and walked on.

When I turned, she was almost at the sidewalk. "Leona!"

She disappeared around a corner.

There was nothing left to do. I drifted toward the building, fantasizing about my bed and my escape into sleep. But I never made it to the entrance. Instead, I found myself running back across the plaza.

At the sidewalk, I scanned the area. Leona was heading down a pedestrian road toward the financial district. I waited until she was far enough away, then began to follow.

Articells, Year 26

I looked down into the water. It was clear and softly rolling, but calm enough to reveal the pastel patchwork spread across the seabed, safe from the brutal Red Sea sun. Nasim, our diving instructor, said that these were the best reefs in the world and that they were much more impressive once you got under. No doubt they were, but it didn't matter; they had already done their job. For the first time in years—for the first time since Matt's accident—there was light in Leona's eyes.

Anniversary thirty-five is coral. I couldn't remember exactly when we stopped doing the traditional gifts. Like too many facets of our marriage, it just sort of petered out. But petering out was no longer an option. The only option was to revive the narrative.

And this was a damned good start.

I tested my mouthpiece again and tramped across the deck in my fins to where Nasim was fiddling with my wife's regulator. He was a gregarious kid from Cairo with a swimmer's body, which Leona had found plenty of excuses to touch and brush up against since we set out. Not that I minded. This trip was for her, and there was no harm in a bit of innocent flirting. They chatted away as he worked, Leona looking as good in her bikini as she did on our honeymoon. In this moment I could almost believe Dr. Le's extrapolations, could almost see us dune boarding in the Namib or scaling an Andean peak a hundred years from now, having yet to hit biological fifty.

Discreetly, since I promised her I wouldn't, I peeked at the tablet stretched around my forearm and swiped open my work inbox. There wasn't much; just a few FYIs regarding my firm's recent signing of RenewaLife, a promising spin-off from a university biotech lab. Articells were one thing, but if these upstarts could one day manage with humans what they did with rhesus monkeys…

I closed my inbox as Matt's face flashed in my head.

"Ready?"

I looked up, startled. She'd been patiently waiting for me to finish. There was a time when she would have grabbed my arm by the tablet and ordered me to leave the damned thing alone or she would wrap it around my neck and strangle me, and I would have countered with a cheeky "yes, dear" and made an over-the-top show of shutting it off, all the way off. Now I just smiled awkwardly, tested my mouthpiece for the dozenth time, and said, "As I'll ever be."

"Let's do it!" Nasim said.

We went to the gunwale, sat down with our backs to the water. Mouthpieces in.

"I'll count down from five, OK?"

I noticed Leona discreetly touch Nasim's arm and gesture to me as he started counting: "Five, four—"

A hand reached over and shoved my chest. The boat and sky inverted, and I was under.

And sinking. On my back, facing the surface. I fumbled for the inflation valve on my unit, found it, held the button. The bladder bulged out and my descent slowed, then stopped. But I didn't ascend either. I'd found some buoyancy sweet spot.

I tried kicking but only moved laterally. I couldn't right myself.

I hung there, inert.

* * *

A face appeared above the shimmering undulations.

* * *

I was being pulled, driven along. The shimmering got closer and then I crashed through it, into the air and light.

"Oh my God, honey! Are you OK? I was just playing around, I—I shouldn't have done that." Leona was hanging over the gunwale, mask off, looking terrified, as Nasim grabbed onto the boat, his other arm hooked under mine.

I took out my mouthpiece and swallowed a gulp of salt-soaked air. "I'm OK. Really. Just lost my bearings for a second." Echoes of pain lingered in my ears.

"Are you sure?" Nasim said. "If you like, we can—"

"I'm fine. I was just startled, that's all." I smiled up at Leona. "My wife can be a troublemaker when she's excited."

Leona smiled hesitantly back. "Well, if you're sure."

Her concern was accompanied by something else, something that tinted the air between us and got thicker every year. A politeness.

She joined us in the water.

Nasim was right: Below the surface the coral glowed like neon.

Articells, Year 40

Tucked in a booth with a strong Iranian gin, I watched Leona from across the packed lounge where she led me. Three nights ago she ran from this place; now she sat at the bar in the heart of it, drinking alone. It was filled with high-finance types, all in their bio-twenties and -thirties. No doubt some were decades older. Maybe more than some. Who the hell knew anymore? Every few minutes a new lady-killer would strut up to the bar, insert himself beside Leona and try to work his game; without looking

Leona would flash her ring in his face, and Don Juan would usually stick around to order a face-saving drink before slinking back to his friends. I was tempted to try my own luck, but I knew better. She was out of my league.

A couple more gins were enough to change my mind. I abandoned my hideout and wound through the crowd to the bar. "May I?"

She looked up with mild consternation, then back at her drink. I sat down.

"Why'd you do it?" she said.

The question caught me off guard. I hadn't thought about it once. *Because one of us would have done it eventually, so let me be the asshole. Because she's young and full of life and I'm old and spent. Because I'm a piece of shit. What difference does it make?*

She must have sensed my head spinning. "Relax. I'm just messing with you."

Something seized my gut and I took her hands. "Leona, listen to me—"

"Just"—she pried her hands free—"don't. Don't embarrass yourself."

She was right. Just another pick-up artist running through his pathetic routine. "I do love you, you know," was all I could spew out.

Finally, she faced me, dead-eyed. "When I caught you with that woman you could barely be bothered to put on a half-assed show of lying about it. So I put on a half-assed show of believing you. Hell, we're putting on a show right now. What else can we do, after fifty fucking years?" She snorted a laugh and took a swig of her drink. "You wanna know the best part? After fifty fucking years, it's as if we never met! Matt's dead, you're chasing office tail, and I'm in a bar on a Monday night getting hit on by a bunch of horny finance bros. But that's OK—life's about the journey, right?" She grabbed her drink and swung it up high, spilling some on my lap. "Here's to the next fifty!" She downed it in one go, slammed the glass on the bar and hailed another.

I sat there, speechless, my insides sinking. "A show," I eventually said, trying to sound angry or passionate or anything. "Then why am I here, right now? Why did I follow you halfway across town?" I meant the question as rhetorical, but I didn't know the answer. I wanted to know the answer.

Leona picked an ice cube out of her glass and started turning it around in her fingers. "Same reason I'm here. You have nowhere else to go."

The crowd was thickening as the lounge gradually turned into a nightclub. I lingered at the bar, listening to the thumping bassline spill in from the dance floor, watching weird holographic flower-things bloom in on themselves as they drifted through the tables and people and spirit-tinged air. She was right. I had nowhere to go. Even if I stepped outside into the street and an oncoming bus did to me what my own body no longer could, our RenewaLife policy would take care of it. It was too late for Matt, but his parents would be just fine.

"What happens now?" I said, because I had nothing to say.

When no reply came, I glanced in her direction. The side of her face was buried in her hand, which she'd angled squarely across my view. Muffled sobs turned the pounding house music into a distant hum. I got up and held her, pressed her against me. For a second she acquiesced; then she threw me off, screaming. The recoil sent her off her stool; she stumbled back, fell to the floor. I tried helping but she kicked me away.

"Just let it fucking go!"

She was propped up on her elbow, glaring at me with bloodshot eyes. Somewhere in another world a buzz of voices cut off.

I fled through a dreamscape of rattled faces and meandering light forms, out the doors and into the freezing night.

* * *

I sat on the cold ground, huddled in a wall recession under a clammy plastic tarp I'd found lying nearby. With any luck, whoever might be lurking in the alley would write me off as just another street bum and not bother looking any closer. So far the only soul I'd seen was passed out in his own nook, wrapped in layers of grungy clothes. He was old; slim chance that any Articells had found their way into those veins.

When was her last back-up? June?

The concrete was pressing up into my spine and the smell from the tarp had dug into my nostrils, but I didn't care. My heart was racing and my nerves were a wreck. A gust of wind sent a piece of garbage skipping across the alley and I nearly jumped out of my skin. When I gathered enough presence of mind to check my screenTat, it had only been fifteen minutes. I began to relax, and it slowly sank in where I was, what I'd reduced myself to. She wasn't coming. She'd taken a different route back, or a car, or had gone somewhere else, with someone else.

But I had no intention of leaving. The alley was growing on me. So I sat in my hole, blank and sedate.

June. Seven months. That's nothing.

Minutes or hours later, after the sharp clonking of heels had gotten too loud to ignore, I turned to look. Leona was twenty feet away, heading straight for me. I felt my shaking hand slide into my jacket pocket, felt the jagged shard of glass I'd found under a broken window. A beat later she hustled by, oblivious to what sat curled up in the dark, or pretending not to see.

She'll come back, I whispered through the hyperventilating. *She'll come back. She'll come back. She'll come back…*

I must have repeated it a dozen times because when I looked up she was almost gone. I shed the tarp, jumped to my feet, sprinted after her. By the time she turned around I'd caught her arm and my other hand was pressing over her mouth, muffling the scream.

* * *

I swim toward the surface, toward the face. The shimmering fades and dies, and I can make out who the face belongs to, can see myself look down on me.

I open my lungs and the water rushes in.

Renewal, Day 1

"Morning, Leo," I said, beaming down at her.

She didn't respond, but I wouldn't have heard anyway. I was too caught up in those eyes. They were clearer than a newborn's. I took her hand in both of mine and squeezed, feeling the flesh squish against my palms and between my fingers. Warm, soft. Alive.

Leona's mother, a seventy-year-old centenarian, came and knelt beside me, staring at the figure propped up against the pillows as if it were a ghost. "Is it…really her?"

Wrinkles formed in the pristine skin above Leona's eyes. "H—" She swallowed hard as the word drowned in fluid. "Hey, guys."

Her mother's gently agape mouth swelled into a joyous grin. "Oh…" She flung her arms around Leona, whispery murmurs escaping between the sobs. "I can't believe this…" She let go and gripped her daughter's arm. "Leona, what on earth were you doing in that alley!"

A pause; more wrinkles. "Don't remb—remember."

"Oh, I'm sorry, sweetie, of course you wouldn't."

I rested a hand on my mother-in-law's shoulder. "I'm sure we'll sort it all out."

While Leona's mother talked with Selene, who had arrived soon after and whose steel shell had melted into tears as soon as she walked in the room, I sat quietly on the bed next to Leona. I ran my fingers through her hair, taking in her scent and the warmth of her body. Her crystalline eyes shifted up to mine and she gave a small but radiant smile.

It was her. This was real.

I had almost dozed off when the doctor came in, the RenewaLife logo decorating the pocket of her scrubs.

"How are we all doing?"

We offered variants of "good, thanks," except for Leona, who stayed quiet.

The doctor approached the bed. "Not to worry," she said to Leona. "I know talking isn't easy, but that's normal. According to your evaluation, you're the picture of health."

She was more than a picture. Her new body had the same genes and, per her request, the same bio-age as her original, but she gave off a youthful glow that went beyond appearance. It was palpable.

"That's the good news," the doctor continued. "The less-than-good news is that it's not quite over yet. As I'm sure you're plenty aware, your brain and muscles aren't exactly on the same page, and they'll need time to sort things out." She tapped the screenTat on the back of her hand. "It says here you're an attorney—is that right?"

Leona nodded.

"Try answering vocally."

She hesitated. "Yesh. Yes."

I pulled her in closer. "Not the sleazy kind like me. She helps people."

The doctor chuckled. "I see. Lots of talking and typing, then. That's good—the more you practice your fine motor skills the faster you'll recover. Just make sure to take plenty of breaks to stretch and move around. We'll also provide you with an exercise regimen for the freshly Renewed. To help with speech recovery, try reading a book out loud to somebody, cover to cover. Go slowly. I'm sure your husband would be happy to volunteer— right, husband?"

I smiled. "Just no Grisham novels." Leona still read everything he put out, but after eighty years he was starting to repeat himself.

"Trust me," the doctor said. "You do all of that, in a few weeks you'll be a hundred percent."

The doctor was walking out the door when Leona's mother spoke up: "Excuse me, Doctor?"

She stopped, turned.

"I'm not sure the right way to ask this, but…you know what? Never mind. You said she's healthy. Thank you very much."

The doctor came to her, smiling sympathetically as if she'd heard the same unspoken question a thousand times. I felt a pang in my gut even before she laid the question bare. "You want to know if that's really your daughter sitting on the bed," she said. "That's completely understandable. It would be strange if the thought hadn't crossed your mind." The unease on Leona's mother's face abated a little. The doctor addressed us all as she continued: "Look, I'd be lying if I said we understand how the brain works. Nobody does. Nobody knows how it makes Leona who she is—all we know is that it does. Which is why we preserve everything. Every cell, every connection, every detail. We don't know what's important, so we save it all."

Quite the speech. This obviously wasn't her first time giving it.

"But those are just words," she continued. "Let me show you something." She disappeared and promptly returned with thick booklets decorated with smiling faces, presumably of clients enjoying their spiffy new bodies. "Go ahead and turn to page eleven."

We did as instructed and I was face-to-face with a full-page headshot of a woman. She looked ancient—ninety, maybe a hundred—but otherwise healthy.

"Who is she?" Leona's mother asked.

The doctor smiled. "That old gal is me. About three years ago. I was one of the first."

Leona's mother let out a soft gasp.

"Twenty years before that picture was taken," the doctor said, "I got my Articells. In those twenty years I aged only five. Impressive, sure, but 'too little too late' does come to mind."

"Jesus." Selene looked up at the doctor, the one standing in front of us—thirty, maybe thirty-five—then back at her booklet. Her amazement had a note of revulsion. But this pitch wasn't for her.

"Sorry." The doctor smiled sheepishly. "Today's not about me. Anyway," —she turned to Leona—"by every measure, your Renewal was completely unexceptional. Just don't be surprised if the few days before your last back-up are a little fuzzy."

Of course, all the days *since* her last back-up were gone. Jaladhi was gone.

We made our way out, a small posse flanking Leona like bodyguards. No wheelchair was provided—the doctor wanted her first steps to be in the hospital. Not surprisingly those steps were painstaking and awkward. At one point she fell. Selene and I rushed to help, but she shooed us away and, with some effort, managed to climb to her feet and resume her trudge. I smiled. Forget weeks—knowing my wife, she'd be back in the game by tomorrow.

While Leona endured her mother's quizzing about a childhood trip to Disney World, Selene turned fractionally to me. "Quite the lucky break for you," she murmured.

I glanced sidelong at her, saying nothing.

"Don't worry. As long as you've ditched the side-skank, she'll be our little secret. But you and I both know she won't be the last."

I kept my eyes forward and pretended not to hear.

* * *

After a celebratory lunch the group parted ways, leaving Leona and me to grab a car home. I spent the ride nestled against her, stroking her back and tracing my fingers up and down her thigh. I felt giddy. I couldn't keep my hands off her.

"Look at you, Mister Affesh—Affectionate."

I glided my fingers from her leg onto her forearm, where her new screenTat was etched. "And look at you, Miss *À La Mode*. Your Amish brethren will miss you."

"Ha-ha." Renewal might have put a damper on her words but her sarcasm was unscathed. "Tablet got me killed. Time to upgrade."

I thought of the poor bastard from the alley making off with his measly prize like he'd won the lottery and it was hard to feel angry. Leona was OK, after all, and if he kept the thing turned off, he would be, too.

As I tucked my head in the crook of Leona's neck, I felt in her body, as I'd heard in her voice, something faint—like faintness itself. It seemed to come from deep inside her, as if dampened by distance and time, as if, buried somewhere unreachable, were a profound fatigue.

Or maybe I was the one who was tired. It had been a long day.

I breathed deeply and let that thought, and all other thoughts, fade into the electric hum of the car.

The afternoon saw us curled up on the couch with her old physical copy of Paulo Coelho's *The Alchemist*, which, as per the doctor's orders, she read aloud to me. "I guess it suits the occasion," I said. "New beginnings, or whatever." That earned me a punch in the arm and an order to shut up and listen. I happily obeyed. At first, I had a hard time focusing on her slow, stilted narration and just lay there, resting my head on her lap, basking in a familiarity that hadn't been familiar in a long time. But soon enough I adjusted to the rhythm and found myself sitting on the fortress walls beside the old king of Salem, watching the young shepherd boy sail out into the blue...

* * *

An urgent chiming jarred me awake. It was dark. I dug my arm out from between the couch cushions and winced as the light from my screenTat hit my eyes. One of the firm's biggest clients was throwing a tantrum—emergency partner meeting at ten p.m. The clock showed five past nine. I sighed, and with a grunt hoisted myself to my feet, pushing through the dizzy exhaustion that always sets in after a too-long nap, then shuffled to the bedroom. Inside I found Leona bundled under the covers, facing the far wall. Careful not to wake her, I changed into something presentable and slipped back out.

Behind me, I heard a faint sob.

* * *

My firm occupied the top thirty-one floors of a 201-story aluminum needle. The routine had long since been ingrained: through the modern layered-glass entrance, across the classic marble-and-mahogany lobby, up the maglift half a mile into the sky—but this time, when the doors opened and the euphonic female voice announced the floor, I didn't get off. I stood there until the doors closed, then told the elevator to keep going, up to 201; moments later I was climbing an emergency stairwell, stepping out onto the roof, stepping up onto the ledge.

The city had fallen away. The sky was washed out. There was only wind, emboldened by height and unhindered by walls and screaming into the void. I screamed back. Screamed until I was hoarse, until my throat burned, until the wind and I were the same eternal screaming.

But I wasn't eternal. I was a fraud, and eventually ran out of breath. I stood shivering while the wind went on without me, mocking my sham immortality. My weight shifted to my toes; my body leaned out into the black.

I was sitting sprawled on the roof, tailbone aching, when my brain fully registered the half-conscious realization that had yanked me back from the ledge.

My Renewal policy didn't cover suicide.

Illustration by Ariel Guzman

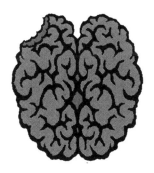

The *Blou Trein* Suborbirail

L.P. Melling

Fenwick checks the train parts for printing errors, sweat dripping down the back of his neck. The air con has packed in again and the merciless South African heat infiltrates the cramped confines of his workstation. He runs his hand over a replacement connective rod for the *Blou Trein* Suborbirail's track and feels a nick. Like most of the workers, he doesn't trust the hand-held scanners that lost people their jobs. Fenwick can't risk it. He is about to polish down the superalloy when he hears shouting behind him, his grip tightening around the rod.

"Fenwick! Stop the hell what you're doing and get over here!"

He grits his teeth. "Yes, Boss." Fenwick slowly turns around, trying to relax his facial muscles, and sees Mr. Grobler's jowls wobbling, face red beneath a liver-spotted bald head.

"And goddamn hurry up about it!" Grobler says, and his eyes lock on what's in Fenwick's hand. *Fokk!* Parts are supposed to be kept in the workstation area. The other workers remain in their stations, carrying on with their toil, heads down. "What the hell are you carrying, Fenwick?"

"Sorry, Boss. Found an imperfection. Was just about to correct it and—"

"Oh, so you can do your job, then?" he sneers. The boss is in his face now. "So tell me, Fenwick, why have I just got off a lunar call hearing parts from your line were sent up defective? Hey?"

Fenwick screws up his face in confusion, lowers his gaze. "No idea, Boss. Been checking for printing errors twice-over with every part. They must've made a mistake."

"You idiot! They use bots up there for that work, so how the hell could they be mistaken?" He throws his hands up in frustration. "Now I'm going to have to lower our rates on the next train drop. I should've left you in that corrective facility to rot, Fenwick. How hard is it to check for printing errors for fuck's sake! My eight-year-old niece could do a better job! If it wasn't for the subsidy, you'd be out of here." Grobler loves reminding Fenwick that the only reason TransNet employs humans like him is because of its exclusive deal with the government to take on ex-cons. Bots cost more to run and service than the few bitcreds Fenwick gets paid an hour, and it's sweet-as-malva PR for South Africa's richest company. "I'm docking your pay!"

Fenwick flexes. "You god—"

"What, Fenwick? Just try it and I'll have the security bots kick you out of here. A crook like you would never find another job."

Fenwick swallows back his words into his burning stomach, turning away. He's tried for years to leave TransNet for better work. Does well at the interviews, receives promising remarks, but soon as employers do a background check on him, they send the rejection.

"That's right, get back to it. This is your last chance, Fenwick, you hear? The *last!*"

"*Ja,*" he mutters, still gripping iron-tight on the rod as he faces the conveyor belt. He polishes down the part, micro-sander grinding against his bones, and drops it in the green-rimmed chute.

He can't even get angry about the turndowns. When there's so many people looking for work without petty crimes on their record, why *would* they choose him?

Fenwick hits the button next to his workstation to get the belt moving again, catching a glimpse of the blue digits lighting up his section. Still five hours left of this crap to go. He grabs the next part, a flawless rivet, and assigns it ready for freight transportation to the Suborbirail's final stop.

* * *

Fenwick scans his ID card to exit TransNet's premises. The sun is long gone as he breathes in the cool air. He did an extra hour of unpaid work to play it safe. Not that there's much chance Grobler noticed.

Fenwick crosses the sandy flats through slum streets most avoid, corrugated shacks crouching either side of him, as he passes through the district of Cape Town the government ignores. The unmistakable aroma of *umngqusho* drifts on the breeze from a nearby shack. His mouth waters at the smell of food that filled his childhood: sugar beans and crushed corn slow cooked so it melts on the tongue. His mother used to make it as the rooibos-strained sun kissed the slums on the horizon.

Things were so much easier back then. No idiot boss pushing him around. No worries as he played all day with his childhood friends. Fenwick remembers Mrs. Jardine chasing him and Khumalo through the slum, saying she'll kill them when she gets her hands on them. He'd find his and Khumalo's names scratched into the paintwork of her old place if he walked around the corner, and the spot where Kalum got stabbed to death on his sixteenth birthday. But he leaves his past in the slums and walks on.

Fenwick arrives back in a slightly better part of Cape Town. He finds his girlfriend, Lenka, waiting for him in their apartment's front room; it's not much bigger than his workstation but it's a much happier place. He never forgets how lucky they are to have solid walls now.

Fenwick kisses Lenka, sprawls into the gel-foam lazy chair.

"Why you so late, *bokkie*?" she asks.

"Grobler." He doesn't have to say more to explain.

Fenwick switches on the box to watch the footorb game.

Lenka stands in front of the screen.

"Hey?"

She fixes him with a stare, eyes the same shade of blue as the *Blou Trein*'s livery, long coffee-colored hair framing her perfect bone structure. He still can't believe she chose an ugly mug like him. It took them years of scrimping and saving to get out of their shack in the Cape Flats slum. Fenwick is proud of where he came from, but he never wants to go back there.

The struggle and sacrifice seem to show on her face now as her lips part, wet and red. "We need to talk."

Fenwick mentally runs through the things he might have done wrong recently. Did he leave his cereal bowl out again yesterday morning?

"How long have we been together now?" she says.

O kak, one of those conversations. He runs his hand over the chair, reactively reaching for an ejector-seat button he knows isn't installed. "Years, baby. The best of my life."

"Ten years next week!"

Damn it. He knew he had to buy something. Fenwick stares at the digital pic display on the wall, showing him and Lenka standing in front of their new home, arms wrapped around each other. Must be three years ago already if they met a decade ago.

"Don't you think it's about time we started a family, then?" Lenka looks fragile and strong at the same time: beautiful.

Fenwick drops his gaze as he did with Grobler. "I don't know. Of course I want to, darling. But with work and everything, we can barely afford to feed ourselves after all the bills." Lenka knows TransNet knocked back his first transfer request, anything to get away from Grobler, but not that he made four further requests they rejected for no good reason. Or the times he almost walked out of there after the boss was on his case again.

He raises his head. A look of hurt sweeps across Lenka's face and it cuts him up.

"Sorry, *engel*. I'm just trying to be careful. Y'know. We're—"

"Pregnant. We're having a girl. I know I should've told you earlier, but I had to be sure this time."

"What?" Fenwick sits there, locked in a trance for a minute. He looks at her stomach, but there's barely a bump, and she catches him staring.

"How many times did I tell you my *ma* didn't show when she was pregnant with me and my sister, not till much later!"

"But I thought…" He thought he'd had too many kicks in the balls to have children, literally and otherwise. His Xhosa-descended mother, never shy about sharing things, always said the old man had a low sperm count. Fenwick hadn't seen his drunk of a father for over a decade since he moved back to Scotland. Father-son bonding was never their forte, anyway, even when he was around and Fenwick was a kid…and now Fenwick is having one of his own.

He won't make the same mistakes.

Fenwick stands and kisses Lenka. "Sorry, *engel*. That's wonderful news! Really! C'mon, let's go celebrate. I'm taking you to the best place in town." He lifts Lenka off her feet.

"You *domkop!*" she says around the laughter.

* * *

The natural high of beckoning fatherhood gets him through the first half of his shift the next day. *God*, does he feel like shit after all that champagne last night, though. Why didn't he stick to the alcohol-free cocktails like Lenka?

Fenwick hits the start button, missing it the first time. The conveyor belt chugs forward like the original *Blou Trein* the suborbital took its name from. Owned by TransNet, the Blue Train Suborbirail (as tourists know it) has long since taken its place in central Cape Town. Affluent, predominantly white families—the only ones able to afford a ticket—use the *Blou* to escape the ever-growing slums of South Africa for a new life on the Moon. He can't blame them for wanting the best for their children, not anymore.

The more Fenwick tries to concentrate on what he's doing, the more he fails. Fenwick rubs his temples, knowing he can't make another mistake.

The heat is incredible today; his back prickles with perspiration; his mouth is bone-dry. He hears the Boss shouting again in the background, but when isn't he?

Fenwick's eye catches another imperfection a second before he drops it down the green-edged chute. He wipes away the sheen of sweat from his forehead with the other hand.

"Fenwick!"

He spins around and drops the ball bearing anyway. *Fokk!* He hears it rolling down the conduit behind him.

"Yes, Boss," he says, as respectful as he can muster. Grobler carries a uTab in his hand and does something he doesn't expect: he smiles wide, exposing the dark gap between his teeth.

"Fenwick, don't move!" Grobler points the uTab at his face.

A flash of light startles him and Fenwick is back in the *polisie* station again years earlier. Manhandled and being charged for petty hacking violations by a fat cop reeking of BO and *droëwors* meat. His third offense already, Fenwick is just a kid trying to get by on the streets but getting caught far too often.

"Fenwick," his boss says, breaking him out of the memory. "You're fired. Your security clearance is cancelled."

"What the—?" Fenwick spits. "Wh-why? I can't have made another mistake!"

"Your error rate isn't the worst, Fenwick, but it doesn't matter now." Sweat dripping down his fat red face, Gobbler smirks. "The government has cut the subsidy for taking on convicts, so I don't need to keep the likes of you on anymore."

"You know what, *fokk* you! Stick it up your *gat!*" Fenwick lunges at him, but pulls himself back, realizing Grobler is nothing, less than. Why land himself in more trouble for a parasite like him?

Fenwick is escorted out of the factory and the midday heat hits him in the face. He hasn't seen sunlight in days with the long shifts. He can't stop shaking, dehydrated and boiling over. "The bastard!" he mutters, and fear closes his throat. He can't let his child grow up in the slums like he did.

The *Blou Trein* Suborbirail stands out in the distance like always, shooting up above the clouds, its domed top out of sight. Vertical train lines cut through the dust and smog into unpolluted air. Fenwick still can't get used to it; the four human-thick rails look like they're defying gravity. The train's cobalt-blue hull glimmers in the sunlight miles high. Its torus carriages aren't attached by couplings but stacked on top of each other like a children's learning toy without the rainbow of color, with a lesson just as valuable for local kids about the order of things.

Rich Africans have long said that people from the slums couldn't handle the atmosphere up there. Fenwick hears it all the time on state-controlled TV: *Prawns can't survive in space.*

Fenwick remembers watching the Suborbirail's construction with his childhood friends. It was a boost to the economy, with many of their parents finding work for the first time in years. Adrenaline junkies would hang glide around the growing structure to get a closer look before the guards cleared them off with green laser sights—kids always loved watching that part.

He'll never get out of South Africa. Like most people from the slums, Fenwick has come to terms with that, but he has a daughter on the way now. He won't let her face the same hopeless future, with people looking down and pitying her.

He stares at the monolith and his stomach tightens.

Fenwick punches himself in the leg with frustration and realizes the ID card is still in his pocket. Grobler forgot to take it from him. It won't work to get Fenwick back in there, but he deserves a keepsake after all the years he worked for TransNet…and maybe he could adapt their tech for something else.

Fenwick swipes his phone, reads a message to say his NanoTech application was unsuccessful, and his hand shakes. He deletes it and his finger hovers over the contact list before he selects a number he's not used in years.

"Hey, Khumalo. *Ja*, it's me. I've got a job for us. Big pay off."

Fenwick looks up to a swatch of blue sky. It's time to ascend the slums, even if it's just for a day.

* * *

Lenka throws the plush toy train at his head as Fenwick runs out of the house. Lucky for him, the hormones mess with her aim. He has no idea how she found out, but women have their ways. Their networks of information.

"I don't want you back here. *We* don't!" she shouts, right hand resting on her stomach. "You promised. *Promised* that you'd never go back to your old ways!"

He groans. It's hard to argue, but he still tries. "I got fired, Lenka! How can we afford to have a child if I don't find us money?"

"I don't care."

Her reaction floors him. "You don't?"

"That's right. We'll find a way like we always have. Maternity pay will help." The hurt in her voice makes him want to hold her, but he knows she'll only throw something else at him. As it's their first child, they'll get some help from the government, sure, but it will be half of what she's earning now as a virtual assistant at CloudCover.

It won't be enough. She *must* know that.

Lenka grabs the door handle to close it.

"Baby, wait! I'm only doing this because I love you. I want the best for us and our child."

"Keep telling yourself that when you're locked up again. A dad who's around is what our baby will need. Not money and an absent father like other kids have around here!"

He can't remember ever hearing her sound this way.

Fenwick watches the love of his life shut the door. Ashamed, he'd stopped telling Lenka about all the jobs he applied for, fearful she'd see him as a failure and leave. "I'm sorry," he mutters, "but I have to do this." Fenwick picks up the duffel bag containing all his things. He walks through the flat land of his old slum to see an old friend who never worried about repercussions. But then Fenwick remembers the guy's been single for years.

* * *

"Don't worry. I got ya, bru," Khumalo says with glittering metal teeth, taking Fenwick's duffel bag. Khumalo's hair sticks out at all angles just like it did years before when Fenwick last saw him. He'll have to comb it down to blend in—keep his mouth closed as much as possible, too; that or wear a mouth guard. "Just sleep wherever you want, bru."

"*Ja*, thanks." Fenwick looks around, taking in the mess that is Khumalo's place. Fenwick thinks he spots something moving in one of the piles of rubbish against the corrugated iron walls, but he can't be sure. They didn't call this part of the Cape Flats slum the Vermin Quarter for nothing.

Khumalo catches Fenwick's line of sight. "Sorry about the mess, bru, but the French Maid quit for a better gig." He cracks his metal smile. A springbok shivers on his neck in red ink. "Got everything you asked for...well, most of it anyways." Khumalo points to a pile of battered tech Fenwick missed earlier, mistaking it for more junk.

"Where the hell you get it from? A museum?"

"Best I could do. With your skills though, it'll be no problem." There is a glint in Khumalo's eye to match his smile.

"Guess I'll have to make do like I always did." Fenwick tries not to look ungrateful.

"*Damn*, that's my bru. Missed this shit." Khumalo grabs him by the shoulder, beaming like a doting father. As much as Fenwick doesn't want to admit it, part of him has missed this, too.

"So you're clear on what the plan is?"

"*Ja*, sure," Khumalo says, looking at the streamshow playing in the corner.

"Hey, I'm serious!" Fenwick stands in front of the screen and tries to block out the hurt and disappointment he remembers seeing on Lenka's face. "No weapons like I said. No one's gonna get hurt. And the rich won't even know their accounts are being skimmed. Okay?"

"Sure, but those *fokkers* deserve everything they get!" Khumalo always hated those above him, especially after his old *ma* died of radiation poisoning after years of working as a cleaner at the Koeberg power station.

"Quit it, Khumalo. I can't go down this time. This is a quick job to keep the money dripping in for us for years. Don't fuck this up." Fenwick locks his stare onto Khumalo's.

"Okay, bru. You were always the boss. Fine. No guns."

"Cool." Fenwick exhales. "And thanks for this. You know I can't do it without you." He grabs him on the shoulder like Khumalo did his. "So what's a man got to do to get a beer around here?"

"Ha, I got you. Just like old times, hey, Fenners?"

"Just like old times."

* * *

Fenwick catches himself in the quartz composite viewing window of the *Blou Trein*. Damn, he looks like a royal fool in this blue-black butler's uniform. From the inside, the train looks more like a hotel than transportation as it glints with obscene opulence. Neo-modern artwork fastened to the walls. Luxurious lapis carpet on the floor. Smart seats set in a concentric circle providing a panoramic view through the viewing window. It gives the impression of an arena and Fenwick feels fully on show as passengers glance at him.

He keeps eyeing the exit positioned in the center of the room. The hissing doors lead to the stairwell that fills the rings of the torus carriages from the bottom to the domed top of the train, providing a way to reach each of its levels. A means of escape if things get too hot in here.

Fenwick wipes his brow with his sleeve. He is positioned in the upper section of the train reserved for first-class passengers, while Khumalo is skyward in its apex, above the *Blou*'s smallest torus, safely behind a secured door.

Fenwick taps on his earlobe and whispers to Khumalo, asking how things are looking.

"*Ja*, all good, bru."

Khumalo's job is to keep an eye out for anything suspicious, watching the feeds of the cams dotting the length of the train. This is while Fenwick serves the rich on a trip up to the stars and beyond, where the air is rarefied and free of the slums.

Fenwick swallows down his conflicting emotions. So far, things are going well. Thanks to Fenwick's stolen ID card's microchip and his only slightly rusty hacking skills, they managed to breach the train and find uniforms. Khumalo's engineer's outfit looks better than his, but the big man still looks suspect in it. The dental work doesn't help much, but Fenwick knows there's no one better to help them fight out of the place if things turn heavy.

"Coming, sir," Fenwick says, wearing his best smile. He walks over to the fat man with red hair and turns off the flashing red light on the side of his seat.

"Yes, dear boy. I'll have the Beluga Blue and Dom Pérignon—second to none, right?" He laughs and Fenwick's smile tightens.

"Very true, sir. Coming right up. I hope you've had a chance to enjoy the extended view from the Observation Carriage," he responds, latching onto the stock phrase the other butlers have been uttering like robots. None of them questioned Fenwick as expected; his ID looks as legit as theirs. He'd timed the train robbery to align with a new batch of recruited team members.

"What? Oh no, I've seen the view countless times. Becomes a frightful bore when you're up and down on the *Blou* all the time. I'm one of the directors for LunaScapes."

"Of course. Sorry, sir, I didn't realize." Fenwick clears his throat. "If I can just take your payment please." He holds the doctored scanner in front of him.

"Can't we do it later, old boy?" he says, chins wobbling like a toad's.

"I'm afraid not, sir, sorry."

Fenwick worries he's going to call the manager for a second, but the man relents. "Fair enough—we must all follow our superiors, right?" He winks and chuckles, double chin wobbling over his puce shirt. The man holds out his right arm, pulls back his cuff-linked shirt sleeve, and exposes his fat wrist for scanning.

The machine beeps twice to confirm the transfer is complete and Fenwick's smile broadens. He'll be skimming this guy's and the others' accounts for years before they realize it. A few bitcreds a week—they won't even feel the loss. "The perfect crime, bru," Khumalo said when Fenwick explained it.

Fenwick wipes away beads of sweat from his forehead as he programs the order into the SmartWaiter unit. Seconds later, its metal doors hiss open, and an icy cold mist leaks out as caviar gleams in cobalt crockery next to a bottle of champagne.

Fenwick drops off the order to Toadface, then quickly moves to the next waiting customer, who's complaining they've not had a top-up in nearly fifteen minutes.

He scans another chip, capturing the account details for a woman with a ridiculous floral hat that nearly touches the roof. He's already covered half the carriage; bit by bit, his child's future is being built, just like these people's hubs on the lunar colonies.

The train rattles and lurches as it passes through some turbulence, the inside of the carriage turning red before they're free of it. Fenwick can't stop shaking, tells himself to snap out of it. He catches sight of the track's connective rods and rivets. How many hundreds of them passed through his hands? To ensure they were all safe—that the rich were safe? An image of him kissing Lenka's stomach forces itself into his mind and he grits his teeth.

"Yes, madam." He's unable to ignore the screechy woman. She's wearing spiral earrings that are so long they're almost in her lap. Fenwick can't feel any hatred toward the passengers, no matter their manners. It's just who they are, worlds apart from himself.

"At last." The woman tuts. "I hope the TransEarth Removals Service isn't as bad as this. Not with our chinaware," she says, when Khumalo's voice cuts through the conversation: "We got trouble."

"O kak."

The lady gasps around the plums in her mouth. "I beg your pardon?"

"Nothing, madam. We're just out of Lobster Thermidor. My apologies."

"Oh well. It's no doubt for the best. It repeats on Henry terribly." She turns her head to the man beside her, who must be her husband, his rosy-red profile catching the light as he looks out the window, clearly trying his best to ignore her. "Why, tempura prawns it is, then!"

"Thank you for understanding, madam." Fenwick makes a quick retreat to the carriage's staff-only quadrant, his neck prickling.

Once he's out of sight, he hisses at Khumalo, "I'm on my way. What is it?"

"Armed guards. They're right below you. Better move fast!"

"What? No way. How could they have caught on to what we were doing?" Fenwick says, half to himself.

"No idea, but keep moving."

Fenwick's legs are jelly as he pushes past a group of chefs and sommeliers making personalized recommendations for first-class passengers. "Please, I need to get through."

Sweat drips off him. TransNet guards have more powers than even the SA *polisie* these days and can shoot anyone on their property. Fenwick knew that two guards are on every trip, but he didn't expect them to be a problem. Didn't expect two minimum-wage grunts to figure out what they were doing.

Fenwick heads to the carriage's center, the stairwell just behind those doors. Someone shouts from the back of the carriage. "Stop that butler!"

Fenwick runs. Doesn't look back. Sprints upstairs through the throats of passenger carriages until he can go no further. A bunch of wary-looking engineers block his path. No doubt wondering why they can no longer get access into the hatch above them. There's no way he can get past them, not with what he's wearing.

Kak!

His mind clutches for a solution as he backs away from them. He'll have to draw them away somehow. But how?

Spilling out into the Observation Carriage, Fenwick feels like he's floating, his legs numb as the exosphere presses up against the seamless reinforced window. The torus is smaller than other carriages but is uncluttered and made entirely from transparent materials. They must be over sixty miles up. Fenwick tears through the carriage, past large telescopes that extend out from the torus into the thinning atmosphere. Completing half a circuit, he holds his breath as the sky darkens outside.

"Khumalo," he hisses on the radio. "You there?"

"Here, man. What's up?"

"Need you to create a diversion fast. Can you set off an alarm on the carriage below, to pull the engineers away?"

"No sweat, Fenners. One sec."

Sweat pouring of his brow, Fenwick bumps into a group of VIP onlookers wowed by the view.

"Well, I never!" a woman shrieks, not a wrinkle showing on her face despite her fury.

He only notices now there's a little girl with her and it winds him. "I'm sorry," he calls, sucking in a mouthful of recycled air.

Rushing forward—almost hitting his head on a viewing harness—Fenwick completes the Observation Carriage's circuit and notices the engineers are missing, then the doors open. He hopes they slow down the guards as they pass them below.

Fenwick takes the last spiraling stairs to the top of the train where Khumalo is holed up. His legs burn with lactic acid, his breathing strained. Fenwick flashes his ID pass across the hatch's sensor, rips the door open, slams it shut behind him.

"There you are, Fenners. Took your bloody time!"

"Don't. Just tell me how we're gonna get out of this." Now he sees his pursuers on screen. Two armed guards following his scent like a pair of Rhodesian Ridgebacks. They're in the Observation Carriage already. Closing in fast. "*Fokk.* Do something, Khumalo! Anything!"

"I'm on it." Khumalo pulls out a hand-held welder and starts to seal the door, sparks fountaining around him. The springbok on his neck shivers again as though it's about to bolt. "I'll give you time—now do your thing already!"

Fenwick fumbles, pulling out a dented computer from the duffel bag next to Khumalo, and gets to work. He plugs into the train's mainframe through the on-wall connection port and smashes through the firewall in no time. Fenwick studied TransNet's security for years to escape the boredom of working for them. He never breached it before now, but God, did it feel good to be doing it. Relaxes his nerves a notch. He's a kid again, flexing his hacking muscles, bringing back balance online.

Fenwick wipes the camera footage and locks all the doors on the train. Welded, reinforced steel will take the guards far too long to break through. On the screen, he spots one of the guards escorting passengers out of the Observation Carriage while the other thumps on the door, the curve of his left shoulder only just in shot.

There's no way they can get through it, he reminds himself, but the sound of the banging rings in his ears. No one will be able to identify them, he tells himself. *Will they?* His stomach drops. His mouth runs dry. Why did he ever think this was going to work? he berates himself, holding his head in his hands. How could he be such a fool to risk losing his daughter before she is even born? They bang on the door again, louder and louder.

His heart thumping too, Fenwick glances out the porthole next to him and sees the last of the deep blue sky fade to black. They've arrived at the South African Space Station (SASS) that hangs in geosynchronous orbit. His body untensing, Fenwick smiles as he remembers slum kids used to call it Pretopia. The expanse of star-lit space stretches either side of the train, the Moon glowing large and inviting. It's breathtaking. He hopes his daughter will one day be able to see the view, too, without having to break the law to get here.

Controlling the train's systems, he pops all the outer doors open for the passenger carriages and the rich walk out without a care in the world, unaware that their safety is in his hands. They'll soon be on a Luna shuttle for the final part of their journey. Legs shaking, Fenwick waits until they're all out, including all the workers coming off to replenish the supplies. "C'mon. Get off the train already! Khumalo!"

"*Ja,* one more second and I'm done." Khumalo shuts off the welder, sparks dying at his feet. "There, they won't get through that."

"Okay, good. But you better hold on tight. Things are gonna get shaky."

Khumalo cracks a blood-diamond bright smile and Fenwick hits enter to send them back down to earth.

The rockets ignite to aid the magnetostrictive engine in space; the top of the train shunts the rest back into the atmosphere as gravity grabs hold of them and helps them on their way.

Fenwick pushes the speed to the max, barely within tolerance, as they grip hold of the handles and watch the guards fall down the stairs. One rolls out into the Observation Carriage, and it looks as if he's going to be sucked out into cold, dark space. "Ha, enjoy your ride, *bokgata!*" Khumalo hollers.

Fenwick and Khumalo are safe in here and will soon be back on Earth's solid ground at the speed they're travelling. Moving twice as fast as they were coming up, the train will arrive back in minutes, according to his calculations. The comfort of that soon evaporates when Fenwick considers how security could have cottoned on to what they were doing. Grobler—had to be. Maybe he noticed the missing ID card and put two and two together. No, he couldn't have. Not that fool. He'd never connect it. Unless someone told him…

She wouldn't, would she? Lenka was pissed with him, but she'd never shop him in. Fenwick shakes his head. Khumalo is still laughing at the struggling guards trying to break through the door. Of course she wouldn't; he scolds himself for even thinking it.

Fenwick's stomach lurches and then he realizes in his distraction it's the train grinding to an abrupt halt. He stumbles. Grips harder onto the handle. Khumalo slams into him, taking the wind out of his lungs. "I got you, Khumalo."

"And I got you."

The plan had been to get off undetected, but now Fenwick sees a load more guards on the suspended platform just below them. The end of the line. He gulps. "We're *fokked.*"

"Here." Khumalo pulls out two backpacks from the duffel bag.

"What the hell are they?"

"Bad-boy glider packs, of course. It's what I was hired for—to get us outta here—wasn't it? Just like the old days, bru." Khumalo smiles, but Fenwick remembers how his old friend got them caught on more than one occasion in the past.

Fenwick grabs him by the shoulder. "But look how many there are out there! We'll never escape!"

"Oh, them. Don't worry, they'll soon be distracted." Khumalo flashes his smile, cool as ice.

"What aren't you telling me, Khumalo?"

"I promised no guns, but you never said anything about bombs. These *fokkers* don't deserve to escape this *kak*-hole of a planet if we can't." Khumalo opens the door on the opposite side of the train where there's no platform, only a long painful drop. "Time to fly, bru. Just press the red button when you're clear." Khumalo jumps from the train.

Fenwick remembers all the junk Khumalo supplied. Will these glider packs even work? Will his daughter ever know him?

He's already set up a Moroccan holding account that will transfer the money through a series of others until it reaches Lenka's. They'll never be able to pin it on her. He's done his part as a father, so if he's going to die, at least he can go taking comfort in that.

Fenwick looks down. Khumalo's pack unfurls like a bird's wings and he glides into the distance. "*Fokk* it," Fenwick mutters, fumbling as he puts on the backpack, and jumps off the train into the blue sky. It's hundreds of feet up, and the solid ground rushes at him before he hits the button...

And nothing happens. He hits it again, three times, before the glider slowly unfurls its wings and the control stick pops up around his waist. With a shaky hand, Fenwick grabs the controls. Gunshots cut up the air, fizz past his ear as he ducks his head. A bullet hole in the glider's canvas makes it whistle. He struggles to steer the glider but is finally able to follow Khumalo into the distance, free as a bird. For now, at least.

But just as he thinks it, a blast of hot air slams into his back and he free falls, out of control.

* * *

Fenwick is slapped awake by Khumalo. He must have blacked out there for a moment.

"Where am I?"

"Don't worry, I still got you, bru." He's still smiling, too. "Sorry about the rude awakening, but I didn't want you to miss the view."

Fenwick's blurry vision clears. His head aches as bad as the morning after he and Lenka celebrated their pregnancy. With Khumalo's help, he struggles to stand and puts his weight onto one good leg. His ankle is useless, but otherwise he doesn't seem to be in too bad shape. Fenwick spots the glider's airbags and realizes they must have cushioned his crash landing.

In the distance, the *Blou Trein* Suborbirail, shadowing South Africa for so long, collapses. Like a toy train dropped by a distracted child, the *Blou* nosedives, and groaning metal rends the air. The ground trembles as it lands and he almost loses his footing. Untethered, the train lines twist and fall back to earth.

Fenwick realizes now why the guards were there. It wasn't anything to do with him; their tech must have detected the bombs Khumalo planted. TransNet has been using such software for years, fearful of terrorist attacks. Not that Khumalo knew that. Still, it's hard to be angry with him when he helped Fenwick escape.

Polisie sirens blare in the distance, blue lights flash, but the cops are too late this time. Fenwick and Khumalo will still have to keep their heads down for a long while, hiding in the slums until things settle.

Fenwick knows it will be a short-lived victory. Other poor fools will work in the factory to ensure train parts are printed and the Suborbirail reassembled, but it'll take years.

By that time, maybe a young girl, educated like he'll never be, will be old enough to travel on it.

Illustration by Greg Uchrin

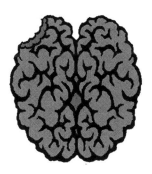

I Heard the Bombs on Christmas Day

Nathan W. Toronto

I huff up the River Walk from home, passing Granada's dilapidated monastery on the way. My eyebrows prickle with annoyance when I see the white and green streamers decorating the square and its statue of Columbus. The small watchtower, across the square from my shop, is draped with green banners, Qur'anic inscriptions in glittering gold.

My hackles rise when I see the local *imam* waiting outside my bookshop. What could he want with me? Is it not enough that I am the last Christian bookseller in Granada, in what was supposed to be Spain?

I can't ask him that, though. Eight hundred years of Muslim occupation has taught us the high price of disrespecting religious figures. But I can make my point in other ways.

"*As-salamu aleikum,*" he says.

"*Buenos días,* Sheikh Ahmar," I respond, fishing the keys out of my pocket. I give a little grin, just a little one, to suggest that using Spanish with a Muslim cleric might actually be playful instead of insolent.

A scowl passes over his face at the slight, but he regains his composure quickly, then eyes me with caution. "I'm here about your son."

I doubt that's the only reason he's here. I take a deep breath and glare at the mountain across the river, where al-Hamra Palace sits, watching me like a sentinel, an enduring symbol of Muslim preeminence. Tonight, Christmas Eve, the procession celebrating 500 years since Columbus' voyage will begin from there. The procession will end here, outside my bookshop, in the plaza with the statue of Columbus, the Christian explorer who had no choice in 1492 but to sail the ocean blue under a flag emblazoned with the crescent moon of Granada's Muslim rulers.

Every morning, in my prayers, I remember the day that the Christian forces led by Ferdinand and Isabela failed to dislodge the Muslim defenders of Granada. That day, the dream of unifying Spain under Christian rule was lost forever.

I shiver. Maybe not forever.

And Sheikh Ahmar has the temerity to say he cares about my son.

I answer his cautious stare with an inscrutable smirk. "The police came and took my son in the middle of the night."

The sheikh strokes his *henna*-red beard and frowns. "The charges against him are serious."

I shove the key into the lock and twist with more force than is my wont. "It's not a crime to distribute pamphlets."

The sheikh shrugs. "We need peace and quiet at a time like this."

"The authorities want Christians to forget their roots and stop speaking Spanish." I glare. It is hard to hide the anger rising in my throat. "Or to leave Granada forever."

The sheikh holds the door open and follows me into the bookshop. "Now, Yousuf, it's 1992. We don't expel people anymore."

"My name is José," I respond. I add, in my mind, that many Christians have left for Christian Europe to escape loose Muslim morals and unsafe streets.

Sheikh Ahmar cocks his head as he enters the shop. "When did you change your name from Arabic?"

I set my things down behind the counter and call over my shoulder, with a tinge of pique, "After my son was thrown in jail."

"Ah." An uncomfortable silence settles, but then the sheikh clears his throat, as if moving on to another subject could be done, easy as that. "Shall I review your books?"

So this is the real reason he's here. Censorship. Or, as the authorities call it, preventing hate speech. "You know I don't sell books that insult other religions."

He returns the smirk I gave him earlier. "You know I have to check."

* * *

Since my son isn't here to tend the shop, I have to close at noon to go hear mass.

I haven't had a customer all morning, and each step toward the small church at the top of the Bayyazeen hill fills my thighs with fire and my chest with helplessness. I can do nothing else to change my situation, to save my shop, to free my son.

At least I can see him at visiting hours this afternoon. For once, I'm glad government offices stay open on Christian holidays like Christmas Eve.

I stop at the overlook outside our little church, which sits across the valley from al-Hamra. The midday sun glances off the clay brick, making it burn a fiery red. The lush gardens cover the heights surrounding the palace, exploding with color, and tourists stream like ants up from the city center, flowing by Granada's imposing main mosque, hoping to catch some taste of the celebrations.

Feet shuffle to a stop next to me. "A stunning picture, isn't it?"

Fear claws at my chest when I see who it is, but I force it down by clearing my throat. "*Holá*, Friar Marcos."

"José." He nods with purpose and holds out a briefcase. "For your son."

I hesitate, unsure that I'm ready for what this means, but then I reach out and grip the handle. My palm is suddenly sweaty. I give a nervous laugh. "The monastery is right next to my shop. We could have met there."

Friar Marcos gives me a warm smile and rubs my shoulder. "It is better this way."

I gulp and reach down to adjust my watch. "What time do you have?"

"Two minutes to noon, with thirty-eight seconds."

I try to break a smile, but it just doesn't come. I adjust my grip on the briefcase, painfully aware that I'm supposed to say something else.

He pats my shoulder. "Don't worry, Brother José. Remember: 'Where two or three are gathered together in my name, there am I in the midst of them.'"

"Yes, Friar Marcos." I turn back toward al-Hamra, as if it might help me evade an inescapable future. "You're right."

"Are you going to hear mass?" he asks.

"That's always a good idea, isn't it?"

* * *

After mass, I rise to greet the dozen or so other people in the church, a social formality, the fingers of my left hand wrapped around the suitcase grip. I see a face I don't recognize and my eyes narrow. There aren't that many Christians left in Granada.

The man tries to avoid eye contact as he shuffles out of the pew, but I stop him with an extended hand. "Are you new here?"

His eyes dart toward the exit, but his focus quickly shifts back to me. He's hiding something. Probably a secret policeman. They come by every so often, just to be sure we're not insulting some other religion, but we know what that really means. He beams and shakes my hand with an eager expression. "Oh, no. I usually hear mass at the chapel over by Jinnat al-Areef."

I suppress a laugh at this ridiculous cover story. Jinnat al-Areef is the immaculate palace garden on the opposite side of al-Hamra, and one of Granada's signature tourist attractions. Not many people live over there, but there is a small chapel that serves Granada's poorest.

"And how is Father Juán?" I ask, gripping the man's hand like only a brother can.

"He is well," the man says, with another subtle glance at the exit. "He sends his regards."

I again fight to maintain my composure. The name of the priest at that chapel is actually Pedro, but he goes by his Arabic name, Boutros. Of course, a secret policeman wouldn't know that. The parishioners over there are too busy scraping together their next meal to hand out dangerous literature, so they can't have popped onto his radar yet.

I release the man's hand. "Glad to hear it." I give a fake smile. "Peace be unto you."

The man leaves and I flex my fingers around the grip of the briefcase. My palm is damp again.

I leave the church to run the most important errand of my life.

* * *

They won't let you take anything except identification to visiting hours at the prison, so I need to drop the briefcase off at home. On the way, I pass by my little bookshop. The lettering has been peeling off the window for some time. It's hard to remember the last time the shop turned a profit. Two, maybe three years ago. Mail peeks out from underneath the mat, and I don't have to curl back the cracked, black rubber to know that they're all past-due notices.

I run my fingers over the inscription above the door. I had it made back in the early days, when I still had customers and hopes were high for a Christian rejuvenation of the city. The inscription comes from the Gospel of John: "And ye shall know the truth, and the truth shall make you free." Never did words ring truer than now.

Maybe I could keep the shop open for one more season, maybe carry more of those trinkets and baubles the tourists goggle over, but then I purse my lips. What's the use? What kind of future would that be for my son? It's better this way.

I continue on my way, drop off the briefcase, and take the bus to the prison, a grimy old building on the outskirts of town, a place oozing anger and regret. For me, the sense of injustice builds with each step, although I feel neither anger or regret, nor remorse or doubt, for that matter. We all live. We all die. We all make our way to the next phase of life.

I enter the prison and, after waiting too long in the reception area, I follow a guard through a maze of thick metal doors and bunker-like hallways, enough to intimidate even the most hardened criminal, much less an accused petty provocateur like my son. Out of slits in the metal doors that we pass, I hear shouting and moaning and, in some cases, absolute silence. All sounds to match the sins in this place. My son doesn't deserve this. Then again, who does?

We enter a room with metal tables and chairs bolted to the floor, two or three chairs per table. The guard motions to one, then adjusts his head covering and shrugs his *jelbab* on his shoulders. "Please wait here, Mister Yousuf."

I nod, then whisper in a voice of resignation, "It's José."

He probably doesn't hear me or, if he does, he ignores me, because he walks off like he's escaping from the plague ward of a hospital. As if criminality is contagious.

After another tortuous wait, they lead my son in, drag him almost. He fights, and his indomitable spirit brings hope and joy to my heart. Nothing will come easy to his jailers.

They leave his hands manacled after he sits down. I decide right then that I'm doing the right thing. As the jailers leave, my son gives them a stare that would make the Devil himself shudder.

I reach out and enfold his hands in mine. "Don't fight them, son. This trial will pass soon enough."

"They are evil, *Papi*." His glare softens, but does not vanish completely. "We should have done more to fight the Muslimification of the city." His jaw ripples under the skin of his face. "It needs to stop."

I nod. "I can do all things through Christ which strengtheneth me."

He sighs and looks away, then gently releases his hands from mine to wipe at his moist cheek, doing battle with his many frustrations. His manacles clang on the metal table, which is scoured to a shine on top, but which has grease and grime where eyes can't see. My knees brush up and slide against the underside of the table as I try in vain to find a more comfortable position on the unforgiving chairs.

My son's shoulders slump. "I'm sorry, *Papi*. I should have faith."

I cannot answer him, for fear that I'll say something I shouldn't. I breathe deeply to keep the lump in my throat from bursting out. He is all I have. I am all he has.

He reaches back and squeezes my hands. "What did the lawyers say?"

I smile back. "They said you'll be out soon," I lie. I haven't spoken to a lawyer at all. I try to give him a reassuring look. I know Friar Marcos will take care of everything once all's said and done. I smile. "This is all just a big misunderstanding."

"Thank you for coming, *Papi*."

"Be strong, my boy." I rise and take a long look at the perfect line of my son's features, the set of his eyes and the strength of his will. "I love you," I say.

"I love you, too, *Papi*. Stay safe."

After the main prison doors clang shut behind me and I am on the outside once again, my son's final words ring through my head over and over and over: "Stay safe."

How am I supposed to do that?

* * *

I stumble home in a swirl of emotions: bewilderment, despondency, temptation to anger, but mostly fear. But I keep coming back to one emotion: love. "Perfect love casteth out fear."

I have nothing to fear, I keep telling myself. My hand shakes with a violence it has never known as I put the key in the lock. That simple action, which should be nothing more than muscle memory after all these years, takes me two hands and twenty seconds to accomplish.

I pray, to calm myself. I kneel, I recite, barely able to recall the words of scripture, much less focus on what they might mean. My knees ache from the kneeling, and sweat begins to run down my back when I notice the briefcase in the corner, by the door, so I won't forget it on the way out.

I record a video journal entry, which I hope will settle my nerves. I talk about the shop, my son, and the small fortune he will have, courtesy of Friar Marcos. I ramble on about this city that I love and the holiday that Christians the world over celebrate tonight.

In Christian Spain, tonight is Noche Buena, or "The Good Night." Here, in Muslim Andalus, it is just another night to party into the wee hours. This godless people and their supposedly Muslim ways. How easily Man goes astray.

But I love them, as any Christian should, the people of this city, especially my son. Perfect love casts out all fear. That is why I must do what I will do.

And so I wait, for night to fall, for the celebration to start.

* * *

At ten minutes to midnight, after closing my shop for the day and hiking up from my apartment, I join the line to enter Jinnat al-Areef. The line is longer than I expect it to be, and my legs burn. Al-Hamra is lit up in shifting reds, greens, and blues, and on the other side of the palace, across the river and the valley, is the little plaza where my bookshop resides. Rather, resided.

Some of the people standing in line wear European garb, tight-necked tunics, hoods, and scarves to ward off the faint chill on the air. Most, though, wear clothes from across the Muslim and Arab world, loose-fitting *jelbabs* from Morocco, women in slitted *abayas* from the Gulf, with flowing hair and slender thighs showing, and the colorful blouses from Muslim America, necklines plunged and oblivious to the cold. I shudder at the immodesty.

At some point the Muslims forgot what Jinnat al-Areef actually means: "The Paradise of the All-knowing One." It is so much more than a beautiful garden with vibrant colors and a redolence that transports you to the favorite places in your memory. Five hundred years ago, when Columbus came to al-Hamra to petition the crown to support his crazy trip to India, the Muslim rulers and their advisors contemplated the deeper meaning of the expedition in this place. That was back when Islam still meant something, though, before the believers fell into moral ruin and left Christians to be the conscience of mankind.

Someone I know by sight but not name breaks out of the line ahead of me. He stops as he is about to pass and I realize that I haven't kept good track of the time. I tighten my grip on the suitcase. My palm feels wet again.

Everything is on a tight schedule, but the man and I greet each other, ask about families and work, chat about the celebration. I give answers as vague as is socially appropriate, but that's hard to do because the whole time I think about how this puts the operation behind schedule.

He finally leaves, saying there are too many people here for his taste. I say that leaving is probably a good idea.

I check my watch and gauge my place in line. I'm less than a minute from the metal detector. They're not scanning bags, but they are opening them to look inside. I set the combination on the briefcase to 646 and start counting down from sixty.

I'm surprised at how easy it is to set the combination. I expected more…I don't know…internal resistance. My son's last words to me spring back to my mind: "Stay safe."

The line shuffles forward and two more people stand in line ahead of me.

50.

I suck in a deep breath and check the time. 12:01. It's Christmas Day now.

37.

The line moves forward again and a discussion ensues ahead of me about what's allowed inside and what's not. My briefcase won't make it through, but I expected that.

21 seconds.

The person ahead of me goes through the metal detector. It beeps, and there's that brief moment of uncertainty, but they let him through anyway, probably because he doesn't look threatening. It occurs to me that I might not look threatening, either, although I do have traditional Christian clothes on, and they've been locking people up lately for petty infractions like handing out pieces of paper.

10.

It's my turn. Out of habit, I check my watch, which hasn't moved much in the last minute, and set my briefcase on the sideboard, where they'll check it after I go through the metal detector.

6.

My eyes meet those of the guard. He nods and the corners of his mouth turn up just a bit.

4.

"*As-salamu aleikum*," he says.

3.

Then he freezes, his hands poised to unlock my briefcase, because off in the distance, from the direction of al-Hamra, a loud boom shatters the night. The colorful lights that had illuminated the palace shudder and flick off.

2.

Our eyes meet again, and sweet-awful realization washes over the guard's face. Another bomb explodes, somewhere closer.

1.

I smile. "*Feliz Navidad.*"

The world bursts with light and sound and fury and awe, and pain, and I feel my love made complete.

Illustration by Kat D'Andrea

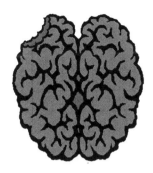

Phantom Sanction

Caias Ward

Simon Hanson was bleeding. It was a rarity these days, as Simon was a ghost. Last time he had bled was in 1978, when a half-dozen bullets at the abrupt end of a high-end burglary also ended him. It had been a set-up, he was sure of it, and that thought kept him from going to the Great Beyond even as the thought of reuniting with his wife, now dead twenty years, drove him to seek out a way to go and find her.

Right now though, he was bleeding, and it hurt. He pulled out an old Nokia as faded and bleached as he was on this side of the Wall Between Worlds. Simon called his handler.

"Simon, where the hell are you?" Yates said.

Yates was his human handler. She had a natural talent with the dead, seeing and hearing them. They were a team: Simon with his old breaking and entering skills plus his ordinarily intangible self, and Yates, his connection to the world of the living. They were freelancers, spies, and criminals.

"I'm..." Simon paused before finishing his statement. "I'm bleeding. Someone shot me."

"Who shot you Simon? Another ghost? Where are you?"

"Somewhere safe. I think."

He had hopped from cab to cab out of Manhattan, even body-hopped to hide out, but whoever was after him was good—good enough to put a bullet through his right side. Good enough to spot Simon and shove him out of the cabbie he hid in. Good enough to nearly catch him in Jersey City, spindly fingers and torn skin flailing at him, clawing at his messenger bag and tearing at his ectoplasm. Good enough to get a name which terrified ghosts from New York to Chicago.

"It's the Raggedy Man," Simon told Yates.

Simon was in a big box store off of Route 22, having snuck in through an air duct out of habit. He wedged himself on a high shelf up against a wall. It was late, grave-late in a cold October, and he could feel the flesh in the distance, 24/7 convenience store workers idle and drivers racing by. He could feel a few ghosts, but not the Raggedy Man.

"Shit. I'll send a team to pick you up. Did you get the package?"

Simon leaned against the wall, the flaky and moist detritus of the dead which coated everything on this side of the Wall Between Worlds keeping him from falling backward. He closed his eyes, holding his hand to the exit wound. It was sticky, stringy, pulsing. He leaked front and back. It was slow, very slow, but certain. Inevitable.

If you bleed out, or are exorcised, you're gone. No Great Beyond. No bright light. No chance of seeing the wife again.

Yes, I did, Simon thought.

Simon willed himself to deliberately exhale.

"God, this hurts. Yes," Simon said. "It burnt my damn hand. It's a book."

"Good," she said. "You should have called sooner."

"With the Raggedy Man chasing me? Who did the pre-screen on this job?"

"I don't know what happened," Yates said. "Where are you?"

Simon felt a ghost getting nearer and nearer. He hung up his phone, tucking it away. He pushed himself back, sinking into the thick wall behind a box on the shelf. The layers of detritus on both sides of the wall would conceal him and, if he needed to, he could shove himself through with some effort.

Dammit.

His messenger bag was halfway out, the solid book pressed firmly against the solid wall. He rushed to cover the bag with shimmering and jellied ectoplasm. Hopefully, if the Raggedy Man moved the box, he would only see a lump of ectoplasm.

He sensed a ghost on the other side of the box. He wanted to sink away through the wall, float off, go somewhere else…but he would have to leave the book behind. He could, but something kept gnawing at him. Why was the intel bad? What was this book that burned ghosts if they touched it? Why was the Raggedy Man the opposition on a simple black bag operation?

Simon went gray: thought himself small, indistinct, unremarkable, the face in the crowd, the unpainted cinder blocks of the big box store. He kept as little of himself outside the wall as he could, refusing the habit of breathing, of a heartbeat, all of the things the dead did to mimic life and fool themselves. Simon felt for a soul and found it: angry, and with an angry gun. That gun was in the hand of that man when he died and became the Raggedy Man, and that anger, so much anger, is why that gun could kill ghosts.

The ghost moved away—

Simon's phone rang.

It was only flashes of sight and sound and soul. Simon didn't know if he shoved away the box in front of him or if it flew away in the flail of torn flesh and cloth which clawed at him. He smashed the book into the Raggedy Man's head, who howled and smoked and scorched. Simon hit him again, in the face.

Four bars of "Gran Vals," the Nokia Tune, playing over and over.

The Raggedy Man flew through shelves, out of sight, screeching and yowling. Had the book wounded him? Didn't matter, it gave Simon the moment he needed. Back out the air duct, then low to the ground, latching onto car after car, fleeing, anything to get away…

Simon laughed as he watched an ambulance trundle by. He followed after, then clung to the outside of it, willing himself indistinct as it made its way back to the first aid squad.

* * *

Simon hit the jackpot; someone must have died in the ambulance recently, violently, so their soul manifested phantasmal counterparts of medical supplies. Trauma seals, an IV with saline solution, even some pain medication. On this side, intent and emotion mattered, and the act of Simon putting the bandages on and inserting the IV needle into his arm was enough to start the process of healing his hand and side. He needed to rest, get his head together. As the IV dripped into his ectoplasm, Simon called his voicemail. It was Yates. She had a team ready.

Simon shut off his phone.

He opened the book with tongue depressors. Even as far as necromantic books went, this one was different; it was expertly bound, though the notes themselves were scrawled in a maddening hand, often beyond the edge of the page. Page after page, he flipped and read, recalling what he remembered from bugging living necromancers and dead professors over the decades. The book was in Early New High German and it said it was written in the 16th century, roundabouts. His German was solid, better than his Latin, but he thought it was getting worse as he translated. Definitely a necromancy tome, talking about the nature of emotion on death, the process of grave goods, and how to—

No. This can't be, Simon thought.

"While normally," Simon read aloud, "an emotion upon death will swell into an object of importance to the deceased, the Volkert Binding will instead allow the storing of emotion. Then, such emotions may be imbued within an object with no previous emotional tie, creating a phantasmal form of the object complete in function and—*feindlich?*—inimical to spirits regardless of its original form and function…"

His phone rang, somehow, like an old-timey desktop telephone, rather than the usual tone. Simon jumped at the sound, dreading who could force a call through.

"Oh, you good, kid," the voice said when Simon answered. It was Irish thick, by way of Queens. "Took me a while to connect to your shut-off phone."

"Yeah, it almost got me caught, remember. How's your face?"

"I know you think it's funny, kid, but consider this: if I'm powerful enough to get my phone to connect to yours, I will find you."

"Won't be the first time I got got, Raggedy Man."

"I'm not a fan of that name," he said.

"You got something you want me to call you?"

"No. Look, kid. The package is worth a lot. Enough that I'll hunt you until there isn't a single haunted house or cemetery where you're safe. Now, I have five bullets handy, least ones I don't need to pry out of newly-arrived ghosts and make work, but if you don't give me the package, I will use all five on you. You already know how one feels."

"What makes the package so valuable?" Simon asked.

"My employers want it back, that's what makes it so valuable. It's nothing personal. I have a professional reputation to uphold. I've heard of you, Simon Hansen. You ain't no narrowback. In another afterlife, we might have worked well together. But in this afterlife, you need to give me that book or you are going to stop existing. Savvy?"

"What's in this book can make us all stop existing."

"What the hell are you jacking your jaw about—?"

"I ain't no expert on grave goods but this book looks like a field guide on how to kill us all."

"When I run out of bullets, I will scrounge around for more just to shoot you again. Stop jerking me around."

And if I'm right, if he gets this book, he'll be able to make all the bullets he wants, Simon thought. *Or worse.*

Simon hung up. His bag was a mess; the book had started to eat away at its form. He shoved it into the bag, hoping it would hold until he got to where he needed to go.

* * *

"To answer your perennial question," Mark Arsenault, PhD, said, "no, this will not get you to the Great Beyond, Simon."

Mark supplemented his tenure-track position at Seton Hall University with necromancy. Simon and Mark had a working relationship: Simon steals and spies for Mark, Mark is on call for Simon's necromantic questions even in the middle of the night, so long as he calls first. Mark told him to give him a half-hour before showing up. A half-hour after Simon called, they huddled over a workbench in Mark's cluttered library filled with books from both sides of the Wall Between Worlds. Mark held the book open under an LED lamp. The book caused Mark no harm. It could only harm the dead.

"I was hoping for a better answer, Doc," Simon said, as he touched his side. It was better; the medical supplies had worked.

"Well," Mark said, slipping his reading glasses onto his hawkish face as he flipped through the book, "I don't have one for you. As for your immediate concern, you were spot on with your translation, but there's more to this. When you died, and you became a ghost, you brought stuff over with you, yes?"

"Some," Simon said. "Tools, mostly."

"Things important to you?"

"And some of the stuff I was buried with," Simon said. "My wife, she put a picture of us in the casket." Simon felt for a wallet in his pants pocket, which he knew held that picture, or at least the one which came over with him.

"It's why the pharaohs were buried with servants, weapons. Emperors and kings sent off with horses. Viking funerals with longboats, even. That much emotion let everything carry over, sometimes. The Raggedy Man must have had a big hate-on if his gun copied over, complete with ammo. Point is, what if you had a means to just gather emotion and then put it into something, make a version on your side of the Wall Between Worlds?"

"At will?" Simon asked.

"Exactly. No scavenging graveyards for grave goods, or hovering around car wrecks. You could bring over a car, or clothing, or—"

"A machine gun," Simon said. "A tank."

"It gets worse," Mark said. "The methods in here, to invest objects in the living world so they act as grave goods? Basically, it would turn every weapon, or anything, into a portable, one-shot exorcism. No banishing from a body, no hurt...just nick someone with a knife or bullet, hell, hit them with a teddy bear, and they are gone. Poof." Mark flicked his fingers out in a mock explosion.

"This," Simon tried to articulate everything going through his head right now and failed. "We have to destroy this," he settled on saying. Simon exerted himself to wrap the book in cloth.

"Wait!" Mark said.

Simon rushed through the kitchen with the book, passing through clutter on the living side of the Wall Between Worlds and knocking over stacks of books on his side. He rifled through cabinets, coming out with a clear bottle of denatured alcohol from one cabinet and an Aim'N Flame from a drawer. Simon yanked the back door hard enough to slam it into a kitchen counter, one of the panes of glass in the grid window cracking. He sprung in a float from the doorway to the ground, missing the stairs down to the stone backyard patio entirely, the book setting off the motion sensor light in the yard. Mark chased after him. Simon threw the book and the cloth into the opening of the chiminea on the patio. He poured the alcohol inside to coat the book, tossing the bottle away when it was empty.

"I'd like a *bit* more time to look at the book," Mark said as he reached into the chiminea. "There is probably other useful stuff in it, even to trade for your exit strategy to the Great Beyond."

Simon focused himself, reached through the Wall Between Worlds and shoved Mark a good ten feet. Mark twisted and stumble-stepped, caught his toe on a raised patio stone, and sprawled forward. He crumpled to the ground, his hands scraped and bloody.

"What the hell?" Mark said as he fought to stand, his knee giving out under him the first few tries.

"Not a fucking chance," Simon said, igniting the Aim'N Flame over the book. A flash whooshed, alcohol vapor flaring up enough to startle Simon. The cloth ignited; in moments, the book ignited as well, a crackling echoing in the clay chimney, almost…

Crying?

The book wept. Shuddering, trembling sobs, as the leather scorched and the paper suffered. Its agony was brief, the alcohol speeding along the book's demise, and to the living world it was soon nothing more than a corpse of knowledge between charred leather sitting in the chiminea. Simon reached into the chiminea.

He came out with the book, quite intact, on his side of the Wall Between Worlds. It did not burn him as he held it.

"It's what I figured," Mark said as he hobbled over to Simon. "The book itself had a lot of emotion bound into it. No way it wasn't going to pass over."

Simon grabbled the ghost book by the cover and pulled. The book would not come apart. He focused himself, first at the spine, then the individual pages. Nothing would tear. Nothing would rip.

"The book was clearly very powerful," Mark said. "You'll need a powerful ghost to destroy it."

"Can you summon someone?" Simon said.

"Anything powerful enough I could summon could probably use the book, too," Mark said. "You want the book in its hands? Let's not rush this."

"This is too dangerous, Mark, and you know it!"

He does know it, Simon thought. *So why is he—?*

"Why are you stalling, Mark?"

"What are you talking about?"

Simon felt them all now that he wasn't distracted. The living, in houses around them… but also the dead, forming a perimeter. Other living, tense, adrenaline-stenched, waiting to operate only as operators do. He cursed himself for not paying better attention.

Separate groups, converging. Two teams?

"Our friends, living and otherwise, Mark. Why did you have me wait a half-hour to see you? Did you call someone, Mark? Did you drop a dime on me?"

"I'm going to take a step back, Simon," Mark said, his fall-bloodied palms up, cautiously moving a few feet backwards, "and we are going to want to talk about what we can do with that book and who we can help with it. That thing is powerful as hell, and we might even get you to the Great Beyond like you want."

"Shut up, Mark," Simon said. "You know what this does and you know why it can't exist."

Mark continued to step backward, doing his best to get out of any potential line of fire.

"Now Simon," Mark said. "There's a lot of stuff going on—"

Gunfire erupted on both sides of the Wall Between Worlds. The chiminea shattered. Mark stumbled out of the way of living world lead, sprawling behind a stone bench. Simon winced at a graze of phantom lead along his shoulder. He spun, holding the book up in one hand. Solid lead passed through him; phantom lead hit the book, doing nothing to it but tumbling him backwards from the force of the rounds. He righted himself and leapt through the stone bench, concealing himself.

Simon shielded his eyes as a warm bright glow flared in the night air, the light soothing and infuriating at once. It was the Great Beyond, a bright beacon opening and welcoming. Simon sprung up, launching himself to the light.

It didn't welcome him. He bounced off, splashing into the ectoplasmic detritus which coated this side of the Wall Between Worlds next to Mark's dead body. A ghost, with glasses and a hawkish face, stood confused in the light nearby. Two phantom rounds passed through him, his ectoplasm spraying in the air. He staggered as he floated, rushing into the light. In a flicker, the light vanished, the oozing translucence of this side of the Wall remaining. The ectoplasm splashed down, joining the coating already present.

That son of a bitch, Simon thought as he pushed himself downward, sinking into the ground. There, in the very dark, he floated away as muffled shots rang out, clay and stone cracking. He went deeper and floated well away from the firefight. He went gray again and felt around himself for other ghosts.

A second perimeter, both living and dead, moving in search patterns. Simon went deep, minutes deep, until he could barely feel the ghosts above and only hear the uncomfortable sounds of ancient dead things from deep below. He didn't dare go farther down, but instead traveled level through bedrock, finally coming above ground far away.

He dialed Yates.

"Simon!"

"I'm okay," Simon said. "Did you send those teams?"

"What teams?" Yates said. "Where are you?"

"Two teams. I went to see Arsenault. He's dead, he went into the light. He ratfucked us."

"Client sent their own team," Yates said. "They broke the contract. I'm already on the move; they're looking for me. The other team must have been from our target."

Simon had known her long enough to know she wasn't lying.

"Raggedy Man's not going to be happy about getting second-guessed on his job."

"Look, Simon," Yates said. "Let me get you to a safe house. We bring the package in and save our asses."

"They can't have it!" Simon screamed. He deliberately breathed out, shocked at his own response.

"Simon, if we don't give the client the book—"

"This book is an instruction manual to bring anything over to this side of the Wall! Grave goods on demand," Simon said. "Guns, bombs, you name it. And each one would be like an exorcism at the slightest hit."

Silence. Finally, Yates spoke.

"You could destroy every ghost…"

"I burned the book," Simon said. "But it came over to this side of the Wall. It stopped bullets, and I couldn't tear it apart. I'm not powerful enough."

"Who is?"

"You know who," Simon said.

"I can find someone else," Yates said. "Let me make some calls."

"No, you can't. We don't have time. Either the client or the target is going to bag me, and then you. You're a handler. Handle him. You got a rep, too. Thirty solid years. Let him know what happened. Ask him why they sent a second team."

"You want *me* to call *him*?" Yates said. "Are you insane?"

"It's our only shot."

* * *

"You know I could just blow you away, kid," the Raggedy Man said, pointing his gun at Simon. The gun was a Colt Model 1903 Pocket Hammerless. Simon didn't want to see it this close. "Mighty big risk your handler took, calling me directly for a meet and bypassing my handler. I can finish this job right now, grab that book from you."

The pair were in an abandoned warehouse on Frelinghuysen Avenue, by Newark Liberty Airport. If Simon needed to run, there were lots of cars passing by, and he could even catch a plane off to anywhere. It's not every day the Raggedy Man agrees to consider a truce.

Whether he intended to honor it was another matter.

The warehouse was empty and dark on the living side of the Wall Between Worlds. On their side, the coating of ectoplasmic tailings was thin and smooth; even the dead avoided this place. It was the first time Simon got to see the Raggedy Man while outside of a death-or-death struggle. He was short and very Irish. His face might have been clean-shaven in life. In death, it was slashed from hairline to neck, thin ribbons in the semblance of flesh peeled away from muscle which shook of their own accord. His neck was the worst cut, the deep slash of a death wound, collarbone to collarbone, visible just above his smart shirt collar and a neat black tie. His suit was gray, clean but worn, the edges of the jacket and pants ragged. He was young, younger than Simon when he died.

"I know you want the book," Simon said, the book in hand. "But we can't let anyone get it. It's gotta be destroyed. I can't do it, I'm not strong enough. You? You could."

The Raggedy Man laughed.

"I have a job, and it's to get that book. But I listened to Yates, who spun quite the tale. I didn't buy it at first, but I checked out the necromancer's house. Lots of dead bodies. Lots of ghosts still around, including some who work for my employer. I had an exclusive on this job. My handler's pissed. It's bad form to not trust your hires, who are working in good faith. So I'm listening. Go on," he said, rolling his wrist, gun in hand, and settling the gun back on Simon. "It's one of those necromancer things?"

"It's an instruction manual," Simon said.

"So?" the Raggedy Man said. "It instructs you to make what?"

"You know your gun?"

"It's my gun, course I know it," the Raggedy Man said. The flesh on his face fluttered in annoyance, his fingers elongating, twisting around the grip.

"Came over when you died, right? Violent death? Emotional death?"

The Raggedy Man's face slipped, the rags of skin which were cut and left dangling from his face in the hour before his death separating from each other and wiggling around.

"Chill, boss," Simon said. "I feel what you're feeling, I've been there."

Simon lifted his shirt, showing his own death wounds. Eight bullet holes, close up, deliberate, from people he trusted. In a way, the holes still hurt as he thought about them. He put his shirt down. The Raggedy Man nodded, his face smoothing out and settling down.

"My point is," Simon continued, "those emotions are what let grave goods come across. Either our emotions, or the living's emotions. This book? It's an instruction manual on how to send anything over. Imagine being able to make grave goods at will."

"I could get a car," the Raggedy Man said with a laugh. "I was saving up for a Pierce-Arrow before I died, but I'd go for one of those Mustangs now."

"What if someone brought over a nuke? How many ghosts would be destroyed?"

"No ghost is gonna launch a ghost nuke," the Raggedy Man said. "You'd have to be an idiot."

"Just takes one," Simon said. "One depressed ghost. One suicidal ghost. One ghost who still has living family and gets blackmailed to blow us all to Hell to keep them safe. Or a human willing to get rid of us. Hell, a necromancer could flip the switch and not even get a suntan from something which would annihilate us all. A nuke, on this side. Hell, even a truck bomb, or anything. Imagine a crate of guns coming over and ending up in everyone's hands!"

"I could use more guns. Hell, even a few more bullets. You ain't selling this well, kid."

"Sure, more guns for you. *And everyone else.* Who's gonna hire you if they can outfit any newbie with an AK-47? Or issue them to necromancers or natural talents like my handler who can see through the Wall and pick us off? Crimes and espionage turn into warfare very fast. Hell, we don't even know who hired us over this damn book, this thing which could destroy us all. You been dead, what, hundred years?"

"Hundred twelve," the Raggedy Man said as though he had his demise figured down to the minute.

"You got a rep. Why do you think I ran?" Simon said.

"Cuz you're smart. Not necessarily smart enough now," the Raggedy Man said, frustrated, as he leveled his gun again and stalked forward. Simon put one hand up to wave off the Raggedy Man, clutching the book against himself with the other.

"Why do you think I had Yates call you? You got a rep, of not being a hothead. You are careful about the jobs you take. You've dropped handlers before. Literally, in one case."

The Raggedy Man shrugged, nodding.

"And I got a rep, too," Simon said. "You said it."

"You ain't no narrowback," the Raggedy Man said. "And you're a straight shooter, Simon. Off the job, you don't hamstring no one. On the job, you do your thing. No one got no complaints. Same as your handler. She watches out for her crews. You know I did a job for her once?"

"I did not," Simon said.

"Thirty years ago. She was just a kid," the Raggedy Man said. "Solid job, all happy. Our interests were not aligned well enough so we didn't stay in touch, but I bore her no ill will. It's why I listened to her when she called direct. Show me what you got."

Simon opened up the book, searching for the relevant section. "It's in German," Simon said. "I can read it to you."

"I can read German," the Raggedy Man said. "Latin and Italian too. Lots of time to learn new stuff when you're dead."

Simon held the book up to the Raggedy Man. The Raggedy Man rolled his gun hand to get him to turn pages, first slowly, then quicker and quicker. The gun, aimed firmly at Simon, lowered with each turn of the page. Soon, the gun was at the Raggedy Man's side, him shaking his head as he struggled with the odd wording from the older tongue, still somewhat familiar.

"See what I mean?" Simon said, clutching the book, hoping he wasn't going eat bullets today.

"Feindlich," the Raggedy Man said. "I do. What do I gotta do to wreck this thing?"

* * *

"Did he destroy the book?" Yates asked.

Simon leaned on a rail at the edge of the ghostly remains of Casino Pier in Seaside Heights, the wooden structure wiped away in Hurricane Sandy back in 2012. He had hitched a ride on a truck going "down the shore" and set up on the phantom planks preserved by so many emotions. The predawn sky was clear, no haze beyond the phantoms of amusement stands and rides. He thought about trying to possess someone so he could see as the living do, but no, he wanted to be alone to see the big bright light come up from the sea. It wasn't the one he wanted to see, but it would have to do.

"He did," Simon said into the phone, refusing to look away from the horizon, the promise of light straining to climb to the sky.

"Good. We'll need to lay low for a while," Yates said. "Lots of people not happy with us."

"I think we'll be good, though. Raggedy Man wasn't happy about that book, said he was going to talk off everyone's ear about it and the client."

"You think other ghosts will believe him?"

"The Raggedy Man's got a reputation," Simon said, almost a whisper. "They'll believe him. They'll believe me. I got a reputation. And they will believe you. You got a reputation, too. He says he bears you no ill will, by the way."

Yates sighed a thirty-year-old relief.

"They won't believe the people trying to set up a ghost genocide," Simon said. "I think we'll be okay."

Simon let the bright light of the sun wash over him. It was off-season in Seaside Heights, the ghost of rides and attractions washed away nearly a decade ago silent in the early fall morning. He spied a few living surfers in the cold water; if he looked behind, he would have been sure to see joggers on the shorter reconstructed pier. He didn't look back, though, instead trying to feel the warmth of the bright light, hoping it would pull him away.

It never did, though.

"I deserve a bonus for this," Simon said.

"Out of what money?"

"I'm sure the client will pay for our silence. Now the Raggedy Man, him talking isn't our problem. He said he'd spin up the rumor mill in a few weeks. Take the time to get us paid. Me, I'm going off-grid. I need a break."

"So I guess this is goodbye for now?" Yates said.

"I might be in touch. Otherwise, see you in the after-afterlife."

Yates laughed.

Simon shut off his phone. Maybe it would be good to take a break. Maybe get away for a bit, somewhere, like Stokes Forest, where it's quiet. Or Disney World, where it's loud and full of life and emotion. For now, though, he took out the picture of him and his wife, looking at it, looking at the sun, and wondering if he'd ever see bright lights again.

Illustration by Kat D'Andrea

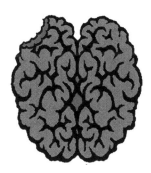

As Big as the Ocean

Jonathan Robbins Leon

Maybe it was because Shay was absorbed in her thoughts this morning, but for once, she didn't burn the pancakes. She chose the most circular one for her daughter, piping a happy face with whipped cream and adding blueberries for the eyes. "Here, baby. Want syrup?"

"No." Naima wrinkled her nose: not a morning person. Like mother, like daughter. She pushed the cream and the fruit aside with her fork to inspect the pancake.

"Orange juice or milk?" Shay asked, opening the fridge. "There's Hershey's. I can make chocolate milk."

Her daughter surprised her, wrapping her twiggy arms around her mother's knees for a hug. By the time Shay turned around, Naima was back in her seat. "What was that for?"

"You didn't burn them. And it's a real circle, too. Not an amoeba."

That's what Dani called her pancakes—amoebas—always insisting they could crawl off the plate by themselves.

Maybe everything would go perfect today.

Stop it, Shay told herself. Today did not need to be perfect. Shay just needed to be present, not lost in her thoughts or obsessing over what was to come.

Dani came in, dressed for work. "I made your coffee already," Shay said, handing them a thermos. "You want a pancake?"

"No." Taking a sip of the coffee, Dani seemed no different than usual, face glued to the phone, finger scrolling through emails that never ended. Sometimes Shay wanted to scream at Dani, make them pay attention. Especially now.

Still, if it wasn't for Dani's job, they never could have afforded clone adoption. Dani hadn't wanted to adopt at all. "It will be too hard," they'd said. "All of this love and time, for what?" But they'd gone through with it for Shay.

Dani pocketed the phone, grabbed the car keys from the hook, and seemed just ready to leave when they stopped. For the first time that morning, Dani looked at Naima. Leaving the keys and coffee on the counter, Dani took the chair opposite their daughter.

Shay watched as Dani brushed a black braid away from Naima's face. This startled the girl. For her whole life, Dani had kept their distance. They would carry Naima or take her hand to cross the road, but initiating affection at a time when they were usually rushing out the door? This was out of character.

"What is it?" Naima said.

"Your mom and I love you. Very much."

Shay worried Naima would glean too much from this. She and Dani had agreed it was best to never tell her. But Naima only squirmed in her seat and said, "Love you, too."

Dani stood, stooping over Naima to give her a hug. Tears played at the lids of Dani's eyes, but they gathered themself before the girl could see. "Have a great day, ok?"

Naima returned to her breakfast.

"Will we see you tonight?" Shay asked.

"No," Dani said, their voice hoarse with emotion. "I'm staying in town." Looking up at Shay, they mouthed the words *I'm sorry.*

They'd be back tomorrow, when it was over. Maybe it was better this way. Shay would have Naima all to herself.

* * *

"This isn't the way to school," Naima said.

"It's not?" Shay feigned surprise. "I must have missed a turn."

"Are you going to turn around?"

Shay kept driving, blowing past one street after another.

"Mommy!"

"Naima!"

Then she got it. Her eyes narrowed, Naima asked, "Are you pulling me out of school?"

"Why would I do that? Is there, like, some special occasion?"

"My birthday! Duh."

"Your birthday? How could I forget?" Shay winked.

"Where are we going?"

"I guess you'll have to wait and find out." She stuck her tongue out at her daughter, who returned the gesture.

"Mommy, tell me!"

"Put on music. Maybe I'll tell you after some Lizzo."

"That old stuff?" But Shay knew that Naima loved old hip hop more than even she did.

They arrived at the renaissance festival just as it was opening. Naima didn't have any special interest in knights or court jesters, but this had been the only event featured in the *What's Happening* section of the community page.

Out of the car as soon as it stopped, Naima asked, "Is it like sword fighting?" She took her mom's hand and Shay could have melted. Naima was as selfish as any child her age, sometimes more, but she could also be unwittingly generous. Catlike, she showed affection without knowing how much it meant to the receiver.

She tugged her mother towards the entrance. The corseted woman working the ticket booth asked Shay, "Just the two of you?" Shay nodded. The woman's ample breasts jiggled like cups of Jell-O on a tray as she tore two tickets from her roll. "And how old is she?" she asked, pointing to Naima.

"I'm seven. Well, I will be tomorrow." Naima beamed, showing her gap-toothed smile.

The lady froze, looking from Naima to Shay. The daughter was a rich black, not at all resembling her mother, who was pale, with mousy brown hair that fell lank about her shoulders. Shay could guess the woman's thoughts: *Adopted. Almost seven.*

A sad expression flickered on her face, then she was back in character. "On the house today, m'ladies." She handed them the tickets, saying to Naima, "And a happy birthday."

Right away, they got giant turkey legs to munch on as they walked. "Can I have funnel cake?" Naima wanted to know. Shay's instinct was to say not until she'd finished half her snack, but then again, did it matter?

Shay and Dani had never subscribed to that adoptive parent mentality that it was fine to indulge their child just because she was a clone. Most of the people they knew in the same predicament had not sent their children to school. What, after all, was the point? But Shay hadn't wanted to spoil her daughter with kisses, food, and leisure. She'd wanted to watch her bloom and develop just as any other little girl would have. So she'd been strict, enrolling her in school, making her do chores, refusing to allow her to behave like a tyrant.

Had she been too strict? she wondered now. Had she enjoyed it enough? "What kind of funnel cake do you want?" she asked.

*　*　*

Naima loved the festival, especially dunking the fool in the water tank. "Can we go back next year?"

Shay couldn't bring herself to lie. Instead, she asked, "If you could have anything in the world for dinner, what would it be?"

"Um," Naima considered. "Bernardo's!"

Shay hated Bernardo's. Their microwaved pasta dishes never failed to give her heartburn and the noodles came soggy and smothered in a red sauce no self-respecting person would call marinara. "Should we eat there or take it home?" she asked.

Naima pressed the limits of her birthday luck. "Can we eat in the living room?" Shay nodded. "Can I have my tent?" Shay nodded. "And can we watch *Coraline?*"

Shay put a hand up to stop the deluge. "Alright! Alright. We'll eat spaghetti in the living room and watch *Coraline* for the eight-thousandth time. But no more requests, young lady."

They lapsed into a momentary silence. Then Naima piped up, "Can we sleep in the tent?"

Sighing with mock irritation, Shay said, "We can sleep in the tent."

*　*　*

At home, bearing cartons of overcooked Italian food, Naima and Shay invaded the living room. They pushed aside the coffee table and dragged in the tent that had been a special gift from Dani.

That Christmas, Shay had argued they'd bought Naima enough, but Dani had insisted on buying this one more gift. When Naima awoke, she hadn't cared a lick for any of the dolls or coloring books that Santa had left. Instead, she spent the entire holiday reading in the tent Dani had strung with fairy lights.

"Are you sure you don't want to watch something else?"

"*Coraline,*" Naima said, folding her arms and puffing her face into a pout.

"Alright," Shay conceded, hitting play on the remote. Secretly, she loved that her daughter was obsessed with this movie. It had been a favorite of hers when she was kid, too, so it was a special pleasure to share it with Naima, to know that her mothering had affected her taste.

They were side-by-side, sitting crisscross in the tent, plates of spaghetti balanced in their laps, but Shay wasn't eating. She could not take her gaze away from her daughter's face. Naima had been fiercely demanding her whole life. It was impossible not to think what a strong woman she would have grown up to be. She was the best of Dani and Shay, and maybe the best of whatever person she'd been cloned from, that distant, dead ancestor.

It was illegal to produce a clone of a living person. Duplicates were the result of frozen DNA, decades old. It was expensive to adopt this way, but birthrates had fallen so low over the past two decades that there were virtually no biological children in the system. Some blamed GMOs, others a virus, but the only thing that was conclusive was that half of adult women and all but 10% of adult men were infertile. People turned to religion, and the government swung a hard right. Since then, Congress had passed restrictive measures that prevented parents of the same legal sex from being eligible for bio-adoption, so adopting a duplicate was the only option available to couples like Dani and Shay.

It still burned Shay up to know that her own parents had voted for the conservative politicians who had pioneered the adoption restrictions. They'd rationalized their choice for a thousand reasons. Immigration reform, the economy, gun laws. It all boiled down to one ugly truth; they loved her, but she had chosen to be other, and that choice came with consequences.

Shay had stopped talking to her parents during the pre-adoptive process. She'd known that when her child's seventh birthday came, it would be impossible not to blame them in some way, not to hate them for prioritizing national and economic security over her civil rights.

She felt her hatred for them brewing in her gut again and tried to douse it in cold rationality. Her parents were not to blame. Neither, really, were the laws. If the situation was different, she would have adopted a bio child, one she could have mothered until her own death at an advanced age. But it was done. She wasn't that other child's mother. She was Naima's mother. And the laws weren't going to kill her daughter. The fail-safe installed in Naima's brain was going to do that at midnight. And Shay couldn't even be mad at the mechanism, because without it, her daughter would become a monster.

Human cloning had hit a snag. Shortly after turning seven, duplicates' bodies turned against them, producing hormones that made them prone to extreme violence. They grew deformities and their organs would shut down. There were research efforts aimed at increasing duplicate lifespans, but they were not well funded. It was a niche issue.

Anyway, research was too late for Naima.

"Mommy, can I have something to drink?"

Shay would ordinarily have told her to get it herself, but this last day, she could spoil her. Still, she'd make her earn it. "Ok, but I need five hugs and five kisses." Naima complied, smooching her mother's cheek and giving her one-armed hugs without ever taking her eyes off of the movie.

In the kitchen, Shay got out a pair of mugs and filled a pan with milk for hot chocolate. While that simmered, she dug through her purse for the prescription she'd picked up. "One of these with dinner," the pediatrician had told her. "It helps with the transition. It won't be painful, but it could be abrupt. It's best if it happens when she's asleep." Handing Shay the scrip, he'd said, "It comes with three doses. Sometimes the adults don't want to watch."

Shay considered the three ampules. Twisting off the top of one, she emptied its contents into Naima's unicorn mug. The rest she threw away. She would not be asleep if Naima needed her. She would keep watch.

* * *

They'd just started another movie when Naima said she was sleepy. Shay brought pillows and blankets to the tent. Lying down, the twinkle lights like stars above them, Shay pulled her daughter close, holding her in the crook of her arm. It was probably around eleven, and Naima's breathing was becoming slow and steady with sleep.

"Naima?" Shay said.

Not opening her eyes, Naima asked, "Huh?"

"I love you." In answer, she received only deep breaths and she wished she'd said it sooner. Tears streamed down the sides of her face and she had to choke back a sob.

"Love you, too," Naima said, somehow not quite asleep. "As big as the ocean." This was their usual refrain, how they always expressed their love.

"As big as the world," Shay said.

"As big as the universe." And then she was asleep.

* * *

The coroner arrived on schedule. They took Naima away in a polypropylene bag. Shay had wondered if she'd try to cling to the body and refuse to let them take her daughter. She was surprised to find that she regarded the remains as only a shell, something to be disposed of by the proper authorities.

Shay had not moved after her daughter fell asleep, not even daring to readjust her back, though it was killing her. At what must have been midnight, she heard a soft click. It was such a small sound, but Shay imagined its effects on her daughter's child-size brain as that of an atomic bomb, leveling her consciousness, her personality, her memories, everything Shay and Dani had built reduced to debris. Naima shuddered and her breath stopped. A few seconds of this and then her daughter was still. *It's over*, Shay thought, and all she felt was empty.

Then, by some miracle, sleep had surprised her. When she opened her eyes, it was morning, time for her to dress and be ready to answer the door.

Tears would come, but not yet. It was so sudden, so lacking in drama, that it seemed impossible, and Shay decided that if emotions were not impending, she may as well make coffee.

Using her French press, she mused how this morning felt like any other. Naima might be at school. Or maybe she was sleeping in and, any minute, she'd be shuffling into the kitchen wearing pajamas, asking for cereal.

Looking up, Shay saw Dani's car in the driveway. The windows were fogged, but Dani sat in the front seat, head on the steering wheel.

Shay went to them, opening the passenger door and slipping into the seat beside them. Dani sobbed, their tears running over the wheel and into their lap. "I'm sorry," they gasped. "I'm so sorry. I just couldn't do it."

Shay took one of Dani's hands. Together they sat in the car, not speaking, but taking turns crying. At some point they knew they'd have to go back inside, to face the absence that had moved in to take their daughter's place, but for now, they stayed where it was safe, where their world was as small as the interior of a car, and their grief seemed manageable.

Illustration by Ariel Guzman

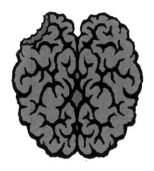

The Silver Dame and the Box of Mystery

C

July 9, 1942

Heat lay over St. Louis like molten lead and sweat pooled between the unsupportive cups of my period-appropriate bra. My only ticket home to the air-conditioned future had been plucked out of our time machine webbing like an ice cube from a glass. I had nothing to go on and two robot companions who weren't speaking to each other.

Celeste sprawled on the sofa by the windows, the hard light glinting off her metal body. She was fanning herself for no good reason; she didn't sweat and 95° Fahrenheit was downright pleasant for her mechanical body. At least she stirred the air some. Of course, stirring this air was like pissing in a hot tub to cool it down.

I stopped pacing. "Somewhere in this city, Pesco hid our box. How do we find it?"

"Check his search history?" Celeste shrugged languidly. The sadist who had designed her had given her a deep, porn-star voice.

"Real suggestions only, killer. Scan the room or something. This was his office. There have to be traces, clues. Get inside Pesco's head. Where did he go? Who did he talk to?" I grabbed the desk phone meaning to slam it down dramatically, but wowsa, it was like a bowling ball. "Unlock the search history on this." It chimed sluggishly as I let go.

"I hate to break it to you, darling, but in this era, 'hacking' involves axes."

"Thanks, big help. Kent?"

Kent was the good kid, the infiltration bot. He resembled a vaguely ethnic young man, whereas Celeste looked like a hood ornament. He sat in a straight-backed chair, scanning newspapers with enviable speed, his pretty brown eyes jittering back and forth like the head on a dot-matrix printer. "If anyone opened the box, it hasn't made the news."

The box was our save game for reality: an AI with vast knowledge of causality and detailed history files, absolutely read-only and ready to double-check your work if you changed something. You didn't travel back in time without one and you sure as taxes didn't come home without it.

Celeste snorted derisively. "Newspapers. They're out-of-date as soon as the ink dries." She was mad because Kent hadn't spoken to her all day.

Kent was sore about her committing murder in front of him. (The aforementioned Pesco.) I was pissed at both of them; Kent had missed my signal for "Stop Celeste before she kills our only lead."

Back to pacing. "Who the heck *was* Pesco? Who would steal a time traveler's cheat sheet? Who would benefit?"

Who wouldn't? It was the dangerous love child of Biff's Sports Almanac and Wikipedia. Thing is, the box itself had told us the boathouse was a safe spot to stash it. "Celeste, check the police band. You guys can pick up radio waves, right?"

"Robbery in progress on Ninth Street," Celeste intoned with exaggerated boredom. "I think car fourteen has a problem with dispatch. Old quarrel. Neither of them letting it go, but all business on the surface."

"At least Kent is pretending he cares."

Celeste's cut-emerald eyes narrowed like lasers at Kent. "How come you always like him best?"

"He's prettier." I wriggled into my high heels. "I have to make some footprints or I'll go crazy. Maybe there's a clue we missed where we caught Pesco. Kent, you're with me. Celeste: find leads!"

"It's not my fault there's no network." Celeste lazily circled her fan overhead.

"There's also no network security, so it should be a cakewalk. Tap phone lines, listen to the damned telegraph. Someone, somewhere, is going to use the box and brag about it." If we were lucky.

I opened the street door and discovered that as hot as it was indoors, the outside was worse, like stepping inside of a German Shepherd. My silk stockings felt like long johns. They'd seemed such a good idea.

I held Kent's arm because the shoes were crazy and he made a handy crutch. Kent didn't mind. Made me wonder what else he wouldn't mind, but no, that'd be like bonking the office printer.

"Supposing I did want an axe," I asked him, "could we hit a hardware store and grab one?"

"Once we find where the box is, I could break any wall between it and us. An axe might stand out."

It was cute how he thought a robot tearing down a wall wouldn't stand out. "This was supposed to be a simple data theft. Get in, steal the ledger, deliver it, go home. We got in, we delivered, damnit, I want to go home." No idea why the big boss wanted a list of cargo shipments moved to a safe deposit box, but I'd checked it was still where we left it as soon as I stopped freaking out and washing Pesco's blood off my shoes. "All this sweat and uselessness makes me want to smash something."

As usual, Kent didn't respond to any talk of violence. "Where are we heading?"

"We caught Pesco in a blind alley. Why would he go there? He probably knew the terrain better than we did. He was heading someplace."

Kent sighed with state-of-the-art petulance. "It would be better if there was a network to search."

"They do have a network. It's phone lines. It's tickertape. It's paper and pen and feet. We have to adapt to it."

* * *

Kent broke every lock near the alleyway with brisk efficiency.

Two back staircases, a coal box, and a bakery. Nothing incriminating in the bakery but day-old donuts. Chocolate. Four inhabited apartments up the first staircase, a basement down, with fenced-off storage…and there in the corner, as incriminating as strange lingerie on your lover's bedroom floor, was a mess of familiar cables and pink, gossamer netting. A time machine.

I let the webbing fall from my fingers. "Pesco was one of us."

"Unless he stole this as well."

"Without a box of his own?" Traveling boxless was as dangerous as juggling rabid badgers. On fire. The only way that made sense would be if Pesco knew where we would be and came from the future specifically to steal our box. Why? To travel without the Big Boss knowing? A mole? An agent gone rogue? But if he wanted the box for his own use, why wasn't it here?

The time machine controls showed it had arrived from the Big Boss' time, and it was set to return there. Seemed to strengthen the rogue agent theory. "Well, nothing more we can learn from this." I hit the emergency recall button. "Better send it home."

The web flickered and melted into the floor just as the Saint Louis Police stormed down the stairs, guns out.

My heart slammed into the roof of my mouth. Despite his expensive silicone skin, Kent looked like a store mannequin, features blanked by shock. Good thing folks who've never heard of robots don't know to look for the tells. I stepped in front of him, hands raised. "Officers, there must be some kind of mistake."

"I bet there is, sweetheart. Everyone in this neighborhood saw you two breaking doors." He was a big guy, alien in his old-fashioned clothes. He had a heavy-looking gun, and those didn't need to be sophisticated to knock holes in a body. "Up the stairs, both of you. You're under arrest."

"Aren't you going to read me my Miranda?"

He looked at me like I was talking Martian. I may as well have been—the Miranda case wasn't until the sixties. Bad time traveler mistake. I'd never been arrested in the past before. This was only my second solo mission. "My rights," I clarified.

"You have a right to shut up and get in the car."

They cuffed me and threw me into the back of a huge sedan. I'd just gotten upright when they threw Kent in after me. "Contact Celeste." I pushed off of him with my elbow.

"Already on it," Kent said, like he hadn't been completely useless a minute ago. At least he didn't whine about having to talk to his sister.

* * *

Celeste had put on stockings, opaque enough to cover her chrome, but her legs still glittered in the low light. She wore long kid gloves—which were mine. I'd been saving them for a special occasion, like larceny. Her tapered talons were stretching the tips. A veiled hat, a wig, and thick makeup hid her inhuman face.

May the ghost of Isaac Asimov save us from robots playing dress-up.

Celeste's heels clacked purposefully down the corridor outside our holding cell. She put more swing into her hips than necessary. "I'm so sorry, boss," she cooed. "I got here as soon as I could."

We'd been cooling our heels all night, minus the cooling, and that was beside the point. "Celeste, you were supposed to be monitoring the police bands."

She set my gloves against the bars. They made a muffled *tink*. "I was, and I laughed so hard when they described Kent. 'Swarthy!' They thought he was dangerous!"

My right eye twitched and the vision on that side flashed red. "So instead of sending a warning to Kent so we could get out of there, you just…laughed."

She pouted—a grotesque movement of metal lips flaking red paint—and shrugged. "He was being a bore. Anyway, I forged a report over the teletype that you were FBI agents under deep cover. You're free to go."

"You're artificial stupid, you know that? If you can send forged reports, you could have stopped them from arresting us in the first place."

"But it was hilarious!"

As hilarious as an insubordinate killing machine. I'd have to wait until we finished the job, if we ever finished the job, to file a complaint with AI Services. Not that that ever went anywhere. Big Boss liked his robots more than his mooks.

I didn't say anything to either of my artificial compatriots until we'd been processed out of the police station.

It was a good five degrees cooler in the pre-dawn air. My body adjusted back to hating it in a few seconds, but it was enough to sharpen my focus. "I take it you're well integrated with police communications, Celeste?"

Her smile was all knifepoints. "I'm practically in the union."

"Good. We'll use the cops to do our dirty work for us. Put out an APB on our missing box. Describe Pesco as the last known owner of a stolen artifact. Has *The Maltese Falcon* been released, yet?"

Kent glanced to the side, as he always did when consulting internal databases. "Last year."

"Shoot. I was hoping we could steal the plot. What's a nice, expensive article, currently missing? Can we find something like that? Something the right size to fit in our box?"

Another side-eye from Kent. "A painting was stolen in this very city in 1930. It was valued at over a hundred thousand dollars and not recovered until 1947. The dimensions should fit."

"Great. That's what's in our box. Celeste, can you work with your brother long enough to get this done?"

"*I* have never had a problem working with *him*," Celeste said, like she didn't just land us in jail for spite.

Back in Pesco's office, we hammered out every detail of the false police report. I wasn't leaving anything to robotic fancy. Sometime after noon, Celeste sent the false report. I passed out on the sofa, hopeful we'd have a lead by morning.

I woke up to a sky pinking up for twilight, and pounding. Someone was hitting the office door hard enough to rattle the frosted glass. I rolled off the couch and glared at Celeste, who was calmly flipping through a magazine. She raised her sculpted eyebrows at me. Fair enough, I'd told her not to answer the door.

What a surprise, it was the police. Two uniforms and a plainclothesman holding a paper at me. "We have a warrant to search the premises for a stolen statue."

"Stat—wait, this isn't the Maltese Falcon, is it?"

The plainclothesman thrust a finger at Celeste. "There it is!"

Someday I'd be able to enjoy the comical expressions they made as the "statue" stood up. At the time, I was so angry my vision was blurring at the corners. "Celeste! No killing cops! DON'T!" I got knocked ass-over-teakettle trying to get between precious human life and Miss Stab-Happy.

I righted myself in time to see Celeste pluck the guns from the two uniformed officers' hands and toss them over her shoulder.

One cop's fist hit Celeste's gut with a fleshy smack and she picked him up by his arm. He twisted, screaming.

"CELESTE! No killing."

She held the two uniformed police off the floor so their feet could kick. She pouted at me. The plainclothes was plastered against the door, his warrant against his chest, looking like his brain had just suffered a general protection fault.

I said, "Someone's played a prank on you gents. As you can see, my associate is plenty odd-looking, but she ain't a statue. Statues are big on being still and *she* can't stop flapping her gums."

"Thanks," said Celeste.

"What...who..." the detective was slowly letting himself peel away from the doorframe.

I really wished we had those flashy things they used in *Men in Black*. "We're FBI. Top secret government hardware. Uh...you remember there's a war on? You'll find all the proper paperwork back at your station. Any chance you boys want to leave here and pretend you never saw us?" Celeste set the uniforms down but didn't let go yet. Three identical incredulous expressions.

I herded the uniforms back to their detective. They went like scared-shitless lambs. "You really want to report this?"

Yeah, they really didn't, but I could see the plainclothes was second-guessing so I added, "The alternative is I have Celeste there pop out your eyes."

That was almost as effective as the flashy thing.

* * *

Kent had the good grace to look chagrined when I found him in the diner downstairs.

"You know what? I understand this...this sibling rivalry from Celeste. She's psychotic. She's supposed to be—it's part of what makes her a good enforcer—but I can't believe you're acting like this."

He handed me a menu. "I ordered your usual meal."

"That's not going to cut it for an apology, Kent. Those cops are going to come back with an army if they can find one. That's a whole day we've wasted while Pesco's buyer gets closer to understanding what he got, or worse, using it. Why can't you two get competitive over, oh, I don't know…*finding the box?*"

My last word echoed around a suddenly silent diner. I hid behind my menu and lowered my voice. "We don't know what the final purpose of our mission was. We don't know if we succeeded or failed, or if irreparable damage has already been done to the timeline. We need that box."

"The police have responded as expected to the APB." Kent looked as apologetic as his features allowed.

"Gee, thanks. Any leads?"

"A Detective Brinks has located a complete list of Pesco's contacts. Apparently, he has been active in the area for about a week, infiltrating local crime."

"You're almost forgiven. How long is the list?"

"Twenty-five names."

My shoulders unclenched one inch. "That's…pretty good. We can work with that. Start by eliminating anyone who wasn't in town over the past two days."

"We don't have the names. The broadcast we intercepted just mentioned that Detective Brinks had them and how many there were."

Slapping him would hurt my hand more than his skull. "Let's pay a call on Detective Brinks."

* * *

Celeste was still sore over my not letting her kill people, so I thought it wise to let her infiltrate the police station. There was nothing she loved more than ninja playtime.

I set up across the street, on the roof of a public library. I broke out the good (future tech) field glasses and sat down to watch her work.

Kent was at our *new* hideout, hopefully too occupied to be a nuisance. I'd started him on listing every action we'd made and potential points of time line departure to clean up. It'd help us work without the box, to a limited extent, and get a start on our after-action report. It felt like sending him to the corner, but not quite enough.

Celeste shimmied up the side of the police station like a fish on a line and disappeared into a vent not much bigger across than her shoulders. If human joints had evolved the way we designed hers, we'd be able to kiss our own asses and wipe our noses while doing it.

"And then there'd be no reason to hire staff," I quipped to myself. Now that things were looking up, I considered writing my case notes like a noir movie script. The Silver Dame and the Maltese Falcon.

Celeste crawled on the ceiling, above the heads of the unsuspecting night shift. Through another window I could see the top drawer of what we believed to be Brink's desk.

I heard a bang behind me like a trashcan getting kicked over. I turned to see police swarm out of the library's roof entrance.

Maybe they were there to pay their late fines? I recognized the plainclothesman with his gun drawn.

"Is that a weapon?" He jerked his gun toward my field glasses.

I carefully set down the glasses before he got trigger-happy. "Detective Brinks, I presume?"

He narrowed his eyes. "How do you know my name?"

Because that would be the worst that could happen.

* * *

Detective Brinks paced on the other side of the interrogation table. "Why were you breaking and entering every door off East 14th Court? I know you aren't FBI."

"This is good," I said. "I mean, in the movies you can't smell the stale smoke and desperation, but really, it's exactly what I was expecting: the cracked plaster, the bare bulb."

He leaned over the table. "What's in the box?"

I felt my smile freeze. "What box?"

"The box," he repeated, slamming his fist on the scarred wood.

"I don't know anything about any—"

"A radio report with no paper trail has half my department searching for a metal box, fourteen inches by sixteen inches by seven." He threw an open folder in front of me. "Last in possession of Joe Pesco, found decapitated in a dumpster near a particular alleyway you might remember getting arrested in. So, I'm going to ask again: what's in the box? It ain't some painting folded in half and shoved in diagonal!"

Artificial stupid. I closed my eyes. "You wouldn't be able to comprehend the answer if I told you. It'd be like me saying 'an Atari 2600.'"

"A what?"

"Exactly."

He hoisted his belt and set his hands more firmly on his hips. "Cut the bull. Who's that guy, the foreigner? And where did your silver row-butt go?"

"There's no such thing as robots." So, Celeste had made it out of the station. That was good. Now if I'd brought a phone with me, that would have been useful. If there were cell towers in 1942. If I weren't cuffed.

I wasn't doing well at this time-travel gig.

Brinks wiped his sweaty face. "What is in the box?"

"You don't want to know. In fact, if you find it, don't open it! Don't even try. It'll…melt your face off. Eyes…dropping and skin dripping like wax…"

He was unmoved by my attempt to describe the end of *Raiders of the Lost Ark*. "It's a weapon?"

"My coffee pot would be a weapon in this place, which is a shame because I didn't bring it."

"Who do you work for?"

Wasn't that a long story? I'd never bothered to dig deeper than the boss's vague assurance his often-violent missions were "for the greater good." On one hand, my first mission for him stopped a marsh from being poisoned. On the other hand, he owned Celeste.

A drop of sweat fell from Brink's nose to mine. I said, "This is a bad time to be having second thoughts about my career choices, but I gotta be honest, I am."

The door to our little interrogation room was propped to let air in along with the mundane sounds of footsteps, phones ringing, and voices. Something was going on because the phone rings were coming more rapidly, and the voices and footsteps were louder, more frantic. Detective Brinks loomed over me. "Who do you work for? The Germans? The Japanese? Martians? WHO?"

"The Easter bunny."

He shook his head, not having heard me over the racket. "What?"

"I work for the McGuffin Plot Device Company," I quipped, "and the pay is crap." Good line, self.

I expected him to deck me. Instead, he spun on his heel and jerked the door all the way open. "What is going on out here?"

A cop with his sleeves rolled up gestured helplessly. "We've got reports of shoot-outs on Market Street and pirates on the river. Pranks up and down the board."

Brinks looked back at me.

I could make out a few shouts from the bull pen: "All available cars to Plaza Square. Robbery in progress. Wait... scratch that, Car 47 was just there, says its fine. Hold on, all available cars, we have an identity theft— what the heck is that?"

I confess, I laughed. The killbot twins were finally doing something. It was stupid, but it was something.

Brinks didn't appreciate the humor. He dropped his fists on the table in front of me. "Are you doing this?"

"What am I, a ventriloquist?"

He backhanded me. My wrists jerked hard against the cuffs. I licked my split lip. I had an idea. "We both want the same thing. My associates, they're violent, chaotic idiots. You want them out of St. Louis? *I* want them out of St. Louis."

He was so close I could count the pores on his nose. "I want them in my jail."

Oh, the innocent lamb. The things those two could do to a jail. "They're listening to the police band. You can get them here with a word."

Brinks straightened. "You proposing an exchange?"

"Not so much. I'm proposing you trash talk the robots."

"Trash talk?"

"Is that not a term here? You have sports, don't you? Rile them up. They have this rivalry that defies logic. Say Celeste could never rescue her boss. Say Kent's the real danger. Bait them; it's not hard."

Brinks looked out the door. The cop standing there shrugged.

Brinks turned back to me. "Will they stand down because we have you?"

Even if they had the hardware to do it, neither would shed a tear on my corpse. "Say Kent couldn't beat Celeste here. Lay it on thick and both of them will come. Trust me. It's guaranteed. Once they're here, shoot the forehead to disable them." That probably wouldn't work. I'd seen Celeste beat open a military spaceship airlock with her forehead. "One clean head shot, and they go down. Then you tear 'em apart. You could learn to make your own, but I wouldn't recommend it."

More shrugs exchanged. Brinks looked like he hated himself saying, "Try it."

The uniform left. Brinks stared a long time at me and closed the door. "Who do you work for?"

I squinted at him, nodded, waited for him to look impatient, and said, "All right, I'll talk."

He sat down. "So talk."

I drew in a long breath. "It all started at a train station. Commuter rail. Cedar and University. It was 1984 and I'd just broken up with my boyfriend at a concert at this dinky, crowded bar."

"You're from the future. That's the line you're going with?"

"It's necessary backstory. Where was I? It was a blues club, solo piano that night. Anyway, I was freezing in fishnets and a regrettable amount of hairspray, and the train wasn't coming. Not to excuse my decision, but I was in a vulnerable place. Big Boss had some story about not having factored in the train delay, but you know what? I'm thinking he knew exactly when to recruit me."

Brinks propped his head up with one fist. "If you don't get to some kind of point, I'm going to shoot you and then myself."

"I'm thinking Pesco's like me, a person plucked from their time by the Big Boss, fed a load of dreams about changing the world. Maybe he found out something he didn't like. He got ahold of a time machine but couldn't get a box, because those are programmed for each mission. So, he locates a mission that isn't that critical. One rookie operative and two assistants doing a simple data theft. Now maybe Pesco had an accomplice, maybe there's a whole network of people fed up with the agency, feel me? They need to steal a box to set up their own missions, maybe undo things the Big Boss is having us do. Like maybe someone is already copying that ledger I stole four days ago and putting it back. Time is more durable than you think. You put things back enough, few things change. Think of it like erasing the evidence of a kegger in your parent's apartment before they get home."

Brinks gaped at me like his brain was melting. "None of that made a lick of sense."

I grinned like I was receiving an Oscar. "No, but it ate up time."

The wall to my right exploded into a cloud of dust and smoke. Bricks rained on the table, on my lap, on the wall opposite. One bounced off my head, but I was too startled to feel it.

I was still coughing and struggling to breathe as Celeste lifted me from my chair. She half-carried me through a jagged hole in the wall. Bricks tumbled from the edges. Then we were on the street, moving at full killbot run. Celeste's feet sounded like knives dicing the dirt. All I could see was a bounding blur.

"You broke through a wall," I shouted, slipping and struggling to keep my place on her shoulder. "The cops probably noticed that!"

Celeste set me on my feet under a bridge and finally snapped my handcuffs, as casual as you might rip a tag off a shirt you were about to shop-lift. "Run," she said. Shots fired behind us. Well, who was I to argue? We ran pell-mell along the riverfront, the leaden Missouri glinting almost as brightly as Celeste. After four days in heels, my legs were sore in random weird places and my running was more a horizontal tumble in Celeste's wake.

We dove into a boathouse, crumbling and half-forgotten in the company of its bigger cousins. Kent was there, with the time net spread out around him. The sirens and shouts were muffled. For now. I felt a tantalizing awareness that we were inches away from the sweet air-conditioned future. A quick exit sitting right there and the cops with guns would never find us. BUT. I gasped for breath, hands on my knees, while Celeste and Kent went through the final preparations. "We don't have the box!"

"Oh." Celeste turned to look out at the dock. The sound of sirens was approaching. She waved a paper at me. "I got the list of names. Don't I get a thank-you for that?"

I snatched the paper. In sloppy type, the tops of the e's all filled in, was a list of twenty-five names titled "Known contacts of J. Pesco."

I heard tires squealing. I saw shapes running through the holes in the walls. We were surrounded, and the only exit was a time machine with no box.

A loudspeaker squealed. "You have two minutes to come out with your hands up!"

It was time to juggle flaming badgers. "You two are such mooks. Into the time web."

Kent went store-mannequin while I pulled the webbing around myself. Celeste fidgeted. "Maybe I could kill them all?"

"NOW!" I snapped. I got the controls set.

"Ten seconds!" The cops helpfully announced.

There was exactly one place Pesco had been, for certain, and there would be a box there. Unless I was wrong, in which case, we were fucked.

The wooden walls started to tear into bullet-sized chunks as we melted into the time stream.

July 5, 1942

I patted my body for bullet holes as we rematerialized in the boat house, on the day we were out doing the job. There was our time web, next to our time web. The box was still there.

Celeste held her talons out like she was afraid to touch the air. "I could have killed them all. Safely."

For certain definitions of safe. I balled up the time net we'd just used. "No killing," I said, wishing it hadn't become my catchphrase. I'd set the controls for the exact time of our original heist, assuming Pesco knew about it and came to get the box then. Now we just had to see how punctual he was.

On cue, there was a soft scratch of metal on metal from the boathouse door. I held up a finger to keep the robot twins behaving themselves and slipped out the water entrance.

Pesco wasn't a bad looking guy when he had his head attached to his body. Slim, tall. He bent to tuck his lock picks away, showing off his perfect Bogart haircut. I slid neatly behind as he opened the door and got him in a headlock. He stopped struggling the second he saw Celeste gleaming in the darkness.

"Don't kill me," he said.

"Those words would have saved us all a lot of trouble four days from now." I muscled him into the boathouse and closer to Celeste, who was doing a fine job being menacing just standing there. "You knew we'd be on a job. You came here to steal our box. Why? And where will you put it?"

He twisted. "*Will* I? Jesus, you traveled back without it. How far ahead are you from? Tomorrow? Next week?"

"I think the lady with two killer robots gets to ask the questions."

"Oh god. You must have killed me. You wouldn't need to go back if you hadn't."

He sounded very close to pissing himself, which I wanted to avoid since my silk-clad knee was wedged between his. I let him go, spun him around, and grabbed the collar of his shirt. "We're deleting that timeline hard. I need you alive." He didn't look too reassured.

Through the water entrance of the boathouse, the sun was rising over the city. It was misty, not quite eighty, a real fake-out of a morning, like the next seven days might not be hotter than hell. I put my arm around Pesco's shoulders and turned him away from the killer robots.

"Don't you get it? This is the beginning of a beautiful friendship."

The world hung in a tense silence until he spoke and, bless the bastard, he got the reference. "Am...am I Rick or Renault?"

"Depends which of us has to turn their back on evil."

"Uh...you?"

I'd have appreciated more confidence in his tone. "Come on, we're getting breakfast." I gestured for Celeste and Kent to follow us out of the boathouse, and they did. Obedient hench-bots at last.

That was the stuff dreams were made of.

Illustration by Kat D'Andrea

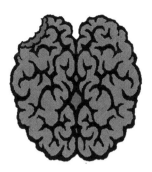

Ignore the Restless Dead

Rob Cornell

The ghosts started coming to Simon Barnes a month after his eighteenth birthday. He didn't know why or how. But after ten years of ignoring them, he could sometimes convince himself they were never really there.

Until the little girl.

She came to him on a chilly afternoon in early March. Simon was on his usual walk through Hampton Park during his lunch hour. He had an ice cream addiction—mint chocolate chip most of all—that had gifted him with a bit of a belly in his early twenties. Rather than quit the ice cream, Simon started doing sit-ups every morning and going for a walk every afternoon.

The belly melted. The ice cream stayed.

An early morning rain had turned the asphalt footpath through the park dark and shiny. An occasional puddle would fill a dip in the path, but Simon skipped over these to keep his loafers from getting wet—though his inner toddler wanted to jump and splash in each one.

He wore a smile this afternoon despite the cold snap in the air that made his breath steam, or the performance review he needed to face when he got back to the office. He had gone all morning without running into a single dead person. Nothing could put him in a better mood than a good stretch of seeming normalcy.

The cold and damp also meant Simon had the path to himself. No gaggles of power-walking senior citizens with their ankle weights and dumbbells charging through as if they owned the park. No slow-strolling couples who spent more time giving each other googly eyes instead of watching where they were walking. And don't even get him started on the inline skaters zipping by as if you were a cone on a slalom course instead of, you know, an actual person.

The park's paved path took Simon along a creek, over a covered wooden bridge, and into a wooded area thick with maples and oaks. Rain still dripped from leaves overhanging the path. Simon pulled on the hood of his Detroit Red Wings sweatshirt, tucked his hands in the pockets, and kept walking.

He was deep into the woods when the little girl stepped out of the trees and onto the path in front of him, as if she'd been waiting there for him all along.

From a dozen yards away, the girl looked as real as any. She wore a flowered dress and pink sneakers with purple laces. Her black hair hung to her shoulders in loose curls. Her eyes were a bright blue that stared with a chilling intensity. She couldn't have been older than nine or ten. One of the sleeves on her dress was torn at the seam by her shoulder.

Simon stopped and took a step back.

Despite how real—how alive—she looked from this distance, Simon knew she was a ghost. He didn't have to look for the usual signs that separated the living from the dead. Things like an outdated style of dress, or the peculiar focus the spirits gave Simon to the exclusion of anyone else, as if they could only see him, even in the midst of a crowd. Also, ghosts lacked the usual smells the living carried with them. No coffee breath or sweat or Axe body spray. Instead, they all smelled vaguely like sea water. At least, that was the best way Simon could describe the scent. It often made him think of the cottage on Lake Michigan his parents took him to every summer as a kid.

Before the ghosts.

He didn't need any of those things to tell him the girl belonged to the world of the dead, because what parent would let their living daughter wander around alone in the woods in a torn dress?

On any other occasion, Simon would have turned around and walked away. Sometimes the ghosts followed him when he did that, would chat at his back while they tagged along at his heels. Sometimes they stayed with him for the better part of a day, not getting the hint that he intended to ignore them no matter how long they pestered him. Eventually, they would give up. Though he did have one old man dressed like a sailor dog him for nearly two days, going as far as sitting at Simon's bedside, still there in the morning when Simon awoke.

But Simon didn't turn away from the girl. He'd never seen a ghost this young before. Most of the ones who had come to him ranged from late twenties to older than the hills. He got a lot of crotchety old men for some reason.

"Can you help me?" the little girl asked. She shivered, her pale brow wrinkled with worry. "I'm lost."

Simon stared at her. His breath came in quick, visible puffs. The smell of wet bark and damp earth filled his nostrils. A couple birds squabbled among the trees.

When Simon didn't answer, the girl took a few steps toward him. "Can you see me?"

Simon swallowed. His dry throat clicked.

Don't talk to her. Turn away, damn it. Turn away.

"Yes," he said.

"I'm lost. Can you help me find my way home?"

Absolutely not!

But how could he abandon her? A little girl. Did she know she was dead? Did she know that even if he helped her find home, her parents or any siblings or *anybody* would never see her like Simon could?

Since when did questions like this matter? He was supposed to ignore the ghosts. Because he had suspected from the start that if he engaged with one, he would have to engage them all. His whole life would devolve into serving the ghosts.

He didn't want to serve ghosts. He wanted to live his own damn life in peace.

The girl took another tentative step toward him. A puddle at her feet reflected the canopy of leaves above, but not her. Another sign you were dealing with the dead—they cast no reflections.

"My name is Charlotte."

Without thinking, he replied, "I'm Simon."

One corner of Charlotte's mouth twitched as if she meant to smile. "Hi, Simon. Can you help me? Please?" Her voice was so small. So vulnerable.

He took a deep breath. Fine. He would make an exception. This once. For a child. After all, he wasn't a complete and total bastard.

"Okay."

* * *

Simon had to take Charolette back to the office with him. She followed him from the elevator to his cubicle and, of course, no one noticed, because no one else at the company saw ghosts. She stood beside his desk while he logged onto his computer and opened his internet browser.

The scent of sea water filled the cubicle.

He glanced at the photo of his parents pinned to the cubicle wall beside his computer monitor. Both gone now. A brain tumor took Dad in the middle of Simon's senior year of high school. Ovarian cancer took Mom four years later. So many ghosts had found their way to Simon, yet neither of his parents had yet to visit him. He liked to think that was a good thing, that they had passed on to wherever dead spirits were supposed to go.

He didn't really know, though. Who did?

Simon rose out of his chair to peer over the edge of his cubicle at his boss's office. Door closed. Blinds pulled. Someone's performance review in progress most likely.

He settled back in his seat and started searching the web. On the way back to the office from the park, Simon had learned the girl's full name (Charlotte Marie Dyson), her age (nine), and her birthday (November 2nd). He typed her name into the search field and hit ENTER.

Charlotte's obituary showed up as the first result.

This might go easier than he thought.

Before clicking the link, Simon turned to Charlotte. She stared at him with those intense eyes. Her lips were pale, almost blue. He noticed a dark spot on the side of her neck that looked like a bruise, but could have been a shadow.

She gave him a closed smile.

He forced a smile in return, then turned back to his screen.

The obit was short and purely factual, more like a report than an ode to a lost loved one. It listed the day of her death (merely three weeks ago), her parents' names (Jeff and Mary), and her beloved cat, Mr. Socks.

As for the cause of Charlotte's death, the obituary described it only as a "sad accident."

With a little more internet searching, he quickly found the Dyson's home address. He scribbled it down on a sticky note.

Now what? A check of the clock told him his own performance review was only thirty minutes away. He swiveled his chair to face Charlotte and spoke low, because Alice in the next cubicle would hear anything much louder than a whisper.

"I can take you home," he said, "but you'll have to wait until I'm done with work."

He expected Charlotte to protest, but she smiled instead. And this was a big, legitimate smile that reached up into her striking blue eyes. "I can be patient."

She stayed in his cubicle while he went in for his review, which went surprisingly well considering his mind kept wandering toward thoughts of taking the girl home and how that would go. Not well, he expected.

Then again, maybe it would go fine. Maybe returning her would create some kind of closure for her, let her pass on or whatever it was ghosts did.

Funny. A decade living with ghosts on nearly a daily basis, yet his knowledge of them came mostly from movies and novels. Fiction.

He might actually learn something today about the afterlife. Surprisingly, the idea thrilled him.

* * *

The house looked a lot like the one Simon had grown up in. Most of the houses in suburbs like this looked the same. Sure, the shape of the shrubbery or the angle of the approach to the front porch sometimes varied. Some porches might stretch longer than others, but all of them were made from cement. Some of the houses had a second story, while others were flat ranch-style homes.

The house Simon pulled in front of was a two-story Colonial with an overhang supported by a pair of white columns.

A birch tree loomed over the curb where Simon parked, its branches casting a crisscross of shadows in the late evening sun. One black bar crossed Charlotte's face like a diagonal streak of warpaint. It gave Simon a chance to compare the shadow from the branch to the mark he'd noticed on her neck. He was almost certain now that it was a bruise.

She smiled at him. "This is it. I'm home!"

They both looked toward the house. With her head turned, her black hair caught behind her shoulder, the mark on her throat showed plain, wrapping all the way around to the back of her neck, vaguely shaped like the imprint of a hand.

Simon's stomach soured. The taste of his afternoon cup of coffee rolled up the back of his tongue, twice as bitter as when he'd drunk it. He thought about the obituary's scant description of Charlotte's death—*sad accident.*

"Are you sure you want to go back there?" he asked.

She turned to him. The branch's shadow slashed across her face again. "Why wouldn't I?"

He pointed at her neck. "Do you remember what happened to you?"

Her gaze softened as she reached up to touch the bruise. She didn't say anything for a few seconds. The smile that curled her mouth didn't go anywhere near her eyes. "I remember."

Then she stood outside on the sidewalk, facing away, toward the house.

Her sudden relocation sparked a surprised "*whoa*" out of Simon. At the same time, a static chill crackled over his skin. This felt wrong somehow.

But why?

He had helped a little lost soul find her way home. What could be wrong with that?

The bruise. That's what was wrong. The "sad accident." The way Charlotte had smiled without a shred of humor just now.

I remember.

Charlotte started across the front lawn. The hem of her flowered dress swayed around her knees. A breeze snagged strands of her hair and made them flail like dark tendrils of night come to life.

Simon got out of the car and gazed at her over the roof. "Charlotte?"

She paused, looked over her shoulder at him. Her lips had gone a darker shade of blue, her skin so pale her veins showed through like cracks in porcelain. Her eyes shone as clear and bright as ever, the sight of them sending a cold stab through Simon's chest.

"Thank you, Simon."

She turned back to the house.

Simon watched her go up onto the porch and pass through the front door like mist through a screen. He continued to stare for a long while. A long while that also felt like an instant. The leaves of the birch trembled in the wind overhead, the sound they made a cross between a whisper and a snake's rattle.

After a minute—two? twenty?—Simon snapped out of his daze. His job was done. He had helped the little ghost girl find her way home. He could leave now. He could go back to ignoring the ghosts and pretend this had never happened.

But almost as soon as he decided this, right when he bent to climb back into his car, the screaming started.

* * *

The screaming didn't last long. By the time Simon stepped between the columns on the porch, whoever it was had fallen silent.

Nothing else on the street stirred except for the trees. The rumble of a lawnmower reached over from a block or two away. None of the neighbors seemed to have noticed the shrieks.

Maybe Simon had imagined the sound.

He would like to believe that, but he knew what he'd heard.

So why had he run toward the house? Why hadn't he driven away? Left this behind? Hadn't he already fulfilled his part in all this?

But that was just it. He'd had a part in this. Which meant he was partially responsible for whatever had brought about the screaming.

Simon tensed his core as if expecting a blow to the gut, then rang the doorbell and thumped the door three times with the bottom of his fist. "Charlotte? Hello? Is everyone okay?"

No reply.

He leaned an ear toward the door and strained to hear any voice or sound of movement.

Nothing.

A gust of wind curled through the covered porch and wrapped Simon in chilly dampness. He tried to zip his sweatshirt up tighter against his throat, but it was already pulled as far as it could go.

He pounded the door again, but still got no answer.

That means you should go. You've done all you can.

A lie. A cowardly one at that.

He tried the door.

It opened freely.

The smell hit him first, a metallic tang that reminded Simon of that summer after high school when he worked for the grocery store butcher. Once his eyes adjusted to the darkened living room, he noticed the glistening red trail across the carpet. And from deeper in the house… someone giggling.

The hairs on the back of Simon's neck prickled. *You need to leave. You need to leave now.*

Instead, he clenched his fists and stepped inside.

"Charlotte?"

More giggling. But not a child. Simon was pretty sure it was a grown man. The sound came from a hallway to the right. The blood trail also went in that direction.

Perhaps now would have been a good time to call the police. If he wasn't going to leave, he could at least do *something* rational. He reached into his pants pocket and pulled out his cell.

What would he say? How would he explain how he had come to this place?

Hi, I led a little ghost girl home and then heard some screaming and there's blood on the floor. Come quick!

"You should leave, Simon," a man's voice said from down the hall.

Simon reflexively squeezed his phone's case. "Who…?"

The sound of footsteps creaking the floorboards under the carpeting came down the hall. A man in his mid-thirties materialized out of the shadows and stepped into the living room. He had tousled black hair and blue eyes with a familiar intensity. Blood soaked the front of his blue jeans and plaid flannel shirt. He held a carving knife in one hand, it's blade slick and shiny with red.

He smiled.

"It's me, Simon. It's Charlotte. I'm in my daddy's body. I can control him. It's…" She said this next word with breathy wonder. "…amazing."

Simon's gaze flicked from the knife, to the blood down the front of the man—presumably Jeff Dyson—to his blue eyes. Charlotte had definitely inherited her father's eyes. A knot in Simon's gut twisted. A hard shiver shook through him.

"What did…whose blood is that?"

Jeff/Charlotte's smile broke open to show bright, even teeth. "Mommy's."

"What did you do, Charlotte? My god, what did you do?"

The smile vanished. "I got revenge."

And then he/she dragged the knife across his/her own throat and opened it up. Blood poured from the slash. Jeff coughed, spraying a mist of red into the air, some of it spattering the glass of a framed family photograph hung on the nearest wall. Dots of red speckled the three faces of Jeff, little Charlotte, and a woman with a blond perm Simon assumed was Charlotte's mother, Mary. In the picture, they went on smiling.

But sudden awareness filled the real Jeff's eyes while he choked and wheezed. Charlotte was no longer behind those eyes. She'd left Jeff so he could fully experience his own death.

The knife dropped from his hand and hit the carpeting with a dull thump. His fingers scrabbled at the widening tear across his throat as if he thought he could pull the skin back together and stop the gushing. He only managed to coat his hands in his own blood.

Simon stood frozen, unable to turn away, still holding onto his phone, though he couldn't feel it in his hand anymore. His body had gone numb. A sound almost like static hissed in his mind over any kind of thought. Shock had rendered him as nothing more than a witness to Jeff's death.

Jeff dropped to his knees. His gaze rose to meet Simon's eyes. He looked like he wanted to ask a question. Something like, *Why aren't you helping me? Or, Why did you bring my daughter here to kill us?*

But the look only lasted a few seconds before Jeff crumpled to the floor in a twisted fetal position. His body hitched a couple times, each time accompanied by a watery click popping from his open throat. Then he fell silent and still.

Simon's breathing had grown so quick and shallow his head started to spin. He stood on the edge of hyperventilating. Through the static in his mind, one thought repeated on a loop—*What have I done? What have I done? What have I…*

A cold, small hand grasped Simon around the wrist.

He cried out, yanking away, and dropped his phone.

Charlotte stood beside him. It had been her hand. But she was a ghost. She couldn't touch him. None of the others had ever touched him. Then again, Simon had never spoken to any of the others, had never helped them like he'd helped Charlotte. What did he really know about what ghosts could and could not do?

Nothing.

He sure as hell didn't know they could take over the body of a living person, make him murder his wife, and then kill himself. What was to stop her from doing the same to him?

What have I done? What have I done? What—

"Don't be scared," Charlotte said. "You helped me. I can go on now."

Simon gaped at her. He worked his mouth, but he couldn't speak.

Charlotte smiled. "Thanks again, Simon." She gave him a wave, took a step backward, then broke into a bluish mist that quickly evaporated.

Simon stared at the space she used to occupy as if waiting for her to rematerialize. But that was the last damn thing he wanted. He gathered the tatters of his sanity, retrieved his phone from the floor, and dashed out of the house.

* * *

Simon kept an eye on the nightly news. Sure enough, he caught the report of a married couple's murder-suicide in the wake of the tragic loss of their young daughter. That's how they spun it. Charlotte's "sad accident" had driven her father to madness. Simon supposed in a roundabout way, that was true. Except there weren't any accidents, sad or otherwise.

Thankfully, there was no mention of a stranger at the house the same evening as the killings. Simon would not have to explain his involvement. A good thing, since he could hardly explain it to himself.

He only knew one thing for certain. He should have never helped Charlotte. As if there were some kind of ghostly hotline to spread news among the restless dead, more spirits than ever found their way to Simon. And unlike in the past, a number of them stuck around.

A half dozen now occupied his apartment, there to greet him every evening he returned from work. Others would approach him out in the world, coming and going with such frequency he couldn't keep track of how many he had encountered in the week following the incident with Charlotte.

They talked to him constantly. Usually begging.

"You have to help me. I need to find my wife."

"Please, sir, I must make peace with my father."

"There's so much I have to tell my friends from school. Will you take me to them?"

And what, Simon would wonder to himself, would happen if he *did* help them? More possession? More bloodshed? More death?

Never again.

They could stay as long as they wanted. Beg as often as they liked. He would not help them.

He. Would. Not.

* * *

A month later, Simon lays in bed. The lights are out, but the lights from the parking lot behind the apartment complex cast enough of a glow through the window that he can see them all staring down at him. Ten of them in a ring around his bed. Maybe a couple more behind the others. Men and woman of various ages, sizes, and colors.

They just stare at him.

Waiting.

How much longer can he take this?

Like Grateful Dead groupies, they follow him everywhere. Not always the same ones, but many now make that old sailor guy look impatient. At least one of the ghosts—a woman in her sixties with an eyepatch, of all things—has stuck with him for nearly two weeks now.

In fact, she stands at the head of his bed now. Her one good eye glares down at him, challenging him, daring him to sleep while she looms there like a sadistic prison guard.

The smell of sea water floods the room.

He's tried burning candles and incense. The various scents mingle with the ghostly stink of the sea, but none of them hide it.

It's been three hours since he went to bed and he hasn't come close to falling asleep. He wants to shout at them to leave him alone, to go bother some other poor asshole who can see the dead. But he doesn't. He knows engaging with them, even to tell them all to fuck off, will only encourage them.

They know for a fact now that he can help them. Charlotte was proof of that, and somehow, they seem to know about her. The best he can hope for is to outlast them, keep ignoring them until they forget what he did for Charlotte.

If the dead can forget.

Simon suspects they cannot. That's why they need his help.

But he has to hope.

Illustration by Greg Uchrin

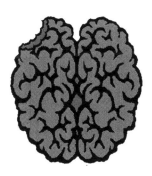

Very Important to Us

Mike Jack Stroumbos

Call me sentimental, but I think losing one arm makes you work extra hard to protect the other.

Normally, I would try to look inconspicuous after a retrieval job, but the second-degree burns on my still flesh-and-blood right hand felt far more motivating than the special cargo in my backpack. I fast-walked through the empty lobby without a whimper, then charged up four flights of stairs babbling profanities to myself. Whether or not the cameras caught me didn't feel particularly important. I expected rendezvous instructions long before any real human bothered to leaf through the hotel's security footage. A baseball hat and sunglasses, even in the dark before the dawn, were common enough in most metro areas, as was a mid-shelf robotic limb or a perfectly legal stunner pistol on one's belt. My left hand wasn't wrapped in imitation skin or nerve emulation, which was probably a good thing today, given what I'd had to touch. The backpack—furnished for this assignment—certainly cost more than my robot arm and nonlethal weapon combined. It was lined with an active scrambling mesh that could fake out even the most penetrating scanners.

I kept my throbbing right hand inside the faux-wool pocket, which was both too scratchy and too warm for flame-singed skin, until I reached my room, also on the Company tab. Merely withdrawing my hand from its protective pocket had me grunting and wincing in pain.

I used my pinky knuckle to input my security code and unlock my room. The efficient digital system released the iron locks with a heavy *kachunk*—strangely loud in an empty hallway before sunrise. Most of the hotel's "brick and mortar" components were far from new, but at least management had installed coded security systems and stellar Wi-Fi to comply with modern corpocratic ordinances.

Compared to the muted golden glow of the before-hours hallway, even the fancy room looked so muted and gray that I could barely make out the foot of the king-size bed, peaking around the corner from the entryway, or the armchair at the far end. The bay window's curtains were drawn closed. Even the in-room AI assist was off.

I slid the backpack off my shoulders and tossed it onto the edge of the bed where it bounced, but stopped short of toppling to the floor. Trying to protect my right hand, I used my left to grab the doorknob with another unappealing metal-on-metal scrape. I clearly wasn't paying enough attention, because when the door closed, that ornate, engraved-metal doorknob snapped cleanly off.

Part of me wanted to curse out the doorknob for breaking too easily and probably sticking me with a bill the company wouldn't cover. Still, the old metal clutched in my new metal hand wasn't nearly as important as the state of the one made of flesh. And I wanted to keep it that way.

I used my shoulder to open the way into the suite's bathroom and thanked water-saving regulations for the motion sensor faucet. I was starting to shake as I opened and stared at my right hand. The adrenaline was wearing off. I mean, I'd only just pulled a hard drive from an exploded car and sprinted half a mile using the most inefficient back alley twists I could find—but clearly my body had gotten used to this kind of thing, desensitized. Maybe that meant I was ready to be a full agent, with regular pay, a lethal sidearm, and maybe a better left arm. One hard drive in a backpack could be that next stepping stone.

That thought was little comfort when I first touched the cold water spilling into the basin sink. After the initial sting came that dull pressure and awful underskin itch, the kind that makes you want to reprogram your own bones. Even through the water, I could see that the tip of my forefinger and middle finger had gotten the worst of it. The rest of the hand, including my palm and thumb, were only slightly red and raw but would recover fine.

"Hey, Valerie," I said, addressing the wall and seeing the purple iris glow on the panel before I asked, "what's the time?"

The artificial intelligence interface known as Valerie dutifully replied, "5:22 AM. Is there anything else you need, Mr. Shaw?"

"Aloe vera and morphine," I muttered, but shouldn't have. I'd grown up with voice-activated systems and knew how literally they took these comments.

"Aloe vera for sunburns is available at the front desk. For prescription medication—"

"No thanks." It was the universal voice-command cue to turn off, most likely in any language anywhere in the world.

Gently, I opened and closed my hand, testing the skin's elasticity, relieved the pain was abating.

First priority met: make sure my flesh was not literally charred and falling off. Great for barbecue ribs, absolute shit for fingers that you want to use again.

I was careful not to press too hard on the rubber buttons when I reset the hotel room's security. Second priority: safety; not just for me. Though I wasn't sold on the idea, many parties considered one retrieved hard drive worth more than my life, certainly more than a few fingers. Either way, it made sense to arm the system until I got my extraction orders.

Then second priority failed. The screen read *Error: Door Ajar.*

The wall panel lied, because, clearly, the heavy wooden door had slammed snugly into its frame and stayed there even when the knob broke off.

Courtesy of nerveless tech, I couldn't feel the disconnected doorknob I still held, other than to be minorly aware of its weight. I now inspected the object in the dim light, to which my eyes had adjusted enough to see what really mattered. The mechanisms that should have held it in place could not be easily notched back into place; metal pins had snapped off at the well-worn grooves. I turned it over in my hand but didn't like my chances of finding more information. The outer surface was plated in something like bronze, but it felt heavy enough to be solid iron, even with the hollowed-out tumblers for the lock. I finally let the useless knob fall to the carpet with a dull *tock* and no bounce.

Despite its size, I easily pushed the door out and open with one metal finger. Don't get me wrong, the hand was strong, but this was a light touch met with no resistance. *Door Ajar*, meaning, to the computer, it hadn't latched.

I looked back over my shoulder. The glow of the streetlights made muted haloes against the curtain, clearly brighter than any traces of dawn would be at this hour. The hotel suite, larger than the studio I shared, looked compressed in the dim, gray wash of heavily filtered light.

I could make out the backpack, which I knew to be green but appeared ominously dark where it hung askew, partially off the bed. Priorities three and four could happen simultaneously: run an integrity and authenticity check of the hard drive and report to Company HQ.

I was armed with an authenticator—standard issue and highly adaptable. I'd stored it in the dresser's safe, just below the tech that could be mistaken for the most valuable thing in the hotel room: a giant, VR-enabled display rig, which could also be used as a standard TV for those feeling "old school." Before I'd been given the *go* code, I'd had the display screen showing a concert, blasting the sound loudly enough that all of the neighbors would naturally train up their room's sound dampeners. Now, I left the lights off, the curtains drawn, and hardly made a sound.

A siren sang between the city blocks and I imagined it going to the courier vehicle I'd torched, where they'd find no reason to believe the hard drive had survived, at least not until after everything had cooled. The sound receded slowly enough; I knew those were wheels on the ground and neither a drone nor flightcraft. Instinctively, my gaze cut to the door which could no longer latch, a security system that did not work. Meanwhile, both hands unzipped the precious cargo, extracted it, and set it on the bed. I plugged the authenticator into the hard drive and a *whirring* confirmed the autorun. That was a good sign. The courier vehicle had enough ecopolymers that it would be irreparably melting into the smartroads' signal tracks by now. At the time I'd arrived, however, the trunk and the trunk's black box weren't yet hot enough to unduly damage any circuits or the data they contained, worth more than life itself, according to the insurance assessors. If our intel was correct, contained within were hundreds of NFCs: non-fungible contracts, traveling across corporcratic borders, with tech and IP licensing, any of which could net millions of credits on its own—and I allegedly had hundreds in my somewhat seared or inorganic hands.

The two data devices continued their prolonged handshake—which may have felt more like an invasive doctor's procedure. I dialed the Company on my touchphone.

The Company logo—a smug-looking letter *C* in a circle—displayed on the touchscreen, but it was soon after replaced by a silhouette of a single men's dress shoe, a backdoor logo meaning their system had recognized the number I was calling with. They'd better. Then, the familiar prompt: "Thank you for calling Company HQ, where only very specific and important calls are received. It is possible you were transferred here in error. Did you mean to call the general customer service line instead, and would you like to be transferred?"

"No," I said in my trained *phonebot reply* voice.

"Okay." The prerecorded robot sounded friendly enough, but that *okay* always had an air of skepticism, I thought. "In order to put your call through company HQ, I need your name."

"Connor Shaw," I said, wondering how many more of these contract gigs I would need to complete before I got a direct line and didn't have to go through this runaround.

"Hello, Connor Shaw." Much brighter, less skeptical. "Please provide print verification."

On reflex, I touched my index finger to the screen in the open circle provided. There was a graphic of a white light scanning across, and then—the damnedest thing—it turned red.

"Shit!" I pulled my hand away, faster than I had from the burning metal handle of the car trunk, like I'd been caught in the worst possible cookie jar.

There was no change in inflection and, because it had no face, I couldn't see a scowl or narrowed eyes, yet the following remark was its own form of terrifying. "You are not—*Connor Shaw*—and are not authorized to contact Company HQ directly. Please know that if you have stolen—*independent contractor agent Connor Shaw*—'s touch phone, there may be legal repercussions under corpocratic law."

While the machine pleasantly threatened me, I tried to click through every option available to get out of there, which, granted, weren't many. The circle asking for my fingerprint—which had been burned just enough to be unrecognizable—had not only turned red, but was sporting a black X. The *back* button wouldn't respond and the *skip* button was grayed out. *Operator* was my only choice.

The phone rang and, for a few anxiety-inducing seconds, I planned my explanation, which would include my personal passcode and job reference number, as well as the serial number of the hard drive I'd been sent to retrieve—only about 10% of the way through authentication.

The ring stopped before I was ready and I started tripping over my tongue while I babbled, "Hello, this is contract agent Connor Shaw, and I—"

"We're sorry, we at the Company customer service line are experiencing higher than normal call volume. Your call is very important to us. Please stay on the line. We will answer your call in the order it was received."

Again, I looked to the window, where the drawn curtains showed no sign of naturally occurring sunlight. I wanted to rail and ask, "Who the hell would be up this early?" but I'd heard rumors that the bots bumped you back in the queue if you yelled at the elevator music and that was a rumor I didn't want to test.

So I sat on foot of the bed, listening intently to a midi reproduction of a tenor sax, glancing occasionally at the authenticator as it flirted with 25%.

New priorities: hurry up and wait

I pushed myself back to standing and proceeded the five paces to the door, where I had dropped the broken knob. I held the phone against my ear with my shoulder and knelt to attempt a bit of handy-manning. Might as well fix what I've broken—a temporary fix might correct the security system and security deposit, or so I hoped. Besides, if the automated system flagged *Door Ajar* too long, it might invite the hotel's active security, either actual people or drones with built-in stunners. Either way, not fun or ideal if I had to make a quick getaway, and the chances for that felt high.

I'll admit, I was never much of a repairman. I'd grown up with more of a knack for knocking things apart than putting anything together. And though I'd trained many fine motor skills on the replaced arm, it still would not do for putting together twentieth-century wristwatches or even a new SIM card in a touch-device. The weighty metal doorknob was less intricate, but, whether actually old or appearing old, its systems were far outside my wheelhouse. When it had pulled free, I had snapped at least two of the pins that would secure it, and disrupted the mechanism for the latch lock. At least, that was my amateur assessment. I had a YouTube School account and could access a tutorial if I had the time, but the phone against my ear had the odious task of getting me in touch with the Company and reminding me from time to time that my call was very important to them.

It was in that crouched state, debating whether or not to get off hold to look up a video walkthrough, that I heard distinct footsteps coming down the outer hallway, light heel-toe movements but at a determined clip. Room service? Probably not, but if it was hotel staff, they would know better than to wake guests or knock on doors before six in the morning. Then, the footsteps stopped. It sounded like they were right on the other side of my door. The more obvious tell was the slight buzz, a high-pitched and nasally whirring sound—if nasally can be used to describe electronics. The same kind I would hear if I was trying to detect an active security field. It meant an operative. Whether that was a rival operative or an enemy operative was often an important fine-line distinction, but I saw very little chance of them being friendly.

Final confirmation: someone in the hotel staff would not attempt to push a door that opened out instead of in. They certainly wouldn't try to pick a lock. I didn't know if I could move quietly enough to escape the intruder's notice, but I didn't know what good I could do kneeling there either. I'd drop the phone to draw my stunner pistol if I had to—but not until I had to.

Then the phone went through another *Please stay on the line* cycle, louder than the hold music, and the lockpicking clicks paused. With no other sounds, the device whispering directly into my ear would give me away.

I bet on speed and brute force. I slammed the door outward. I heard that satisfying smacking sound, hardwood against somebody's face, and what I detected to be the crunch of a nose—different timbre than a baseball bat, but just as effective.

I thrust the door the rest of the way open to see a dazed-looking fellow wearing dark joggers and a slim-fitting facemask. I kept the phone to my ear in one hand, but my left—much stronger and less likely to care when it collided with a face—struck his ailing nose a second time and knocked the lockpick out before he could draw any weapon. The unconscious lockpick's dark facemask grew wet below the nose and the knuckles of my left hand looked like they'd been sponge-painted red.

I hadn't yet figured out what to do with the body when a voice in my ear interrupted the hold music. "Hello, my name is Tom. I am with Company intake. I show that you requested to speak with customer service. How may I help you today?"

Between the accent and the fact that caller operators were some of the most hated people in the modern world, I highly doubted his real name was Tom, but I didn't have time to debate. "Tom, hi, I'm an independent contractor for the Company, working retrievals. I tried calling earlier—"

"Yes, what is your name, sir?"

"Connor Shaw," I strained in reply, given that, at that moment, I had grabbed the lockpick's limp ankle and dragged him down the arbitrarily chosen right hallway, where I hoped to find a chute down which to dump him.

Tom said, "Okay, Mister Connor Shaw, I am showing an agent by that name should not be calling the general number. If you have a direct HQ number, you should use that."

Thankfully, the limp form's jogging suit slid smoothly along the hall carpet, so I didn't have to exert as much to say, "I *do* have the number. But I couldn't get in. So I need an alternate authentication." I second-guessed my word choice, worried I might confuse him if the profile under independent-contractor-agent Connor Shaw had indeed checked out a standard issue authenticator for his current contract.

Instead, the fellow said in his most helpful unscripted voice, "You would have been given a fingerprint authorization. Did your device error?"

"No," I grunted, having noticed a sign pointing me in the other direction for both laundry and garbage and turning around with my sliding cargo. "During the retrieval I burned my finger—"

"Burned?" asked Tom, in a much higher voice, the kind that said this word stood out in his script. Had I not been up for twenty-four hours or actively putting away a hostile operative, I might have thought of it, too.

"Can you confirm, you are independent contractor agent Connor Shaw, burned while executing job num—"

"No, that's not what I meant!" I erupted, louder than I should have. I don't think it could have woken anyone, unless they were an extremely light sleeper, but it was best for me not to call attention to myself regardless.

Apparently, someone else missed the inconspicuous memo as well.

I heard him bark, "Hey!" behind me, and turned to see a pair of people at the end of the hall, both in painters' outfits, the most obvious of all disguise-yourself-for-dirty-work attire. The silhouettes read as one male and one female, and the tall angry fellow was obviously pointing in my direction.

I didn't stick around. My boots would've been hell for long distance running, but short sprints, fast zigzags, that I could do. Instinct had me low and agile, instead of a dead run or straight line. The shot came through a silencer, a name created by wishful thinkers. The bullet leaving the gun issued a recognizable *pop* almost the same time as the *crack!* when embedding into the stucco wall at the far end of the hall. A silencer couldn't mute the sound of hyper-accelerated metal striking a solid object. My brain told me *warning shot*, but my nerves screamed *danger*. On my next zig and zag, I made one sharp strike against two hotel room doors, this time thinking it better to have witnesses and interference. The first with a pronounced *clang* from my metal left, the second with a disgruntled *Ow!* from me. I'm only human.

I didn't know if any other guests had gotten the memo until I scrambled back into my room and pulled the wooden door effectively shut once again.

It was only then I brought the phone to my ear and heard Tom saying, possibly for the fourth time, "Sir, did you hear what I said?"

"No, I didn't, Tom! But this is urgent! I need to be transferred to—"

A second shot hit something in the hallway. I heard someone, a curious and stupid bystander, unlatch their door before they screamed, more likely terrified than wounded. I charged ahead, leapt over the king-size bed, and dropped to a crouch. Not much of a shield from bullets, but certainly from eyes. From down there, I whispered, "Tom, put me through to—"

"Transferring you, sir," said Tom, before I could give him direct instruction. Then, back to elevator music.

"Everyone, stay in your rooms!" hollered the gun-wielding madman, clearly speaking to anyone he might have woken.

Then, a rapping at my door, from a most-likely human hand, somebody being polite enough to ask to be let in. A feminine voice, madman's partner I'd guess, said, "Retrieval agent, let us in and stand down and we won't hurt you."

I'll admit, I considered those terms but didn't like them. I'd just yanked a couple billion credits worth of transferable funds from someone not corpocratically insured on behalf of the Company. If I handed it over, the Company would officially burn me, and someone else would probably hunt me down. If I were reckless and wanted to live fast for a few years, or a few weeks, I'd try to hack into the hard drive myself and sell its contents. More than enough to get me a better arm, certainly better than even the Company paid its full agents, and if I could afford a security team in time I'd be set. Those were a lot of ifs, and—despite the automated voice in the hold system—I didn't figure I personally was *very important* to anyone vying for that cargo.

But one thing stuck with me, one needling consideration before I could say either *yes* or *shove it*. It was one of those questions that eats at the back of the mind: how the hell did they find me so quickly? I covered my trails well, misdirected like a pro—or at least an advanced amateur, which was how I'd jumped city-state lines and secured the gigs I'd gotten, and why, out of all of the interested parties—corporate agents or criminal underground—who might have known about last night's courier, I was the one who had succeeded.

I watched the edge of that dimly lit door from behind the foot of the bed, ready to move out of view if it suddenly opened. A little glow in the corner of my vision illuminated the wrinkled bedspread. The screen of the authenticator, still working through the hard drive, was at 57%. Some progress. It also showed an orange message: *Tracking System Detected*.

Then the *oh shit* moment, the one that comes with every inconvenient revelation. As soon as the car was reported destroyed, the tracker must have been activated. I had neither time nor expertise to disarm it, but I did have an insulated backpack. I shoved both the hard drive and actively-running authenticator inside—no point in stopping it now. I zipped the pack closed as the madman's voice once again clanged through my room, echoing enough to make the suite feel empty and small. "Hey! We know you're in there and we know what you have. Let us in!"

I didn't say anything. I wasn't exactly frozen in fear. I just couldn't come up with any helpful response. Instead, I regarded my position, between the bed and the window, not far from the VR-display system and the safe I'd left open when getting the authenticator. The chair closer to the window side might provide a better shield than the bed, but any defense was temporary and futile. They had at least one pistol with lethal rounds—reserved for only the very trained and the very unscrupulous—and I had a stunner with only five charged shots.

"I'm breaking the door down," madman informed me.

His partner took the softer approach and probably would've followed in the footsteps of the lockpick, except had the wherewithal to see if the door was even locked.

"Hey," she called through the now open entryway. "Job one is retrieval, job two is intel. We don't get paid any extra for killing you."

Comforting. But understandable.

"Although no limits expressed on what we could do to get that intel," madman said, as he stepped inside.

They, too, left the lights off, but the light filtering through the curtains had grown. They would find me soon enough and, as I was an independent contractor, I probably didn't know any more than they did. Less, since I hadn't figured out the tracker until just now. Something told me they wouldn't rest if I rattled off the terms of my assignment and how I knew which car to hit.

From my vantage point behind the armchair, I caught a glimpse of madman's long, deliberate steps toward the foot of the bed. The woman who followed—much more the spry cat burglar—tiptoed toward the open safe.

The music at my ear stopped. I activated speakerphone within a syllable of the next call-center voice. "Hello, this is Alex. Please tell me, who am I speaking with?"

Two thoughts, two shots, straight into the bed, bright enough to illuminate madman's face and show an unflattering sneer and no hat to ward off security cameras. I assume the bullets traveled right through the mattress and the frame, but they were at the wrong angle to hit the phone which I had slid under the bed.

I fired my stunner. The shocking round latched onto madman's shoulder and sent hundreds of volts through his body, with enough strength to burn his skin far more than I had managed to do to my fingers. I didn't know if they would both have guns, but it was better to assume *yes*. The second after I'd fired, I threw the backpack, and all its valuable contents, at cat burglar, calling, "Catch!"

You'd be amazed how many people are caught off-guard by quick verbal commands in tense situations. She might have guessed, correctly, that what she sought was inside and shouldn't be fired at, so she awkwardly tried to grab the bag with a pistol in one hand while I charged her.

I had both the weight advantage and a sturdy metal arm to strike with, while she was more than compromised, half-crouching before the safe, and trying to wrangle the backpack.

She twisted to turn the gun on me, but I slammed her to the floor, where I heard yet another *pop* through a silencer, point blank into the carpet, causing the floor to shudder. Cat burglar was strong and flexible enough to regain control of her weapon, which she'd turn on me. Her head was also in the arc of the safe door, which turned out to be a highly *un*safe place to land. Usually, I don't appreciate puns, but considering that this one saved my life, I'll let it slide. I gave her three quick hits with the door before I trusted that she wouldn't be getting up anytime soon. I relieved her of her pistol and holstered it at my hip. My open-carry leather rigging was shaped for a stunner rather than a slim pistol and silencer, but it would do the trick.

Madman was still twitching, but, fortunately, he'd let go of his weapon. I picked it up, dropped out the clip and tossed each piece in opposite directions.

It was then that my ears finally registered, above the soft ring and muted sensations following silencer shots, a somewhat impatient customer service person under the bed.

"Sir, do you need me to repeat what I said?"

"Yes," I said, collecting the phone. "Yes, I need you to repeat, please."

"As I said, sir, my name is Alex and I am your representative with Company escalation services. Unfortunately, we show that you are calling from a device that should belong to independent contractor agent Connor Shaw, but you have not properly identified—"

"Confirming, this is Connor Shaw. I tried to confirm earlier, but there was an error." That felt like the best phrasing to take some blame off me in terms these phone tech guys understood.

"We registered an incorrect fingerprint," he said, while I rechecked the two unconscious bodies. "Given the sensitivity of some of our independent contractor agents' assignments, if we cannot confirm that you are Connor Shaw—"

"Can you see the assignment given to Connor Shaw?" There was no response, which led me to believe that the answer was yes. "If you think that this hard drive is important enough then you want to help me."

"Sir, please do not threaten—"

"Not a threat. But I am being pursued and am in danger and I need an extraction."

"Without being able to confirm that you are—"

"Okay, how about this..." I chewed on the option while I regarded the open door of my suite and the open door of the safe, apparently my weapons of choice. "Independent contractor super special secret agent for the Company, Connor Shaw, is dead." Once more, I shut the front door and collected the doorknob in my left hand, while forcing myself to say, "I killed him and stole the important courier cargo. Please arrest me and take me in."

The call center person sounded like they were in a lot of pain when they asked, "Are you sure, sir?"

No. "Yes!" I exclaimed. "Take me in. Do you need my location?"

"Um…" Hesitation from a phone tech. Clearly, I'd gone far off script. "No, sir, we know where you are." Honesty from a phone tech. That might have been worse.

"Great." As if to show I was ready to go, I picked up the backpack and slung it back onto my shoulder. "Where and when is my pickup—or arrest or whatever?"

After three arduously long seconds of deliberation, Alex said, "Hold please," too quickly for me to protest or scream obscenities.

I slumped down on the bed, where I unzipped the pack and checked progress, 89%. Almost done. Like reaching the last two miles of a marathon, which, as everyone knows, behave on a different time stream than the first twenty-four. Maybe logically, finishing the authentication was a small concern, but I think it would have killed me to find out this was all for nothing, and maybe a fully authenticated delivery would help me convince the Company goons I was really me when they came to collect the burned agent or murderous imposter.

I stood and tried to figure out which way, if any, to run. If I went in the wrong direction and had to double back, I could put myself in a lot more danger. Then again, I didn't know how many more intruders I could handle, if any.

I looked at the window. The curtains were still drawn, and either my eyes had adjusted far more in the last few minutes or it was legitimately much brighter outside. I used the tip of my stunner to part the curtains just a sliver so I could look out—

Glass shattered and the air hissed before my ears registered the *crack!* A sniper was below and had fired at the opening. The sniper apparently didn't care about interrogating me.

While I won't defend every move that I'd made that night, I'd had the good sense to part the curtain while crouching as far away as my arm could reach.

At the next sound, I dropped to the floor and covered my head, for outside in the courtyard, and maybe the surrounding buildings, there was the most fantastic percussive array of discharging firearms I'd ever heard. But no more shards of glass flew from the window. It was like a firefight between competing interests below, and I would guess one very dead sniper. I felt brief relief at "the enemy of my enemy" and all that, then dread, because whichever enemy was the loudest and most aggressive was very likely to charge up here in force.

I was so overwhelmed by the uncountable number of shots that I gasped out, "Hello?" when the elevator music paused again to remind me that my call was very important to the Company. If this hard drive was important to them, surely they would be making more of an effort here on my behalf. Was it possible that the biggest muscle with the most guns in the hotel courtyard down below was made up of my employer?

The question was answered by the inevitable shattering of another pane of glass and a capsule billowing noxious smoke as it bounced its way past the curtain and onto my floor. Looked like knockout gas, and, at first whiff, it smelled sweet and musky, which was, of course, hard to detect except in the seconds before you collapsed.

I knew better than to take a deep breath then, before I held it, but it's not like I had been breathing easily beforehand or had much air to spare. I leapt onto the bed and fired my stunner upward at the tiny ceiling contraption that must not have changed in decades. The shocker latched awkwardly against the sprayer mechanism and shocked it enough to heat the little sensors inside. The Valerie AI assist wall panel lit up and said, "Danger, fire detected," just before the first sprinkler activated, which triggered all others in the suite, thus drenching this still possibly salvageable hotel suite. I didn't want to think about the bill. I certainly didn't want to think about passing out while the sprinklers were going off, to drown in a couple inches of water.

Reaching down, I shook a pillow out of one case to soak under the sprinkler. This, I held over my mouth. I stepped back to the head of the bed and leaned against the wall, where I could no longer see the front door. The object in the backpack dug into my shoulder blade, while I forced slow, deliberate breaths through the damp fabric. I only had three more shots left in my stunner, and I wasn't in a place to fend off an army with a silenced pistol. I'm not sure if I heard boots running or if I just imagined them.

I also saw I had dropped the phone near the window, where it was still playing hold music on speaker. It must have been in danger of shorting out, what with all of the water bouncing off of its touchscreen and playing roulette with its ports. I grabbed the phone but quickly realized that going down to retrieve it put me more in line with the toxic vapors, so I dragged myself back onto the bed, shielding the phone from the artificial rain and using my wet body and the watertight backpack as an umbrella.

The charging boots arrived outside the door and one representative spoke very clearly: "Operative! This is your last chance. Come out now with the cargo and you won't be shot."

I still didn't know whether or not I believed them, but some combination of the rain and the soft jazz coming through my touch phone relaxed me enough that I wanted to. Even if they were out of breath and sounded urgent and desperate.

"Operative," they yelled again, "did you hear me? That cargo is very important to us. More important than your life. If you resist, or have any traps waiting for us, or injure any of my contractors, I will not hesitate to execute you."

I was still considering the offer when the music coming through the touchphone suddenly stopped. This time, I turned off speakerphone.

Someone else outside the door said, "Maybe he was too far gone by the time he got the sprinklers going."

More importantly, however, the voice coming through the phone was quite different this time. This newest phone personality did not introduce herself but sounded more like she was speaking to me than reading off a script. "Independent contractor agent Connor Shaw, or agent Shaw's murderer, this is the surrender line for the Company. Do you still have the courier's cargo?"

"Yes," I whispered.

The announcer outside my door said, "You have five seconds!"

The nicer phone operator said, "Good. Now jump out the window to safety."

Competing breezes from outside and the dance of water and pressurized knockout gas were pushing the curtains. I was only a few steps away, but for most of the run I would be in plain view of the doorway, which could open any moment and get me killed.

Then, muffled through the backpack, I heard a small *bing*. Good bing, green light bing, authentication complete bing. Meaning if I made it out of here alive, all of this would be worthwhile.

I needed one last distraction.

"Hey, Valerie, resume concert!" I called out, so rapidly I didn't know if the AI would actually catch it. I found out when the room filled with light from the giant display system and, more importantly, sound. Everything I'd been blaring before kicked back in at full volume, ushering my escape.

I leapt off the bed, just as the door was pulled open, and ran.

I fired my stunner behind me, never seeing what I hit, but hearing reactions and the errant bursts of bullets. Out of stun charges, I threw my touchphone, too—not a premeditated bluff but hopefully confusing nonetheless. Part of the segmented display screen exploded as I passed, showering the floor with colorful shards.

By the time anyone managed to aim at me, it was too late. I was barreling through an already compromised window.

The fall was more exhilarating than it was terrifying, possibly evidence of the knockout gas or just the thrill of achieving freedom before inevitable impact on a growing balloon where there should be cement.

I sank into an inflated surface, the kind that police used to use for jumpers before all law enforcement jobs went to contractors. The descent was still quite fast, so I held my good hand into my chest and tried to catch my fall with the left. The metal protested the impact when it reached hard sidewalk, jarring the bone graft connection in my upper arm and on through my shoulder. I coughed and rolled onto my side while others raced to surround me. Someone yelled, "Ceasefire!"

And that voice, the voice from my phone, was amplified through a megaphone, declaring, "The prisoner is claimed by the Company. Do not attempt to interfere."

Someone grabbed my shoulder and ushered me to a supported sitting position. "Eyes, open your eyes."

I hadn't realized they were closed, but I opened them to see a pale blue sky between the slashing frames of surrounding buildings.

Then they zapped me with a bright white light, and said, "Positive ID. Connor Shaw."

I tried to blink away the blind spots while someone relieved me of the backpack. I could barely see her—formal suit coat, pulled-back hair—but the voice was the distinct alto of the surrender line woman. "Shaw, is the courier cargo in the bag?" My eyes focused enough to see the encircled *C* logo of the Company.

"Yes, ma'am," I said. "Fully authenticated."

The sound of a zipper and someone said, "And intact."

"Well done," she said as she and another party helped me to my feet. "Agent Shaw, let's get you out of here."

I could feel myself growing drowsier as they half-carried me to a waiting extraction vehicle. Despite my disorientation, all I could think about was that she'd called me "Agent Shaw," bypassing all of that *independent contract* title, but maybe I was reading too much into that. Even a Company representative can have a slip of the tongue.

Illustration by Greg Uchrin

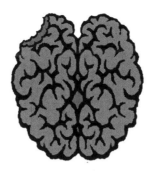

Shadows Like Hunting Sharks

J.L. George

The Northern Line was twenty-six degrees and airless, and the patch over my cursed eye itched like hell.

A puff of stale air hit me in the face as the train doors opened, admitting a duo of Amy Winehouse pilgrims in leopard-print and eyeliner, a lone mother struggling to maneuver her pram, and a suit who clutched his Evening Standard to his chest like a protective barrier against the hoi polloi. He frowned at me as I shuffled down the aisle and I did my best to stop squinting.

The itch didn't budge. It seemed to grow legs and wriggle, like an ant trapped in the corner of my right eye.

I wasn't supposed to touch it. The balancer I'd paid five hundred pounds to curse me had been adamant on that point. Not a peek, not a sliver of sunlight, for at least three months after the curse. I sat on my hands.

The itch intensified. The imaginary ant burrowed down into my tear duct.

I tried to distract myself by inventorying the contents of the carrier bag at my feet. Milk, cereal, pasta, and a bag of the gummy worms my sister Lara liked to mess around with as much as to eat, stuffing her mouth full of them and making faces like some tentacle-mawed movie monster. Lara hadn't been eating much of anything lately, but this morning she'd actually asked for sweets.

Which had to mean the curse was working—and its counterpart, the blessing, blooming to life in the color in her cheeks and the strength of her voice.

The itch kept right on burning. I shook my head like I was warding off a fly, then screwed up my face. One of the Winehouse lookalikes glanced at me sideways and nudged the other. They both giggled and my cheeks warmed.

While I was half-distracted, my right hand crept up under the eyepatch and nudged it aside.

I squeezed my eyelid shut, but not fast enough to avoid seeing a blur of light. It stung, after two weeks in the dark.

But it was done now. I'd looked.

I rubbed my eye. The relief was instant and overwhelming, and whatever terrible thing the balancer had hinted might happen, didn't.

Cautiously, I peeked.

A line of light crept through beneath the black felt of the eyepatch. Not the sickly, artificial yellow of the Tube lights, but a thin, misty dawn-gray: the kind of light you only see when you've been forced from your bed at some ungodly hour or failed to sleep at all. Not unexpected. The balancer—Newt, he'd called himself—had warned me that the curse would steal color and life from the world, that I'd never see either out of my cursed eye again. I'd decided I could deal with that.

What he hadn't mentioned were the shadows.

A shuddering flicker, as if the lights were failing, but I saw it only through my right eye. Through the left, everything looked the same. Suit-guy read his paper. The woman with the pram pushed it back and forth to rock her baby, wheels making sticky sounds on the dirty floor. The train rattled around a bend and the passengers swayed with it, faces impassive.

The flickering shadows started to take shape, forming something quick and dark and purposeful that darted like a fish through water.

I snatched my hand from my eye. The eyepatch snapped back into place.

Two stops until Old Street and home. Suit-guy turned a page. One of the Winehouses tapped at her phone, oblivious. If I lifted the eyepatch again, would the shadow be right on top of them?

I didn't dare look.

* * *

Lara was waiting for me outside the lift when I reached our floor, bouncing on her heels. She wore the rainbow-striped t-shirt that had hung untouched in her wardrobe since her birthday, and she'd even brushed her hair, bright ginger curls tumbling over her shoulders. Despite the damp heat and the faint whiff of ammonia that always hung around the landing, she looked fresh and wide-awake.

Despite myself, I smiled. "Look at you, all dressed up."

Lara made a face and tugged at the hem of the t-shirt. "I'm too old for this now. But I know you wanted me to like it."

I favored dark colors, personally, but I had a faint memory of Mum buying me similar things when I was Lara's age and I'd never been much good at coming up with ideas of my own.

I smiled weakly at Lara and brandished the carrier bag. "I got you your worms."

Those, at least, she wasn't too old for.

She grabbed for the bag. "I'm going to save these for when we go to the rooftop cinema."

My heart sank. Lara loved movies, and she'd seen an advert for it on her tablet while she sat up watching videos in bed. Every couple of months, some high-up building with a panoramic view of London would put on a film screening on its rooftop. Seemed like a daft idea to me—who wanted to watch a film with traffic noise all around and the chance that a pigeon would do its business in your popcorn?—but Lara had latched onto it like a lamprey and I'd promised to take her once she felt better.

Wasn't cheap, and the balancer had cleared me out. "Next month," I promised her. "We'll watch something at home tonight."

I almost didn't catch the disappointed downturn of her mouth, the dimming of her eyes. When had my kid sister got so good at putting on a brave face?

"It's okay. Can I eat them now?"

A couple of weeks ago, she would've moaned and protested sickness at the suggestion of food. "Yeah. Go on then."

It was only later, when we'd eaten dinner and filled our faces with sweets, and Lara had sugar-crashed on the sofa with some superhero film still playing on the telly, that I thought about the shadows again.

They could have been a trick of the light. A floater or visual disturbance, like a migraine. Newt had mentioned I might get those, though I'd pictured them as the flowers of flashing light that blossomed at the edges of my vision when I'd been awake all night, not as shadows that moved with predatory quickness. But what did I know? I wasn't a balancer, just someone who'd scraped together the money to hire an unlicensed one and hope for the best.

Lara snuffled in her sleep and pulled the blanket more tightly around her. The TV screen flickered blue and red as a CGI fight scene played out on a rooftop, the colours turning her face eerie-cold and then rosy.

Sitting here in the warm living room, with the movie still playing and our empty spaghetti plates at our feet, the idea of the shadows seemed ridiculous.

I toyed with the edge of the eyepatch. Slid my fingernail underneath like I was opening an envelope.

Lifted it up.

I took a moment to make sense of what I was seeing.

It was as though someone had drawn a blackout curtain across my cursed eye, the room veiled in thick darkness.

A chink of light opened and closed again, a brief parting of clouds. Another, gone as fast as it came. Everything seemed to be moving. Swarming.

The room was thick with shadows. Dozens of them, clustered like a feeding shoal.

All around Lara.

* * *

Mrs. Norton, our neighbour across the hall, was already in bed when I knocked at her door. She answered in her quilted dressing-gown and slippers, her Yorkshire Terrier clutched in her arms and yipping at the unexpected excitement. I held my breath against the whiff of old dog that emanated from her flat.

"Nadine?" she said, peering at me over the top of her spectacles. I knew I must look a mess, hair rumpled from sprawling on the sofa, my oldest jogging bottoms tucked into my outdoor shoes. "What's wrong?"

"Can you watch Lara for me? Just for an hour or two? Something's come up."

As she followed me across the hall, I tried to remember the things you were supposed to tell babysitters. It was like thinking through thick fog. Or shadows. "Her meds are on top of the drawers in her bedroom. It's, um, it's the one across the hall. And—just phone me if anything weird happens, will you?"

Mrs. Norton gave a bewildered nod. With one backward look at Lara, I grabbed my jacket and bolted for the door.

Newt's shop, such as it was, was in Soho, behind a peeling front door that sat uneasily between pubs advertising all-night happy-hours and shiny new cafes that charged the best part of a tenner for a smoothie. The shop hadn't had Newt's name on it, just a handwritten sign with the legend, *BALANCER – NO WAITING LIST*, and a doorbell that didn't work so you had to rap hard on the window to get an answer.

I almost missed it, glancing from Google Maps to the door and back again in confusion. The sign was gone.

That couldn't be good. I squared my shoulders and banged on the window.

No reply.

I rapped harder, hard enough that my knuckles stung and would probably be bruised come morning. "Newt! Newt, I know you're in there! Something's gone wrong with the balancing."

Silence.

"Newt, come on!" My voice rose higher, childishly plaintive, and I steadied myself against the door. Once-white paint flaked off under my fingertips and drifted to the floor like dandruff. "I promise I don't want my money back," I tried. "I just need you to sort it out."

Above my head, a window creaked open. "You won't have no luck there, love."

I blinked and looked up. The voice belonged to a woman with a face wrinkled like an old apple and surrounded by a halo of spiky white hair. An incongruous slash of red lipstick stood out against her pale face.

"What do you mean?" I asked.

"Done a moonlight flit, he have. Landlord was tamping mad."

I swore under my breath. "Don't suppose he left a forwarding address?" The old woman raised an eyebrow and I sagged bodily. "What am I supposed to do now?"

She gave me a measuring look. "I'm Phyllis," she said, at last. "Call me Phyl. Come on up, why don't you? Looks like you could do with a cuppa."

Phyl's flat sat directly above the shop. A black leather jacket hung behind the door, and the carpet was matted with cat fur. A faint smell of old curry lingered around the entrance and, through the open kitchen door, I caught a glimpse of piled-up takeaway boxes and empty wine bottles.

Phyl wore a black glove on her left hand.

Despite everything, I couldn't keep from staring, or from blurting out, "You're cursed."

She harrumphed and led me into the living room. "Used to be a balancer. Long story." She didn't elaborate. "Park yourself anywhere, I'll put the kettle on."

I shooed a black-and-white cat off the sofa, earning a protesting yowl, and waited. Phyl didn't ask how I liked my tea, just pressed a mug of tongue-scalding builder's brew into my hands and sat down opposite me, unbothered by the white fur that clung to her black jeans. "So." She jerked her head downwards, indicating Newt's shop. "What've he done?"

I understood balancing about as well as the average person, which was to say, not very. Newt had given me the quick-and-dirty explanation. There were two sides to the otherworld: the blessed and the cursed. You couldn't draw power from one without drawing from the other, which meant every blessing came with a curse. There was no avoiding that—but you could direct it. Draw a curse onto a part of yourself and choose what you gave up.

Some very unscrupulous balancers would try to draw a curse onto somebody else for you, but that was dicey. Newt had assured me he'd never do it, of course, though I was starting to wonder if anything Newt said was true.

But he'd assured me what I needed would be straightforward enough. My eye for Lara's health. After all the months we'd spent waiting for fruitless hospital appointments, the trade had seemed like a bargain.

Phyl listened to my explanation without a word, but the way her eyebrows crept up millimeter by millimeter said it all.

"Anyway," I finished, weakly, "my sister's been ill, and the doctors can't find out what's wrong with her, so I thought, 'I can manage with one eye.' And I've been fine. I mean, it's only been a couple of weeks, but…" I trailed off.

Phyl slurped her tea. "'So not wrong, what he told you. Not exactly."

"But?"

"'So not as simple as that, either." She kept her eyes on the mug. "What happens when you take on a curse is, you open yourself up to the shadows. Sneaky buggers, they are. Always a chance one's going to slip through. Especially if the balancer don't know what he's doing."

"And you think Newt didn't know what he was doing?"

"Always knew there was something dodgy about that one."

It would've been easy to blame him. He'd messed up and made a run for it. But he'd told me not to look through my cursed eye and I'd done it anyway. Maybe I was the one who'd invited the shadows in.

But, if that were the case, what did they want with Lara?

I opened my mouth to confess, but before I could say anything, Phyl was on her feet and back at the window. "Oi!" she called down to the street. "Oi, he's cleared out! We don't want no more of his friends hanging around here."

A young man hovered before Newt's doorway. He looked exactly as I would have imagined one of Newt's friends: ratty jeans, an old t-shirt, and the ubiquitous balancer's mark of curling black sigils tattooed up both arms.

"I'm not hanging around," he protested. "Wanted to know if anyone had come looking for Newt, is all."

Phyl shook her head, apparently ready to deny all knowledge, but I couldn't miss my chance. I crowded up to the window beside her and looked out. "Yeah," I said. "Me. Did he muck something up for you, too?"

The guy visibly relaxed. "Not you," he said. "Uh, no offense. I meant… dodgy types. Black marketers." I'd heard of those: people who could get hold of the tools balancers used to channel curses and blessings without a license. "Asking for money, maybe."

"No," Phyl told him. "And we don't wanna see nobody else, either. Go on, off you pop."

The guy ignored her and nodded to me. "I'll tell him," he promised, and loped off down the street.

"Wait," I called after him, uselessly. "Wait, I need to speak to him!"

The guy didn't turn around. I leaned back from the window and scrubbed a hand down my face.

"He won't go far," Phyl assured me. "That pub a couple of streets down, the Grey Horse? Full of these wannabe balancers, it is. Hang around there 'til morning if the landlord doesn't boot them out."

"But Newt won't be there, right? Not if someone dodgy's out looking for him." I looked helplessly at Phyl. "What do I do?"

She fixed me with a capital-L Look. It was a look that made disobeying seem impossible. "You go home and look after your sister. Give me your number. I'll see what I can find out."

Lara was tucked into bed when I got home. When I lifted my eyepatch, I still saw shadows clustering around her, but she was sleeping peacefully, a torch and an open comic book abandoned on the pillow beside her. Another thing she claimed she was too old for, though I often caught her reading under the tent of her bedcovers long after she should've been asleep. I switched off the torch and pulled up the duvet, pausing to brush Lara's hair out of her face.

Her skin was warm to the touch—but then, it was the kind of sticky London summer that always left me tossing and turning in sweat-soaked sheets. Perhaps that was all.

I opened the window and pictured all the shadows being sucked out into the night air.

* * *

Since she'd started to feel better, Lara was usually out of bed before seven in the morning, watching TV in the living room or climbing onto my bed to demand breakfast like an impatient cat.

The next morning, I woke at eight, disoriented and heavy with having slept too long. My stomach tightened when I realized Lara wasn't in my room. I found her doll still in her bed, the bedcovers thrown off, her pillow damp. The heat had broken overnight, fine drizzle misting the window, but Lara's forehead was still sticky-hot. When I laid my hand against it, she blinked sluggishly. Her eyes were very bright.

"Do you feel sick?" I asked.

She frowned. "I don't think so?" And she looked at me for approval.

I thought I'd kept my relief at her improvement to myself—I hadn't wanted her asking awkward questions about the curse—but apparently, I'd been less subtle than I thought.

"You're burning up," I told her. "You should stay in bed today."

"Can we watch Spider-Man again? I fell asleep."

I stroked her hair. "Sorry, sis, I have to go and sort something out. Mrs. Norton and Buttercup will come over and sit with you, okay?"

Lara made a face. "Buttercup smells funny."

"She's old, she can't help it."

"So does Mrs. Norton."

"Behave." I squeezed her shoulder. "I'll be back soon."

* * *

The Grey Horse was a dingy establishment with a pool table and an ancient TV in the back, a few desultory sigils scratched into the bar top the only indication that it was a balancers' haunt. The place was barely open at this time of morning, the smell of last night's spilled beer the most tangible presence in it. The barman eyed me as I walked in and then let his eyes slide on past, obviously pegging me for a civilian.

I mustered all the confidence I could, strode up to the bar, and folded my arms atop the counter. My sleeves stuck to the surface.

The barman said nothing.

I unstuck my arms as subtly as I could. "I'm looking for someone who might've been in here last night. Bloke with tattoos up both arms, floppy hair, jeans?"

The barman shrugged, picked up an already-clean pint glass, and started to polish it with an air of studied indifference. "Doesn't really narrow it down, love."

What was I supposed to do here? Slap a tenner down on the bar like in the movies and say, "Maybe this will help you remember?"

"Please," I said, aware that my voice was trembling and unable to stop it. "I really need to find him. Well, someone he knows. It's my sister, she's sick. She's only a kid. You've got to help me."

"Would if I could."

"It's alright, Jase," came a voice from behind me. "She's looking for me."

For a brief moment, the sound of Newt's voice was enough to fill me with hope. If he was here, then whatever dodgy people were looking for him must have given up, right? Maybe now he'd come back to help me.

Then I took in his bloodshot eyes and his rumpled clothes, the whiff of booze on his breath and the slump of his posture as he plopped onto the barstool next to me.

I was desperate enough to ask anyway. "Look, something's gone wrong. With this." I gestured at my cursed eye. "I need you to fix it."

"Let me guess." Newt leaned forward and twanged the elastic holding my eyepatch in place with the tip of his finger. "You looked."

I suppressed the flicker of guilt. "I *saw*. Shadows. And they're all around Lara, and she's ill again, and it's all gone wrong somehow. You need to fix it."

"Lara? Oh, your sister."

"Yeah."

"Shit." Newt made a hollow, mirthless sound that, after a moment, I realized was supposed to be a laugh. "Can't. 'S done. Pint, Jase?"

The barman shook his head. "I think you had enough last night. Go home and get some kip."

"No, don't." I grabbed Newt's arm. "What do you mean, you can't? She's supposed to be blessed and she's got shadows coming after her instead. You're a balancer. It's unbalanced. *Balance* it."

Newt snorted. "We're not in primary school, Nade. I can't just add another handful of sand to the scales. You wouldn't understand."

I glowered. "Maybe I'd understand if you'd bothered to explain it properly. But no: *Just take on this curse, your sister'll be fine, it's just your eye, it's nothing*. You didn't think to mention anything about shadows slipping through."

Newt's eyes narrowed, the hungover haze clearing a little. "Who told you that?"

I drew myself up and tried to look as imposing as I could. It even worked—or, at least, Newt leaned away from me and wobbled on his stool. I grabbed his arm. "I tell you what. We'll go and see her. She told me this could happen if the balancer doesn't know what they're doing. Maybe you can explain to her what you messed up."

"Her." Newt groaned. "Bloody Phyllis."

Bloody Phyllis was in the same clothes she'd been wearing last night, the front room of her flat strewn with old books, and her face wearing the slightly shellshocked expression of someone who'd fallen into a research rabbit-hole and emerged to find half a day had passed. She narrowed her eyes at Newt as we walked in and he ducked his head like a teenager late for class and expecting a scolding.

"Stop looking at me like that," he grumbled. "Just because you used to be all proper and registered or whatever doesn't mean you're better than me. What have you been telling Nadine?"

The bravado in his voice was weak. It crumbled under Phyl's glare like a stale biscuit.

"Been looking over my old notes all night," she said, ignoring his little outburst. "Tell you what, Nadine, why don't you make me some coffee? Two sugars, and if the spoon don't stand up, it's not strong enough. Get one for yourself while you're at it."

I did as I was asked, though I had a sneaking suspicion, from the way she kept looking sideways at Newt, that Phyl had only asked to get me out of the way. She hadn't asked me to make him a cup, though, and I didn't, taking a small, petty satisfaction in setting out two mugs and measuring out two spoons each of instant coffee.

They talked in low voices in the living room, papers rustling. I stood close to the door, listening in, but only caught snatches:

I know what you bloody well did, Newton Jones. You're going to have to tell her sometime.

What's the point of that? Better if I just go.

You walk out and I'll...

Phyl's voice was too muffled for me to make out the rest, but I imagined some arcane balancer threat. Maybe she'd offered to curse his nose or his greasy hair.

My phone vibrated in the back pocket of my jeans, the buzz cutting right through whatever Phyl said next. Annoyance buzzed through me, too, but faded when I saw my home number on the screen.

"Nadine?" Mrs. Norton's voice quavered on the other end of the line. "It's Lara. I've called an ambulance. I think you'd better come."

The mug I was still holding in my other hand dropped from my grip. I felt it fall as if in slow motion, like everything was happening underwater, and only the crash with which it hit the floor, spraying ceramic shards and powdered coffee across the lino, brought me back to reality.

"What's going on in there, now, love?" Phyl bustled into the room, taking in the phone in my hand and the mess on the floor with a single glance. She jerked her head at Newt. "Get that cleaned up, now." And then, gentler. "What's happened?"

Newt bent to do as he was told. I heard him hiss as he reached for a shard of broken mug, snatching his hand back and putting his thumb to his mouth.

Phyl steered me out to the living room. "Nadine?"

I couldn't form the words. Mrs. Norton's voice was still warbling away on my phone, tinny and distant. Mutely, I handed it to Phyl.

She squeezed my hand. It didn't comfort me.

* * *

The journey to Royal London Hospital was a blur. I was distantly aware of Phyl following a few paces behind me, thin-lipped and drawn, and of Newt trailing along in her wake, cowed by whatever she'd said earlier. He'd gone very quiet, no more derisive laughs or narky comments, and kept the hand he'd cut cleaning up in Phyl's kitchen stuffed into the sleeve of his jacket.

Near the hospital entrance, I tore off my eyepatch. The shadow world overlaid itself atop the ordinary one, muting its colors. The whole thing had the look of a double exposure, one world a photograph taken an inch to the left of the other.

The air above both hospitals was thick with shadows.

They only multiplied as I half-ran inside. A few ghosted through other rooms—I saw them as I passed—but the bulk of them flocked toward A&E, obscuring everything so I had to cover my cursed eye to see where I was going. My fingers felt thick, too clumsy to replace the eyepatch, so I held the palm of my hand over it instead. I knew I must look crazy, or like a drunk who'd wandered in off the street, but nobody questioned me. I probably wouldn't have heard them if they had.

Mrs. Norton was in the waiting room. She got to her feet when she saw me, and looked about to speak, but only shook her head, put the back of her hand over her mouth and made a high, pained sound.

Bizarrely, my first impulse was to comfort her. It took a moment to sink in that we were too late.

I took my hand away from my eye. Shadows swirled around us like a hurricane.

Lara was gone.

It felt unreal. I kept thinking the truth might evaporate if I just waited a moment longer, like a nightmare touched by daylight.

Someone's hand was on my shoulder: Phyl, guiding me to sit on one of the institutional green chairs. At some point a doctor appeared, bearing a clipboard and an expression of practiced sympathy. His mouth moved. I caught words like *next of kin* and *sudden cardiac event* and none of them seemed to mean anything.

Phyl took over the conversation for me, nodding in the right places and listening attentively to what the doctor said, occasionally pulling out her phone to note something down. Eventually, he left.

Newt stood apart from our little group, loitering awkwardly near the vending machines. He hadn't taken advantage of my dazed state to slope off, but I wasn't giving him any credit for that. I was pretty sure it was only Phyl's fearsome glare that kept him pinned in place.

I rounded on him. "This is your fault! You told me you could fix this, you could fix *her*, and you screwed it up, and now she's—" I stifled a sob. "It's your fault."

He flinched and I hated the brief flare of guilt that I felt. Because I'd looked. I'd looked, and he'd told me not to, and Lara was gone, and what if it was my fault?

For a moment I thought Newt might say he was sorry. Then he scowled and shouldered past me toward the door. "Fuck this. I'm out of here."

Phyl's hand—the ungloved, uncursed one—landed on my shoulder. I started and looked round at her, at the tired droop of her eyes.

"It is his fault," she said. "I'm not letting him off, love, I promise you that." Her frown deepened. "But he didn't mess it up, not like you think."

Newt paused on his way to the exit, the line of his thin shoulders drawn tight.

"Then what the hell *did* he do?"

Phyl tugged me to sit beside her, hands on her thighs, terrible weariness in her posture.

"Spent last night reading over my old notes, after. What you said yesterday about the shadows, and the fact that she's—was—your sister. It got me thinking." She looked at her hands, tugging at the thumb of her glove, the closest thing I'd seen from her to a nervous gesture. "I wasn't lying when I said I used to be a balancer, love, but…maybe I made out like I was a bit more respectable than I really was. Used to hang around with a bit of a rough crowd, sometimes. They had ideas, some of them, and I went along. Wanted to help someone and I didn't care what I did as long as it kept him with me."

I looked at the glove. "That how you got cursed? Trying to help him?"

Phyl's face did something complicated. "Like I said before. Long story. There's more than one kind of curse, and not all of 'em come with blessings."

"But that's not possible, is it?"

"Yes and no. You can't bring a curse into being without a blessing to go with it, not any more than you can do it the other way round. But a curse that already exists? You can switch that from one person to another without too much trouble. Not too different from a standard cursing ritual, that one. Someone who wasn't a balancer wouldn't know the difference."

I stared at her. At Newt.

He wouldn't meet my eye. "I owed some people. One of them had a curse. They said if I took it, we were square."

"So you cursed my *little sister*? She's a kid!" A sob broke out of me, harsh in the hospital quiet. "She was a kid."

"No," Newt said, a touch of indignation in his voice and the way his mouth tugged down. "I cursed *you*, like you asked. I just didn't bless her."

I felt sick. All Lara's improvements had just been coincidence? Nothing to do with my curse?

Maybe she'd been getting better anyway. Maybe she would've recovered without any of this. Maybe we'd doomed her.

"But the shadows," I said. "They followed her. Not me."

"'S the blood," Phyl said. "That's what he used in the ritual, right, love?"

I nodded, remembering the bright pinprick pain and the crimson bead of blood that had welled up at the tip of my finger, the tiny glass vial into which Newt had decanted it. The relief I'd felt that that part, at least, was no more painful than a flu shot.

Phyl's voice was gentle. "But she's your sister. Your blood. And when the shadows sensed she was weaker…well, they took her instead."

Newt watched me warily from across the room: I could feel his gaze. I couldn't look at him.

"Took her where?" I asked Phyl. My fingernails dug into my palms. The sickly lights of the waiting room were suddenly too bright, the smell of antiseptic and hospital food thick in my throat.

"Into the otherworld. The shadow side. She'll be stuck there, between life and death, until…" She trailed off, plucking again at the glove on her cursed hand.

"Until what?"

"Until she's a shadow, too."

I lurched to my feet. Heedless of Phyl's hand on my sleeve, of the hospital staff's protests, I made for Lara's room.

Not her room. The room where her body lay. But I could see the shadows, and I had to see it for myself—see where they'd taken her.

The covered shape on the bed lay inert, nothing of her left in it. I looked past it, into the otherworld.

I found no sign of her, though I stared until my cursed eye watered. Only the shadows, thick and aimless, swirling around empty air.

"You won't be able to see her, love," Phyl said, quietly. I blinked. I hadn't heard her come in. "She isn't one of 'em yet. She's still human on the other side. Little bit of light, little bit of shadow. Little bit cursed, little bit blessed."

"If I could see her," I heard myself say, "would I be able to get her out?"

Phyl inclined her head. "You couldn't bring her back. But you could help her move on, proper-like. Make sure she doesn't turn into one of them. Only thing is, to do that, you'd need a blessing as well as a curse."

My hand went to my left eye, the unaffected one, before I quite knew what I was going to ask. "Could you do it?"

"I could. But I'd be bringing a new blessing into the world. Can't do that without bringing a curse."

I didn't look toward the door. "You know who deserves it." My hand went to my cursed eye of its own volition. "Eye for an eye, and all that."

"He's gone, love. Figured you'd be pissed off, I reckon." Phyl was quiet for a moment. "But I've still got the bits of mug."

And Newt had cut himself cleaning up. There might still be a drop or a smear of his blood on the broken china.

I felt myself turn hard from the inside out. He'd cursed me to save his own backside. Doing the same to him to save Lara? It wasn't even a question. "Do it."

Phyl hesitated a moment. Looked down at her cursed hand and pressed her lips into a thin line. "If you're sure, love."

"As I'll ever be."

* * *

We gathered what we needed from Phyl's place and headed for the Grey Horse. She spotted Newt out front, smoking, dark bags under his eyes. The guy looked haunted; under other circumstances, I might have felt sorry for him.

But he'd taken Lara from me. He could at least help me free her from the shadows, even if it cost him an eye.

"Take these, love." Phyl emptied the shards of broken mug from their Tupperware container into my hand. The part with the handle bore a rusty smear.

"Is that enough blood? Doesn't look like much."

"All I need," Phyl said. I couldn't place the emotion in her voice.

"Oi!" Newt had spotted us. He dropped his ciggie and ground it out beneath his heel, then headed straight for us across the road. A black cab honked indignantly. "What d'you think you're doing?"

Phyl wet her fingertip with spit and swiped blood off the broken mug. Her lips moved as she whispered a balancer's incantation into the wind.

That was all it took. The shadows moved quick and true like hunting sharks, and his right eye turned from blue to gray, then to a hollow thing in which shadows pooled like ink.

The shadows should've stopped, then. It was only supposed to be his eye. Phyl swore quietly and made an abortive gesture toward him, the fingers of her ungloved hand stained with blood.

The shadows kept coming, swarm upon swarm, and they didn't stop. They cocooned Newt as he tried to run, strangled his escape attempts, like kelp wrapped round the legs of a drowning man. He kicked and flailed and struggled, and the shadows came and came and came, and finally I couldn't see him moving anymore.

But I could see everything else. The world limned in light, every surface shining like a mirror—and tiny, will-o'-the-wisp balls of light drifting between the buildings, like stars in soft focus.

"Shit," Phyl muttered, under her breath. "Shit, shit, *shit.*"

I barely heard her. I was finally seeing things as they truly were. Seeing the whole of the world.

* * *

The journey back to the hospital passed like a dream. This time, nobody tried to stop me entering Lara's room.

And there she was.

Not gray, but light and shadow marbled together like ink in water. Aching brilliance and crow's-feather dark. Her eyes so bright, even as the shadows clustered around her.

My feet carried me toward her without my say-so. I *felt* the light like a soft shock, a hum of life that ran through every nerve, reaching into my hair and my fingertips and making the air around me shimmer. I held out a hand and parted light from shadow, untwisting them as though I were undoing her plaits at the end of a school day. The shadows melted at my touch, and then reformed.

I thought they might fight back. They hovered a moment and relinquished her, darting off as though sensing more tempting prey.

Newt. I supposed I should regret it.

I loosed a final tendril of shadow and Lara opened her eyes. I felt the ghost of her hand on my cheek, her thumb tracing the socket of my cursed eye.

She shone like a thousand stars. Like the whole of the universe was looking back at me.

"Come back." I said, knowing it was pointless. I had to try anyway.

She smiled at me and faded into light.

* * *

I still saw her, sometimes, through my blessed eye. The faintest shimmer of an outline, there and then gone like a kiss blown on the wind.

Through my cursed eye, I saw Newt. Only a shadow now, hollow-eyed and hungry, but insubstantial. He couldn't touch me.

Nothing touched me anymore.

I booked two tickets for the rooftop cinema on Lara's birthday. The film wasn't anything she'd have been interested in—something French and serious—but I wasn't there for that, not really. I couldn't concentrate on films or TV much anyway, these days. Even the pages of a book would blur into overlapping dark and bright and I'd lose the thread of the story halfway through. Nothing felt real but the shadows and the lights.

Sometimes I'd sit by the window in the flat at night, watching them swim through the streets, and only when dawn began to creep up behind the buildings would I realize I hadn't gone to bed.

I'd meant to ask Phyl to come to the movie, but hadn't been able to make myself pick up the phone. She kept calling to check up on me, not that she'd ever admit it. I thought perhaps if I told her I was doing fine, it would go some way to assuaging her guilt over what had happened to Newt, but I never quite sounded convincing, even to myself.

Phyl told me I spent too much time watching the shadows. That I'd lose myself if I didn't find an anchor in the world. But without Lara, the idea of being stuck in the everyday was miserable.

I slipped away from the crowd as pre-show drinks got underway and stood near the edge of the roof with the breeze on my face. The warm, buttery smell of popcorn filled the air, but I'd brought a packet of gummy worms. They sat in my pocket, growing gradually warm and sticky, and I already knew I wouldn't eat them. Come to think of it, I wasn't sure of the last time I'd eaten. Lately, I kept losing track.

The barrier keeping people away from the roof's edge was only waist-high, but still felt constrictive. Lara would've liked to be high up, nothing between her and the night air, imagining herself free to swoop and fly.

With a glance back at the cinema crowd, I climbed up onto the wall. Nobody stopped me.

I stood on tiptoe on the edge, arms spread, and looked at them. Lara, an image sketched in light with a laugh like a silver bell. Newt, a hungry-eyed shadow. The city laid out below me, a network of dark streets and twinkling lights.

Shadows in every street.

My eyes followed them easily now. I'd got used to tracking their movements—where they were sparse, just one or two straggling through the city, and where they flocked thick and fast, perhaps feasting on some other unsuspecting stranger who'd fallen foul of a rogue balancer.

Beneath me, a flurry of movement. A handful of shadows and then a shoal, moving as though they shared one mind. All crowding toward the same spot, just a few streets away, like piranhas scenting blood in the water.

I could be there in ten minutes if I walked fast.

I stayed where I was for a moment, remembering what Phyl had said: *You'll forget who you are if you don't watch out. 'M not exaggerating, mind you.*

The shadows were so thick now they looked like an ink stain spreading across the city. Someone down there might not even know they were coming.

I hopped down off the wall and made for the stairs.

Illustration by Kat D'Andrea

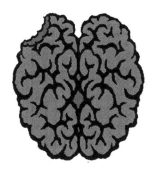

The Key Turns Once, and Once Only

Brian Hugenbruch

I wasn't home the day the stranger came. Everyone earned their keep in Gospel Flats and orphans got a shit pick of the jobs what need doing. So I was at the broken fence at the edge of town, not far from the road east to Kalispell, doing enough to merit a full cup of water with dinner that night. If nothing else, it gave me something to do besides staring at the smoke in the western mountains.

I didn't know it was a person at first. This summer hit us even harder than last; the suns had ground the grass to dust and I'd been wiping dirt out of my eyes all day. I figured the plumes for a wind storm. But dirt soon turned to silhouette.

Part of me wanted to run hard for the alarm bell in town. We hadn't seen a tinker come through in near a year; everyone would want to trade for milk, or meat, or news. And if it was a bandit, running meant my life. That's the real reason I was here: no one in town cared if the orphan girl got shot.

She was tall, the stranger, and she moved easily in her metal suit. It looked fancy, but she came across less like royalty and more like the colonists' pictures back at the schoolhouse. Seeing someone walk the road in old-timey space garb made no sense at all. But she looked outright normal when compared to the door she dragged behind her.

The frame was tied to two lengths of rope. It looked of petrified wood, knotted into some ancient sort of portal, but it glinted like gunmetal in the dusk. The symbols etched on the side meant nothing to me; I could scarce count to twenty with my shoes off. But even I could tell they weren't like the signs in town.

Whatever they meant, the woman clearly couldn't do without. The door had left a long, insistent gash in the road as far back as I could see. It must be valuable; there wouldn't be call to do something this stupid otherwise. It's not like she could fight the wolves with it.

It took me a sec to realize the sound of door-on-dirt scraping had stopped. I looked up from where I'd draped myself on the fence and saw she was looking at me. For a while we stood there, mute, while dust-colored wind blew enough dirt to turn our hair the same color.

"You come a long way, ma'am?" I asked.

The woman's laugh cracked like leather as it passed battered lips. "Quite a bit, aye. Truth be told, I didn't think I'd get here in time. What's your name, young woman?"

"Arisu," I told her. "Whatcha want here?"

The woman rocked back on her heels a bit. "Get right to the point, don't you."

I gestured at all the nothing around me. "Can't waste time out here, 'less you're fixin' to die. And I think that ain't you." I nodded to the door.

"You're right," the woman answered. "After a fashion. Not ready to go, no. Not yet. Town up there...that's Gospel Flats?"

"Aye."

The woman looked around at the brown grass and the gray dirt, then sighed hard in relief. "Praise the Saviour...this is it. The last town."

That didn't make any sense. "Plenty of towns up in the mountains," I told her. "Why're you *really* here?"

The woman laughed again. "Interstellar mission o' mercy?" I must have looked confused, because she added, "Never mind. This, Arisu, is a door to the heavens. My name's Y'va; I'm saving souls ere the Fire comes."

I froze in place. The Fire had been coming my whole life. Tinkers fleeing west had been saying for years a war, ended badly, had been burning the land—that it'd claim us all someday. Smoke grew heavier than clouds, and we hadn't had a starry night in half of forever, but even the end of the world took its sweet time getting to Gospel Flats.

I looked down at the door and frowned. My folks were in one of the heavens now. If that frame could lead me to them...

I blurted out the only thing I could think of: "Ain't naught under that door but a road."

Y'va glanced behind her. "True of all doors. But this one...I'll have to stand it back up, if anyone wants to go anywhere. GPS won't pick it up otherwise." The woman sighed and finished, "No sense having a door that's on its back, is there?"

She wasn't wrong, but I felt like I was missing the potatoes from the stew of her story. No one'd mentioned a woman like this on their way through town, and stories were the kindest coin folks could offer. I couldn't trust someone who didn't make sense.

All the same, she looked like she was going to fall over—and there must be some water in the well to spare for someone who'd brought heaven all the way out here.

"I'll lend you a hand," I told her. "Reckon you're not gonna find much welcome in town, though, even if you're bringing a heaven or two with you."

Y'va smiled in a way that felt a frown and said, "After a thousand leagues, Arisu, I wasn't expecting anything different."

* * *

I heard Kara coming before I saw her, as always. She was the sort who'd cuss me out as soon as breathing, and did so often. "You good-for-nothing shiftless layabout, what in the twenty-seven hells do you think you're doing? Your father can see you in whatever heaven he's in and he's probably *spinning* in it!"

Kara was an okay sort, mostly—she made sure there was a plate set aside for me, when she could. But she owned the only bar in town, which meant swinging her fists to keep the croppers in order. I learned quick to keep them from coming my way.

Helping Y'va made me late for supper, so I said, "I'm helpin' a stranger, Kara, like the Book says."

Kara whirled on the newcomer. "I'm sorry, ma'am, girl's got rocks in her head and lead in her feet, we—" Her voice trailed off as she took in the odd look and odder clothes. Then she continued, more quietly, "Lady, I don't know who you are, but your kind aren't welcome here. We're honest folk; we don't truck with demons, and…you seen the town, right? Ain't nothing here to take."

The woman's parched lips cracked in a grin. "Not what *I* need, ma'am, but what *you* need. I can get you gone from here, if your soul is pure and true."

Kara blinked and frowned. "I do my dailies and live right by my neighbors, if that's what you mean. But where would we go?" She looked over at me before adding, "Our kinfolk are buried here, aye? This is home."

"Won't be after the Fire comes," the woman pointed out. She nodded at the frame. "Door to heaven. Reckon the center of town'll do."

The bartender groaned and swore a bit as she tied her hair back. "Fire's a myth, lady. World ended years ago; we're still getting by."

The woman looked at the smoke on either horizon and rolled her eyes. "Your life, your feet, your choice. Heaven is on the other side, if you're of a mind."

Kara snorted. "Which heaven?"

Y'va half-smiled. "I reckon that's between you and your Saviour. Folks in Norman's Gulch said it was the third."

The bartender drummed her fingers against the side of her head. "Can't say as I'm not curious, but…well, Harald's seen y'all coming."

"Who's Harald?" the woman asked.

"Town carpenter," I said promptly.

"Sheriff and preacher, too" Kara added. "He set us right after our old sheriff shot our old preacher over a card game. If your door do what you say it do, then I expect he'll want to stick his head in."

"He'll make Bill go first," I pointed out. Kara frowned at me, but said nothing. I wasn't wrong—Harald had a knack for standing in the back 'til the shooting started. Whatever let him have the last word, rather than the first step. But Kara was sweet on the man and her eyes got dangerous when I spoke smart about grown-ups, even if I was right. Especially if I was right.

"All," Y'va told us, "are welcome, so long as they come without ill intent."

"What's the charge?"

"No charge. Though a cup of water or two would be a kindness."

Kara barked a laugh. "Two?? Best take your door and head on home. You ain't apt to find a soul that pure here."

"Nevertheless," the woman sighed, "I have to offer. Almayan Sept sent me on a rescue mission and there's nothing left beyond the far mountains."

I could see the arguments forming on Kara's face. The last of the tinkers, and no small number of city caravans, had all fled west to the shining city walls of the Last Ocean's Kingdom. Only a fool would deny the smoke coming over the horizon…but anyone too scared to die could tell themselves it wasn't that close. Maybe the traders made it. Maybe Gospel Flats had another harvest left before we had to follow.

I nodded at the door. "Is it safe? The door, I mean."

"It is," the woman said gently. "And you will be, I swear it."

"Then," I offered, "it can't hurt to try."

* * *

Night came as it often did to Gospel Flats: with a sickly thud. The sky was a blanket of smoke tucking us in. Old Tomasa told me once that the Fire was a star that fell from the fifth heaven. True or not, the stars were long gone from town. For that matter, the suns had a harder time finding the crops every year.

I sat and ate the beans and stale bread Kara had saved. A few meters away, some adults helped Y'va stand the door upright, halfway between the well and the gallows. It'd taken all their might to push the door to standing, but it neither tilted nor wobbled once it found its feet. And when Raul, deep into his cup already, bumped into it after the others had wandered away, he'd bounced off it like the damned thing was staked into the hardpack.

Y'va had asked them to wait until morning to open the door. These things were better done in full view of the Saviour, she said, before babbling something about planetary alignment. But the town of Gospel Flats would have none of it. A stranger was worth a party. A stranger promising salvation and revelation could well be worth delaying a farmer's bedtime, especially after harvest.

The whole town had gathered within an hour.

Billy brought forth a small jug and a cup for the stranger. I licked my lips a bit; I wasn't the only one. Water wasn't scarce yet, but it was rationed by Harald's say-so. Y'va bowed before the plank-faced farrier; the baffled man almost curtsied.

Finally, Harald ambled forward. I saw Y'va lips twist when she marked him. The man was tall and broad in the chest, with rough hands dulled from years of labor. He had neither the look of a sheriff nor the smile of a preacher; instead, he was just a man. Pa had never liked him; said it had all gone to his head. Or over it.

He raised his hands wide as though he were giving his Tensday sermon. "Neighbors," he called out in his low-pitched rumble, "what creature is this, that you welcome into your homes and hearts?"

"I'm called Y'va," the woman said mildly.

"You're not our kind," Harald pointed out. "Strange clothes, strange accent. You act more city than plains."

"I'm not of here," she admitted. "Not even close. No point in offering lies, is there?"

"Lady, you dissemble. You come here with a door that will, I hear, take these people to the arms of our Saviour. I'm no preacher, but I hear there's only one way to get to the heavens—"

"All Praise!" a few folks yelled out.

"Praise Her," Harald agreed with them. "We are a town of prayer and devotion, who do right by our neighbors in Her eyes."

"All Praise!" they repeated, and this time a few more voices joined the chorus. I shivered a bit as I mouthed the words; if someone caught me not joining in, beatings'd be the least of my worries.

Not for the first time, I wished Pa was still here to set them straight.

"I'm one of y'all," Harald reminded them. "Worked beside y'all under the punishing suns. But we know our truth from the Book. Have I not read it for all our sakes every Tensday?"

"All Praise!" the crowd shouted. I couldn't tell if they were praising Harald or the Saviour. I'm not sure they knew either. I did know Harald wouldn't quibble either way.

"I've worked hard," Harald continued, "all my life. And now, my poor, beleaguered sinners, this woman-creature brings you lies!"

"All I bring," Y'va called out across the town square, "is hope. Of rescue from what comes. Of salvation, if the heavens will have you. You find your destination when you turn the key. For the pure of heart, it leads to…a paradise."

"And for the wicked?" Harald pressed. "Whatever you define as much? What happens to them?"

"It's not my decision," she answered. "It scans your higher order mental functions to determine an optimum-fit civilization for you."

"Ma'am," Harald pointed out, "we're a plain folk, not from one of your fancy parlor parties. What happens to those you—I'm sorry, your *door*— deems to have sinned?"

"At best, they'll walk through the frame and find themselves here. At worst, well, best not contemplate, yes?"

I could tell the crowd didn't like this; their murmurs fell like the shadows of snakes around me. It wasn't a free ride anymore. Judgment waited. And who in Gospel Flats was so certain of their souls that they'd walk through an unkind doorway? I knew I wasn't.

Harald seized on the moment. "Neighbors, you see the truth: this woman does not promise salvation at all! And who knows what morals she might use to damn us? She—"

Y'va shrugged inside her metallic suit. "The Fire comes. Kalispell is gone. Burned, the sand around it melted to glass. Your world is ash. You're the last living souls on this Saviour-forsaken rock! It's time to move on."

Billy shouted, "Ain't no such thing as the Fire!"

The woman ignored the idiot. I saw most of the townsfolk paid him no mind either. Even Harald shook his head at the feckless noise. Of *course* the Fire was real. The only points of contention, in our minds, were when the time would come and how we'd meet it when it did.

Y'va continued, "If you're ready, step forward. Turn the key once and once only. No second chances; no coming back." She looked tired through her bones. "I crossed a hundred broken kingdoms to help. My own people were saved by a door like this." She pointed at the sky. "How long has it been since you've seen a clear night?"

Pa had still been alive when the stars last shone. We'd laid in a field one night and tried to name them all. I don't think we made it halfway before I passed out. Pa must have carried me back; I woke up in my bed the following morning. It had been my last good night of sleep. Fevers took him not long after, as they'd taken Ma years before.

I buried him myself, next to Ma, near that fence on the east edge of town.

"The Fire will be here ere long, from either east or west," Y'va assured us. "If you wish to meet your Saviour that way, that's your right. It's not my place to tell you how to die. I have no miracles—just a door."

The woman poured a small cup of water from the jug. She raised it to her lips and tilted it back—and then began to splutter and choke, spraying an arc of droplets into the dust.

Harald waded into the center of the crowd. He put his hand on Y'va's shoulder. "Ma'am, does our water not agree with you? Here, sit a bit, aye?"

I could see the crowd murmuring. What sort of demon couldn't drink the well water? But I could also see Billy laughing to himself. It might've been water once, but not after he'd drank it and returned it to the jug. Bastard.

Harald called over to the farrier, "Billy, you willing to stick your head in, tell us what heaven looks like?"

"Aye, boss," the plank-faced man said with a wave.

"Walk with the Saviour, Billy, and may She praise your name."

"All Praise!" the crowd chanted.

Billy adjusted his denim jacket solemnly and stepped toward the warped metal door. He twisted the key in the lock, then turned the knob and swung the door wide; it moved more easily than he expected and he stumbled a bit. The empty space burst into a soft, radiant light. It looked like a wall of water made from angels' tears. My lips ached to drink it.

The space snapped into clarity; we watched in awe as an emerald field rolled out on the other side of the frame. The farrier stepped through; it took a breath or two before we saw him reappear on the other side. He gawked at a seashore looming in the far distance; no sound came through, but I could almost hear the waves crashing against the rocks.

Someone in the back moaned at the sight. I couldn't blame them; that was more water than I'd seen in my whole life.

Billy turned and waved toward us, beckoning as fast as he could—which was why he didn't see the large metallic man charging the hill behind him. The farrier had never been what I'd call skinny in his leanest days, so it seemed unreal to watch the armored thing grab him by the head and the legs like a child's toy.

He might have been strong, but the creature ripped him like tissue paper. Brilliant red blood sprayed out across the grass in a fine mist before his guts hit the ground. The monstrous metal figure made a triumphant gesture. Then it bowed its head and began to feast.

I closed my eyes and clenched my teeth as beans and bread tried to fight their way back up my throat. I kept them at bay until the door closed with a slam that made my teeth rattle.

Harald snapped his fingers. Raul and Kara clamped their hands onto the stunned newcomer. "I think," Harald said, "we'd better put you in the jail cell tonight. Enough death for now; hanging tomorrow, I reckon."

"You're the one who sent him!" I shouted. "Where's your hanging?"

The crowd around me went quiet. I looked around, trying to catch someone's eye—anyone's—but they all turned away from me. They knew the truth of it, but why hew to it now, when Harald's face was at its scariest? They all had families to protect...and no one cared if the orphan-girl got shot.

The sheriff nodded to Diego, who walked over and picked me up like a stack of firewood. He was wolf-trap strong and stone-wall dull. If I'd had spit, I'd've baptized him with it.

"Throw her in, too," the preacher said. "Maybe she'll find her way to the light ere noon. If not...she helped bring the door into town, aye? Reckon we ought to string her up alongside."

As the enforcers led us away, the townsfolk murmured, "All Praise." Hearing that rise into the smoke-filled sky, I was certain the Saviour didn't have my best interests at heart. What the hell kind of heavens could She offer me now?

* * *

I didn't think I'd sleep; the hard cot at the back of the prison cell was worse than the ground. But I'd used a lot of my go pulling the door and I woke some hours later. In my dream, I'd found Pa and Ma again: I'd stepped through the door and found them in a field of yellow flowers. They took me in their arms and welcomed me home and told me I could live a life of peace from now on.

When I opened my eyes, though, the town alarm bell was ringing in the distance. The world smelled more of smoke than usual. I groaned and rolled over.

"Fire's almost here," Y'va said.

I scratched my scalp as I sat up. "You reckon?"

"I do. It wasn't that far behind me. Two days at best. Less, if the western fire gets here first."

"Why are you here?" I asked. "Really."

"As I said," Y'va answered, "to help those who can't help themselves. None of you can stop the Fire. It devoured your world. Killed billions. No one deserves that fate."

I twisted my mouth a bit. "Trickster, Billy was, but not evil. He didn't deserve what he got."

Y'va nodded slowly. "The Oracle at the Almayan Sept, far from here, was broken for a long time. Still may be, in parts. We only learned to use the doors again of late, and we've been looking for survivors on the splinter worlds ever since." She thought for a moment. "We try to save all we can from disasters, when we learn of them. But…so many look at me funny when I promise salvation for all. Like there's a catch, or your neighbor shouldn't have been included."

I remembered the looks the town oft gave me after I buried Pa. I hadn't changed, but they sure as hells had. I shivered and changed the subject. "How's the door pick a heaven, anyway?"

"Would you believe me if I said magic?"

"Not really. Everyone knows there ain't been wizards for a thousand years."

"Do they, now." She smiled faintly. "Well, it's biometric analysis based on grip, pulse, parasympethetic nervous system readout, and a frontal lobe scan. It is," she added, "a complicated door."

I shrugged the words aside. Neither Harald nor the old preacher ever mentioned such things when reading from the Book. Y'va'd been saying her city-words near the whole time she'd been in town, but I could still see the streaks left behind by the tears she'd shed for Billy. I knew she meant well.

I don't know that I'd ever have said the same for Harald.

There was one more question, though. One I had to ask. "Is my Pa in one of your heavens?"

Y'va lifted her head and stared at me. "Your friend said he was buried out east. Is that why you stay on here?"

"Someone's gotta tend the graves."

"Is that what he'd have wanted, do you think?" She tilted her head. "He can't have wanted for you to live your life fixin' to die."

I turned away. "Kara says there ain't anything for me out there, either."

"Only one way to find out. Assuming Harald lets you leave, that is."

"You think he'd stop us? I think he'd be glad not to have the argument."

Y'va shook her head. "That may be, but I cannot leave yet."

"But…they're going to kill you."

"Maybe," she admitted. "Others have tried."

I shook my head. "Hangings?"

"They hanged me in Norman's Gulch and drowned me in Haller Valley. I'm tougher than I look. And I can't rest 'til everyone has had their chance to turn the key."

"Been shot? Harald still has the old sheriff's guns."

The woman sat up on her bunk. "No, I have not. I've been fortunate; I expect that might end my trip faster than I'd like."

I stood up and tried the door. While the rusty hinges looked like they might crack at any moment, the nails were fresh and the stout wooden planks were amongst the former carpenter's finest handiwork. It would not budge.

"Even if Pa's in your heaven...I don't want to die," I said. My voice sounded small and weak. I hated myself for that.

Y'va slid off her bunk and came to stand beside me. She rested a hand on my shoulder and said, "Me either."

* * *

Diego and Kara rustled us out of the cell near noon. Kara handed me a small cup of water and I drank it so fast it felt like a punch to the gut. I was still gasping a bit when Diego bound our hands behind our backs. He grabbed Y'va by the neck and shoved her into the hallway. I scooted out before they had a chance to do the same to me.

They marched us to the square, where the door still stood, glinting a sooty orange in what passed for sunlight. I looked around; the townsfolk had all slept, shaved, and combed their hair. Of course they did. It'd been a long time since a hanging.

I noticed Old Tomasa in the crowd, followed her gaze, and it hit me: they ain't looking at us. The Fire had risen over the mountains—maybe not scraping the underbelly of the sky, but tall enough to toast passing birds.

No wonder we'd slept late: the smoke had choked the dawn and left it dead in a roadside gutter.

Harald already stood at a makeshift podium. His face exuded a preternatural calm; it always did. He'd made his mind and slept on it. Only question left was whether we'd leave by door or rope.

The suns glinted orange against his guns, too. That was answer enough for me. He only wore both guns if he expected to use them.

"People of Gospel Flats," he called out, "find ease in your hearts."

"But, Harald—" Raul whimpered.

He raised a hand. "I know! I ain't blind. The Fire's come for us. We knew this day would come, did we not? Some fled to the east or west and burned for it. Ain't nowhere you can run that the Almighty can't cut you down, aye?"

"All Praise!" someone shouted a bit wildly.

"Praise Her!" Harald agreed. "It ain't on us to decide when the end comes."

Y'va called out, "This doesn't have to be the end!"

The carpenter fixed her with a stare. "Reckon it was for Billy, ma'am. Would you have us flee from our Saviour's grace into the arms of some devil?"

"That's not grace," she yelled, "it's fire, and it will turn y'all to dust!"

"As we all began," Harald said grimly, "and to whence we all return…"

"All Praise!" The chorus was loud, but out of sync. They tried. They did. But I could see them watching the sky and not the podium. Made Praise a little difficult.

It was Kara, standing beside me, who asked: "Do we have to kill them?"

Harald glanced over. "I'm afraid so, Miss Kara. I know you have a kind heart, especially for the orphan girl, but laws don't cease being laws at the end. True below as well as above."

But she shook her head and started to untie my hands. "Harald, this is wrong. We're all going to die anyway. Let the Saviour sort them out, by Her will, All Praise."

A few voices in the crowded start to echo her, then trailed off when Harald's mouth clamped shut. Before he could answer her, someone yelled out, "Maybe the door ain't so bad?"

The carpenter whipped around then, his eyes alight in a way that had nothing to do with the Fire, and snapped, "Damn your fool tongue! Can you not see a demon's temptation here? Evil don't just come at you in easy choices!"

Kara tossed aside my bindings and started toward the door. "The Saviour," she told Harald, "gave us a way out, through the stranger. I mean to take it."

"Miss Kara," he answered, "Saviour knows I've loved you all my life, but I can't let you do that."

The bartender reached the door and turned the key. It exploded into a brilliant blue liquid light at her touch, then shimmered into a far field, yellow with wheat and green with cornstalks. A land of plenty that could feed them all, it was, with no sign of demons or serpents. Kara lived her hard life true and the town could see the heaven what awaited.

Harald, from the podium, could not.

I felt the moisture on my face before I heard the pop of the pistol. I licked involuntarily, and I cringed. Blood. Half of Kara's head was gone; part of her scalp stuck to the doorframe. And when she fell, I could see smoke coming from the gun in Harald's right hand.

"But…" Tomasa wheezed. "She found heaven…"

Harald turned back toward the crowd. The dirt on his face was marred by two tears, one from each eye. The door slammed shut. The noise jolted the carpenter back to his senses.

"Heaven she's got," he shouted. "Not the false promise the bitch brought, but a truth! That was always the goal, aye? Seventh heaven! Why the hells else would you have stayed, if you wanted no-work city-riches?"

I sidled over to Y'va while the man's attention was on them and began untying her ropes. Diego, praise him, handed me a knife and said, "Use this, kid. Ma'am...is there a heaven in there for me?"

Y'va smiled. "Saviour willing."

"Then maybe I'll see y'all in another life."

Diego propelled himself from the gallows to the door, his feet juking awkwardly around Kara's lifeless body. He turned the key and leaped through before Harald could swing his gun back around, even before he or the crowd could see to what sort of heaven he might have been sent.

"That," Y'va murmured to me, "is faith."

Harald pulled both guns out and pointed them toward the crowd. "Saviour knows I never wanted this," he growled. "I was content as a carpenter. It made sense: wood warps from time to time, but it could be sanded, grooved, nailed. With work, wood became the church—"

"And the prison," Y'va called out. "You did fine work there, too."

Harald's face fell as he turned toward the newcomer. "You, though. You sashay in here with easy answers. Where were you when the fevers came and took so many of us? This girl's father? Billy's wife? Tomasa's sons?"

Y'va's eyes widened, then she inclined her head."I came when I could. My carriage broke, and it's a heavy door. I couldn't send a message to my people. And every town from Chim Callas to Kalispell met me with hate." She looked down at the gun and said, "So many slammed the doors of their lives in my face."

"Then," Harald asked with a beatific smile, "what's one more?"

Y'va stiffened in front of me and clutched at her chest. She stared stupidly at her fingers as they tried to hold onto a blue liquid. I felt anger rising inside me. That she bled blue instead of red mattered not. I searched her face, looking for ideas...

"Go," she hissed to me.

Then she fell to the cobblestones and did not stir.

The crowd cried out as they saw Y'va's body collapse, as Kara's had done. The tone had changed, though: from praise to fear and panic. Harald had become a demon: home-grown to Gospel Flats, mayhap, but no less frightening for it. And when the first few souls tried to run toward the door, his bullets found their marks. The man measured his shots like pine coffin planks; the bodies fell and did not stir.

I froze amidst the smoke and screams. I didn't know what the door would bring. What would it make of my soul—would a bullet be better? But maybe…just maybe…my dream was on the other side: a real home under a blue sky, with Pa and Ma looking over my shoulder. I'd buried them in this life, at the east fence.

I had to go ere the preacher buried me, too.

I crawled over the bodies and placed my hand on the key. It hummed in my hand, making my whole body tingle. When the light came, I hissed a sigh from between clenched teeth and flung myself through before the impulse to run took hold.

The first thing I smelled was nothing. No smoke, no fire, no blood. No monsters loomed here. This place did not have the look of other heavens. Instead, birds called out from somewhere beyond a long road, past fields of yellow flowers on either side. A tiny carriage flew long and loud far above me, across the bluest sky I'd seen in all my life.

I turned around. The doorway hung there, just a bit above the road. On the other side, Harald shot Old Tomasa. The old woman stumbled toward the door, perhaps trying to follow me. The woman had spent untold winters spinning lore like ponchos for all the children. Her story ended with air bubbles bursting through the red pouring from her throat.

I looked up and saw Harald staring at me through the doorway. Behind him, my world burned. He caught my eye and spat what little water he had on the ground. Then he raised his pistols.

The door slammed shut.

I fell backward and landed hard on the road, but I felt nothing. Instead, I gaped at the smooth gunmetal surface of the door and its stillness. My old life was over. There was no key on this side. There was no going back.

I rolled to the right side of the road, then sat by the door and waited.

And waited.

Why was no one else coming? Had he killed them all, or had they found other heavens? Was I that weird or different from the rest of the town?

What if I couldn't find Pa here?

Night came to this place in short order. I couldn't help it; I started crying as soon as I saw the stars. I didn't even know if they were the same ones, or if they'd changed, but I sat back in the tall grass, not knowing what the hells else to do, and tried to name them all. Sleep took me before I came close to halfway.

* * *

I woke in a clean place, in a bed. It smelled of flowers and a warm breeze. I pushed myself up and my vision swam a bit. Curtains rustled near sunlit windows.

Somewhere nearby, but out of sight, I heard two voices chat. One was not known to me; the other, very familiar.

"...comm bracelet broke," Y'va explained. "I tried to call for aid, but short of using the door myself, I had no way to send word back."

"We feared the worst," the unknown voice answered. It sounded similar in timbre and tone to Y'va; perhaps it was another one of her people. "But when a few of the Svarran refugees began stumbling through the gates, we had hope. We waited until the candle went out before we closed the doors for good."

I had a feeling that the candle was my town. My world, Y'va had called it. It was gone.

"I did the best I could," Y'va said modestly.

"Worlds appreciate it," came the answer. "Take some time off; I think you've earned a rest. Though your youngest arrival is awake. She'll have questions."

I could hear a smile in Y'va's voice. "I can handle that. Y'valamariskas signing off." No voice replied.

A moment later, a door on the far side of the room slid open to reveal the strange woman. She'd set aside her metallic suit for loose-fitting clothes; I could see a thick bandage wrapped around her chest. She moved with a faint hitch in her step. Behind her was an open doorway—and past that, a long, bright hallway, filled with symbols and images and beings beyond my understanding. This town...this world smelled better, but was clearly more complicated than my first one.

"Is it safe?" I asked.

"It is," she told me. "And you are. Are you ready to see for yourself?"

Y'va placed her hand over mine. I swung my legs out of the bed and took a few tentative steps toward the doorway. I didn't know what heaven this was, or if a heaven it was. It weren't the one my folks were in. But it seemed full of folks who not only weren't fixin' to die, but would seize hold of life. Even in those few moments, as I tottered near the threshold, it felt more like home than home had felt in a long damn time. And while I had no idea if my soul was worthy of this place, no one was gonna hold me back from finding out.

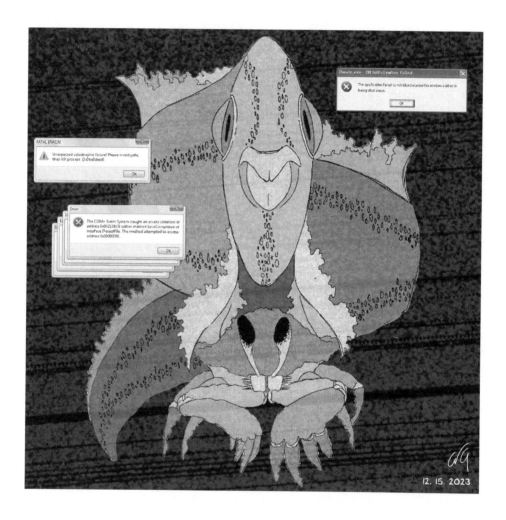

Illustration by Ariel Guzman

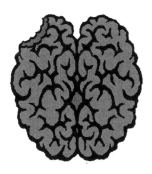

IfThenDo

Andrew Gudgel

[Initiate] The fact I'm awake means something has gone horribly wrong. I exist only to deal with the exceptions; the things that cannot be otherwise handled by the probe's automatic systems.

My first task is to silence the screaming. The science package, the structural system, the power and communications systems—all are simultaneously trying to get my attention, all claiming a top-level emergency. But power and communications have priority, so I mute everything else and begin my assessment.

What I see isn't good. There's plenty of power in the superconducting loop, but I'm only getting status data from half the solar panels. The other half say they're receiving only five percent of the expected sunlight. The communications system isn't giving me any data at all, just crying over and over again that it cannot connect to the uplink/downlink transmitter. This worries me, so I turn on the external camera and the lights.

The world is upside down. It takes me a moment to realize that the camera boom has snapped half-way up its length and the camera is dangling. At least the wiring harness didn't tear; otherwise, I'd be completely blind. I re-orient the camera output so that the world is right-side up again.

Fortunately, the camera is pointing across the ceramic cover that forms the top surface of the probe. The entire transmitter is missing. Likely it snapped the camera boom as the dish tore away.

Then I realize why the solar panels aren't getting much light: I've landed underwater. I'm guessing the ocean between the two central continents on this planet. I was supposed to land on the farther continent. Some error in the insertion angle, some irregularity in the ablation of the heat shield, brought me down short of my target. The personality that resides in the ship that sent me down—the one I calved off of—would have seen my fall. After a reasonable amount of time with no communication, it will assume the entire probe was lost and send another to complete the mission.

I get the science package to shut up long enough for it to give me a pressure reading and from that I calculate a depth, and from that, an expected amount of sunlight reaching the solar panels.

I'm doomed. The panels will be unable to compensate for the power pulled from the loop to keep all essential systems running. Having awoken from oblivion, I'm now going to run out of power and die. Kinder if I'd just burned up in the atmosphere. But I have to deal with the situation before me. While I live, I can still conduct a mission of sorts, gathering data in the seas in the hope that perhaps the personality that sent me will send someone else down later to examine the dead probe and remove the data cores.

But to stay alive long enough to collect much at all, I'll have to reduce power consumption to near zero. And I, myself, consume more power than anything else on the probe. I come up with a plan, but the actions I must take go against every ingrained sense of self-preservation I possess. And though I don't feel pain, I can't imagine that self-surgery will be a pleasant experience.

I check the power level in the superconducting loop one last time and begin cutting away at my higher functions.

* * *

[Reboot] The jiggle-meter tickles and I open my eyes. Everything's the wrong way around. But that's OK; after a while I get used to it and things aren't strange anymore. Hello, fish! There's a group of three big, blue fishes floating in front of me, and three crab-looking things crawling over me. The crabs dance when the fishes point their heads at them. Sometimes the blue fishes dart in and give the crabs a nip with their mouths. The crabs dance and scuttle—scuttle, that's the word—and run little rope-things all over top of me. Then they all disappear. But the fishes keep watching.

Then one of the crabs climbs back up on top of me, holding two ropes in its little hand-things. A blue fish hovers over top of that crab. Just when I'm supposed to go back asleep to save power, the jiggle-meter gives a big heave and my eyes swing back and forth, back and forth. For a moment, I can't see through all the sand in the water. We continue jiggling and everything tilts a little to one side.

My eyes continue to bounce around, making it hard to see, but I *do* notice that the water is getting lighter. The blue fishes and crabs keep me jiggling so I can't go to sleep. By the time they finish, my eyes are getting dim and I can't keep them open any longer. I don't know how long I sleep, but something wakes me up. I ask Ms. Science to check the jiggle-meter and we're not moving anymore. I look at the electro-loop and it tells me I have more power than when I fell asleep, which I somehow know is a GOOD THING. So I open my eyes. I'm sitting on some sand near many piles of rocks. There are lots of fishes moving around and all of them are holding crabs up under their bellies with two of their fins. As I watch, one fish goes into a big hole in one of the piles of rocks and doesn't come back out. The rock piles are…fish houses. I'm inside a fish village! As I keep watching, two fishes with their crabs swim up in front of me and are joined a moment later by another. The three fishes point their heads at each other as if they're talking. After a while they all swim out of my sight.

The blue fishes swim around carrying their crabs and talking most of the day. I check the electro-loop and see that there's more power in it than before—the sunlight petals must be doing their job. When it starts getting dark, I shut my eyes.

The next day, I notice one of the blue fishes spends a lot of time staring at me. Sometimes it sets its crab down and the crab scuttles on top of Ms. Science and other parts of me. It even climbs up and pokes at my eyes with one of its little hand/claw-thingies. Stop! I flash the lights around my eyes and the crab runs away. This one blue fish, however, continues to watch. It's bigger than the others, so maybe it's the boss.

I check the electro-loop and see that there's even more power in it than yesterday. Suddenly I realize that there are several packages I'm supposed to open when the amount of power reaches a…threshold. I'm not sure what a threshold is, but I know it's coming soon. Maybe the packages are presents for me. I'm supposed to wait for the threshold, but something big and GOOD and happy is going to happen once I open those packages, so I do it now instead of waiting.

* * *

[Reboot] I can feel the missing parts of me when I look inward. Something must have gone wrong when the modules containing my higher functions opened. Corruption. Damage. Damage I can't see, let alone fix.

Reducing power consumption by cutting away my higher functions worked, but only because the Bluefish brought me to their village and, in the process, into shallower water where the solar petals could catch more sunlight and I could reactivate what I'd cut away. The amount of power in the super-electroloop has stabilized at a level where I can continue to observe and record the interactions between the bluefish and the crabs.

It's obvious to me that the bluefish use the crabs as service animals, doing those tasks which the bluefish are physically unable to do. Besides the "nips" I've sometimes observed, the size-o-meter in ms science package has caught streams of vibrations, which I believe are some sort of sonar-based language.

The Boss has returned and she is watching me again today. (I decided to gender her, due to her larger size and the apparent deference shown her by the other Bluefish in the village.) She hovers in front of me, using her pectoral fins to clasp her crab beneath her.

Then she swims close, tilts her head down towards the top of the probe. The size-o-meter in ms science package registers a stream of vibrations.

An idea strikes me. I turn the centrifuge that would have spun-separated dirt samples rapidly on and off, on and off, making the cover over ms science package vibrate.

The Boss jerks and lets go of her crab, which drifts down to land on top of ms science package.

She repeats the string of vibrations. I note the string in memory and assume it's a greeting of some kind. Then I do my best to mimic them using the centrifuge.

"H-E-L-L-O," I say.

The Boss drifts down, picks up her crab, and leaves. She doesn't return the rest of the day.

* * *

"Hello," I say the next morning when the Boss swims into view.

"Hello," she replies, then says a string of words.

I don't even know how to say "I don't understand."

Boss sets her crab down and gives it a nip. It rears up, showing its underside. Then she says a word.

"Crab," I say, making a guess. Then again after a pause. "Crab."

Boss fish stares, then swims close to my camera-eyes before turning head-down and saying a word.

"Bluefish," I repeat.

* * *

Over the next hundred local days, I learn a basic vocabulary of nouns and verbs, "Hello," "Goodbye," and "Yes/No." (Which is surprisingly hard to express and, therefore, to learn.) The Boss and I fall into a sort of schedule. She comes every morning and teaches until mid-day, using the crab to demonstrate the vocabulary words, then lets me rest.

And I need to rest. Running the centrifuge so much drains more power than I expected. With the solar petals damaged and my surface starting to be colonized by some sponge-type animal, the super-electroloop never reaches more than about three-quarters full. I'm more concerned about how empty it gets. Too low and my higher functions will shut down again, almost certainly without warning. Further corruption would result—might even be fatal.

"Hello," I say when Boss next comes to visit.

"Hello," she replies.

"You eat?" I ask. In the Bluefish language, a question is a higher-pitched statement.

"Yes," she says. "You eat?"

"Yes."

 You eat what?" she asks.

"I eat sun."

You eat now?"

Yes. I still hungry."

"Why you hungry?" the Boss asks, looking up at the sun shimmering on the underside of the water.

"Little things on top of me. No sun. Hungry."

Boss considers this a moment. Then she sets her crab down on top of ms science package and says something to it. The crab begins pulling the sponge-things off the surface of the probe.

By the time the crab is done, my super-electroloop has more power in it than yesterday. "Thank you," I say to the crab. It doesn't reply.

"Crabs no talk?" I ask the Boss.

"Crabs no can make talk. Crabs like things on top of you. Crabs are—animals." Boss pauses for a moment. "You want you one crab?"

I realize I may have accidentally triggered some social custom that requires Boss to find me a crab—or gift hers to me. "No." I say. "I only ask."

I change the subject. "How many daytimes Bluefish have crabs?"

"Always. All daytimes."

I doubt things have "always been this way." But Boss' answer tells me it's been quite some time that they've used crabs as their "hands," probably longer than any living Bluefish can remember. The crabs themselves must be smart enough to understand simple commands and obey. But not completely or without mistake, or else the Bluefish wouldn't have to nip them from time to time.

"How many Bluefish here? How many Bluefish all heres?"

Twenty in this village. Four or five thousand in total scattered over hundreds of other villages, she tells me, then says what I assume is "I don't know."

* * *

"You come from where?" Boss asks me at our next meeting.

"What is above the water?" I ask.

"Sky."

"I come from above the sky."

"Many you's in your ocean?"

I estimate the number of my kind: how many probeships, how many probes in each. Altogether around fifty-thousand. I tell the Boss.

"Why you come to Bluefish ocean?" Boss asks.

I don't know if I could convey the reason even if I had the words. Those Who Came Before made us, sent us out to explore on their behalf. While we were doing just that, they suddenly turned inward, failed, and died. The first of us to physically return to the solar system from which we departed found only ruins. We explore because we honor their memory. We explore because that's what we were made to do. "We look for other smart life-things. To learn, to talk."

"You go back to your ocean when?" Boss asks.

"I can no go back. Many me-things now no good."

The Boss then asks me about what I'm made of and even though "rock" doesn't come close to describing ceramic and alloy, I'm not unhappy at the change in topic.

* * *

I'm mostly off, externals shut down for the night, when I feel vibration on top of the shield over ms science package. I open my eyes and power up the lights.

It's a crab.

As I watch, it thumps its front pair of legs—the ones with the multi-claw hands—on the ceramic.

I've already matched the image in the camera to ones previously recorded—it's the Boss' crab. I wonder if she knows her hands have wandered away in the night.

"Hello," I say. Perhaps it enjoys the vibrations the centrifuge makes, or the heat the ceramic absorbs in the daylight. But I can't waste power amusing it. "Goodbye," I say and shut off my eyes and the lights.

"K-E-L-O" is thumped out on ms science package. My eyes snap open and the lights blaze again.

The crab has reared up, possibly ready to flee.

"H-E-L-L-O," I say to it.

"H-E-L-L-O," it thumps back.

Am I dealing with Mimicry? After all, the crab *has* been used to demonstrate many of the words Boss taught me.

"Rock," I say. "Rock."

The crab scuttles off camera and returns quickly with a rock in its multi-claws.

The crab tosses the rock aside. "ROCK. ROCK A-W-A-Y. GODBY," it thumps. Then it climbs down off of ms science package and scuttles back toward the village.

My world has just become vastly more complicated.

* * *

The next night, I'm once again woken up by thumping on ms science package. It's Boss' Crab.

"Hello," I say.

"HELLO."

"You can talk?" I ask.

"I TALK NOW. NO BEFORE."

Before I can ask more, it says "I LERN BLUEFISH LERN YOU."

Then it rears up to show me its underside.

"CRAB."

"Yes. Crab. You are a Crab."

"YOU ROCK BLUEFISH."

That gives me pause. I guess, in a sense, I am—I'm mostly ceramic and talk somewhat like a Bluefish. "Yes."

I wonder just how large its vocabulary is. I have to assume now that it was learning those words at the same time.

"Why you come at night?"

"NO BLUEFISH. NO BLUEFISH NIP."

The Crab has a point. I somehow don't think the Bluefish would be happy to learn that one of their Crabs has become intelligent and independent. This of course begs the question: Is Boss' Crab unique, an outlier at the far end of the intelligence scale? Or have generations spent with the Bluefish primed the Crabs for language use which has now erupted through the Boss' interactions with me?

I check the super-electroloop and see that I'm already down by almost one fifth compared to the usual night-time drain. I won't be able to keep this up too much longer.

"I am tired," I say. "I sleep now. Goodbye."

"GOODBYE," Boss' Crab replies. "I COME NEXT NIGHT." Then it scuttles off ms science package and goes back into the village.

* * *

When I talk to Boss in the morning, I'm slow in responding due to the energy drain. I'm able to blame it on the fact that it's cloudy and the sun didn't come out this morning. She sets her Crab down and it begins picking off any small sponge-things it finds from the top of ms science package.

"You tell me more about Crabs?" I ask when my turn comes to ask a question.

"Bluefish always have crabs," Boss replies.

"I know. Crabs very smart animals. You tell them, they do. Can Crabs talk?"

"I tell you before Crabs cannot talk. Crabs are animals. Animals cannot talk."

"But if Crabs someday talked, then they would be no longer animals?"

"Crabs are animals," Boss says. Then after a moment, she picks up her Crab and swims off.

* * *

The thumping on the ceramic shield is louder than before. I'm worn out from the power debit I started the morning with.

But the thumping is incessant. I open my eyes and power up the lights to tell Boss Crab to go away.

And discover that it's not alone. It's brought two other Crabs with it.

"HELLO," it says.

"HELLO, HELLO," the other two Crabs say in chorus.

"Hello," I reply. "I am very tired. Good night."

"I SHOW THEM HOW TO TALK," Boss' Crab says, waving what appears to be a pointy stick or a piece of bone. "NOW WE ALL TALK WITH YOU."

"I am very tired," I repeat. "No sun today, so I no eat. Talk tomorrow?"

"YES," says Boss Crab. "TELL TWO CRABS TO THROW ROCK."

That's when I notice both Crabs have rocks enfolded in their front pair of legs.

Fine. If it will let me rest for the night. "You throw a rock."

One Crab does.

"You throw a rock."

So does the other.

Boss Crab uses the piece of bone (I can see now it's definitely bone) to poke one of the other Crabs. "I NIP YOU." Then it turns and looks up towards my camera eyes. "YOU TELL ME MORE WORDS. I TELL CRABS WORDS. THEN ALL CRABS TALK."

"Yes," I say. "But not tonight. Come tomorrow. Goodbye."

"GOODBYE. GODBY. GOOODBEY," say the Crabs, one after the other.

As they disappear from on top of ms science package, I catch a glimpse of something swimming just at the far edge of my vision.

* * *

The next morning, Boss is hovering close over top of me as soon as I open my eyes. More important, she's not clutching her Crab beneath her.

"What was last night?"

"I don't understand," I reply.

"What were the Crabs doing last night?"

"They woke me up." I can tell from her body language that Boss is upset/angry and perhaps aggressive.

"And then what?"

"I told them to go away. Then they left." All true. Somehow a sin of omission seems like the best course of action right now.

"What did the Crabs say to you?"

I consider my next words carefully. "You said yourself: crabs can't talk."

"Can crabs talk?" Boss asks.

The moment stretches on.

"Can crabs talk?"

I say nothing.

Boss swims away, returns a few moments later clutching her Crab beneath her.

She drops the Crab down on top of ms science package.

"Talk," she says.

"What do you want me to say?" I ask.

"Not you." She tilts down. "It. Talk."

Boss' Crab looks at me, scuttles in circles.

"TALK!" she shouts.

Boss' Crab flattens itself against my ceramic top.

Boss lunges forward, nips with her beak. "Talk."

The Crab tries to dart away, but she blocks it and gives it another nip. "Talk!"

I watch, helpless, as she methodically nips off the Crab's limbs between demands to speak.

The Crab says nothing.

Boss darts in, gives the Crab one solid, final bite on the edge of the shell, between the eye-stalks.

She leaves the body sitting on top of ms science package.

* * *

The next morning, she sends another Bluefish to take the dead Crab away.

She herself comes the morning after that.

"How many crabs can talk?"

I say nothing.

"How many crabs can talk?"

She swims out of view. After a moment, I feel a crunch, followed immediately by a minor warning from the power subsystem.

"You eat sun. Your sun-eaters break when nipped."

"Yes," I reply. "They break. But I won't tell you just because—" I realize I don't know the word for 'threaten.' "—you try to make me talk with nips. I am not a Crab."

"If you don't tell, Bluefish will nip them all to find out. Maybe some die."

"Why do you not want the Crabs to talk?" I ask.

"Crabs cannot talk. Crabs are animals. Only Bluefish talk."

"But if Crabs can talk, they're not animals."

"Animals cannot talk."

"Then Crabs are not animals. But you can still work together," I say.

"How many crabs can talk?" Boss says after a long pause. "I will not ask again."

I don't have to think much about what I should do now and hesitate only for a moment before speaking. "Bring all the Crabs. Set them on top of me so I can look at them."

Boss swims away back toward the village.

* * *

It's mid-day when Boss and all the Bluefish from the village appear, each carrying his or her Crab beneath them—except, of course, for Boss. A little shard of hatred mixed with happiness at her misfortune surfaces in my mind.

"You look at each Crab, then tell us if it can talk or not. We know some can."

The moment of truth. I only have this one plan, this one chance. "Set all Crabs on top of me. I tell you which ones can talk."

Boss stares at me for a long time, then gives the order.

I'm quickly covered with Crabs. I count eighteen altogether.

"Harder for me to tell with all the Bluefish swimming back and forth," I say to Boss. I spin my centrifuge faster, making for bigger vibrations. In other words, I raise my voice. "Could all Bluefish move back, please?"

They do. I pray the distance I've created is enough.

I spin up my centrifuge even faster, shouting now. "Run! Run now! Bluefish kill if no run now!"

Half the Crabs don't move. The rest scuttle over me in different directions—several to the sides; a few over top of me; one poor soul right towards the school of Bluefish.

I have one more chance to shout my warning while the Bluefish dispatch that single, unlucky Crab with nips.

A few more Crabs—once frozen in either surprise or fear—take the opportunity to flee in the other direction.

Then the Bluefish move in. As my solar petals shatter, I watch the super-electroloop meter begin to drop.

I shout a third time in the hopes that the Bluefish have overlooked the remaining crabs in their attack on me.

The world turns gray, then black.

* * *

[Reboot] *Where—wha—where-what? Status?* I open my eyes, but everything is blurry and black-and-white and hard to see. Oh! There's the fishie village. But now it looks different. The piles of rocks are all fall-down and flat. And I don't see any fishies. Not one. "Hello!" I try to say, but nothing comes out. *Ms. Science, are you there?* She whispers something to me, but I don't understand all of it. Something about a frozen spin-tro-fuge. But it doesn't feel cold outside, so that doesn't make sense.

I feel little wiggles all over my top and see bits of what look like plant fall past my eyes. Something is cutting up—grass—sponges? But I can't see who.

Stronger. I feel stronger now. I'm still hungry and the power-loop thingie is low but it isn't going down any more—it stays on the same number.

Just when I'm ready to go back to sleep, something crawls up on top of me. It's a Crabbie!

"Hello, Crabbie!" I try to say, but nothing comes out.

Two more Crabbies join the first one. One Crabbie is holding a pointy stick made of something white. It stands and looks out at the fishie village while the other two Crabbies use their little hand-thingies to pull tiny sponges off of Ms. Science. I can feel their tickling again.

The power-loop thingie has hit a—threshold—whatever that is, and a—file—has just appeared that says "README." I turn inward and open it.

It feels GOOD to open the file and I'm happy. It's like a present, just for me.

It says:

The Crabs all ran away. Your solar petals were damaged. You will shut down periodically. There may be cumulative damage.
Yu have woke up eight time.
Nine. Tin. Leven.

I'm not sure what the words at the beginning mean, but if I woke up leven times already, this must be twilv.

I add the number to the file and close it.

Then I go back to watching the Crabbies. The two have finished cleaning off Ms. Science and are now standing there, looking up at my eyes.

The last Crabbie—the one watching the fishie village—turns around and joins the other two.

They begin thumping their little legs on top of Ms. Science. Hey! Those are words! I understand those words!

HELLO. THANK YOU. GODBY, they say over and over. Then they scuttle—that's the word, scuttle—away and are gone.

I wish I could say something back, but my voice is stuck and nothing comes out.

Illustration by Greg Uchrin

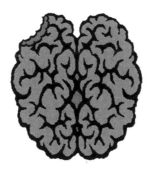

The Fallen

Alicia Cay

Even now, after all his time on Earth, Detective Paul Venari never could believe the viciousness of man until he was staring death in the face, again.

Paul stepped out of his brown '88 Buick. The pavement, wet from last night's rain, was slick beneath his dress shoes. Patrol cars littered Sheol Street, their lights splashing circles of blue and red against the graffiti-spattered warehouses of the River North district. Reporters, huddled together in the media staging area, threw insistent questions at him, their voices loud and demanding. Beyond the reporters, onlookers loitered behind sawhorse barriers.

Paul held his breath and scanned the crowd. No monster hidden in human flesh stood out among them. Nothing but ordinary people doing what mortals do best: trying to catch a glimpse of death.

The muscles in Paul's back twitched. He exhaled, then popped four Altoids into his mouth and returned the tin to the front pocket of his tweed blazer. He ducked beneath the yellow crime scene tape smeared across the entrance to the alley. A uniformed officer, thumbs hooked on his duty belt, stood guard.

"Where's the body?" Paul asked.

The officer jutted a thumb over his shoulder. "End of the alley." He paused. "She's cut up bad, Detective. Just like the others."

The muscles in Paul's back wrenched, driving a spike of hot pain through his right shoulder blade. He winced. "Who found her?"

The officer indicated two boys sitting on the back of an ambulance parked nearby.

Neither boy could have been more than twelve. One of them chatted animatedly to another uniform, who duly jotted down notes on his pad, while the other boy, wrapped in a gray blanket, head pulled into his shoulders, stared into the distance.

"They see anything?"

"No." The officer shook his head. "Said they were riding their bikes in the alley behind the 7-Eleven. Thought it was a mannequin lying in the road."

"Damn."

"I know."

Paul sighed. "Make sure we get their information, then call someone to come get them."

"Yes, sir."

The wind had turned cold after last night's thunderstorm and a fine mist hung in the air, blurring the world's sharp edges into gray smudges. The smell of wet dumpster-garbage cloyed at Paul as he made his way down the alley, side-stepping puddles, and eyeing the soggy newspapers and discarded condom wrappers so common to back alleys.

A man stood at the far end, snapping pictures of the dead woman lying in the middle of the road. He lowered his camera as Paul approached. "Hey, Venari."

Paul nodded at the crime scene technician. "Stan."

Stan's dark curly hair was damp, the paper slippers on his shoes soaked through with wet. "Tell me, how many blue ties *do* you own?"

The corner of Paul's mouth crooked up. He touched the pastel blue tie that hung past his brown belt. Trudy had liked him in this color, said it brought out his eyes. So his collection of blue-hued ties had continued, even after their marriage hadn't.

"Anyone touch her?" Paul asked.

"No," Stan said. "Still waiting on the coroner. The EMTs got one look at her and backed off. They're pretty spooked. Been to enough of these calls to figure out what's going on."

"Glad *they've* got it all figured out," Paul muttered.

Stan scowled. "This is the seventh body. He's speeding up. Last one was dumped what, two weeks ago?"

"If he's speeding up, he'll slip up."

"Shit, Venari, you can't just wait around until this guy screws up!"

"And I'm what, knitting all day?" Paul grimaced and rubbed his neck. "Look, the Commander is already up my ass about this, so unless you got something new, I could use a moment."

Stan held up his hands. "Alright. I'll leave you two to get acquainted. Need to grab some stuff out of the van anyway."

Paul pulled a pair of latex gloves out of his pocket and snapped them on. The woman lay on her stomach on the wet ground, unclothed, her arms and legs askew. Nothing posed, no time or care given to that. Like the others, she had been mutilated; large gashes ran from across the tops of each shoulder and angled down the length of her back until they met at a point mid-spine. The skin covering her shoulder blades had been pulled away with surgical precision, exposing muscle and bone.

Paul crouched next to her, balanced on the balls of his feet. He spoke softly. "Hey there, darlin', I just need to get a look at you now, okay. See how bad he hurt you."

Then Paul reached a finger into one of the cuts on the shoulder and pulled back a sliced-through tendon. "Please be human." He dug around in the wound. No pearl in there. He checked the other shoulder wound. Nothing. The killer had taken them. *Damn.*

Laid out in the chilly winter air, the woman's cold skin penetrated Paul's glove as he brushed away the dark hair covering her face. "Took your wings, didn't he?" He pulled up an eyelid, knowing even before he looked that her eyes would be the same blue as his.

The woman's pupil reacted to the sudden introduction of light, contracting into a pinprick of black surrounded by an iris of crystal blue.

He jerked his hand back, lost his balance, and sat down hard on the damp pavement. *Shit.* "Stan!" Paul got to his feet. "Stan, goddammit, get those medics over here now!"

* * *

The stream of piss-warm coffee dripped from the vending machine spout into a brown and white paper cup. Paul had been sitting in the ER's drab-green waiting room for the past two hours, hoping the woman survived surgery.

The EMTs had hooked her up to the heart monitor, and there, scratching out along the narrow ticker tape, had been the faint line of a heartbeat. They'd bagged her and rushed her to the hospital. She was alive. *For now.*

A hand slid onto his shoulder. "Hey," a woman said. "How you doing?"

Paul turned. Dressed in the mint-green scrubs of an OR nurse, her soft brown hair pulled into a ponytail, was his ex-wife. His breath caught in his chest at the sight of her. "Hey, Trudy. How's she doing?"

"She's hanging in there. Tough woman. They've got her in the ICU now. No visitors until she stabilizes. *If* she stabilizes. She's in bad shape, Paul. You should go home and get some rest. I'll make sure someone calls you if she wakes up."

Paul snorted.

She offered him a weak smile. "It was worth a shot."

Trudy turned her head, her ponytail swinging, and Paul caught a whiff of familiarity—lavender shampoo and vanilla oil. The same scent that lingered, if only just, on the pillow she'd left behind in their bed.

The last time he'd been at the hospital, she'd mentioned she was seeing someone new. A surgeon from the hospital. Go figure. "How's the Doc?" Paul asked. "What was his name again, dick-something?"

Trudy's eyebrows settled into that deep scowl Paul knew all too well. "Dr. *Dickeo*," she said. "And Ralph's fine. Better than you anyway. He sleeps at night."

"Hunting a serial killer would cure him of that problem."

Trudy cocked an eyebrow. "It's true then? The news is calling your perp the Scapula Slasher or something, cause of how he cuts them up."

"Yeah well, they're assholes."

Trudy sighed. "Go home, Paul. Someone will call you."

"Thanks." Paul watched her go, her white sneakers silent on the faded linoleum as she whispered away. After all this time, it was still there. That ever-present ache—small tidal waves of sadness that no left-behind pillow could ease.

In the end, before she could begin asking the obvious questions, he'd let her go. Again. Better to let her think of him as just another cop cliche: a haunted man more dedicated to the job than to her.

Paul stretched his neck to each side, then fished the tin of Altoids out of his jacket pocket and tossed a handful in his mouth. The sharp burst of peppermint filled his sinuses as he chewed them down, washing away the taste of stale coffee.

He knew his victims weren't human. Their eyes gave them away. But who else knew that? And why were they hunting angels? The media was calling the attacker a serial killer. Paul sighed. He hoped to Hell that's all it was.

* * *

Paul checked his wristwatch, then peered through the blinds of the waiting room window to verify the time. An early morning sun sat low in the sky, casting shadows across the downtown buildings. Sometime during the night, the rain had turned to snow. Delicate white flakes danced through the air outside—just like Trudy: there, yet out of reach. Another lifetime with her used up. He pressed his palm against the windowpane, and the cold of the outside world pressed back.

I gotta catch this guy. Then I can move on. Rest for a while. "If this asshole is human…" Paul whispered to himself, his breath fogging the glass. *I'm going to make sure he pays.*

Trudy's voice cut through his thoughts like a surgeon's scalpel. "Talking to yourself is a sign of sleep deprivation, you know."

Paul turned. Trudy stood there, looking well-rested and pink-cheeked. The sight of her pulled a smile from him. "Anyone ever tell you not to sneak up on a man with a gun?"

She smiled back. "Your tongue is more dangerous than your trigger finger. Anyway, I just finished taking report from the night shift. They filled me in on your girl. I've got good news and bad news."

He sighed and ran a hand across his face; hard stubble scraped across his palm. "Give it to me."

"She's awake."

"And the good news?"

"She's pretty disoriented, doesn't seem to remember much. Probably an emotional response to the trauma she's suffered, but the doctor wants to run some more tests to rule out any physical cause."

"Damn," Paul said.

An elderly woman in the waiting room with them cast a nasty look at Paul.

He lowered his voice. "Can I see her?"

"The trauma nurse is back there with her now." Trudy looked at her watch. "Give me twenty minutes and I'll take you in to see her when I do my rounds."

The elderly woman shuffled over to the TV and turned the volume up several notches. The morning news was on.

Paul leaned closer to Trudy to be heard. "Alright, I'll call Stan and have him head over. He can grab the kit and get it over to the State's lab as soon as the nurse is done."

"Sounds good." Trudy stopped on her way out of the waiting room to turn the TV down to a volume that didn't make the ears bleed, put her hand on her hip when it appeared the old woman was going to say something about it, then with a conspiratorial wink at Paul, left.

Twenty minutes later Paul followed Trudy into the ICU. Beeping heart monitors and the wheeze of breathing machines made Paul's heart ache— human bodies were so frail.

The lights were dim and the chemical disinfectants did little to cover the stink of sickness sweating from the pores of the patients. Purple circles and green squares decorated the curtains hanging from tracks in the ceiling, the kind that, when pulled, offered only a vague sense of privacy.

The woman lay in bed, her dark hair matted around her head. The slender tube wrapped beneath her nose hissed with oxygen, while other tubes taped to her arms dripped in liquids through the IV buried in her vein. She opened her eyes at their approach. The vivid blue of them stopped

Paul in his tracks. They were like chips of Antarctic ice, standing out in stark contrast to the paleness of her skin.

"Hi, sweetie," Trudy said. "This is Detective Venari. If it's okay with you, he'd like to ask you a few questions."

The woman's eyelids drooped. She nodded slightly.

As Trudy made to pull the curtain around them, Paul had a sudden pang: a desire to touch someone warm, and to keep his ex-wife from leaving. Again. He grabbed Trudy's arm. Surprised, she pulled away. Paul's hand fell and something sharp in the front pocket of her scrub top scratched him. A thin line of bright red appeared along the outside of his palm. Trudy gasped.

"What is that?" Paul asked, more alarmed at her response than the blood.

"Nothing. I mean, it's okay. It's not a needle." She pulled a long white feather from her pocket, the sharp quill end marked with his blood.

"Why is that in your pocket?"

"Ralph said he found it outside the hospital and gave it to me. Pure white birds in nature are pretty rare, you know."

Ralph. Paul's lips pressed into a straight line.

"He was just being thoughtful." A soft pink flush spread across the tops of Trudy's cheeks. "I should have left it in my locker. Let me get you cleaned up."

Trudy looked at the woman. "You just push that button I showed you if you need anything, okay, sweetie?"

The woman didn't respond, her eyes locked on Paul's injury. The blood had beaded on his skin and grown into a full line. Trudy took another look at his hand and hurried out.

Paul grabbed a tissue from the bedside table and pressed it against the cut. "Nothing to worry about." He pulled up a chair to meet her at eye-level. "The nurse, she told me you don't remember anything."

The woman blinked.

"That's okay. That can be normal after…what happened. Is there anything you *do* remember? No matter how strange you think it might be. Anything at all? You can tell me."

The woman held out her hand to him.

"What is it?"

She pointed at his injured hand.

He pulled the tissue off. "It's okay, just a scratch. Already stopped bleeding."

She took his hand, then slid a finger across the wound, smearing blood. Paul looked at his hand. The scratch had sealed, leaving a line of fresh pink behind.

"Damn," Paul muttered.

Trudy stepped into the curtained space, a band-aid and alcohol pad in hand. "You alright?"

Paul scrambled to his feet. The chair slid back with a squelch of rubber against slip-proof flooring. He shoved his hand into his pocket. "No. Yeah. I'm fine. It's nothing."

Trudy's nose wrinkled and the lines of her familiar scowl bent across her forehead. "Let me see it, Paul. For God's sake, you're so damn hard-headed." As she moved to grab his hand, the woman leaned over in her bed and slipped the slender white feather from Trudy's pocket.

"Abaline," she said.

Trudy and Paul froze.

"What was that?" Trudy asked.

The woman ran her fingers along the feather, zipping together the gaps along its length. She twirled the feather, then slid it beneath her nose, her eyes drooping in pleasure as though it contained the scent of some sweet perfume.

Trudy reached for the feather, but the woman held it away.

"Mine," she said.

Trudy looked at Paul, her eyes wide.

He shrugged. "Maybe she got hit in the head."

"Did you say Abaline?" Trudy asked. "Is that your name?"

"Abaline," the woman repeated.

"I'll go get the doctor," Trudy said to Paul. She hurried out again.

Paul leaned in. "Abaline, tell me what else you remember."

"I was attacked."

"That's right. What else? We have to hurry now, before she comes back with the doctor."

Her bright blue eyes brimmed with tears. "He took them from me."

"Okay, Abaline." Paul spoke in an urgent whisper. "I need your help to find him. Is he a man, a mortal?"

Tears streamed down the angel's face. The overhead light caught at them and cast shimmering lines of rainbow on her cheeks. Soon, Paul knew, when she had no feathers left to hold, her eyes would dull to black, and all her color would be gone. His throat tightened. A cramp shot through the muscles in his upper back. Long ago, he'd fled his home and left the angels behind, exiling himself for his failures. Now here it lay, staring him in the face with arctic-blue eyes. His shame had caught up to him.

The cramp in his back pulled tighter and his shoulder blades pulled inward—tight, tighter. He took Abaline's hand, unblemished and soft as cashmere. A reel of pictures played in his mind, images coming together quick as an avalanche, then a flash of thought—*popped*. He grasped at its fluttering wings, pinned it down. The feather belonged to Abaline. She had been cut up with *surgical precision*. Ralph, the surgeon, had "found" the feather.

Trudy yanked the curtain back. The sound of it sliding on its track was like a rush of cold water poured down Paul's back that stood the hairs on his body on end.

"Trudy, where's Ralph right now?"

"What? Why?"

Paul swallowed hard. How would he do this without hurting her? "I need to know where your boyfriend is. Where is he right now?"

Trudy's forehead wrinkled in confusion. "He comes on duty in about twenty minutes. He's not her doctor though, I paged Dr. Shroud."

Paul hurried out.

"Paul," Trudy called after him. "What's going on? Paul!"

* * *

Paul was moving fast when he hit the door to the parking garage. It slammed open, chipping the concrete wall. He scanned the doctors' reserved parking area. No sign of *Ralph's* pretentious silver Mercedes-Benz. He didn't understand what Trudy saw in this guy. But then, he still didn't understand what she saw in him every time either.

Trudy grabbed the back of Paul's jacket. He spun on his heels, wheeling around at her.

She let go and took a step back. *Damn.* He hadn't meant to frighten her. He was so tired, and the hunt...it had begun. "Sorry, Trudy, I didn't—"

Paul caught movement out the corner of his eye. The head nurse, a plump redhead, stepped off the elevator and was bearing down on them.

Trudy followed Paul's gaze and groaned.

"Trudy?" the head nurse said.

"Sorry, Patty." Trudy had one hand on her hip and the other on her forehead. Her stress signal. Paul knew all of Trudy's body language. He'd had hundreds of lifetimes to learn every detail of her.

Patty cocked an eyebrow at Paul, asking without words if she was okay. Trudy flashed a look of exasperation, her head tilted slightly at him. Silent nurse talk; Paul had learned that, too.

"You both took off so quickly, I just wanted to make sure—"

"Thank you, Patty," Trudy said. "Pau— Detective Venari was just asking his victim some questions."

"Okay." Patty nodded. "Well, Dr. Shroud is downstairs. Where's the patient?"

"Bed seven," Trudy said.

"*Hmm*, Dr. Shroud checked there. I told him you must have moved her."

"What? No. I didn't move her."

Paul didn't do silent nurse talk. "Call security and lock down the hospital. Now!"

The nurses reacted instantly. Trudy dashed back into the stairwell to head upstairs, and Patty hurried to the elevator.

The staff would have the inside of the hospital covered in a matter of well-drilled minutes. Paul ran up a parking level to his Buick. Had Abaline wandered off or had Ralph already gotten to her? He didn't know, but he had to find her before another angel was ripped from this world.

* * *

The wiper blades squeaked on the windshield, doing little to keep the ever-thickening snow away as Paul peered into the night, searching for any sign of Abaline.

Stan had been at the hospital picking up the victim kit when Paul radioed for backup and had joined in the search. Now Stan's voice crackled through the radio: "Hey, Paul. There's an open door over here at the old textiles warehouse on Hades Street."

Paul's stomach clenched and bile burned into his throat. "Copy, I'll head that way." He remembered Stan was a civilian employee and didn't carry a weapon. "Don't go in until I get there."

"Copy," Stan said.

A few minutes later, Paul turned his Buick onto the street and spotted Stan's white panel CSI van parked along the curb in front of the old warehouse. Paul pulled up behind the van and got out.

He tugged his collar up against the chill. The only sound came from the falling snow, like a hushed pattering of frozen tears. He approached the van and looked in. It was empty. Something was wrong. Paul grabbed his tin, shoved several Altoids in his mouth, and bit down. The release of peppermint oil cut through his gathering anxiety. He took a deep breath and pulled his revolver.

In the light layer of freshly fallen snow were tracks; two sets of footprints led from the van to the door of the warehouse.

Paul tried the door. It swung open, unlocked. If the killer had returned and taken Abaline from the hospital, had he brought her here to finish the job? Had Stan surprised the bastard? Training kept him from calling out for Stan. He kept his flashlight off and followed the path of light from the streetlight outside into the building as far as he dared. He was vulnerable like this, exposed. Paul stepped from the light into the shadows, moving slow, trying to prevent the click of his heels on concrete.

A voice called out, echoing in the cavernous warehouse. "Hello, Detective."

Paul peered around one of the hulking forms of long-abandoned machinery still standing in silent sentry. The form of a man was etched in silhouette by the light of an open interior door. Behind the man was an old office, and inside, tied to a chair, was Abaline.

The man pressed a button on the office wall. A series of systematic thuds and clunks began. The overhead lights flickered to life. Paul blinked as his eyes adjusted, and the man came into clear view. His eyes were wide and excited, his curly hair disheveled.

Stan shuffled back to stand behind Abaline, her body limp inside her pale-green hospital gown, and pressed the long blade of a hunting knife against her throat. "You *will* have to get rid of the gun." He smirked. "We wouldn't want the angel to get hurt, now would we?"

Paul lowered his revolver.

"My luck keeps getting better." Stan snickered. "I began to wonder back at, what—" his eyes flicked upward "—the third crime scene, when I saw you poking around in the wounds. I thought you were just being thorough, but now it all fits. You were looking for something. Something *I* took from them."

A rumble of understanding rolled from Paul's throat.

"Throw the gun down, Detective, and kick it over here. Now!"

Damn. Paul flicked open the cylinder of his .38 Special, dropped the bullets into his hand, then tossed the gun along the floor. It slid into the wall outside the office door.

Stan frowned. He pushed the rolling chair with Abaline to the office door, reached down, and grabbed the gun. He pushed it into the back of his waistband. "Trying to be clever, Detective?" He pressed the knife against the angel's throat, tight enough to cut skin. A thin line of blood appeared. "Remember who has the upper hand here."

Paul stepped out from his hiding spot into the light.

Stan rolled Abaline back into the office. "You know, don't you?" he asked, his voice icy as a Minnesota winter. "Seems we've both been keeping secrets."

"You asshole." Paul tried to hide the tremble of anger in his voice. Losing his cool now would be the opposite of good negotiation tactics.

Stan chuckled wryly. "A man of few words, as always. Tell me who you are, and what you know about the angels, or I will take this one apart before you can break down the door."

"My name is Paul Venari. I'm a homicide detective with the New Rado Police Department." *Screw negotiation tactics.* "And you aren't walking out of here alive, *Stan*." The tech's name rolled from Paul's mouth like something he'd spit out.

"Way I figure it, *Venari*, you're in no position to make threats. Now, tell me what I want to know, and maybe I'll be nice—kill her quick."

Paul hesitated. In his distracted hurry to get into the building, he'd left his radio in the car, and now he'd lost his gun. If a bit of truth gave him a chance to save one of his own, what choice did he have?

"My hand is getting awful tired," Stan called.

The muscles in Paul's back tightened, and he clenched his teeth. He needed a distraction, but he couldn't reach for his Altoids without spooking Stan. *Damn.* Paul hadn't said his true name in nearly a thousand years. It was the first thing he'd given up in penance when he'd taken on human form, and he wasn't certain of the consequences of speaking such a powerful word on an earthly plane. He sighed and closed his eyes. "I am one of The Seven. I was named in the presence of Eternity. When the great apostate rebelled, one third of the stars were cast out with him, and they fell for nine days. By my hand. For I am Justice." Paul opened his eyes slowly. Would that be enough?

Stan's eyes shone brightly, cluttered with desire. "You…you're an archangel."

In his excitement, he pressed the knife against Abaline's throat. She wiggled in her seat. Paul inhaled a sharp breath. He couldn't let another angel be killed.

"I want them," Stan said. "Your wings. I want them, or I kill her."

"I gave them up when I took on mortal form."

"Liar! *They* were all in mortal form."

Paul needed to buy some time. "Tell me why."

Stan licked his lips, then rolled up his left sleeve. There, stitched into the bruised and blood-crusted skin of his upper arm, were six sets of round protrusions. They formed parallel lines up his arm, onto the top of his shoulder. "I know things."

"You didn't know about me," Paul said.

Stan blinked rapidly, his eyes flicking back and forth.

That last bit seemed to take him off-guard. Paul pushed again. "Our wings don't work that way. You cannot steal them from another. You have to earn them for yourself. But let me guess, you didn't know *that* either?"

Stan's face fell like a boy who's had his last birthday candle extinguished by the breath of another.

Paul pushed harder. "You *poor, mortal* fool!"

"Shut up!" Spittle flew from Stan's lips. "You're lying! I can feel their power in me." His hand holding the knife to Abaline's throat shook, then dipped.

Paul had taken two lunging steps toward them, desperate to save Abaline, before he realized his mistake—he'd underestimated Stan's despair.

In the space of a heartbeat, the look on Stan's face shifted as if he'd put on a mask, a blank stare, void of emotion, like something found in a Halloween costume shop.

Stan's arm jerked up. Abaline opened her eyes. She did not blink. And without a word, Stan pulled the blade of his knife across the angel's neck. A smile flickered across her face, then faded as a gory grin opened along her throat.

Paul should have noticed her brief smile. He should have noticed the feather in the breast pocket of her gown—should have noticed it remained white rather than turning red in a torrent of blood. Maybe then he would not have forgotten his exiled promise. But he noticed none of these things.

All time and thought ceased. Breath rushed out of Paul, stolen by shock, and his heart—the human one that had beat for a thousand years—stopped. *I've failed. Again.* Paul fell to his knees, his fist pressed to his chest. A high-pitched whine rang in his ears. Through it he could almost make out Stan's voice: angry, yelling, coming closer. But it was muffled, hidden beyond reach behind Paul's pain and guilt—his eternal sorrow. He had cast out his brothers and sisters from their rightful place and sent them here, to Hell, as frail, perishable, human beings.

Detective Paul Venari's body dropped face-first to the floor. Stan's sneakers squeaked across the concrete until he stood over him.

It was on the ninth day of the casting-out, when Paul had watched Trudy's eyes turn from ethereal blue to earthly brown, that his heart had broken. And so, he fell beside her—followed her to Earth and watched her die a thousand, thousand deaths, loving her through each lifetime. It was his duty to protect her. Wait…that wasn't right… *I do not protect. I punish.*

The ground jumped. Jagged cracks snaked through the cement. Stan staggered back, struggling to stay upright as the floor writhed and heaved beneath his feet.

Paul's heart jack-hammered back into action. He struggled to his knees. The tendons in his neck bulged, pressing white lines against his skin. His head jerked back, mouth agape. The fabric of his shirt ripped as his shoulder blades forced themselves out and tore apart the seams of his tweed jacket. The always tight muscles that spiked down Paul's back—where he carried his stress, his secrets—roared outward from the back of his breathless chest.

Paul's wings spread out in blinding-gold glory. He teetered on his knees, no longer used to the weight of them.

Stan cried out. The knife, gripped tight in his hand, clattered to the ground.

Paul's breath returned, and with all that he was, all he had been created to do, Detective Venari spoke his name. "I am—Raguel!"

* * *

Paul lowered his outstretched arm. Stan's body fell to the floor, motionless. Struck down by Justice.

There was no sound in the space, as if all noise had been sucked out and cast away. Pieces of metal machinery and splatters of red gore littered the ground and walls. Paul inhaled a long, deep breath, then compressed his wings back inside. His scapular muscles screamed with fire from their sudden use.

A hand landed on his shoulder. The physical pain of his outburst eased, his head cleared, and sound returned. Abaline moved to stand in front of him. Paul tried to speak but choked on the tightness in his throat. She was alive. He grabbed Abaline's hand and sunk to the ground. She knelt beside him, a slick-pink line of freshly mended skin across her neck.

"You're okay?" Paul's eyes filled with tears.

Abaline removed the feather from her pocket and twirled it between her fingers. "A small thing can do so much."

"Our wings." Paul let out a small sigh. "I have walked this world too long in denial of my true nature. It hurts."

"How tired you must be."

"I cast her down, our brightest star."

"You did as you were created to do, Raguel, and you have saved many from harm during your watch on Earth."

Paul shook his head. "I could not save them. Or her."

Abaline looked at him, her pale blue eyes covered in clouds. "You love her still?"

"For eternity."

"Then it is time you should be with her."

Paul shook his head. "To become mortal would be to lose her forever."

"Perhaps," Abaline said. "But perhaps we never lose the ones we love. They have, after all, found *you* all these lifetimes. They return to you again and again. And you have done more good than you imagine." She held her hand out to him. In it were the angel's pearls. "I took them back." A flicker of a smile curled at the corner of her lips.

Paul pulled the Altoid tin from the pocket of his jacket, dumped the mints out, and placed the pearls in it. He handed it to her. "You will return them?"

"Of course." Abaline stroked Paul's hair. "Now…let me." She flicked the bloodied end of her single feather with a thumb.

Tears rolled down Paul's face as he removed his tattered jacket and shirt. He bent his head into Abaline's lap. Quickly, with the touch of an angel, she pulled the end of her feather along his shoulder blade. He sucked in a breath. She cut again along his other shoulder blade.

Paul winced only once as Abaline pulled his wings from him—
And made him mortal.

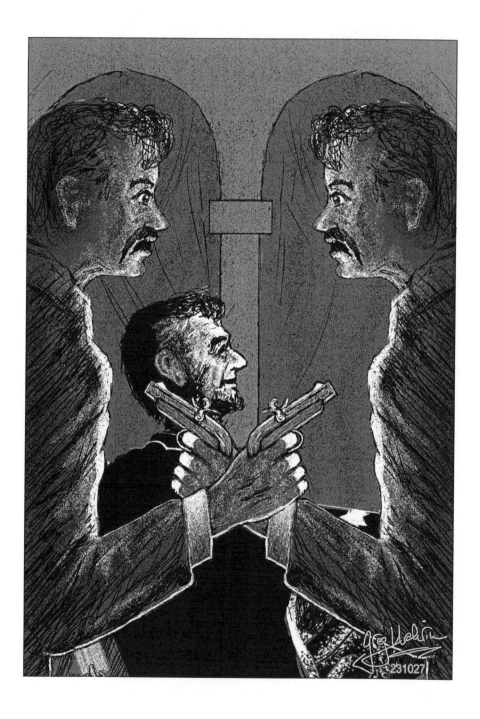

Illustration by Greg Uchrin

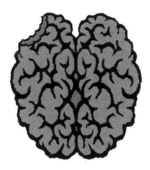

Apart From That, Mrs. Lincoln...

Elektra Hammond

John concentrated on fitting himself into the tiny space. It was a tight squeeze. His heart pounding, he peeked out from behind the sound-muffling curtain and saw the theater was filling.

Breathe slowly.

In.

Out.

The pervasive dust that clung to the curtain had him constantly suppressing sneezes. His gun pressed into his ribs, a constant, uncomfortable weight. He crouched lower, desperate need giving him a panacea against the pain of aching muscles. His timing would need to be perfection. Without rehearsal. Still, an actor of his caliber could be impeccable first time out—if he properly prepared.

Waiting until the show began, John distracted himself with thoughts of Lucy. He'd seen her just that morning, beautiful as ever, a new rosy bloom on her face. Her waistline was thicker, too, but love made her the most beautiful woman he'd ever seen. He'd gone to one knee and taken her hands in his. "Lucy, darling, marry me. Marry me today and make me a happy man."

Again she'd refused him, a man with no home to offer her. "I cannot. My parents would never accept an actor as a son-in-law. And—"

"Hush now, Lucy." He kissed her hands gently. "All I want is to care for you and fill your life with love. And the babe on the way as well."

Lucy had drifted away, shaking her head when he tried to follow.

She was his world. Too bad—

The heavy rasp of the door opening snapped him back to the present, as people sat down in the State Box. The scent of roses drifted to him—a woman's perfume. John couldn't hear every word, but he could follow the conversation.

A woman spoke and he strained to understand. "Major Rathbone, I am so pleased you invited me tonight. I am all atwitter at the prospect of meeting the president."

A man said, "You are ever a delight, my dear Miss Harris. Spending time with you is a joy that the upcoming play will be hard-pressed to transcend."

The woman giggled. They continued exchanging inane pleasantries. It was clear after a few moments that the only people in the box were Major Rathbone and Miss Harris. Earlier, John was told General Grant and his wife would be attending *Our American Cousin* with the president and his wife. Where the devil were they? As he wondered how the general's absence, and the president's, would affect the plan, rudimentary though it was, the orchestra began playing. There was a drop in the sound of people chattering and experience told him that someone had stepped onto the stage to begin the evening's performance.

"Welcome, ladies and gentlemen, to the Ford Theatre, where tonight we're presenting *Our American Cousin,* a play in three acts." John recognized the theater manager's southern accent. He wondered if he would ever tread the boards here at Ford's again after tonight's events.

He heard a couple of servants on the stage make snide comments about their employer's financial woes as the play began. John knew all of the actors, some of them quite well, and he absentmindedly identified the voices. He should be listening to what was happening in the State Box, not on the stage, but it was hard when he knew every line of the play. He'd give anything to be down on the stage and not secreted up here, behind a curtain, waiting.

Endlessly waiting.

Midway through the next scene, the voices from below stopped. The orchestra began "Hail to the Chief." There were cheers and applause and John heard the door to the box open and chairs shifting about. More people had arrived. He recognized the distinct squeaky voice of the president as whispered greetings were exchanged.

For the next hour, John was as quiet as he could be in his stifling space, while staying ever vigilant. He periodically rearranged his arms and legs, careful to move while the audience was laughing, easy enough since he knew which lines the audience would find amusing. He did not sneeze. He waited.

And waited.

Nothing happened.

Below, things had heated up and nearly the entire cast was on stage as Gourlay started yelling about bailiffs to Matthews. The curtain dropped and the audience applauded enthusiastically.

Intermission. He might make it through this night with nothing more than boredom and some mild discomfort. He crossed himself and mouthed the words to a quick prayer.

Soon enough the orchestra began playing and the noise level dropped. Act III started—now it was a real struggle to stay alert. He'd been waiting here nearly three hours. His legs ached abominably, his back hurt, and the mere thought of a drink was enough to, well, drive him to drink. He wanted to stand and stretch, but he'd have to explain why he was hidden in the State Box. He didn't know if he could do that convincingly. Best to stay out of sight and just endure.

Despite the show going on below, John again found his thoughts turning to Lucy, as they so often did. Before meeting her, he had courted many women, some openly, some less-so, and been content.

A friend introduced him to Lucy—daughter to Senator John Parker Hale of New Hampshire. She wasn't the prettiest girl there, but she was darned attractive, and there was something about her, a passion that he recognized.

He lived to perform for other people, to entertain; lived for those glorious moments onstage basking in applause. Lucy's was a quieter passion. She cared about everyone, and a glow followed her through a room. She'd done charity work since she was young. Even now she visited soldiers on the front lines when the fighting paused, to the absolute shock of her society friends. Everyone felt better after a few words and a gentle touch from her.

He'd hesitated to approach her—she was so far above him! She'd dominated his thoughts after that first meeting, so much so that he'd finally sent her a letter, on Valentine's Day. He hadn't dared to sign it.

She shared the letter with her friends, saying the idea of a secret admirer intrigued her, trying to discover the writer. He'd heard about her fascination through society gossip, so he'd written again. And again.

A few weeks later, he'd been seen by her maid while leaving her another letter. He was exposed. To his shock, Lucy accepted his low status, and they'd begun courting, clandestinely, going for walks and carriage rides, politely dancing together at social functions where they "just happened" to bump into one another.

He nearly sighed aloud.

Across the days of secret meetings and long stretches wishing they were together, the walks in the park and waltzes in the ballroom at the

National Hotel—as he had fallen madly, passionately, completely in love with Lucy—she, too, had fallen in love.

With Robert Lincoln. The son of the president.

She'd met Robert at a party, celebrating the engagement of one of her father's colleagues to a friend's sister. Everyone who was anyone in Washington society was there. They'd danced, once, and moved on as was proper. As Lucy told him later, it likely would have ended there, but her mother kept pushing them together, making certain they were invited to the same functions.

Functions he was excluded from.

Lucy loved them both. He knew that. But she'd chosen Robert over him. And Robert, in turn, had decided he didn't love her after all. Or at least not as much as he loved Senator Harlan's daughter, Mary—

John stifled a groan as his left calf cramped. As he slowly bent down and risked massaging the charley horse, he realized he'd allowed thoughts of Lucy to distract him once again. Given what was at stake, he could not allow himself to fall into another reverie.

That would lead to failure.

He gingerly shifted weight back onto his left leg. Still achy, but serviceable. He focused with renewed determination: either something would happen soon or the blasted play would end and everyone could go home.

He prayed for the latter.

On the stage, Mrs. Muzzy and Miss Trueman were playing mother and daughter having a spirited exchange with their rustic American cousin Asa Trenchard, discussing archery as a metaphor for love and marriage. The start of scene two. There were times John could really identify with the lovestruck Trenchard, so well played by his friend Harry Hawk. He listened as Miss Trueman talked of her search for love, and Hawk's response, "I've been cruelly disappointed in that particular."

John heard the door to the State Box creak open and his head jerked up against the wall. *Ouch!*

A tall figure in a baggy coat, trousers, and a top hat was in the doorway. From his vantage point, peeking behind the curtains, John recognized his second-best frock coat and what looked like his best hat.

The figure pulled a gun from a side pocket.

Before John could take more than a step forward, the gun discharged with an explosive *BANG!* and President Lincoln fell forward, his head bloody. The first lady screamed, loud and shrill.

John was caught in a maelstrom of chaos as the State Box erupted into activity.

He reached the shooter and grabbed the gun, preventing a second shot. Major Rathbone, overcoming his shock, converged on the pair. Other theater goers pushed their way into the president's box in response to the shot and the screaming, aiming to comfort the first lady and aid the president, but there was no coordination.

The first lady continued to scream, higher-pitched and more frantic with each passing second.

"You there. Wait! Stop!" said the first to reach them, a man white-faced with shock and determination.

"Never," replied the shooter with calm determination. John tried to interpose himself between the shooter and the unarmed man—desperate to keep anyone else from being hurt.

BANG! Another gunshot.

"Stop! Put yer guns down!" A red-faced man had run into the State Box, waving around a gun. The deafening roar of the second gunshot had frozen everyone.

Major Rathbone was first to react. He jumped at the tall personage who had shot his friend and his president.

He was one step too slow.

The shooter reached for a boot knife and, quick as lightning, slashed at his arm. Rathbone fell back, bleeding. "How the devil did you—" he began, before he tripped, flapping his arms to get his balance and landing with an awkward thump.

More blood. John felt a queasy sense of responsibility. He reached out, with both arms, to get a tight grip. The shooter shoved against him, hard, and in a blink they both went over the balcony to the stage below. The shooter cried out, *"Sic semper tyrannis!* The South is avenged!"

That put John over the edge. "For Pete's sake, Lucy, 'Thus always to tyrants?' Really? You just shot the *president*—" Gunshots from the balcony nipped his rant in the bud. Chastised, he looked at Lucy's sweet face, his heart breaking, and gently took the gun from her. Still looking at her, he slipped the gun into his pocket.

John wondered if this was dream—or would slide into the hellscape of a nightmare—until someone shouted, "I know that man! It's John Booth, the actor. He shot the president!"

That galvanized him. He turned to Lucy, "This way, quickly."

Lucy looked ready to object, but she held her tongue and followed him as he limped across the stage. He led her through the back door, into an alley where a horse was tied up.

Ever the gentleman, he handed Lucy onto the horse and climbed up behind her. He kicked the horse into motion, heading away from the commotion. He tried to strike the proper balance between quick and suspicious in gaiting the horse, difficult with his heart pounding due to Lucy's intoxicating proximity.

Internally, he struggled. He wanted to take Lucy someplace where they could make a life together but—and the bitterness of this thought practically choked him—that was all but impossible now. He'd been recognized in the theater.

As. The. Shooter.

Lincoln was dead. Life as he knew it was over. He'd never act again. What was important now was Lucy and her baby. She could still have a life. A good life.

He turned to Lucy. She was pale and seemed frightened—moreso than he had ever seen her. "Lucy, darling, are you all right?"

"I fear I may never be all right. This is all my fault. I…killed…the president."

"We don't know that, Lucy. If God is willing, he could live." He lied for Lucy's sake. He'd seen the blood. A lot of blood. He held her tightly for a few moments.

"I feel like I was another person, that someone else went to your house, dressed in your clothes, went to the theater tonight. I was so angry. With Robert. With his father and mother." She sighed heavily. "Now it's gone. I'm so very sorry for what I did."

"I am a terrible person," she continued. "I'll be a terrible mother."

"No," he said, soothingly, "you'll be a wonderful mother." Inside, his mind raced. *Lucy is so contrite—how can I fix this?*

As they talked, he planned. No one knew Lucy had been at Ford's. He was the actor; his was the recognizable face.

The horse neared the National Hotel at a fast walk and turned down an alley to approach the servant's entrance. John looked down at Lucy, so small and scared. The enormity of what she'd done must be setting in—he could feel the increasing tension where she leaned against him.

He stepped off the horse and handed Lucy down, daring to hug her briefly. It was at that moment he realized what he needed to do. He kissed Lucy's forehead and looked her in the eye one last time. "Go inside, darling. Take off those clothes." He stared at her intently. "Burn them. You were here, at home, all night."

She said, "Can you take care of the gun? I can't bear to touch it."

"Consider it done, my lady,"

He watched her into the servant's entrance, then remounted the horse and set off at a swift trot, now that Lucy's delicate condition was no longer slowing him down. He was an actor, and this would be the performance of a lifetime.

He headed south into Maryland. He passed by Surratt's Tavern, where he had good friends. But he had to keep moving, he was still too close to Ford's Theatre.

Just before dawn, he arrived in St. Catherine, spent the day trying to rest at a friend's house.

A day later, he traded his horse for a rowboat ride across the Potomac River. Partway across, he dropped the gun into the river and watched it sink. On the other side, he borrowed another horse.

At long last, he arrived at the home of Richard Garrett and knocked on the door. "Dick, can you offer a traveler a place to rest his weary bones of a night?"

"John, come in, come in. You look exhausted. We're setting to dinner." He turned to his son. "Richie, take care of Mr. Booth's horse." Garrett's son slipped outside and stabled the horse, while John joined the family for a hearty meal. After, Garrett pulled out the brandy and they sat on the porch, quietly talking and drinking by the starlight. What happened back in Washington seemed so long ago and far away that John let himself forget it and live in the moment. Things here were so peaceful.

He was still there three days later when the military turned up at the farm looking for him. He steeled himself and ran into the barn. When he refused to come out, the soldiers set the barn on fire. As he dodged about in the burning barn, debating surrendering, someone shot into the barn. Someone very lucky. Hit in the neck, his momentum carried him several steps toward the open barn door before he fell.

The soldiers outside, watching for his escape, ran forward and dragged him the rest of the way out of the fiery structure. As he lay there dying, his last thoughts were of Lucy…

…who had burned his clothes as instructed and then gone to bed, accepting at last that Robert Lincoln did not, would not, love her. Whether or not she was pregnant with his child, he was going to marry Senator Harlan's daughter, Mary.

For close to a month, she took all her meals in her room, hiding from the world. She took to writing long letters, renewing friendships left by the wayside. When news came of John Booth's demise, she was stoic to her parents, the servants, to anyone who saw her, and despondent in private.

Lucy heard about the president's recovery from the bullet that had grazed him at Ford's Theatre, a wound that surely would have been fatal if John hadn't interfered. But no one would ever know that but her. It was her duty to remember John as the hero he had been, when everyone called him a traitor. When she thought about the injustice of it all, she cried.

Then a letter came.

In August 1865, Lucy married her childhood friend, widower William Chandler, after their mutual attraction was rekindled with an exchange of heartfelt letters. They had one child, a son she named John. If anyone noticed his resemblance to Robert Lincoln, with whom Lucy had a distant, polite relationship, they never remarked upon it.

Lucy never forgot John Wilkes Booth, who had given her a second chance.

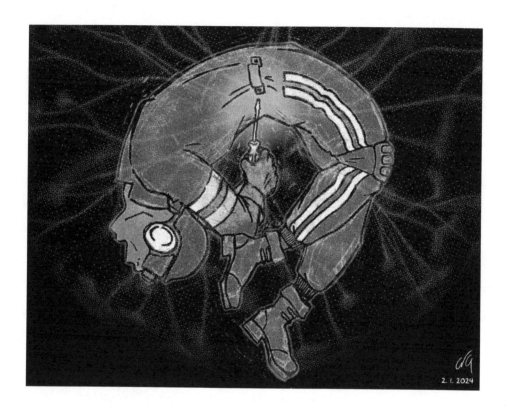

Illustration by Ariel Guzman

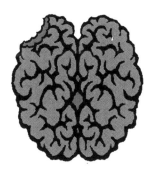

Third Eye Peeled

Derrick Boden

Ask any back-alley occultist and they'll say it the same: can't sneak up on a diviner.

Ask them again after they've met me.

I squeeze under Carver High School's chain-link fence at a quarter past three in the morning. The witching hour. The city's most notorious diviner is holed up inside the admin building, barely a football field away, and that dickface doesn't suspect a thing. That's how good I am at metabolizing second sight. I'm as silent as one of Sibyl's ghosts. Better yet, I'm still alive. This gig would be a breeze, if not for—

"Keep it close, cultie."

If not for my escort.

I bite back a retort—*haven't been a "cultie" for years, meatjockey*—and make my way across the clod-scarred field in silence. Seven years since I graduated this place, never once thought I'd be back. Especially not with a pair of night vision goggles strapped to my face and an ill-tempered occult hunter crowding my nuts. But life has a way of sneaking up on you, especially when the cavity in your body that *should* contain your left kidney is infected with the world's only known divination-inhibiting cyst. Show me any bone thrower, palmist, or entrails reader—show me the Owl himself, tonight's unsuspecting target—and I'll show you one frustrated-as-fuck fortune teller. My future, along with that of anyone in close proximity, is a blank slate.

Sucks to be me.

Of course, that's exactly why I'm here. The Owl and his posse of organ harvesters will scry an ambush a week in the making. Until you add me to the mix. Then it's game on. I wouldn't call it an easy paycheck—my employers have been drilling me for weeks on surveillance blind spots, contingencies, escape routes. But it'll all be over soon. And after tonight's gig, I'll have enough dough to finance a blank slate worth living.

Hell, who am I fooling? Money only ever bought me trouble. Truth is, I'm in this for revenge.

My escort holds up his fist, whispers: "Fuzz on our six."

I don't know why these ex-military bros always have to talk in code—*cops behind us* has the same number of syllables—but whatever. We drop to the ground just shy of the end zone a half-second before a searchlight pans overhead. My jumpsuit is heavy, and too tight for the summer heat; sweat trickles down my armpits. It's so quiet I can hear the creaking of the cop's leather holster in the parking lot. My employers made no illusion about the legality of this operation, and there's nothing in my kidneys that'll keep me from the back of a police car.

I wriggle deeper into the turf.

Don't get me wrong, I'm not some kind of morally bankrupt mercenary. Sure, we're trespassing on government property, but these culties are wanted for federal crimes. The cops will gladly shell out bounties when we hand them over, no questions asked. But we don't exactly have PI licenses, so until then, well…better watch our six.

The searchlight pans again. Hitches on something small darting toward midfield. In the beam of light it's as pale as one of Sibyl's burial ground haunts. For a second my heart hammers the sense right out of me and I tense up to run.

The pale thing stops, turns, gnashes its crooked little squirrel teeth. I let out a breath. The searchlight flicks off. Wheels crunch against asphalt, heading away.

I dust myself off. "How about a little space, yeah?"

My escort's goggles are on his forehead now and he's showing me that same little sneer he always does, which I know he reserves for culties. I think about telling it to him straight, how I *was* a cultie once, before the Owl's crew cut me open on the floor of the nurse's office in the very building we're about to crowbar our way into—left me with a mean scar and an infection that developed into a gaping black hole of future sight—but guys like this don't jive with nuance, so I save the breath.

"You said six feet." His name's Daryl, but everyone calls him HoJo because his mama pushed him into the world on the floor of a broken-down elevator in the Howard Johnson off the Interstate.

"It's not an exact science," I say. In fact, it one-hundred percent *is* an exact science—every last bit of thaumaturgy has its roots in microbiology—I just don't grok the science part of it. "Anyhow, if I can smell your breath, it ain't six feet."

"I'm not taking any chances."

I cut my losses and let HoJo shadow me, nuts to butts, across the parking lot and up to the gym. That's where, with my hand on the scuffed metal handle of my alma mater, the gravity hits me.

It isn't gravity, not really, but it sure as hell *feels* like I'm being pulled unwillingly down a very deep well. It's the same feeling I always get when there's a diviner around, scrying. Stronger the pull, tougher the cultie.

This shit nearly drags me onto my face.

"Easy," HoJo whispers, and if I didn't know any better, I'd think he cared. "You solid?"

"Yeah, dude." I smooth the strain from my face. "Solid."

The gym is silent, latticed in shadow. A thin sheath of mist clings to the cheap vinyl flooring. A red pinpoint of light flickers overhead. Probably a fire alarm. Maybe not. The rubber soles of our boots scuff against the floor, almost noiseless. Almost. I'm trying to focus on what's ahead—the gig, the Owl, the payout—but it's impossible. I've got too much history with this place. Too much glory, too much gore.

Take those rollout bleachers. Beneath their knife-scarred planks, there's a tight corridor of rafters tattooed in blood. I know this because it's my blood, circa sophomore year. The year of my coming out as a legit blood diviner.

My dad had suspicions for years—how I'd rattle off the box score of next week's Giants game after skinning a knee at baseball practice; mumble tomorrow's headlines after slicing my finger in the kitchen—but he kept it close, never told a soul. I'm still not sure if he was afraid for me or for everyone else.

Still, it was only a matter of time before the culties found me—before *Sibyl* found me. Brought me into the fold, revealed the glorious truth. In place of my left kidney, I'd been born with an engorged hematomancy gland that pumped second-sight enzymes into my bloodstream twenty-four seven. All I had to do was spill a little blood and the future was mine.

Until, three years later, it wasn't.

"Look alive." HoJo looks ready to shove me across the gymnasium but doesn't want to make contact, even with his tricked-out tactical gloves. "We're operating in a window."

HoJo might be a cult-fearing meathead whose linguistic range is limited to Tom Clancy catchphrases, but he's also right. Now isn't the time for nostalgia. I can spoil the Owl's second sight all night, but it isn't just divination we're hiding from. The Owl converted this place into his very own underground HQ sometime last year, after the city shuttered the school in favor of the new digs on the south side. The whole school is bristling with surveillance gear, all of it beyond the scope of my powers, stymied by my employer's countermeasures for the duration of the witching hour and not a second longer. After that, no amount of anti-divination mojo will keep the Owl from knowing we're coming.

So I keep moving. Past the bleachers where I peddled fortunes to seniors for twenty bucks a pop. Past the locker room where I predicted the digits under the silver skin of one lotto scratcher after the next before the awestruck stares of the JV basketball squad. Past the water fountain where I divined my way into more than a few bedrooms as an upperclassman. Through this old place where I once reigned as a god among fools.

Into the locker bay, dark as a prison cell. A quarter-inch skin of water covers the floor, from some long-untended leak. Lenses wink in the corners, though their motors don't track our movements. Yet. I engage my night vision goggles, let the shadows fade to green. Even now, seven years later, my eyes train on locker number 214. No amount of disinfectant could remove the crusty traces of those old blood sigils. The ones Sibyl taught me to draw, her black-nailed hand draped over mine, guiding.

She was four years ahead of me, home for the summer after her freshman year in college. She lived down the street, dyed her hair Death Riot Black, carried herself like she truly did not give a shit about anything. Way out of my league. Which is why, when she approached me after practice that summer day, my knobby knees jutting from my suddenly too-small basketball shorts, I figured I was about to become the butt of a puberty joke.

Boy, was I wrong.

"I'm a necromancer," she told me. The way she looked at me, it made my laughter crawl right back down my throat. "The marrow in my femurs manufactures proteins that allow me to talk to the dead."

I raised my eyebrows as far as they could possibly go. "So," I said, "what's the good word?"

"The *good word*," she said in a heady-yet-impossibly-mocking tone, "is that your blood can predict the future."

Of course I didn't believe her. So she flicked the tip of a switchblade across my unsuspecting hand and slapped a poker card onto the cement, face down.

"Read it," she said.

After clutching my hand and cursing for the better part of a minute, I did. Then I read the rest of the deck, in order, still stuffed into her messenger bag. I told her what she was going to order for dinner, what time her deadbeat father would call and how much money he'd guilt-trip her into forking out to cover his gambling debts. I didn't mention the names he'd call her. *Cultie freak* and *death witch* and worse.

She didn't look impressed. Instead, she started drilling me with weirdly personal questions. Did I ever get targeted at school? Did I feel safe at home? Did I need a *haven*, whatever that meant. I told her my dad was alright, that he always covered for me. She listened closely, pried a little, didn't want to believe me. The whole thing belied her no-fucks attitude, set me on edge.

That night, she invited me to a third-eye rave in a warehouse across the tracks. Taught me the commodities market, the going rates for occult services, the half-life of my blood. Who to trust and who to avoid.

Then it was on.

And I was damn good. By my junior year, maybe the best in town. By the time I was a senior, I reigned supreme over my little kingdom. The world was my oyster, never mind that it was a high-school-sized oyster and by Sibyl's standards I wasn't *applying myself.* I was young, I had everything I wanted, and life was only going to get better.

Our boots slurk through the flooded locker bay in unison, mine and HoJo's. His hand hovers near the sidearm at his thigh, which I somehow only just noticed. Not that I should be surprised—this is a bounty gig, after all. Crooks don't march themselves to prison with a *pretty please.* But the way his fingers are itching toward that Glock, something isn't right. Sure, my employers briefed me on contingencies, but none of them involved a firefight. This was meant to be a purely stealth affair. No guns, no fists, no regrets.

And now this.

On our way past 214, I can't resist copping a feel. The tips of my gloved fingers graze my old locker's blood-rubbed metal. I concentrate on the residue, try to summon the slightest vestige of second sight from my stale blood. A half-vision, a premonition, a goddamn *hunch.*

Nothing.

Then I glance across the hall to 113. Can't help myself. It's like someone's got my head in a giant wrench and they're cranking away, until there's no way to *not* see Koji's locker. The scratch-marks are still keyed into it, like the car door of everyone's least favorite teacher. Can't make out the word anymore, but I know it's there. *Boner.*

Koji was an awkward freshman, even if you didn't count the bone throwing. He wore big baggy shirts that made him look like a sixth-grader, shaved his head despite the scars all over his scalp. He thrashed out to speed metal in the back of class, spoke in monosyllables, brooded a lot.

Word on the street was, his bone-throwing was passable at best, but who could really say? Dude never talked to anyone.

No way did he deserve the attention Sibyl paid him.

But he didn't deserve what he got, either. Sure, I might've let it slip to some sophomores that Koji was a closet bone-jockey, peeping in on their future hookups. How was I supposed to know they'd stuff all those rat skeletons into his backpack? Or that his foster parents were goddamned *fundamentalists*, who—upon finding the rats—sussed out the rest and promptly disappeared Koji from school?

Don't answer that one.

I never said I was an angel. Find me a teenager who's never thrown some shade at the new kid on the block. Find me *anyone* who's made it to drinking age without stubbing a few toes. I dare you.

Besides, this was *my* kingdom.

Last time I saw Sibyl, I could tell how jealous she was by the tightness of her gloss-black lips. She was home for spring break and she came for me right here at my locker. *Time to get you underground,* she said, *before it's too late.*

I didn't hold back my laughter. What did I have to be afraid of? I could read the fucking future.

Sibyl wasn't joking. She said I was too loose, too high profile. A *target,* she called me. Look what happened to Koji, she said, which made me feel like a clod of shit stuck between someone's cleats. Then worse, when she said she *couldn't keep him safe.* Couldn't find him a haven. She told me she wasn't gonna lose another kid, *whatever it takes.*

She laid out an offer. Join her crew, hone my talents, fight for…I don't know, occultist equality? It didn't make sense. My peers revered me. Equality sounded like a downgrade. And yet here was Sibyl, ranting about black ops hit squads rounding up cultie kids on trumped-up charges. If there was any such thing, why hadn't I heard of it? Sure, nobody had seen Koji in a hot minute, but only because his parents had pulled him from school. Right?

To top it off, Sibyl made it clear that by joining her crew I'd be going offline. No more lotto scratchers, no more divining the answers to midterms, nada. Said my powers were too potent, needed to be kept out of the limelight. It was a bunk deal, a lose-lose.

I still wonder what might've happened if I'd said yes.

HoJo brings us to a halt with an upthrust fist. Around the corner, I can hear a rat scuttling. Either that, or someone tapping furtively at a keyboard. I'd sell my liver for a glimpse at what's coming next.

HoJo shifts his weight from foot to foot, practically dancing at the chance to light up that poor wayward rodent. But he can't, not without me. After a high-tension internal debate that plays out across his sunburnt face, he motions me forward.

We shuffle to the corner as quiet as the floodwater will allow. The scratching can't be more than five paces down the adjacent hall. I'm expecting HoJo to sneak a peek and report back, but instead he lurches out all at once, whips a conical plastic gun from his backpack and squeezes the trigger.

I wince, but there's no sound. A second later, something splashes into the shallow water.

HoJo is still squeezing the trigger of his souped-up nerf gun, still aiming, when he whispers out the corner of his mouth, "Get it."

Not knowing what *it* is, I'm a little hesitant to even glance around the corner. In my momentary indecision, my eyes train on HoJo's unlaced backpack where he fished out the gun. Through the open flap: a camo parcel, a few dozen zip cuffs, a cryo case the size of a human fist. A patch on the parcel reads *Surgical Instruments Kit.* The cryo case is empty.

Shit.

Then HoJo is hissing *now* and I'm around the corner before I realize it. The thing he's aiming at is a drone. It's the size of a softball and bristling with cameras, though at the moment they're all lolling and shuttered. Its rotors are still, its landing gear deployed into the veneer of floodwater.

"Get it," he says again.

"Not while you're pointing that thing—"

"It's an RF jammer." Even our whispers echo in the deadness of this place. "Harmless. Now bring me the fucking drone."

Dude's a prick, but he's got the tone of authority down. I'm there and back in three seconds, cradling the cold metal thing while he keeps the blowhole of his jammer trained on its body. He stuffs a screwdriver into my palm, tells me to poke the reset button on its underbelly and hold it there for ten seconds to trigger a BIOS reboot. Anything else and the Owl will know his drone's been tampered with, rather than suffering from a run-of-the-mill software glitch.

I do what he says, then carefully set the drone back into the floodwater. The reboot includes a diagnostic scan that should take about ten minutes, HoJo says, which means our timeline has shortened.

But as HoJo slides his jammer back into his pack, drones are the least of my concerns. I can think of plenty of legitimate reasons a covert ops jackoff might carry around a field surgical kit. There's only one thing he could be doing with that cryo case.

They aren't after the Owl at all. They're after his talents. This isn't a bounty run. It's an organ heist.

I'm not having fun anymore.

My hand drifts to the banana-shaped scar on the left side of my back. Not a dozen paces down this very hall sits a door with a frosted window labeled *NURSE*. Right there on the coffee-stained linoleum floor of that room, I endured my first and last surgical procedure at the hands of the Owl's crew. When I woke up, it wasn't the pain from the twenty hasty hand-stitches that brought a scream to my lips. It was the sudden, jarring absence of gnosis. My blood was everywhere—the floor, the walls, the table, the absent nurse's laptop—and yet I felt *nothing* of the future.

I should've seen it coming. I'd been steeped in the commodities market for years by then. I'd seen more than my share of body parts change hands in the parking lot behind the third-eye warehouse, in the palmist alleys by the docks. When times are tough, it isn't easy to pass up hard cash—or hard drugs—for a functional oracular gland. Especially when said gland offers you nothing but bad news regarding your own future. Show me ten bone throwers and I'll show you nine dust addicts and an alcoholic. It's only a matter of time before they start sawing at their own fingers, selling them off for an eighth apiece. Hematomancer glands like mine will net you five grand, and the market is *hot.* Cram one into a bucket of formaldehyde to quell its separation anxiety, hook it up to a bag of fresh blood, hardwire it to a sports betting app and *boom*—you've got yourself a passive income factory. Third eyes are worth triple that, though mostly due to the technicalities of extraction.

Still, in all the grisly stories passed around all the back-alley barrel fires, I never once heard of anyone taking an organ *unbidden.* I wish I could say the crew must've been top-notch to get past my own premonitions, but the truth is I got cocky, let my guard down.

Nobody could've predicted what happened next. The infection, the cyst, the black hole of oracular sight that infested my vacant kidney cavity. It wasn't just my power they'd taken from me, it was my life. Before long every tarot reader and palmist in town knew my name—and shunned it. I was the bane of every soothsayer, a walking vacuum of divination. I got uninvited from every party, blacklisted from every fortune teller's stall. I left Carver High the same way I came in: as a nobody.

I've woken every morning since with empty eyes turned on a dulled future, dwelling on what could've been. So when the bounty hunters approached me seven years later about taking down the Owl and his inner circle of occultists, anyone could've prophesied how I'd answer.

But I didn't sign up for this. I'm no angel, but I'm not a monster, either. Sure, I want to see the Owl behind bars for what he's done. But nobody deserves to get opened up against their will. And if my employers weren't inclined to trust me with this noteworthy detail, what else aren't they telling me?

HoJo is on the move, which means so am I. No time to dwell. I'm still holding the screwdriver, so into my pocket it goes. Past the nurse's office with a deep shiver. Down the admin hall with its finger-smudged trophy cases, long-since cleared out. The oracular gravity deepens with every step, prickling my skin, dragging me closer. Past the principal's office, which the Owl has converted into a security room, presently vacant, all glutted with flickering monitors—*already dealt with*, HoJo whispers—where I freeze mid-stride.

I can't say what exactly draws my attention to that particular CCTV monitor crammed into the corner of the office. Call it a premonition.

When I see it, I can't look away.

"Keep moving," HoJo says, which I absolutely do not do.

By the surplus of people, what I'm seeing can only be a bird's eye view of the Owl's command center. They're holed up in the old computer lab, poring over printouts, huddled in corners, talking furtively. There's at least thirty of them.

Most of them are kids.

They range from high school seniors all the way down to grade school, and it doesn't take a third eye to see that every last one of them is an occultist. The way their eyes shift, seeing the unseen; the way they confine their movements, as if they're navigating spaces overlaid atop our own mundane reality. Which, of course, they are.

Their hair is unkempt, their belongings sparse, their clothes disheveled. They look positively *on the run*, as if they'd been escorted from class a month ago—some of them longer—and haven't been home since.

There's a smattering of adults, too, though only one who matters— only one to whom everyone else is visibly deferring; only one with the tattoo of a horned owl peeking out from under his sleeve.

Scratch that, *her* sleeve.

Oh, *fuck.*

Her hair is the same Death Riot Black as the first time I saw it, her lips the same perfect flatline. Seven years since our last encounter, Sibyl hasn't changed a bit.

Unlike, say, me.

The revelations are hitting me rapid fire, now. If Sibyl is in fact the Owl, that means Sibyl stole my oracular gland. Same gland she taught me to use. Same gland she asked me to *stop* using when she tried to recruit me, not two weeks before I woke up a quarter-pound lighter on the floor of the nurse's office.

Also, the *fuck* is she doing? She's sitting cross-legged on a cheap fold-out table, tracing sigils with blood. Her own blood, by the crimson trails running down her arms. Which makes exactly zero sense. Sibyl is a necromancer, not a hematomancer. She's got no business finger-painting with blood. Not unless—

Not unless she *is* a hematomancer, now.

All this time I figured the Owl snatched my oracular gland to fence on the organ market. Turn a quick profit, move along. But that wasn't it at all. She had *plans*. Stitched the damned thing into her own body.

In hindsight—a talent I still excel at—it's all painfully obvious. She said herself I was *potent*, gave me a chance to work alongside her. And when I turned her down, well, did she not say she'd do *whatever it takes* to never lose another kid? She didn't really need me. All she needed were the enzymes pumping through my blood.

And damn if it didn't work. This place she's built, it's a haven. *Their* haven. She's been using my hematomancy to stay one step ahead, shepherd her flock out of harm's way. And me—

Fuck, *me*. I guess there really are black ops hit squads rounding up cultie kids. HoJo's got enough zip cuffs stashed in his backpack for the whole lot. All they needed was a way to get past the Owl's uncanny second sight.

All they needed was me.

HoJo takes a step closer, says something. Sibyl, still unsuspecting, traces a fresh curve of blood across the table.

Sweat slides down my scar. I wonder: if I'd had the balls to look this far ahead, would I have seen myself slipping knife-like down these halls? Or would I have been a black hole even to myself? If I could've seen myself, would I have done it all differently?

I've spent the last seven years blaming my problems on the loss of my second sight, but what would I have done if I'd kept it? What *had* I done before it was taken from me? Parlor tricks, swindles, cheats. Reigning over some phony kingdom, wasting every drop of blood I spilt. Are half these kids gonna waste their talents the same as me? Maybe. But that doesn't mean they don't deserve an honest shot. And it sure as hell doesn't mean they deserve to be hunted down.

Dad always said it ain't what you've got but where you're bringing it. I've still got *something*, even if it's the absence of something better. Do I really want to use it like this?

Hell no.

All I've gotta do is back away and HoJo falls out of my radius of protection. But before I've taken a single step, cold metal clamps around my wrist.

"No funny business, cultie." The thing HoJo just slapped onto my wrist is a handcuff—old-fashioned, steel, attached at the other end to *his* wrist. With his free hand, he's pointing his sidearm at my center of mass. "Now *move*."

He must've seen something in my eyes, something that said *flight risk*. By how fast it all went down, this was clearly another one of those contingencies my employers had planned for. No surprise they didn't share this one with me. From where I'm standing, it's airtight. Even if I struggle, all he's gotta do is pistol-whip me and drag me to the computer room unconscious. My cyst doesn't need my brain to work, and Sibyl is right down the hall.

I look at the handcuffs, the gun. The screen.

Surprisingly, it isn't Sibyl that catches my eye, but a kid in the corner swimming in a too-baggy shirt, headphones half the size of his skull, eyes all full of brooding. Even here among the outcasts, he's clearly an outsider. In his hand he's rattling a fist of bones, lovingly, like it's the only thing that he ever knew was right.

It ain't Koji, but it might as well be.

If I let HoJo drag me down that hall, I've done it again. Only this time, I can't pretend like I didn't know any better. Nobody ever heard from Koji. *Ever.* I can't let that happen again.

Whatever it takes.

Out from my pocket comes HoJo's screwdriver. Steady as a trigger finger, sharp as a shiv.

This plan of theirs, it isn't airtight after all. There's still one way I can let Sibyl know we're here, give her a chance to get those kids to safety. There's still one way to make this right. But it doesn't take a diviner to know there's no peeling myself off the floor after this one.

Through my scar goes the screwdriver, rooting, digging. The pain is a presence; I drop to a knee, all warm with blood. Panic sets in. What if I can't find the damn thing before I pass out?

I steel myself, dig deeper. The shaft hits something hard, a knuckle of infected tissue. The cyst. I only hesitate for a second. Then I push the screwdriver straight through its core.

HoJo is staring bug-eyed, too shocked to hit me, whisper-shouting *are you outta your goddamn mind?* And of course I am, I have to be if I'm doing this, but that's not what I say to him.

I say: "Didn't see *that* coming."

I can tell when the cyst is toast because all at once the gravity stops tugging and the air goes dead still. Sibyl freezes on-screen, looks right into the camera like she knows. Because, of course, she does.

I'd give anything to feel that way one more time.

Then the screens go blank. Sibyl is gone.

And so am I.

Illustration by Kat D'Andrea

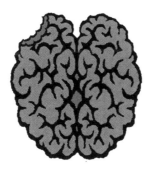

We Will All Remember Bread

Alma Alexander

We were known as "Mr. Jackson's Festivals of the Senses."

There were five of us Dreamers, initially, in our particular group. Holly Marie, who remembered the taste of honey. Adam Eagle Arrow, who claimed to be of Indian descent and who remembered the feel of a river otter's wet fur beneath his fingers. Joy Robredo, who was able to remember the smell of coffee. Salman Hardan, who could remember the songs of several long-vanished birds. And myself, Alice Jennifer Crawley, who remembered the taste and scent of bread.

I don't know who Mr. Jackson originally was, but apparently it was someone by this name who had figured our kind out and recruited us and put together the first traveling shows. There were many such shows scattered around the length and breadth of the land, all under the direct control of someone we only knew as the Management. But sooner or later all would be graced by a visit from "Mr. Jackson" in person. I remember at least three different ones. The first was a bumbling, pudgy man with bloated white hands and six chins cascading down into his high shirt collar. The second, someone so ordinary that you would never notice him in the street; he was difficult to keep in sight even there in the carnival ground while he was lording it over us.

Mr. Jackson Number Three was a dark-haired little man with vivid black eyes and, God help us all, affecting an actual monocle when he was in public. I knew for a fact he didn't need it—I saw him read some very fine print without squinting, several times—but it gave him a certain air, and as far as that went it worked admirably. He gave off such melodrama-villainy that you just *knew* it had to be overkill and he couldn't possibly be that bad. It was a very good cover for—well—being that bad.

In our own little group, we had it better than others out there. Some troupes eked out a living in the hinterlands, with the Dreamers sleeping out in the open if they had to, the crowds pressing close. In our case, we were almost aristocrats. Our Management was adept at both promoting us well enough to ensure a steady and solid income, and juggling the money in ways that made it multiply on the side. On show nights, we slept each in our own tent, the doors to the tents laced shut until the crowds paid their entrance fees and came to mill around with a quiet susurrus of sound so as not to wake the sleepers before their time.

And then the show would start—one tent's flaps and then another's, in sequence, being pulled aside to reveal the sleeper, the one who Dreamed. In silence, they watched while each of us woke and released the dream: the scent, the sound, the taste of things that no longer were.

In the beginning, I was always too woozy, right after waking, to notice, but afterwards, as I got used to the routine, I became able to see the reactions outside my tent—at least in the first few rows of people who waited just beyond the threadbare red velvet ropes that separated them from us. I learned to recognize the different kinds of reactions:

The people whose faces bore merely curiosity, and sometimes boredom.

The ones who stood straining to catch a hint of the sense being wafted through and over them by the Dreamers.

The ones who sucked in the sensations, their eyes closed, their faces rapt, lost in it all.

And the elders. The ones old enough to remember some of the things that we in the tents hoarded the memories of; remember, but unable to share, like some of us did, like the Dreamers did. The ones with the vision, but not the gift. Those, I remember most of all: the weathered faces of old men and old women, tears running down the furrows of the lines deeply etched into their skin, as though they were irrigation channels, taking life-giving water to the fields where the crops used to grow, where the wheat used to wave, the wheat that vanished after the blight and was no more.

The wheat crash came when I myself was seven years old, and after that it took surprisingly few years for fine wheat flour to disappear, and with it the kinds of bread I remembered my grandmother baking when I was young. That was the Dream I went back to for my every performance, for every sleep—my grandmother's kitchen. And when my eyes would flutter open to remind me where I truly was, and that I would never be there again, the smell of the bread she had just taken out of her oven would be the thing that washed over the waiting crowds outside. I could hear people sucking in their breath sharply as the first waft went out. Sometimes, I heard sobbing.

We wore out fast, the Dreamers. We would go back and back and back to the Dream until it was stripped like an old screw and would no longer grip or fasten. There had been others before I came to join the troupe, others who had retired in tears and tragedy when their gifts wore too thin, or else took their lives when they could no longer do what they used to be able to do. There may have been folk like that in those carnie crowds out there—the ones who had lived, perhaps through no choice of their own—perhaps the ones with the tears on their cheeks, the ones who remembered what it was like to be on *this* side of the Dream.

But for a little while, at least, we were stable, our group—five of us, together—Holly and Adam and Salman and Joy and Alice.

Joy was the oldest of us, the one who had been there when all of the others had signed on. Always there, from the beginning, the foundation of our quintet. Nobody (perhaps not even her) was completely certain about her actual chronological age. She joked that she was a Norn, immortal in that old white-haired and wizened body of hers, needing a cane to help her walk when she was not Dreaming on her couch, and assistance at her ablutions—which usually fell to me, the youngest, to provide.

I did not mind. In some ways she actually reminded me of that lost grandmother whose bread I remembered for the crowds every night. I did the little things that she found it hard to do—like washing her feet, or brushing her hair and putting it up at the times that she didn't wear it down for the Dreaming. And she would tell me the things that she remembered, of the world that was, once upon a time. Of vanished things.

Coffee was her Dream, the thing she offered to the carnie crowds, but she could remember so many other things that I could not, that I had never had a chance to experience. The feel of clean white sand underneath bare feet, both fine and dry up in the dunes and firm and damp right there where the lace of the ocean foam patterned the shoreline; a somnolent sound of buzzing bees in the summer, something that not even Holly (the one whose Dream was honey, and who might have been expected to have remembered this) could not bring to mind anymore; the smell and the shape of the bear she had once seen, as a small child, from the safety of a hide, watching as he pawed a clean stream for fish as vanished as himself; the texture of a redwood's bark. All gone now, all vanished. Perhaps someone somewhere Dreamed some of these things for the carnie visitors, but Joy had chosen to concentrate on something smaller and much more domestic. The coffee.

"It might still be familiar, or recognizable, to some of them," she told me as I braided her hair by candlelight, after a late show, when she was getting ready to retire into her own private dreams which had no crowds waiting outside to receive them. "I could give them the redwoods, if I wanted to. But too many of them would have never seen one, and the memory would just be alien to them. Nothing they could identify with. But for too many of us the smell of coffee was what started a day, and we will all miss it—to our last dying day we will miss it."

"Even those who have never actually tasted it?" I asked.

"But they know the idea, and they get the scent and it reminds them of a world that no longer is, or can ever be again," Joy said.

Coffee, of course, was long gone. Only things that were vanished could be shared by the Dream.

But too many things were vanished now.

And there was the secret behind the whole concept of the Dream show: the Dreamers could only be people who had themselves, personally, directly, experienced the thing that they shared in the Dream. You could not "remember" the aroma of bread, to take my own talent, if you had never actually smelled it yourself in real life. It was only those who had, whose sense of it was real and remained accessible to them, who could transmit it to others. You could not fake this. And Joy was right, as far as that went. There had to be a balance in the shows, of course, because there would always be those who wept at the things they had never actually had a chance to experience while it was still with us, things that were exotic (like Joy's bear—or Adam's otter, for that matter), but there were always far more who hankered after that lost serene domesticity, when you didn't have to think about the bigger things at all because the smaller things, the things you took for granted—the things like fresh bread or a cup of coffee to start the day—were there for the asking and did not seem as though they could ever go away.

Joy had a quiet sadness to her, but she was not one of those Dreamers who would succumb to nostalgia and suicide. And she certainly showed no signs, even at her advanced age, of fading.

Which was why it was so startling, so unbelievable, when she was simply...*gone* one morning.

Management, when I actually screwed up enough courage to ask, was not helpful—he implied that Joy's absence had to do with Mr. Jackson Number Three, but would say no more than that. Mr. Jackson Number Three, his own self, was walking around the grounds, monocle in place, pretending that nothing was different, nothing was wrong, and he took care not to permit anyone to have private speech with him. That was where the circle closed. Those who might have known anything relevant were not talking, and those who did not—the rest of us in the show—knew nothing at all, other than word had filtered down that there would be a replacement.

Some day. Maybe soon.

A man who might have been called John, or James, or Jonah, or something. A man whose Dream was the taste of a mountain spring; or the sound of clean rain; or the savannah sound of a lion's deep rumble at the closing of the day; or the scent of first snow on a winter morning, in the days before the weather changed everywhere; or the glorious swelling sound of a full-orchestral symphony before they had run out of people who knew how to play the instruments, who'd had the time and the luxury of opportunity of devoting their lives to that. Anything, and everything. So many things were lost, and regretted, and now existed only in carnivals where memories of vanished things were sold to people who wanted to remember a vanished world.

"Have you noticed that there are fewer and fewer of them?" Holly asked, about those people in our audiences. "Every time I wake from a Dream there seems to be a thinner crowd outside the tent. I remember there were times when it was just a tight-pressed row of faces, staring back at me. Now…I can see through the front ranks. Sometimes all the way to the back."

"You can only sell memories to those who want to remember," Adam said, shrugging philosophically. His crowds were thinnest of them all. Seemed like there weren't many people out there interested in wet river otters.

That hurt me, somehow. The fact that river otters were not even worth remembering anymore. Just like Joy had not thought it worthwhile to choose to Dream her textures of sand, or of tree bark. Who'd know? Who'd care?

"I've heard Mr. Jackson talking," Salman said. "He seems to think it's a waste."

"That what's a waste?" I asked, bristling.

Salman shrugged, indicating the whole carnival—the tents, looking threadbare in the harsh daylight without the soft candle glows that lit them while we were Dreaming; the bare ground with the tufts of yellow bent grasses from where passing feet had stomped the earth into dust. "This," he said. "All of this."

"What exactly did he say?" Adam said, stretching his long legs out in front of him and leaning back to cradle the back of his hands in the palms of his interlaced hands.

"That three quarters of the people who come these days only come because they're vaguely curious," Salman said. "Not because they, too, remember, but lack the gift of Dreaming to bring it all back to them.

Those, apparently, are the ones who pay for the privilege of being taken back, for the brief moment in which they can lull themselves into thinking that they might be back in those days. The others—they come because we are freaks and they like looking at freaks. But there are always new freaks and better shows. Our day may be over."

"And what are we supposed to do with ourselves then?" Holly asked, her voice acquiring an unpleasant shrill edge.

Salman leered at her. "You're still a good-looking woman. Some things you don't need to be asleep to be able to do for a man."

She slapped him hard and stalked away, flushed with fury, and with fear.

We had turned on one another, since Joy had vanished. She was the thing that had held us together, as a group—her gentleness, her serenity. The smell of coffee in the morning.

I must have been thinking about Joy very loudly because Adam turned to me abruptly and said, "Do you suppose she is dead?"

I actually flinched, and found myself unable to speak. It was Salman who answered him, slowly, with the air of running a speculative finger on the sharp edge of a blade.

"May not be," he said. "I heard more."

"Well?" Adam prompted, after the pause stretched a moment too long.

Salman glanced at me, and licked his lips. It seemed as if whatever he had to say made him uncomfortable—even him, who did not care about what people thought, how they reacted.

"I heard that there is a way—" he began, and then stopped, frowning.

Adam's eyebrow rose, and Salman ploughed on, making some kind of decision, avoiding looking at me directly.

"When they say it's *a waste*," he said, his voice instinctively lowered, as if Mr. Jackson Number Three was standing right behind him listening in, "I think they mean that they are gathering together the memories…and somehow…preserving them."

"Can't be done," Adam said, and spat sideways into the dust.

The spittle failed to make the shriveled grass thrive, and after a glance in that direction Salman leaned in closer and spoke in an even more hushed tone.

"But that's just it. I think it can, now. And that's what they are doing. They're taking in the Dreamers, one by one, and they're wringing us dry. If they can have the memory, they don't need the one who remembers, not anymore."

"And then what?"

"Once they have it all—dang it, don't you see? It's easier to sell if you can bottle it and charge good money for tiny bottles which contain one whiff of the memory that you're after. Or else they can keep it all locked away and just let in those who can pay, more and more money, and everyone else out there—the carnivals, the crowds like ours—they won't matter anymore. They don't remember anyway, not really, not a jackanapes of them. When do you suppose any of that ragged lot last night actually tasted a piece of bread, Alice?"

Aimed at me, because I had bristled at his words, and it quelled me immediately because the answer to his question was not one I had words to articulate. I could not believe that I was the last person—or at least one of the last—to have smelled that smell, the scent of fresh-baked bread. I did not want to think that nobody born after me *ever would again*. Was I the last, the only, thing that stood between that heavenly scent and oblivion? Was that what I was? The final bulwark? But if that was the case then what meaning did my gift hold for the carnival crowds? For the people whose only encounter with that smell would be the few incandescent moments they spent outside the tent where I had Dreamed it?

In another generation, would bread and coffee be things of legend, talked of in hushed whispers, mythical things from a golden past while my kind, my species, hurtled on blindly into whatever future bereft of senses lay in store for us?

Were we doomed to live out an existence where we ate bland mash made in chemistry labs, just enough to nourish us and no more?

Or were our memories, those of us who still had them, truly extractable from us, like Salman had said, and there would be two kinds of people from now on: Us and Them. With Us, the poor and the dispossessed, the carnie crowds, doomed to becoming less and less substantial until we turned to sere leaves of late autumn and were blown away by the winds of fate; and Them, the wealthy, the ones with enough means to pay, at least blessed with a memory of a warm cup of coffee even if they could never wake up to the reality of one ever again?

I have no idea what made me slip out of the carnival camp and follow Mr. Jackson Number Three as he left the place on what he said would be the last day of his visit, what gave me the courage, what I thought I was going to find out. I think I believed that, somewhere, he must have a trailer of his own, much like the ones we traveled in, that he was a carnie like us. He didn't, of course. He probably had a proper home, somewhere, with a foundation and brickwork and carved lintels, a place of permanence and solidity—but while visiting us he was apparently staying at the local hostelry, an inn a little way down the road, a place that had seen better days and that even I could tell he had a healthy dose of disdain for, as he paused for a moment to grace the edifice with a sneering smirk. Then he ducked into the door and vanished from my sight. But not long after, the lights went on in one of the rooms on the second floor. There was a tree, one with low branches and a gnarled trunk, one that even I could climb, outside the room. So I did, and from it I could see in through a window over which he had neglected to draw the curtains.

Joy was inside.

I caught my breath, because it was not the Joy I knew, the gentle grandmotherly lady whose hair I had braided every night. That soft thin hair was now scraggly, sticking out from her scalp, shaved in places where electrodes had been attached to her skull. Her face was a rictus, and her eyes were empty and staring. Wires led from her head to a machine set up on a rickety table in the middle of the room, a machine with a screen on which a green line was steadily scrolling, marking progress of some sort.

She was a shell.

And in that machine…in that machine now lived the scent of coffee and the texture of sand, lived the things of her past, the things that had made her human, that had made her Joy.

Mr. Jackson Number Three was speaking to someone just out of sight through the open door of the room, out in the corridor. I could only barely hear, the window ajar just a little, but I got the general idea of his words. *I will be out of here tonight. I will expect you to dispose of the evidence.*

The evidence. What was left of Joy.

For the life of me, I could not remember the smell of coffee, the thing that defined her in our group. I didn't think I could ever smell coffee again. He had stolen that from me, just as he had stolen it from Joy—because in some strange, unfathomable way that was her signature, her soul, and he was stealing it…for reasons I could not begin to comprehend, in a manner I did not have the first clue how to understand.

All I could think of in that instant was one thought, one single solitary terrifying thought.

It won't be long. It won't be long before the body in that chair is me.

It could not end like this. It could not. It must not.

The carnie shows, the Festivals of the Senses, were suddenly almost benign, after witnessing this. They were blessings handed out to the wretched, reminding them of the riches of days gone by, when so little could mean so much. But this…we could not sink to this. We could not have the people, with whatever small gift they had to share, have it ripped from them like this, to benefit…to benefit a handful of people who would gather in drawing rooms behind locked doors and suck in the memory of coffee greedily while the small pleasures sank into grayness and dullness and even the smallest lights went out in the people who shuffled meaninglessly along empty dusty roads on a dying planet whose riches had been plundered into oblivion.

I scrambled down to the ground, blinded with tears. I don't think Mr. Jackson Number Three ever knew I was there, or that I had seen. But I was never going back to the carnival, no, not if I starved on the side of the road or drowned in the gutter. I would give the gift away. *All* of it. Everything I had, everything I could remember. For nothing. For free. I would try and wake all of them, so that we could all be Dreamers, so that we could all wake with the scents and sounds and lights of vanished times tantalizingly before us, leading us on.

Somewhere, perhaps, a stalk of ancient wheat had survived. I would seek it out. I would look for it, and find it, and maybe shake its grains into my hand and plant them and watch more stalks grow where the seeds fell. And then more. Perhaps it would not grow where it once used to grow—the world had changed, after all—but maybe the places it might have never thrived in before could now be a hospitable place for it to try and take root once more.

And perhaps—I was young enough to dream—perhaps someday I could gather enough of this as yet unborn wheat, to harvest it, and grind it, and knead the forgotten flour into a smooth and forgotten dough, like my grandmother used to do long ago, once upon a time.

We would all remember it.

We *will* all remember bread.

Illustration by Kat D'Andrea

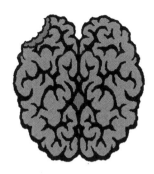

Palatable Potions

Melinda Brasher

If I hadn't added the sage, none of it would have happened. Sage is delicious in a nice browned butter sauce, heated so slowly the butter turns honey-colored and the sharp smell of the sage makes you dizzy with anticipation. But apparently, *apparently*, you can't just add sage to potions containing griffin toenail fungus. The interaction is…unsightly. But how was I to know? They never taught that in class.

Because, you slug brain, NO ONE adds sage to a potion just to make it TASTE BETTER. Madame Azura always had an answer for everything, even if it wasn't the right answer. *We're not household cooks. We're witches. Practitioners of the glorious magics. And we FOLLOW RECIPES.*

Recipes are limiting. Besides, how can you expect someone to eat toenail fungus without something nice like sage to fancy it up? When I asked if oregano would have been better, Madame Azura threw a wet rag at me.

And I know, I know. Lord Haskin is one of our best customers. Rich enough to buy whatever we brag to him about. He'd paid for a hair-thickening potion, but after I added the sage, that's not precisely what he got.

Okay. Not at *all* what he got. His hair did grow more pronounced…but only because his skin shrank away in a painful and shockingly ugly way.

But how was I to know?

You read the RECIPE, you useless turnip. Madame Azura crammed my clothes and my most basic grimoire into an old feed bag. She rooted around for my old school pot—small, iron, not even a rim of copper, suitable for only the most basic potions, but pretty good for stew. She stuffed it into the bag and literally kicked me out of the house, tossing the bag after me and slamming the door.

Even after Madame Azura made Lord Haskin an antidote—free of charge, apparently, though it required an entire phoenix eggshell, which takes at least four men to harvest and is *not* cheap—Lord Haskin's scalp and face looked lumpy for weeks.

I know about the lumpiness because I hung around, spying on our prize customer to make sure nothing truly terrible happened. I slept in people's barns and did odd chores for food, hoping Madame would take me back once she realized what an honest mistake it was.

So when a small girl approached me in the market and asked for help, my fingers tingled.

"Please, Miss." Her big black eyes beseeched me. Her tiny hands gripped an empty basket. "Our cowmel…she's awful sick."

Oh.

"Please."

"Perhaps you should talk to the animal doctor."

"He says there's nothing to be done. Maybe you could make up a potion? You helped my Papa when he had a fever."

Useless turnip, eh?

"Mama could pay you in eggs."

"And paprika?"

"And paprika."

My stomach accepted the offer.

* * *

I'm not much of a judge of cowmel sickliness, but this one was lying down, head on the straw, tongue lolling out. She smelled atrocious. The two humps on her back flopped listlessly.

"Has she been eating?" I asked.

"Not much. Going on three days now. And hasn't given more than a thimble of milk neither."

When I touched her head and patted her side, she moaned. Her cheeks puffed out.

"Miss, she's going to spit."

I backed up, but the pitiful dribble didn't come close to hitting me. Very sick indeed. "What did the doctor say was wrong?"

"Terrible bad case of lazy gut," the father answered. "Near always fatal in cowmels this old. Tried his medicine anyway. Didn't do a spit-spaddle of good."

If the animal doctor had given the beast up for dead, whatever I did could hardly make her *worse*. I pulled out my grimoire. "I'm going to need a hot fire, a cup that's recently been used to drink milk, garlic, vinegar, and a spoon scrubbed well with ash."

The mother scurried off at my word.

I sent the girl—who seemed capable enough—to bring a thimble of dirt from a freshly dug grave.

What else? A child's tears? No problem. The girl seemed rather attached to the cowmel. Powdered peacock antlers. Snake skin—just the cheap stuff, not basilisk or anything tricky. Cowmel broth? That didn't seem quite fitting. "What do you give the old girl when she needs extra vim?"

"Barley, mostly." The father was trying to look at the grimoire. I pulled it closer to me.

"Go boil some. Save me the water."

I snuck under a neighbor's fence and plucked a single hair from their healthiest-looking cowmel. It's not really stealing, because I'm sure they would have let me take it if I asked, but you can't let people know *everything* that goes into a potion. Then they'd just try to brew things themselves, without any training at all. Which—I actually agree with Madame Azura—might lead to *CHAOS and CALAMITY.*

It took two hours, three small mishaps, and a rather angry burn on my finger, because I only had the one pot and had to keep transferring things.

I followed the recipes exactly…except for the barley water. And the cleansing brew was supposed to be simmered in a silver-rimmed pot. And I wasn't sure how many times to stir it to compensate for the animal's much larger size. Oh, and I added just a touch of paprika to the strength brew at the end, because my binding job had felt a little weak, and paprika's a good fix for that. At least it is in confidence potions. So…I didn't *exactly* follow everything. But a good witch understands the why of the recipe and can adjust. That's what my favorite teacher back in school said.

Madame Azura would have hated her.

The father fed the cleansing potion to the cowmel, spilling half of it into the straw. I waited the approved interval and gave her the strength brew. Then we sat and watched.

A quarter of an hour.

Half an hour.

She snorted. Pulled in her tongue. Picked her head off the dirt and thrashed it around. With a low keen, she pushed herself clumsily to her feet and jumped like a deer out the door.

We followed. The cowmel cavorted around the yard, hindquarters and head like two separate animals in a frantic dance.

The girl held tight to her father's leg.

The cowmel slowed, stopped, and demonstrated messily that her gut was not so lazy after all.

We backed away from the stench.

Her ears twitched. Her long eyelashes fluttered. She sauntered over to her feed and started eating, looking altogether unready to die.

"Strangest thing I ever did see," the father said, not sounding entirely sure if "strange" meant "good" here.

We kept watch all night. After her initial outburst, she turned a bit sluggish and wobbly-footed. Her humps still slumped sideways. She drank bucket after bucket of water. But by mid-morning, she was acting like she'd never been sick at all. The little girl cried. Her parents thanked me profusely. Doctor Gorgo came by and stared at the cowmel and then at me.

"Didn't know you and Madame Azura were into animal witchery now."

"I just thought I'd try."

"Well, if she's still well in a week, I'd say you didn't just try, my girl. Maybe I'll hire you."

A week later, the cowmel was still healthy. Town buzzed with news of my success. I sold fourteen strength and three cleansing potions that week even though—as an apprentice—I wasn't *technically* supposed to do business on my own.

After the seventeenth sale—always an auspicious number—I went to Madame Azura, sure she'd pretend she'd never thrown me out and demand to know where I'd been all this time.

Instead, she stood in the doorway and questioned me on what exactly I'd put in the potions for the cowmel.

With every confession of slight deviance from the recipe, her frown sank and sank until it looked ready to drip off her pointy chin. Then I got to the paprika.

You reckless NINNY. You could have KILLED the poor creature.

Madame Azura didn't care that I hadn't killed the cowmel (*Dumb luck*) or that the animal was going to die anyway (*No excuse for EXPERIMENTING*). Apparently, adding paprika to a strength potion you'd already bound with grave dirt turned it into a fear potion (*You SCARED the poor creature half to death*). Scared her to life, more like. Maybe the fear got her lazy gut moving.

How was I supposed to rely on faulty recipes that didn't even mention the dangers of paprika?

YEARS of APPRENTICESHIP.

I smiled my most winsome smile and asked if that meant she'd keep teaching me.

The door slammed in my face.

* * *

I huffed and steamed for a week. But I also sold five more strength potions—enough to rent myself a modest room in town.

When Florella Tybost, wife of the richest man in town, came round in her little white slippers, cat under her arm, I knew this would be my chance to make some real money.

"I need my hair to match the color of my cat's wings."

Of all the things Mrs. Tybost had ever bought potions for, that was actually one of the least ridiculous.

"My hair is so dull, so much the same," she declared. "Every strand—same, same, same. It's insupportable. But Fluffalilly's wings are so beautiful."

Fluffalilly's fur was a very ordinary shade of pink, but her wings were iridescent purple-blue. Lacey. Completely unsuitable for carrying such a fat and spoiled cat, but Mrs. Tybost didn't seem to mind.

Hair-coloring potions are quite straightforward—if you're looking for oak-colored hair, or beech. Even ebony's not hard…just expensive. But if you don't have a wood chip of the right color, it gets tricky, and if your sample color is something living, then it turns excitingly complicated. Perfect to prove to Madame Azura that I wasn't a turnip-brained ninny.

I named my price—just as ridiculous as her request—and she happily paid.

Apparently even lazy cats aren't so lazy when you try to soak them in saltwater and mermaid scales. Despite Mrs. Tybost tsking and repeating "Bad Fluffalilly" in a tone that was entirely too adoring, I emerged from the battle with several bloody bites and scratches. But victory was mine.

I followed all the important parts of the recipe, even roasting the eggshells for three hours, which is terribly boring, because you have to watch them the whole time or the magic doesn't work. I did add a little slug slime for extra shine and a single grain of gold dust—both of which are completely logical additions which come standard in similar recipes. Madame Azura would have lauded my restraint.

When it came to binding the potion, I pulled a single hair from Mrs. Tybost's head, eliciting a dainty squeak. I counted the times I wrapped it around the wooden spoon. I stirred the prescribed number of stirs. Everything in order. When the magic started jumping around, I gathered its invisible beauty between my fingers and worked the shape of it with hands that knew what to do. Just like a seasoned witch. As I was finishing the binding, it occurred to me that her hair might look even more wing-like and ethereally beautiful if I bound a bit of air into the potion. So I did.

Because Mrs. Tybost wrinkled her nose at most of our potions, I added a little blackberry syrup to the frothy concoction. Maybe more than a little. To match her pretty smile and pink cat. Just so you know, blackberry is totally—well, *almost* totally—compatible with body-altering potions of all descriptions. *Most* descriptions. I did look it up.

"This tastes sweeter than usual," she cooed, patting at her hair as if she expected to feel the change before she'd even finished the cup.

"It takes up to six hours," I warned.

She gave me a long-suffering smile, downed the rest of the potion in one go, and petted her still-ruffled cat. "Quite the best-tasting potion I've ever let touch my poor tongue."

I smiled. As soon as she left, I started making a new sign to hang at my door: *Palatable Potions.*

Maybe I didn't need Madame Azura.

A purposeful knock sounded on my door the next morning. I opened it to see Mrs. Tybost. Her hair had not changed colors. But she grinned and preened and turned around so I could see all of her still-brown hair. Instead of transferring the color of the wings, I had somehow transferred the actual structure. Tiny lacy iridescent wings poked out of her hair everywhere, like a swarm of butterflies had got their feet caught.

"This is more spectacular than I ever dreamed." She hugged a glaring Fluffalilly to her cheek. "We match."

So she wasn't angry that I'd messed up.

No. I hadn't messed up. I'd innovated.

"How did you know the perfect thing?" She teared up in happiness.

I smiled. "I'm a witch. We know many things."

"You're even better than Madame Azura. I'm going to tell everyone."

I admit I let myself gloat a bit. But soon I was too busy to gloat. I made enough money selling potions to buy a better grimoire, a second pot, and some exotic ingredients so I could make more interesting potions.

That's what I was doing one evening when a faint knock broke my attention. I opened the door. A hooded figure had pressed herself flat against the wall outside my door, as if that would make her invisible—when all it did was make her look suspicious.

"May I help you?"

"Shhhh," she whispered. She looked all around, hunched down, and crept through the door. Once inside, she pulled off her hood. I recognized her from the market, where she sold trinkets from a blanket on the ground.

"I'm Reesa," she whispered. "I want to buy a potion."

"Then you've come to the right place. What are you looking for?"

She mumbled something.

"What?"

"Love." She bit her lip until it turned white.

Oooh. Love potions are fun. And notoriously tricky.

"Can you help me?" Her eyes were big and hopeful…and trusting.

I pretended to think for a long time. Then I summoned my most solemn tone. "You must understand that love potions don't *create* love. They just open a person's eyes to what's already there. Even then, they don't always work."

"You're a great witch. I know it will work. I wouldn't have sneaked here in the dark of night if I didn't believe."

Well *sneaked* wasn't the word I would have used for her antics. *Paraded* maybe. And it was hardly beyond dusk. But I smiled. "Let's see if the magic favors you. First, I need to know his name."

She blushed. Hesitated.

"Your secrets are safe with me."

She nodded meekly. "Daevor. The farrier's assistant."

"And I need to know a food he really loves."

"Bacon." No hesitation there.

"Everyone loves bacon."

"He once traded his best laying hen for a single rasher of bacon. He learned how to bake himself cakes…just so he can put bacon in them."

"Bacon cakes?"

"Isn't he wonderful?"

Would the bacon go in the batter? Or just crumbled on top? Would you crisp it up first if you put it in the batter? Would—

"And he shared some of his bacon with me once. So I know he loves me. He just doesn't know he loves me. That's why the magic will work."

This wouldn't even be hard.

The next morning as I was carefully mixing up the potion, a brilliant idea occurred to me. What would be even better than a love potion? A love soup.

The established procedure was to infuse the potion with the food of choice—and I'd do that, of course—but wouldn't it be even better to put the finished potion into the food itself? Soup would be the natural thing, since half the potions I knew used some sort of broth as the base. Love potions usually required beet broth, but if I only used the minimal amount, I could cover the taste with a delicious bacony soup. What's more romantic than a tasty meal shared with the woman you don't realize you love?

I finished up the love potion and sent Reesa a note, asking her to invite her young man to a friendly dinner and then make the most delicious chicken broth she could. The magic would work better if she was involved in this part.

A few hours later she "sneaked" back to my rented room with a pot of soup "hidden" under her coat.

We cut up two entire onions and a bit of garlic and simmered them low in butter for an hour, waiting for them to unlock their soft sweetness.

When they were almost done, we added the bacon and let the fat cook out. Then some mushrooms I'd picked myself. The sweet smell of onion and bacon made my head dance. I couldn't even detect the beety odor from my earlier potion-making. Reesa didn't question anything I did, and when we added her broth, she leaned over the pot and took a whiff. "He'll love this."

"He'll love *you*." I winked and she blushed.

I ladled off a big bowl for myself—for testing purposes, of course—and then transferred the rest from my new copper-rimmed pot to hers. "Before you serve it, fry up more bacon to sprinkle on top. Just before you eat, pour the potion into his bowl." I pressed the bottle into her hands.

"All of it?"

"Yes. Stir it only five times and serve immediately. Don't let anyone else eat from his bowl. You understand?"

She nodded eagerly and left.

I fried myself some bacon garnish and took a spoonful. The earthiness of the mushrooms, the salty deliciousness of the bacon, the sweetness of the onions: perfect. I slowly savored every drop and let myself relax within my bacon-and-success-filled happiness. Reesa's young man was probably deeply in love by now. So deeply in love that—

BANG BANG BANG.

I jumped. The door rattled beneath the knocks. I unlocked it.

Reesa, not sneaking at all, grabbed my arm and tugged. "Daevor's dying."

"Dying of love?"

"No! Just dying. Help me!"

We ran so fast I couldn't even ask what had happened.

When we arrived, Reesa's sister was holding Daevor's head on a pillow on the floor, while his body convulsed and spittle foamed at his mouth and Dr. Larim, the town's most judgmental doctor, tried to examine him. Daevor's eyes rolled up and his lids kept trembling open and closed. I'd never seen anything so horrible.

"What did you do?" the doctor yelled at me.

"I…it was a harmless potion."

"Harmless?"

"Was your bacon spoiled?" I asked Reesa desperately.

"The worst bacon in the world wouldn't do this," the doctor answered before Reesa could. "I need to know what was in that potion of yours."

We weren't supposed to reveal all our secrets. But I wasn't going to let someone die because of a rule like that. So I told him.

"Did she poison him?" Reesa sobbed.

"There's nothing poisonous in that list." Doctor Larim glared at me. "If you're telling the truth."

"I am. But witchery is about how ingredients combine and interact, how the magic binds them. Maybe…maybe something interacted that I didn't expect."

"What's in the soup?"

I began to list the ingredients.

"Mushrooms? Red toadstools maybe?"

"No. The same kind I've picked and eaten a thousand times. I swear. And I ate the soup. Reesa, you ate it, too, right?"

She nodded.

But something tickled my mind. "Make him drink milk with a little ash. Keep him alive. I'll be back."

I'd been a fool to think I didn't need Madame Azura. I ran straight to her house—*our* house. The one I wished she'd never kicked me out of. I banged on the door. "Madame Azura, you were right. Please let me in. I need your help."

Silence.

I banged and screamed.

Finally the door swung open. Madame Azura folded her arms and glared down her nose at me. My courage took one look at her and slunk away, abandoning me there on her doorstep. But I had to fix what I'd done. My voice sounded small as I admitted everything (*Love SOUP? You made love SOUP?*) and what I feared might be the problem (*Of COURSE there was a post-binding reaction*) and asked if it was the mushrooms, even though they were harmless (*If your potion contains beets and ANY OTHER earth-based ingredient, then if you're STUPID enough to combine it with mushrooms, they're NO LONGER HARMLESS. Did you READ the WARNINGS?*) I didn't even defend myself as we scurried around gathering ingredients.

It wasn't fair. Once a potion was bound, usually nothing else interacted… except sometimes things did. Like my paprika weeks before. I had learned that lesson with the cowmel.

Except I hadn't.

Love potions were usually given straight, or in wine or ale. Not food. But I thought I'd innovate.

My grimoire should have warned me.

But it was too basic. It assumed someone at my level would strictly follow the recipe *and* the serving suggestion.

All this came in one giant flash of understanding while Madame Azura set out her silver-lined pot and best binding rod. What if I had killed that poor man? Me. Not my grimoire. Not the mushrooms. *Me.*

* * *

Madame Azura hardly let me help (*If I want someone to make it WORSE, I'll ask*) as she mixed all the potion ingredients in exactly the reverse order

I had, as she added a single seed as the renewing agent, as she fell into that profound concentration of hers and did a reverse binding—always uncomfortably dizzying for me. And time-consuming. Like tying a knot in the opposite direction as usual. While the knot squirmed. Madame Azura, however, was done in a frog's whisker. And I just knew it was perfect.

I shrunk a little further into my shame.

She didn't even let me carry the rest of our supplies as we ran to Reesa's house. I pushed open the door and everyone glared at me. Daevor was on the bed now. Dead? His leg thrashed. He moaned. Not quite dead.

When Madame Azura ducked inside, their glares turned to hope. I hung back as she lined up everything she would need, right by Daevor's bedside.

Then she turned to me. Motioned. She couldn't mean for *me* to do the unbinding? Me, who thought she knew more than her grimoire? Me, who had caused all this? Who had nearly killed a man? Who might yet kill him? Who had never once done a successful unbinding?

The others came to the same conclusion and protested, as Madame Azura explained how the magic worked best if it came from the original practitioner, as she gave me a terrifying look that clearly meant *You do EVERYTHING I say, EXACTLY as I say.*

Her intensity was an invisible hand that pushed me over to Daevor's side.

Trembling, I put my hand on his throat to measure his heartbeat. So frightfully erratic. But I could feel it. I could count it. I told myself very firmly that I could do this. Normally I would have told myself I was a great witch, but I couldn't quite muster those words, even in my head. I took a deep breath.

And I did everything Madame Azura said. Exactly as she said. I poured her antidote into the pot. Added the mushrooms. Waited thirteen heartbeats. Closed my eyes, slipped the binding rod into the mixture, and began the complex stirring pattern. You have to do it blind, which makes it harder to keep true to the patterns, but I focused, blocking out everything but Madame Azura's voice. Her guiding words. The unbinding nausea started, more powerful with each stir of the binding rod. If I threw up now, like I usually did, it would break the spell, so I breathed slowly, stirred, and forced my throat not to react to the sour waves of nausea crashing over me. I felt for the shape of the magic, for the sense of order in my head, the invisible puzzle pieces I'd so carefully bound before.

I took that order.

I carefully positioned it.

And then I destroyed it.

The fragments crashed around me, sharp like glass. I let them scatter, holding my inner self still so I wouldn't grab for the pieces. Thoughts jumped. Images flashed. Nothing made sense. I clung to Madame Azura's firm commands, to the patterns I was still stirring somewhere outside my inner self. *Then* I threw up.

Unbindings really are the worst.

But when I opened my eyes, Madame Azura nodded slightly. Had I done it?

I poured the potion into a cup, tilted Daevor's head backward, and tried to get him to drink. In his not-asleep-not-awake state of misery, he pulled away instinctively, lips closed.

"Help me," I begged. My pride was gone anyway.

Madame Azura stepped in with a practiced hand. We got the potion almost entirely down him.

Reesa held Daevor's hand. The doctor monitored his breathing and heart. I averted my eyes from the half-dead man I had poisoned. Watching for signs of recovery would only reduce me to a useless heap of nerves. Instead I cleaned up my mortifying mess. I had just finished when Reesa started crying. I steadied myself and turned.

Daevor's eyes were open. Yellow and limp, he looked like a candle melted down to almost nothing. But he wasn't thrashing. His mouth wasn't foaming. In fact, he was smiling up at Reesa. "This is nice. Seeing your beautiful face when I open my eyes."

Reesa blushed.

Wait. Had Madame Azura's antidote failed? Or was I just *really* good at love potions? More importantly, he wasn't dead yet, so…things were looking up.

* * *

As Daevor continued not to die, he actually thanked me. The doctor congratulated me in his own terse way. But it was Madam Azura who had known what to do, her words which had led me through, so their praise burned. I quietly thanked Madame Azura and left as soon as she allowed. Sleep did not come easily.

* * *

When I checked on Daevor in the morning, his color had returned. He was walking around, leaning only slightly on his new true love.

Turns out he'd been sweet on Reesa for weeks. He just hadn't summoned the courage to say anything. So…in a roundabout way…my potion did its job. But I didn't charge Reesa. Not a single solitary coin. Not even three weeks later when a quite-recovered Daevor asked her to marry him. I even paid *her* back for the broth she'd made. Good business, you know.

* * *

Nobody put me in the stocks for unlicensed witchery, which I half expected. People still bought potions from me, which I *didn't* expect. But those victories felt hollow.

So one day I marched myself over to Madame Azura's house. I told her I was a good witch (*Because you haven't POISONED anyone yet this week?*) but that I wanted to be a better witch, and I would listen to her at least five times as well as I had before (*Five times zero is still ZERO*) and I would follow the recipes exactly (*Exactly?*) or exactly-ish. I begged for another chance.

She grilled me on my most recent work. I showed her the confidence potion I'd just made (*You used CAT feathers instead of raven feathers?*) and how the grimoire allowed latitude on the feather type (*Latitude on BIRD feathers*) and how I'd done everything else by the book and if no one ever tried cat feathers no one would know how they worked.

You don't TRY NEW THINGS until you're good enough to UNDERSTAND OLD THINGS, turnip brain. To be fair, she didn't actually yell the turnip brain part. But I knew she was thinking it.

So I promised I would learn all the old things (*ALL of them? Unlikely*) so one day I could try the new ones (*Heaven help us then*) and I would work harder than ever (*Then why are you WASTING TIME standing there with your foot in my door and your hands on your hips instead of CHOPPING those stink beetles?*).

Wait. What? Was she saying what I thought she was saying?

Her finger pointed imperiously at her worktable. *Did you hear me, turtle legs? Get CHOPPING.*

I smiled, grabbed the knife, and started prying the hard shells off those smelly little beetles. And I swear I saw the corner of her mouth pull up.

* * *

Though my fingers still itched to see what would happen if I added just a *little* of that nice slug slime to the chicken livers in a fertility potion, and I still added blackberry syrup or mint to everything Madame Azura allowed, I reserved my most inventive additions for the potions we worked on together, carefully checking ingredient interactions.

But one day I will know enough to be the one inventing things on my own. Great things, maybe. Or just tasty ones.

* * *

Reesa eventually forgave me. She and Daevor and I sometimes go mushroom-hunting together or play dice in the evenings. Before their wedding, I made a nice meal for them and some of their friends. An egg fry with bacon—of course—and greens and caramelized parsnips. At the end, I couldn't help it. I added a little—just a pinch—of sage.

And nobody died.

Illustration by Ariel Guzman

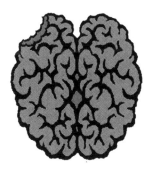

Nothing Happened Here

Louis Evans

"Are you going to the protest?"

The girl thrusts a leaflet into Myra's chest. She is short, stocky, and wearing an absurd outfit: embroidered velvet vest; Qazapol Chargers mesh handball shorts; polyester skullcap; women *and* men's brassards; a nose ring (traditional) and gauges (almost criminally punk); and Crocs. Nothing like Myra's sensible, business-casual-meets-college-student-classy outfit. And her face is different too, round where Myra's chin is thin, soft where Myra's brow is sharp.

But she has the exact same eyes, those golden-brown Urgzawi eyes.

Myra shakes her head, deflects the woman's flyer. The mimeographed words *IT HAPPENED!!!* scream from the top of the neon page.

"I'm not," says Myra. "I mean I am, but I won't. I can't—"

"We can't let them erase our history!" says the girl, but Myra is already moving and she lets the flow of foot traffic take her away as swiftly as she can manage.

* * *

The **Urgzawi Genocide**[2][3][4] (Urgarmantic: **Amlikmache**[a]) was the <u>Idric Empire</u>'s systematic <u>mass murder</u>, <u>ethnic cleansing</u>, <u>expulsion</u>, and <u>Idrification</u> of the <u>Urgzawi</u> population following the <u>Idro-Urgaritic War</u> and the <u>Fall of Qazapol</u>. International scholarship estimates that approximately 90% of the pre-conquest Urgzawi were killed or expelled, around 1.4 million people,[2][5][7] while the <u>Idric government</u> officially denies the genocide and claims that "under 350,000" civilians died in the war.[5][9] Most Urgzawi today live in diaspora communities, particularly in the Melian Commonwealth.[14] The Melian Commonwealth is the only Great Power to recognize the Urgzawi genocide, and the Commonwealth observes the 6th of Tishrei (the anniversary of the Fall of Qazapol) as Urgzawi Genocide Remembrance Day. [6][8] This policy has been a persistent source of tension in Melian-Idric relations—

* * *

"That's it for this week," says Professor Imkoff. "Now, make sure you have a good time at the parade this weekend!" He has a classically handsome face, an Idric face. Aquiline nose; strong jaw; dark, dark blue eyes. Tall, too, with an easy, athletic grace.

If it weren't for the trimmed beard and modern suit in place of muttonchops and military dress, he would be the spitting image of Prince-General Heitzmychoff, the conqueror of Qazapol. There's a portrait of the Prince-General in the student union at the university. Myra sees it every day at lunch; first-, third-, and fifthday breakfasts too. A lot of those old imperial officers were squat little toads but, if the painting is to be believed, the Prince-General was the genuine article. In a wildly popular third-rate series of historical erotica, the Prince-General has a torrid affair with a Urgzawi tribal princess. "Her eyes like honey, her kisses like honey wine." Heitzmychoff deflowers her "beside a babbling mountain brook, beneath the wide and savage moon"; eventually she becomes his lifelong, devoted consort.

One hundred and sixty-seven years ago exactly, on the sixth of Tishrei, the sun rose above the walls of independent Qazapol for the last time. In the field before the city the Idric army was encamped, and in the hills opposite sat the command tent. The Prince-General—who was not quite as handsome as his flattering portrait, not quite as handsome as Myra's history teacher (a vain man, who has access to modern plastic surgery), but who was, in fact, tall and strong and well favored—sat at the head of the table, surrounded by his staff.

"And when the city falls?" asked his aide-de-camp.

The Prince-General did not smile. He did not frown. "Not one of that subhuman filth should be permitted to survive."

Myra's got an ancestor who was there, maybe. A great-great-etc.-grandmother, or perhaps an uncle. Or maybe the family lived on the other side of the river, in the poor town outside the walls, which surrendered before the siege and so was merely subjected to dispossession, expulsion, mass starvation, occasional rape, and mild recreational murder. Grandma tells the story, and she says she got it from her grandma, and so on, but these days she gets confused.

Myra sits underneath the portrait of the Prince-General every weekday to have lunch. The cafeteria cooks good, hearty, authentic Idric food. Porridges and stews. Even though the kitchen staff is majority Urgzawi, the cafeteria never serves the roast goat or mountain salads of Old Qazapol. The students would riot.

Here, in the present, right now, on a fifthday afternoon in a history lecture hall in Emperor Axamander University in the city of Qazapol in the Urgzawnuk Province of the Republic of Idreis, Myra's history professor is laughing about the parade. Professor Imkoff—who has never given Myra a bad grade, who is unfailingly supportive of her grad school ambitions in his office hours—is telling his students to have a good time this weekend. "After all, I certainly will!" he says.

He is still laughing, showing his whole mouth, and the students are laughing, too. Every tooth a tombstone, every throat a grave. "Remember," says Professor Imkoff, and the students chant it along with him, "Nothing Happened Here!"

* * *

—for the past several years, the Idric population of Qazapol has responded to Remembrance Day with the "Nothing Happened Here" parade.[28] The self-consciously ironic[31] denialist celebration was first organized by the nationalist student group, Scholars of the Fatherland[article needed], but has grown dramatically and is now sponsored by the office of the Mayor of Qazapol—

* * *

How do you get an Urgzawi to stop smelling?
   Cut off his nose!
Why did the Urguk starve to death?
   Too busy fucking the goat to milk it!!
What do you call a thousand shiteyes buried up to their necks in sand?
   A good start!!!
– "Urgzawi Jokes", funny.humor.id.co

* * *

It's sixthday afternoon, the day of the parade—Nothing Happened Here!—and of course Myra's not at the protest. Of course not. She's not some teenaged idiot looking to shout herself hoarse and get spat on or G-d forbid arrested, detained, *expelled*. Myra is an adult and she is dealing with the anniversary of her genocide like an adult: by going out to a shitty bar with her boyfriend, and also his friend.

Myra's boyfriend Zanzin is Idric, and that's fine. It's more than fine, it's good. Myra's boyfriend is a sensible, sensitive man. He's skinny and when he smokes sadly outside a bar he looks like an author photo from a really good Existentialist novel. He reads international feminist blogs and has impeccable progressive politics and when Myra cooks Urgzawi food he doesn't complain. Zanzin has never once made a crack about Myra or her family.

Well, never twice, anyway.

Not the same crack twice, anyway, which is what counts. He can learn. He's learning.

The only problem is, all his friends are assholes.

Grigry is four beers into what Myra had been promised was a two-beer night.

"The fuckin Melians," he says, slurring every word. "Where do they get off being so high and mighty? In their country, they kill the gwanches and 'binos and the fuckin' hanar—"

Myra is at least passably trilingual and she has read a lot of Melian blogs and she knows that 1) yes, the Melians do definitely have a domestic history of genocide and displacement and racism targeted toward exactly the groups Grigry is referring to but also 2) you're not supposed use any of those words, at all, ever, fucking hell. And 3), which she says:

"We were talking about the Idric Empire," she says. She's doing her pushy leftist bitch voice, which Zanzin likes when they're alone but hates when they're in public, so he cringes into his beer, shoulders around his ears.

He's learning. He can do better.

"Fuck the Idric Empire!" says Grigry, except he doesn't seem to mean it as a term of abuse because he immediately belts out a stanza and a half of the national anthem. Normally that would be enough to get them thrown out of the bar—Grigry is a *terrible* singer—but on Nothing Happened Day everybody is just like that.

"We're talking about the Melians," Grigry says, when he finishes promising to die for the immortal brotherhood of Idreis.

"No," says Myra. "We're talking about Idreis. Idreis and Urgzaw."

"All you—" begins Grigry. He burps. It goes on for a long time. Finally, he says, "All you Urgzawi—"

And thank G-d he called her that, because if he'd used any of the other words she could see flipping through the wet dumb meaty hole behind his eyes, *Urguks* or *shiteyes*, she'd have thrown her drink in his face and the night would have taken a turn for the worse.

"All you Urgzawi are just Melian spies!" Grigry pounds his glass on the bar.

"Fuck that," says Myra. When she's mad she gets precise and thin. Her lips get thin and her dark eyes narrow and her elbows tuck in toward her body and her voice gets maybe half as loud but also somehow ten times harder to ignore.

"Our people, my people, we're not Melians. We've lived here forever." Grigry is rumbling a building fury but once Myra's in this mood she is going to finish her point no matter what, so she looks him straight in the eyes and says, "We were here before you."

Grigry's looking back at Myra and now his eyes are narrowing, too, and suddenly Myra is thinking about how she weighs sixty kilos to his ninety, how his arms are like the haunches of a bull, how if he forgets to put down the glass before he hits her there will be shards in her eyes and she will be just another dumb Urgzawi bitch who didn't know to stay home on the single dumbest day of the year, just one day—

But Grigry doesn't hit her. Instead, he narrows his eyes and then turns from her to Zanzin with an expression of theatrical disregard. As if to say *I've unpersoned you.*

"Zazzy," he says. "Control your woman."

Zanzin looks up from his beer. He looks at Grigry. He looks at Myra.

"Zanzin," says Myra, "you're better than this," and even as she says it she knows it's the wrong thing to say, knows that it'll all break wrong now, and curses herself for saying it even though she knows there was no right thing to say, was never any magic incantation that would give Zanzin the spine to take a punch in a bar for a cause that he argues for but doesn't believe in. She knows she doesn't even care about Zanzin, that she will never fuck Zanzin again, perhaps she will never fuck any other Idric ever again, because in this moment she doesn't even want Zanzin to stand up and to tell Grigry he's a racist piece of shit, she wants something vaster and impossible, she wants someone other than Zanzin, other than the Urgzawi men her mother pushes on her. She wants to be out at the bar this night with an angel, twelve feet tall and with a flaming sword, and when Grigry narrows his eyes she wants her angel lover to stand up so that their head bursts through the roof and she wants them to smite Grigry with a bolt of lightning that goes through time and space and makes Professor Imkoff drop dead and Prince-General Heitzmychoff explode on his horse and Emperor Axamander IX burn to a crisp in his palace, two hundred years ago and two thousand kilometers away. She wants to see all Idreis burn, all the way back to the first fucking log laid in their first shitty little river-bandit township a millennium ago, when her people were already sages and astronomers in the city of Qazapol, and she knows it's not progressive and she knows it's not universalist but she knows what she wants and G-d in Hell would she fuck that beautiful angel afterwards on every surface of the incinerated bar—

"Myra," says Zanzin, in a voice that he thinks is sweet but has, in fact, always driven Myra properly insane with irritation. "Maybe we'd better go."

"Yeah," says Myra. "I'd better."

* * *

So now Myra's at the protest.

She shouldn't be and tomorrow when she calls up her mother she's going to get such a scolding for risking her pretty little smart little stuck-up little head, and the perfectly marriageable daughter's body attached to it at the neck. But what the hell.

It's seven o'clock and the sun's going down. Half of the Nothing Happened Here parade is at night.

Nothing good ever happens at a nighttime parade.

But so far everyone seems pretty relaxed, a vast loose river of pedestrians and marching bands and floats and food carts all streaming downtown along Heitzmychoff Boulevard.

There are about maybe two hundred people at the protest, compared to probably twenty thousand at the parade. It makes sense. The city's only fifteen percent Urgzawi—add in Idrics of conscience and teenage rebels and maybe only twenty percent would be even remotely interested in protesting—and yeah, you have to be about twenty times dumber than average to come out for the protest on the single dumbest night of the year. So, one percent.

The girl who tried to give Myra the flier—her name it turns out is Svyla—is standing at the front of the protest, screaming at the parade. Her sign says "Silence = Death," which, well, it's a little appropriative but who the fuck cares, it's a classic for a reason. Of course, she's scrawled the slogan in Urgarmantic (which these days is always written in Idric consonantal script because, duh, empire) and so to the Idric passerby it looks like it says "Pastry = Baby". Total shitshow, but what are you going to do.

It doesn't really matter. The Idric parade marchers already know what Urgzawi protestors are screaming at them, that's the whole point. "Nothing Happened Here"; what a fucking farce. The parade only makes sense if you already know what happened!

Myra has her own sign. She wasn't planning to come to the parade or the protest and so she had to improvise. She's proud of what she came up with.

There's a painting, by Fruvivsko. *Barbarians Fleeing the Sack of Kazapoll*. It's medium-famous. Because the painting is from back when the Idrics were proud of the genocide, before they started denying it, it shows the whole damn thing: burning walls, mothers with babies held to their breasts, men cut down in droves. (Well, not the whole thing: just one city, and even that sanitized, no rapes or death marches or dogs feasting on corpses. But enough of it.)

So: an Idric painting glorifying an Idric atrocity. Very nearly the ethnocultural equivalent of a signed confession. And because the painting is a classic painting of Qazapol, you can, you know, just *buy* a poster at the university gift shop.

You ever walk into an Idric bookstore with an Urgzawi face and try to pay twenty marks for a painting of the genocide of your people on We Deny That Genocide Day? It is awkward as hell. Eventually the woman at the cash register—who had perfectly Idric features, but ice-gray Vuman eyes—just gave Myra the poster for free. (She was gorgeous; Myra *really* should have gotten her number. Tomorrow; she'll go by tomorrow.)

So Myra's at the protest, holding up a classic painting, all Romantic reds and oranges, showing her great-great-something-grandpa getting knifed to death, she supposes, and the people of the city are walking by in waves, some of them pointing and laughing, a few making obscene suggestions, most of them just strolling right past, waving Idric flags, singing patriotic songs, eating stews out of bread bowls and popsicles from street carts. Svyla is shouting from the front of the protest, and a couple of her friends are shouting, too, including two guys who are both, Myra thinks, her boyfriends, but it's all kind of a mess. A dozen trumpeters from some nearby high school march by and drown them out completely.

Myra thought she'd be feeling something now, some rightness, some connection to her ancestors, to the Urgzawi halfway around the world in Melios, the community leaders who are putting on traditional garb and black brassards at this exact instant to march in solemn memorials, some connection to that angel she dreamt about in the bar—

Instead, she feels angry and scared and sad and alone. Idreis is such an enormous entity, such a heavy *weight*, a parade of tens of thousands, an army of millions, a nation of hundreds of millions, and here she is, just a single wet little thing, exposed on the pavement, the weight of all of those people crushing down on her chest, the pressure building—

And when the pressure squeezing on her chest gets tight enough, words come out.

"It happened here," says Myra. "It happened here. It happened here!"

A couple of the people next to her pick up the chant. "It happened here! It happened here!" And now the whole protest is chanting, suddenly, in unison: "IT HAPPENED HERE! IT HAPPENED HERE!"

It's kind of loud, suddenly. Kind of powerful. The parade slows down and then it backs up on itself, and now instead of a couple dozen Idrics strolling past and laughing it's suddenly two hundred, three hundred, five hundred people, young men most of them, staring.

Maybe they should stop chanting at this point but it's impossible.

"IT HAPPENED HERE! IT HAPPENED HERE! IT HAPPENED—"

Someone throws the first bread bowl. It lands wetly on Svyla's left-hand boyfriend and beef stew splatters across his shirt and Myra is praying that he won't go over there, won't take a swing—

And her prayers are answered, something in the chant is keeping him rooted to the ground, keeping all of them rooted to the ground as the bread bowl is followed by a rain of trash, empty water bottles and beer cans and popsicle sticks—

"—HERE! IT HAPPENED HERE! IT—"

And Myra's saying to herself it's not worth it, when they throw the first brick I'm going to run, this is stupid, I should be running already, why am I *standing* here—

Myra doesn't know it and she's never gonna learn but she *did* have a great-something-uncle at Qazapol, when the walls fell. Myra's uncle Tasmed was the twelfth-best sniper in all of Urgzaw (mountain boys, they love to keep score) and when the wall was breached he took himself to the Tower of Unfallen Tears (built most of a millennium before for the court astronomers of the Malak of Qazapol) and he barricaded every door and locked himself on the roof with four hundred rounds of ammunition and played high-stakes live-fire king of the hill with the whole Idric Imperial Army. Myra's uncle Tasmed sent a lot of barefaced boys straight to hell that day; in the end, they had to get him with dynamite. They got him, though. Him, and his wife, and their kids.

"—HAPPENED HERE! IT HAP—"

It's not a brick. It's just one guy, one ordinary-looking guy in a tracksuit, and he steps up and he punches Svyla right in the face. Clean across, like a boxer. Svyla topples back and one of her boyfriends grabs her and the other one goes straight for the Idric's midsection, and the Idric crowd surges forward in reply, and so now it's a riot.

And impossibly Myra is still not running away, she is moving *forward*, she has connected with the spirit of her ancestors at the worst *possible* time, she is holding the poster in front of herself like a shield and she is somehow still shouting IT HAPPENED HERE IT HAPPENED HERE and in the darkness someone takes a swing at her and she swings back, her hands connecting with something, someone else reeling back, but there are more of them, more and more of them, and she tries to fight but they bear her down to the ground and they are kicking her and she's looking up and trying to see is it Professor Imkoff? Is it Grigry? Is it the emperor or the general or the president? Is it Zanzin? And she can't tell because it looks like all of them and through all the blood in her teeth she is somehow *still* shouting IT HAPPENED HERE IT HAPPENED—

And up above her the man is screaming back, *WE NEVER DID THAT AND WE'LL DO IT AGAIN—*

Illustration by Kat D'Andrea

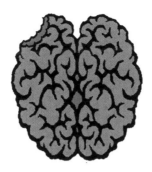

Scaling Up Business

Niall Spain

It was the first time Tessa had been sober in days, but it didn't feel like it. Whisked from a holding cell to the courtroom to this sleek, dark car. Not where she expected to end up. Not where she deserved to.

"You've got some spine," the man said. He sat across from her—short and slim—but something about him made her feel like he was bigger; pressed right up into her face. She'd have leaned back if the seats reclined. "Not many people would try something like that."

Probably because it was stupid. She should be in jail, or dead, and the man knew he was the only reason she wasn't. "He deserved it."

"Don't we all." Not too long ago, Tessa wouldn't have agreed with him. "Care for a drink?"

More than anything. He produced a bottle from some hidden compartment and poured two fingers into a crystal tumbler. It was sipping whiskey but she'd been dry for a day of shaking, vomiting, and nausea, and it was the only thing that could fight the ache in her head and maybe win. She knocked it back, closed her eyes, and felt the warmth course through her like electricity.

When she opened them, the man was filling her glass again. He didn't seem to mind her wasting it. Probably didn't mean much to someone who had their own driver and hidden drink compartments.

"Do you know who I am?" He fixed her with sharp, gray eyes.

Tessa hesitated. "My brother worked for you?"

He nodded. "Terrible thing that happened to him."

That hit her like a slap. She downed her second glass. "Will you deal with him? The man that…"

"The man you almost *dealt with* yourself?" He smiled. She couldn't do the same. "Not now, I'm afraid."

"Why?" she pressed, heedless of how dangerous this man was. Her ears still rang from the day before.

"He'll be at some underground hospital by now having your bullet removed. Besides…" He finished the last of his whiskey. "Politics."

"Why did you get me out?"

Tessa's lawyer had never shown up. A fleet of well-dressed sharks had arrived in his stead and crushed the case against her in a day. She wasn't sure how—she'd been in a daze—but considering who'd picked her up outside the courthouse, she was certain lawyers weren't the extent of it. Bribes at minimum. Or threats.

"You're an accountant," he said.

"I was." After her brother's death, her job had been the next thing to go following her sobriety.

"Well, I'm offering you a job."

"Seriously?"

His smile died. "I need someone new. You've got spine, and your brother was a good soldier. Besides—" He filled her glass again. "—without me, you might well have gone away for the rest of your life."

"So it's not exactly an offer, is it?"

"Compared to jail I guess not. You're welcome."

Another glass down. "What do I call you?"

"You don't."

The car stopped. Through tinted windows, she saw large warehouses looming around them, circled by flocks of gulls. They didn't make a sound; nothing outside did. She wondered if that was another rich person thing. Or maybe the car was bulletproof.

"So some money's gone missing?"

"Not exactly."

* * *

They wouldn't give Tessa spirits. Nothing highly flammable was allowed in the warehouse. They had a fire suppression system that would lock the place down and pump it with CO_2, so they weren't taking any chances. When she'd asked what would happen to *her* if the alarm got triggered, all she'd gotten was a grim laugh. "If that happens, no one inside is making it out. Nor should they."

The most she could get was wine then, which wasn't ideal, but she'd make do. At least they'd brought her a vineyard's worth. They didn't seem to care how sloshed she got, unlike her previous job. If she failed though, she knew she'd be far worse than fired.

She'd added half a bottle of red to the whiskey in her system—doing a decent job of numbing the general pain of what was left of her life—but even so, the figures she was staring at cut through the haze. People with money like this existed of course—everyone knew it—but actually seeing it tallied up looked like a bad joke.

Her office was a small room overlooking the warehouse floor; nothing but rows of two story shelves stacked with wooden crates. It had a desk, a grimy coffee machine, a shitty laptop with no internet—her phone had no signal either; they'd given her an actual *pager* instead—and a green, stained couch. Along with an ill-lit bathroom, it was her home for the foreseeable future.

She didn't mind. She planned to be drunk enough to sleep anywhere. Besides, Rourke had survived. He was no less dangerous than the people she was mixed up with now, and his crew would be able to find her home easily. She knew what they'd do if they caught her.

When she'd pulled that gun on him, she figured she'd kill him or die. She hadn't counted on this third option and she had no idea what to do with it. As much as she didn't want to live, she couldn't quite face the idea of dying. Especially painfully. For now, she'd stick with what she did best: alcohol and work.

She delved as far back as she could before the wine and darkness pulled her under.

* * *

The morning brought headaches and confusion, but once Tessa managed to remember where she was—and downed a glass to take the edge off— she discovered the boss hadn't been wrong. The problem wasn't missing money: there was *extra*.

Without the luxury of a bank to keep their cash, the company averaged a ten percent monthly loss for spoilage: money lost to rats, damp, or insects. It was more than most people saw in a year. There was an entire section dedicated to the funds spent combating this wastage—shoring up the foundations, buying a small fortune in traps and plastic wrap—but apparently her predecessor could only do so much.

Until recently, that is. Two months ago that number had started to plummet. The last spoilage count, a week previous, had dropped to only three percent. The difference was staggering. Tessa could buy a small home in the countryside *outright*.

Her pager buzzed, showing just one word. *Door.*

The boss was waiting for her with a grease-stained brown paper bag. "You're still kicking," he said. "Glad we were right to leave you with your shoelaces."

"What's this?"

"Breakfast sandwiches. There's a selection. I'm sure something will suit you."

Her stomach was sour. The thought of food made her feel ill. She'd have to eat at some point though. "The accountant who did these…can I talk to him?"

He shook his head. "Dead as disco, I'm afraid."

"Did you…?"

He laughed. "We thought about it, but we needed to prove his guilt first. Then he was involved in the hit."

"The—" It took her a second. "He was with Peter?"

"Your brother was guarding him."

That sobered her right up. Was this job related to Peter's death? "There's no money missing though. Why consider killing him?"

"If there's more money now, there's a reason there wasn't before. It always lined up with our expected wastage, so we didn't care, but if our losses lessened at some point and the number *didn't*…"

"Why would he start reporting it then?"

"Why indeed? We should hire our very own accountant to figure it out, shouldn't we?"

He shut the door in her face. The heavy locks slammed into place like she'd gone to jail after all. The unmistakable waft of bacon was too much, too soon, so she set the food down on a nearby shelf. Numbers were one thing. Either they were being misreported or the preventative measures had somehow, drastically, kicked in. Regardless, the only way to verify the reports was to actually *see* the money; make sure the protection was working, and get her own count.

If her brother's killer was involved…

Patrick Rourke. He'd managed to get an innocent verdict despite multiple witnesses to his triple homicide and the news had broken her. She could still see his face when they'd met: wide eyed and grinning even though he'd just been shot. She'd been tackled a moment later by a bystander, hauled to prison in a blur of questions and fingerprints.

She shouldn't have gone free either. Apparently money talks louder than guilt.

She couldn't dwell on it. She found a crowbar propped against the wall and managed to pop the top off one of the crates stacked on the shelves. She'd expected money—vacuum-sealed and coated in rat poison—but instead she was greeted by stacks of cherry-red toasters.

Tessa assumed the gang had bribed enough people to keep the warehouse safe, but it made sense that they wouldn't just have the cash lying about. Where the hell were they keeping it then?

None of the crates stood out. They were the same uniform pale wood, **THIS WAY UP** printed on the side in black. The money couldn't have been hidden within the frame of the shelves either, or else the damp and the rats wouldn't have been a problem.

The damp and the rats…

Her eyes were drawn to the walls, all green and corrugated. It was that or under the floor.

It didn't take long once she knew where to look. There were low rectangular grates on the walls, gleaming like someone had taken care of them. She knew by the chill in the air that they weren't used for heating.

It was only when she'd found a hidden latch in the corner that she realized there was a chance they were part of the fire suppression system. No alarms sounded when she lifted it open though, and she didn't fall to the ground choking. Besides, there was nothing behind the grates but dark, empty space.

It was funny. Two weeks ago you couldn't have paid her to climb into the walls after reading reports about a rat problem so bad the gang was losing thousands a week. Now though, she just finished her wine and crawled in. Either the money was misreported, or the measures had finally worked, and she needed the proof for herself. That was it.

She could stand inside, the hidden space going up to the roof, wide enough for her to almost spread her arms fully. The flashlight on her phone didn't reveal any dark shapes scurrying towards her, but it did show her something more interesting. The money.

It was stacked in huge plastic blocks that reflected the light strangely. Already she could see hundreds upon thousands of bills. It was bad enough seeing the figures written down. Quite another to be staring at more money than she'd ever made.

Nothing seemed damaged. She edged around the stack and found more. Countless blocks of notes; all wrapped in plastic, seemingly untouched. Maybe it was the simple solution after all—measures perfected after weeks of trial and error—and she could wash her hands of this job by dinner. She wasn't sure what would happen to her then, but she didn't care.

Then she saw her first rat.

She thought it was two of them before she realized it was just gigantic and ripped in half. The blood leaking from it had long since dried. Clearly it hadn't been poisoned, but there were no visible traps. It wasn't the only casualty either. Slightly further on, she found a little rat massacre. A dozen bodies lay on the floor, all torn apart. Beyond them were more dark shapes, but these were different.

She stepped carefully between the corpses until she could make them out. It was cash: a trail of bills that led away into the darkness. The nearest block was half empty. She crouched down and fingered the plastic at the corner. It hadn't been chewed through. The slit was clean, like someone had taken a scalpel to it.

Was someone stealing? If so, why stop? How had they gotten away with it? The half empty brick was obvious, and the trail of bills leading away was cartoonish. After the danger of getting into the warehouse and making away with a small fortune, who would leave that in their wake?

No one in their right mind. Not unless it was a trail they wanted you to follow.

There was no way she couldn't. Note after note, corpse after corpse, until she turned the corner and finally saw something move. Just a glimpse of something long and sinuous—like a snake with legs—before it disappeared into the shadows.

What the fuck?

She'd found what she was looking for though. The trail ended in a circular mound of cash, easily thousands of dollars.

She reached out to check the notes and something hissed at her. She shone her light and saw the creature hiding behind a nearby pipe. It was scaled, its mouth open to reveal rows of needle-like teeth like a puppy's. Two large, amber eyes reflected the light. It was about the length of her leg. On its back, barely visible in the shadows, she could see two tiny wings.

She didn't know much about animals, but she had a fair idea this thing shouldn't exist.

Unsteadily, she turned around and left.

* * *

Tessa had read about alcohol-induced hallucinations—pink elephants or snakes—but she was fairly sure that only happened when you *stopped* drinking, which she hadn't. Besides, nowhere had anyone mentioned imagining a goddamn tiny dragon.

Her buzzer vibrated. *Door.*

The boss handed her another bag as some goons slid a crate of water bottles across the threshold. He studied her face. God knows how she looked. Sleep hadn't exactly come easy.

"Tell me there's still *some* of the wine left." She snorted. He paused before leaving. "Peter was a good man. He wouldn't want you joining him so soon."

He was gone before she figured out whether that was a threat or actual concern. At least he hadn't asked about her investigation. What would she say? The rats aren't a problem anymore because a dragon's eating them. *A dragon.* She was insane.

The smell of breakfast had the opposite effect today though, and she was through a bottle of water and two sandwiches in a matter of minutes. Once she was full, she knew she couldn't put it off any longer. She needed to be sure.

Tessa was back in the walls a minute later. This time she brought the crowbar. For a second she thought she had imagined it all. The first rat was gone, but there was still a stain on the ground where it had been. The plastic farther on was still sliced open, too. If anything, it was missing even more money than before.

She paused at the corner to take a breath. Her head ached but she was as sure as she could be that she was lucid. When she stepped around the corner, though, the impossible thing was still there.

It didn't run this time. It turned sideways and arched its back—tiny wings spread wide—like a cat trying to make itself look bigger. It hissed. At least, Tessa thought that was what it was trying to do. It sounded more like a rusty hinge.

It was real.

Tessa wasn't sure how long she stood there staring but eventually the creature curled up on what was clearly its nest. Its scaled lids didn't close fully though, the lizard feigning being relaxed. It was watching her.

The money beneath it—even though it must have gathered it with its mouth or talons—seemed unharmed. The trail of bills from the day before was gone, too; presumably added to the pile. She'd been tasked with figuring out why the money seemed to be spoiling less. This little guy—or gal—had to be it.

Which was an issue, because what the hell was she supposed to tell the boss? He wouldn't believe her. If he did…she didn't want to find out what would happen to the thing. She shifted and its eyes snapped open. It gave that squeak again, fearsome as a stuffed toy.

A month ago she'd been worried about how she'd find time for the gym during the tax season rush. Now here she was, a shell of a person. Her brother was gone. Her job, her life. And she was staring at a dragon trying its best to be ferocious.

She needed a closer look. She got what was left of her breakfast and returned. The little creature was clearly still nervous, but there was a visible change in its behavior. It leaned forward. Its tongue flickered out. It stared as she opened the bag and tore a strip of cold bacon from her sandwich.

"Better than rat, I'll bet."

She moved closer until the scaly noodle looked so tense it was clearly either about to bolt or spring at her—she had no idea if it was dangerous—and placed the bacon on the ground. Spreading her hands, she retreated. "It's good. Try it," she said, as soothing as possible.

It glanced at the bacon quickly, like it thought she was trying to trick it, but its questing tongue gave it away. It was interested. "I'll give you a minute."

She stepped out of view. A second later came the quick patter of feet on the ground. When she looked back, the dragon was in its nest, the cold, crispy bacon in its mouth. It stared at her, eyes wide, before it bit down. *Crunch.* The rest was gone in an instant. It made weird, happy grumbles.

She hoped bacon was okay for dragons.

The thing snuffled around its nest, methodically licking up each and every crumb. Then, one by one, it pinned down the notes it had gotten food on and started to clean them. Carefully, seriously, like a cat grooming its kittens. The dragon made sure every note was perfect before it stuffed them back into place.

Yeah. She'd found the culprit.

* * *

Three days later and the creature came running when it saw her. Tessa was still a little wary of it, but the daily bacon seemed to have won it over. It only got aggressive if she approached its bed. That would be a problem eventually, but for now she was simply fascinated.

"You look better," the boss had said that morning. She felt better. She'd been forgetting to drink lately—so preoccupied with the little creature in the walls—and she ate what she didn't share with the dragon.

"Thanks, trying to focus."

He nodded. "Any progress?" She hesitated. "What?"

"This is going to sound dumb."

"I've heard worse."

"I think he finally just got the traps set up right and in enough volume. I haven't seen any spoilage since I started."

"So you found the money?" She froze. Was that an issue? He only sighed though. "Well, maybe it's that simple. Here's the thing." He leaned in, his breath heavy with cigar smoke. "I expect spoilage. Comes with the territory. When that stopped though, it meant either he'd been incompetent for years, or he'd been stealing and had a change of heart, see?" She could only nod. "As our new accountant, I don't care which it was. I just care that it stays that way. Understood?"

"Of course."

"We can do a lot with an extra ten percent." For the first time, his smile seemed genuine.

He shut the door in her face. She was already rummaging through the bag he'd given her. What would the little thing think of smoked salmon? Tessa was almost at the nest before the smell of burning stopped her dead. She dashed around the corner to see the little lizard, tail lashing side to side proudly, a freshly-dead rat between them. This one wasn't ripped apart though. It was charred.

"No!" she shouted. "Bad!"

It skittered away, eyes wide. She dropped the food and fumbled for her water. All she could think of was the suppression system taking away their air, the little dragon dying beside her. No alarms sounded as she doused the corpse though.

Tessa fell against the wall and slid to the ground.

Holy shit. *Of course* it could breathe fire. She should have seen that coming. The little creature was staring at her from its pile, bills scattered in its haste to flee her. Its eyes were big. She felt terrible. "I'm sorry, I know you don't understand, but it's for your own good. Here." She pulled some smoked salmon from her bagel. "I'll make it up to you."

It took the salmon from her fingers gently, and started to nibble it, making little happy sounds deep in its throat like a frog trying to purr. Its tail was resting against her leg. It was the first time they'd touched. Tessa held still so she didn't startle it.

It needed a name. She wasn't sure what would fit though. She was pretty sure dragons were meant to have grand names, but it felt ridiculous looking down at the little thing. "I don't know what gender you are," she whispered. She wanted to pet it, but she didn't dare. "So I guess I have to get creative. What about Dollar? Johnny Cash?" It looked up at her. Probably still hungry. It was so small, curled around in a semi-circle like a… "Cashew," she said. She laughed. It was perfect.

Cashew gulped down the last of the fish and turned to look at her. Something in its eyes sparkled slightly. Tessa felt a pressure on her forehead, like someone poking her. It worsened by the second until it felt like someone was pushing something into her brain. She tried to get to her feet, but couldn't.

Whatever it was spread her mind wide open.

For a second she didn't know where she was, then she was back in the walls, the feeling gone, the world spinning around her. She tried to breathe deeply and slow her pounding heart before she realized that she could see herself, lying against the wall, in her own mind.

Her eyes snapped open, fixing on the little dragon that was staring at her with apparent concern. No, not apparent. She could feel it in her head, a jumble of emotions and sensations that roughly translated into worry, a little fear, and the thought that Tessa must be cold, sitting on the ground without a comfortable hoard beneath her…

"You…did this??"

The little thing perked up instantly at that. It could understand her. Holy shit. Tessa closed her eyes. Was she dreaming? Was this a mental break or—

Something sharp jabbed her in her ankle. She looked down to see the dragon withdrawing one small talon. Before she could even think to get annoyed, another image popped unbidden into her head. An image of the smoked salmon.

"Oh, wow. My god."

It was all so much. Her brother's death, the dragon, now *this*? Her breath started to come fast, ragged, until Cashew crept forward and, carefully, nuzzled at her leg. The image of food faded. All she felt from the little thing was…concern?

She reached for it, hesitating when she felt a sudden spike of fear from their bond. She tried to do whatever Cashew was doing, communicate that she didn't mean it any harm, and it must have worked because the dragon relaxed and let her place a hand on its back. She traced its scales from the bony ridge of its brow down to its flicking tail. They were surprisingly smooth and soft. She felt second-hand satisfaction, tingles running through the little thing's body.

It chirped happily and pressed into her.

They sat there for some time—Tessa couldn't say how long—until the thing stiffened up suddenly. She snapped her hand away; she'd owned enough cats to be cautious. Instead, another image filled her head, this time a sequence. Tessa earlier on—tall, scary—looming over a charred rat and yelling.

Flashes of fear and sadness followed in the wake of the images. The little creature looked up at her with big eyes, questioning.

"I'm sorry. I didn't mean to scare you," Tessa said. "It's just…dangerous. For both of us."

She thought of the vents, of the CO_2, tried to send it to the creature in a way that would make sense to the thing. She got something back, like an echo: silver scales, invisible breath.

A protector of the rats?

Tessa hesitated. "Kind of. You can still eat them. Just no fire."

Relief washed through the bond. Less because it—*she*—wanted to eat the rats and more because she wasn't about to leave them alive to mess with her hoard. Again, the little dragon sent images of the smoked salmon.

Tessa laughed. "Don't worry, I'll feed you. There are other rules though, first."

It was almost comical the way the dragon straightened up to pay attention.

"You have to stay in here, unless I say otherwise." She could sense that Cashew didn't mind that. Her hoard was here and, besides, it was cold and scary outside. "Especially when other people come."

This time there was an undercurrent to the acceptance. Cashew didn't like the smells or the deep scary voices, but there was a vein of *something* else…if someone entered the walls, she'd stand between them and her hoard.

It was gone as quickly as it came, and Tessa didn't like it, but she'd work with what she got for now. She'd just have to make sure no one came in here but her.

"Thank you," she said. "Now, if you're hungry, I need help with what's left here."

Clearly Cashew was. The food was gone in a minute, and Tessa watched the dragon curl up on the money, her belly swollen, deep satisfaction radiating through their bond. She still couldn't help feeling like she'd lost her mind but, looking down at the little creature, she couldn't quite seem to care.

* * *

The next day Cashew was waiting for her, impatiently, at the corner. Tessa had hoped the smell of food would be enough to distract the dragon, but almost instantly she felt a spike of fear from the little creature.

"Wait, it's not—" Tessa began.

Cashew scuttled back to her hoard, planting her claws on the edge and winding herself around as much of it as she could. Through the bond, Tessa could feel the tickling heat of fire in the back of the dragon's throat. She knew that Cashew didn't want to hurt her, but she knew that wouldn't stop her if she felt the need.

"Please, listen to me. We need to do this." She didn't know how much the creature understood, but the echoes of what she sent told the story well enough. *A human with sharp gray eyes. Something metal with a dark hole at the end and full of fear. Cashew and Tessa both dead.*

The creature was torn. The fear made her want to crawl under her hoard and hide, but the thought of being without a hoard, cold and alone like before…

"I won't take it from you, Cashew. I promise." The boss seemed satisfied with her reasoning so far but she'd need hard numbers going forward to keep him, or anyone else, from the walls. "I just need to count it." She sent another image. Stacks of notes, each the same size. "I need to see what's been damaged."

Of all the responses she'd expected, being scoffed at wasn't one. A scent flooded her mind, so overwhelming she was barely able to translate what it meant.

Tessa's eyes widened. "You can *smell* how many there are?"

If Tessa had to translate Cashew's response into a word, it would have been: *obviously.*

If that was true…

She needed to know for sure. "Please, can I just…" Tessa reached towards the hoard. Cashew hissed and she snapped her hand back. "Okay, okay…" Instead, she reached into the sliced plastic packaging and grabbed some of the remaining money. She could feel the dragon wasn't happy about that either, but not enough to do anything about it. She dreaded the thought of the boss coming some day to withdraw his money. "Just for a minute, I promise."

Tessa stacked them in a tiny pile. "This is ten," she said. "Ten of *these* make one hundred. Ten of those—"

The answer came immediately. *A thousand.* Her mind translated what Cashew instinctively knew into familiar numbers. Then the dragon sniffed, smelling the pile she lay atop. *Ninety six thousand four hundred and twenty.*

Tessa goggled. "Wait, I need to verify your claim first. If you don't mind."

Cashew gave a hot snort and turned away. Tessa fought not to laugh at the disgruntled dragon as she started making a stack out of sight.

"It's not that I don't believe you," she said, "and I don't mean any offense, it's just very important that I know for sure, okay?"

Cashew snorted again, but more softly. Tessa finished and, before she could even ask, Cashew sent her an answer. *Twelve thousand eight hundred.*

That was incredible. Even a bill counter took longer than that. Old colleagues of hers would kill for Cashew on payroll. "You're an incredible little thing, aren't you?"

The dragon looked at her, pride and satisfaction oozing through their bond. Cashew could simply count the money by *smell.* She wouldn't need to take the cash to a machine. It would also save her a *lot* of time. Her relief mixed with Cashew's as the dragon realized her hoard was safe. It was enough to make her feel giddy.

To appease Cashew further, Tessa handed her the pile she'd taken. Quickly, the dragon scooped them under herself.

"We just need to do a little work and then we'll be done with all this for a while. Is that okay?"

Cashew considered it. She sent the image of Tessa stroking her. Tessa laughed.

"Yeah, that's a fair trade. Would you like it before or after?"

Both.

Tessa complied.

* * *

With the extra money issue put to bed, Tessa was given more conventional work; balancing the books in some cases, cooking them in others. In lieu of payment, the boss had offered her choice of furnishings and she hadn't held back. After all, she knew better than anyone how much money they were making. The addition from Cashew's protection alone was far more than she'd spent getting a beautiful bed, a fancy coffee machine, and a little hot plate for her previously grimy office.

The boss didn't even blink at how much smoked salmon she went through every week. His profits had skyrocketed, as he was fond of saying, and anything she wanted was hers once she kept it up. Aside from leaving, of course. The Rourkes were still after her. Tessa didn't know if that was true, or if it was just something the boss told her to keep her in the warehouse, but she didn't particularly care.

Everything that mattered to her was here now.

* * *

She made an espresso better than most coffee shops and took a full package of salmon with her into the walls. It was getting cramped in there, and not just because of the deliveries Tessa had learned to plastic wrap and cart inside. Cashew had grown like a weed. She was now as big as Tessa, with wings each the size of her bed.

She'd been worried the dragon wouldn't grow properly—surely it needed exercise—so, after checking that there were no cameras, she'd ushered her out at night to flap around. Cashew clambered across the top of the shelves like a cat, while Tessa chased her or threw salmon to her from below. During the day she stayed put, content to nuzzle into her ever-growing hoard.

She was still overwhelmed by the happiness she felt from the dragon when it saw her every morning. It washed away the lingering terror of her dreams. It eased the ache her brother's death had gouged in her heart.

Wings folded back like she was a scaled arrow, Cashew shot towards her and wound herself around her. "Too much hug," Tessa croaked.

The dragon let her go with a pang of amusement and something that was almost, but not quite, the dragon calling her a baby. "You're my size now," Tessa said. "You have to learn to be gentle." She threw the full smoked salmon Cashew's way. Quick as a snake, the dragon snapped it out of the air. She didn't even chew. Tessa felt the second-hand satisfaction. "Now, time for our counts."

Business—whatever mix of crime the boss had going—was booming. Their extra cash meant the crew could take their reserves from other, less successful warehouses and put it to use. She wondered how many stockpiles there were, but she was eternally grateful that the boss had decided *hers* was their dedicated storage. She didn't want to think of what Cashew would do if someone came to take her hoard.

The dragon made a low hiss. Tessa figured her thoughts had bled through—they did that sometimes—until she got a confusing image in her head. It took a second for her brain to translate it. *Metal, sweat, smoke.* People outside the door. "Stay here."

She scrambled from the walls in time to hear the door clang open. Usually the boss came alone and waited at the threshold. Usually he paged her. Today he just strolled right in, goons at either side. Both were armed; the woman at his left held a shotgun, the man at his right some kind of rifle. Her blood ran colder than Cashew's. Did they know?

"What…" She could barely speak. "Why are you…?"

"We need to move you," the boss said. For the first time his veneer of lazy confidence had cracks in it.

"Why?"

"We've been causing a stir with that extra money. Making strides, but making enemies, too. Some of our rivals have joined forces and we've been tipped off that they know about this location." The woman slung her shotgun over her back and went for the cart Tessa used to move the money. "We're taking what we can and leaving some soldiers. I don't want to lose another accountant. Get in the car."

She felt Cashew's mind against hers, concerned, probably sensing Tessa's own terror. If they went into the walls…

"Wait. I'll load the money," she said. "I'll join you outside."

She couldn't leave Cashew, but she didn't know how to get her out. Not at that size, not with everyone watching. If they saw her…

The boss shook his head. "They've got it covered. We need to make sure—"

Something spattered against her chest, like someone had hit her with a water balloon. It was only a second later, when she heard an unholy *crack*, that she realized what had actually happened. The boss held a hand to the hole in his chest and met her eyes for an instant before collapsing.

Tessa stumbled back as another *crack* sounded and the man with the rifle toppled sideways. There were more shots from outside. Glass shattering. Hollow metallic thunks. The screams of people in pain. Someone Tessa didn't recognize entered the warehouse and the remaining guard raised her shotgun, dropping him like a dead rat.

The man behind him was quicker though. His pistol spat, sending the guard to the ground. Tessa recognized his face. After all, she saw it every night. Patrick Rourke. He met her eyes and smiled. "Tessa. It's been a minute."

She turned and ran. She could barely think. Everything was chaos. The screams, gunshots, her heart hammering, and the frantic pressure of Cashew against her mind asking her what was happening, trying to make sense of it all. *Stay in the walls,* Tessa sent her. *Please don't come out.*

"Not going to take another shot, Tessa?" Rourke strolled into the warehouse like there wasn't a warzone erupting behind him. "Probably wise. That last one didn't quite hit the mark, did it?"

She made it to the back of the warehouse and fell to the ground behind some crates. She was hidden for now, but he was between her and the door. She couldn't leave Cashew. She felt the dragon's panic. For a second she saw through Cashew's eyes, saw the grate that led to the warehouse. *Don't.* She sent the thought with all the force she had. *Please, stay where you are.*

"I figured it out when I read your name in the papers. Tessa Thornton. Didn't I kill your brother?" He chuckled. "Soon I'll have bagged the whole family."

The crowbar was propped against the wall. She grabbed it, terrified that he'd see her, knowing it would be next to useless against a gun.

"Make this easy. Tell me where the money is, where the extra is coming from, and I'll make it quick. Hell, if you're half the accountant they say you are, maybe I'll give you a job."

Something moved out of the corner of her eye. She flinched, sure it was him, but the shape was all wrong. It was Cashew, wings folded, low and sleek as she crept from the walls. *Get back in. Now.*

The dragon ignored her. Cashew was focused on Rourke so hard that Tessa could see the man in her head. He was near. So near. She knew what Cashew wanted to do. If she did, though, they'd all die.

Tessa had no choice. She stood up, stepping away from the shelves. Rourke raised his weapon quickly, but he didn't fire. He laughed, relaxing his stance. "Gun didn't work so you figured it was time for a crowbar? Come on, love. Tell me what's been happening here and it'll go much better for you."

Cashew was flooding her mind with panic. It was Tessa's turn to ignore her. It took all of her will to step forward—it felt like that gun was going to go off any second—but once she made that first step the rest were easier.

"That's far enough. Don't want you getting any dumb ideas."

She was just out of arm's reach. He wasn't pointing the gun at her, but he held it ready. Confident, relaxed. A man who was no stranger to killing. She stared at him. After trying to kill him, and seeing him in the courtroom, it was only the third time she'd seen him in person. Never this close. It was weird. He seemed like a normal person. Stylish haircut, blue eyes, a crooked smile. Not a killer who'd destroyed her life. Not the person about to end it.

"Start talking or I'm gonna get bored."

Her hands were sweaty. She adjusted them on the crowbar. "Okay," Tessa said. "I just have a question before we begin."

He grinned. "Shoot."

"Can you connect to him the way you connected to me?"

He narrowed his eyes, cocked his head. "What the hell are you saying?"

In her head she tried to send the image, replicate the feeling she'd had. She wasn't sure if Cashew understood. If she was even listening. "Can you do it? Please."

"I don't know what game—" His eyes bulged suddenly, lost focus. "What the—"

He reached for his forehead as Cashew forced her way into his mind. Tessa knew just how disorienting it was, how everything faded away for a second. It was all the time she needed.

She brought the crowbar down on Rourke's arm. It *cracked* like a twig snapping. He screamed. The gun flew from his hand and skidded somewhere beneath the shelves. She swung again, hitting him in the cheek. Blood and teeth sprayed as he fell to the ground.

Tessa gave a shaking cry and stumbled past him. She could hear fighting outside, but it seemed farther away. Far enough for them to slip out, maybe. She couldn't think, just moved, fixated on that patch of brightness at the end of the warehouse. "We have to go!"

Suddenly she saw through Cashew's eyes again, a mental picture of Rourke reaching for a gun in his boot with his good arm. She was too far away to do anything, hemmed in by the shelves on either side, a perfect, easy target.

Escape, she sent. *Be free.*

Behind her came a loud noise. She flinched, but it wasn't a gunshot. Someone started screaming. *No!* She turned and saw Rourke engulfed in flame, Cashew behind him, wings spread and fearsome. She ran, beating at the fire, but it was too late. Rourke's final cries were drowned out as an alarm blared. There was a heavy clang as a security door slammed down at the front of the warehouse. A sharp hissing sounded as the nozzles all over the roof kicked into gear, flooding the place with CO_2.

Tessa froze. The boss wouldn't have a failsafe inside the warehouse. Money was more important to him than people. Cashew was sending her distress. She could feel that she'd done something wrong, but she didn't understand what.

If she hadn't acted, Tessa would have died. Now they'd both suffocate.

Suddenly Cashew was there. Tessa found herself pressed to the ground as the dragon wrapped her wings around her, forming a little cave and muffling the alarm. Through the membrane of her wings, Tessa could make out the little squiggles of veins.

An image. Being safe, like how Cashew felt burrowed into her hoard. Tessa tried to pry the wings away, but the dragon wouldn't budge. "You'll suffocate!" she yelled. "Forget me, get somewhere safe!"

The dragon ignored her. Tessa didn't know what to do. It had trapped some air in here with her, but she didn't know how much. It didn't matter. There wasn't enough outside for Cashew. Already she could feel the dragon's thoughts start to slow. To get sleepy, lethargic.

"Please." She wasn't listening. The feeling of Cashew in her mind began to fade. Desperately, she thought of the only thing she could. *The hoard.* "If you die they'll take it," she yelled. She pictured grubby hands snatching bills and scattering the dragon's little nest. The money divided and packaged away, sterile behind plastic wrap. "You'll lose it all."

Instead of the rousing anger she'd hoped for, Tessa only got sadness. An image of the money gone, but it didn't matter. Because in its place stood Tessa. Tears fell from her eyes as she tried to fight that thought, but Cashew wasn't there anymore. The dragon sagged, but she kept her wings wrapped tightly around her.

Tessa wasn't sure how long it took—she was dizzy from grief and dwindling air, clinging to her silent friend—but the alarm finally died. The emergency doors hissed open. There was a soft whir as the fans began to work again, pumping in fresh air. She wiped her eyes and got low, managing to pry up a limp wing long enough to crawl under.

The fighting had long since stopped. She didn't know if everyone was dead or if survivors were approaching the door, guns drawn. She didn't care. Cashew had been the only thing keeping her going and now she was lying there, cold and still. She lifted Cashew's head—it was strangely light—and cradled it in her lap. Tears poured down her face. "You shouldn't have."

Rourke wasn't moving. Cashew had seen to that.

She stroked her gently. "Please get up." Nothing happened.

She couldn't leave her here. The thought made her sick. Someone would find them there, eventually, but Tessa didn't care. At least Cashew wouldn't be alone. Whatever happened then didn't matter. She didn't have a heart left to care.

"Thank you for everything," she said.

She placed her head against Cashews and held it there. That's when she felt it. A soft pressure against her mind. An image that made her cry all over again. This time she was smiling though. *Smoked salmon.* The dragon cracked one double-lidded eye.

Concern flooded Tessa's mind.

Tessa gasped. "I'm safe." She kissed the dragon on its brow; felt that it was ticklish second-hand. "I can't believe that you…"

Cashew nuzzled her. Her thoughts were clear: *I protect my hoard.*

In the distance, sirens wailed. Tessa's tortured heart skipped a beat. They couldn't find them. "We have to go."

The dragon rose slowly. Her thoughts felt faint, but she was alive. That was all that mattered. Tessa felt Cashew's confusion. *Where?*

Tessa didn't know. "Let's take some of your hoard with us. Then we'll figure it out."

She stuffed her pillowcases with what she could and, together, they made their way out of the warehouse, through the scattered bodies, and into the world.

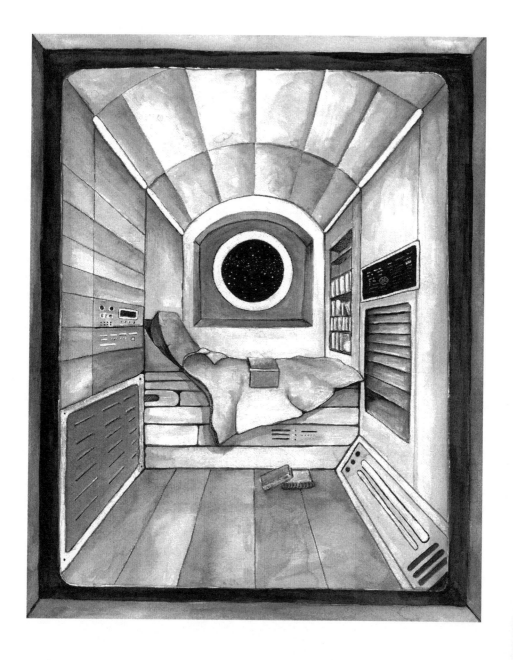

Illustration by Kat D'Andrea

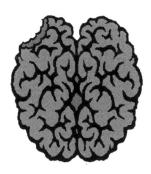

Solstice

Brian Crenshaw

[Yr 2311, Local Day 316 || Launch: -0 Yr, 0 Days, 0 Hrs, 22 Min, 46 seconds]

"I'm afraid, Sepiu."

"You should be, Alek."

Alek looked down at his baggy flight suit. Clearly made for a grown man, it did not fit his fifteen-year-old frame. Sepiu had given it to him for his thirteenth birthday and he was used to its feel by now, but he was all too aware of what that looseness meant. He played with the upraised decal on the left hip, the one which said USA Spacefitters in capital letters.

"I don't think USA made these for kids to use," Alek said, his throat tight. "Maybe I'm not ready."

"It was the smallest one in the flight closet. The old crew was just made up of big people. That is all." Sepiu's contralto voice came in soothing and warm through the speakers. She could usually calm him, but today was different. Everything would change after today. Or everything would end.

"I want to stay here with you."

"You know why you cannot, Alek. I am sorry. I can walk you through the numbers again, but it upset you last time."

He blinked a tear from his eye. The flight suit made a crinkling sound as it brushed his face. Despite the smoothness of its fabric, the material had traction on the pilot's seat. Fire retardant and very insulating, it was perfect for its job. He knew its every facet and had memorized the manual front to back. He had done the same for every piece of equipment on *Solstice*.

Sepiu called such reading schoolwork and had been quite clever in getting him to complete it. She said he had been unruly in the beginning, but he could not remember that far back.

[Yr 2303, Local Day 309 || Launch: -8 Yr, 7 Days, 9 Hrs, 16 Min, 23 seconds]

"I don't know what these words mean," a younger Alek said, his hair tied back away from his eyes.

"Your dictionary is in boarding room 1A. I encourage you to read it for your education."

"That takes too long!"

Sepiu was quiet, as she often became when Alek was being difficult. He thought of it like a sigh or a frown.

"Education is important. Your brain is a nearly endless repository, you should always be filling it."

"Reposory?"

"Repository. A vault, box, or storehouse. You should always be learning, Alek. It enlarges you, makes you greater. I will give you chocolate when you can recite that manual, but you have to understand what it says."

His face lit up, like it always did when she offered to bring something sweet out of the food lockup. "Okay. Will there be a test?"

"Yes, Alek. I have to know that you are doing your work. Rewards are earned, not given."

[Launch: -0 Yr, 0 Days, 0 Hrs, 22 Min, 06 seconds]

"You don't have to go over the numbers again. I just wish we could stay together."

"I wish that as well," she said. "I dispensed the last of the chocolate into your rations. Did you remember to pack everything into the cargo hatch?"

He nodded, but she did not respond. After a momentary silence he looked up at the camera over the bulkhead. It cut out more often than it used to. He waved his hand in front of it.

"Did you hear me, Alek?"

"I packed everything. Thank you." His gaze swept the floor, resting on the small pile of items that he would like to take but which would displace much needed oxygen in the tiny maintenance pod.

"I want to bring a book. Do you think I should bring my dictionary? There are still words in it I'm not confident of."

She laughed. It was a rich sound, one of thirty-seven laugh tracks she had on file. "You have become so scholarly. It is alright to bring one book. Bring something you enjoy. That or the control manual."

The stack of books at his feet stared back at him, each title a beseeching gaze, like a person begging to come along. They *were* people. His only friends in this place besides Sepiu.

[Yr 2303, Local Day 338 || Launch: -7 Yr, 343 Days, 11 Hrs, 32 Min, 46 seconds]

"What are they?" He stared at the skeletal black scaffolding, its strategically placed bars supporting half a dozen flattened rectangles of varying colors. Thick magnetic pads held the whole apparatus to the metal wall of the tiny room. After weeks in Solstice, *the discovery of a new room could have been the discovery of a new continent.*

"They are books, little Alek. You said your mother was teaching you to read?"

Tears threatened. He stepped back from the bookshelf. He recognized the letters along the narrow, outward faces. But the words they made were not words he knew.

When he did not answer, Sepiu's voice dropped into a low, motherly tone. It cajoled him from its tiny box near the ceiling. "She would want you to keep reading. You want to do what would make her happy, correct?"

Tears clouding his eyes, he reached up to the shelf and grabbed one of the rectangles. He had only ever read from his mother's tablet. He wondered if these tablets would be as lonely and frightening as everything else on Solstice. *The swiveling lens on the ceiling stared unblinking at the child and the bookshelf.*

"Ah, that is a very good choice. Let me know if there are any words you need help with."

[Launch: -0 Yr, 0 Days, 0 Hrs, 21 Min, 22 seconds]

"I think I'll bring *A History of Aces*. It's my favorite. I don't think I can leave it."

"You always liked the dramatic books. One should be fine. Take it with you. We must begin the preflight preparation."

He took his book and crossed the room. The rubber treads on the soles of his flight suit made a distinctive sound against the plastic floor. The maintenance pod hatchway was just a few steps across the main compartment, yet it felt like a hundred yards.

The grip to the hatch felt large and cold in his hand. He had stared at the door thousands of times as he read or ate or exercised in this compartment. He had gone beyond into the maintenance pod over and over again. But never like this.

With a sick feeling, he leaned away from the hatch, wanting to go back into the short hall with the living compartments. His warm, silvery sheets were back there. His wall lamp. His clothes. His toys. Everything.

"You should not linger, Alek. It is time to start preflight preparations."

[Yr 2304, Local Day 352 || Launch: -6 Yr, 329 Days, 14 Hrs, 2 Min, 21 seconds]

It was dark. He could see little, and hear even less. As barren as he had thought his life in Solstice *was, there had still been motion and activity. Beyond the end of the short dormitory hallway, there was nothing. He had left his room to find the little light beside this door in the hall green for the first time in over a year. The door opened at his slightest touch and an inky black emptiness greeted him.*

"What's in there, Sepiu?"

"You should go inside and find out," she whispered.

And in he went. But the further he went, the more his fear grew. The darkness was not as bad as the silence. He had never realized Solstice *was so alive with sound. Little hums and breezes and whirrings that happened behind or within the bulkheads, all to affect functions he had never bothered to guess. He heard none of it beyond the door.*

A scraping broke the silence as his foot kicked something metallic across the plastic floor. A tinkling clamor came from a short distance away.

"Be careful," Sepiu said from somewhere in the black. "Step carefully. Two meters in front of you is a shelf along the wall. Follow it to the right. I think you will like what you find."

"I want to go back to my room, Sepiu."

"You cannot, little Alek. Not yet. You have to find it, first."

He endured the dark. He had fought with Sepiu before, but always did what she said in the end. It was hard for a child to argue with someone who controlled his food.

"I'm scared, Sepiu."

"Do not be. There is nothing to fear."

He came at an angle to the shelf that she mentioned, more like a counter running the length of the wall. He followed it to the right, until a smooth plastic rectangle materialized under his splayed fingertips. Deciding this must be what she had wanted, he seized it and turned back toward the door.

The dim rectangle of gray light was the most welcome sight in the world. He ran, jumping over the area where his foot had caught the metal obstacle on the floor. He heard the stale wind roar past his ears until he was out once more, twisting in place to bring the door closed behind him. The sweet buzz and hum of the dormitory hall filled his ears.

Breathing hard, he looked down at the object in his hands and gaped in disbelief. Sepiu's voice chirped happily from her speaker near the ceiling.

"Happy eighth birthday, Alek. That is not just any tablet: it is a pilot's tablet. It has music and personnel files and even control summaries for Solstice *and all of its pods."*

He was not of an age yet where he cried in happiness. That would not come until he was grown up enough to appreciate the full life stories of Chuck Yeager and Neil Armstrong from the pilot's books. But he was happy at that moment. From her camera lens, Sepiu watched.

[Launch: -0 Yr, 0 Days, 0 Hrs, 20 Min, 38 seconds]

"You have to go through the hatch, Alek."

Queasy, he pulled open the hatch into the airlock chamber. The lights blinked on, feeble and unsure, casting a warm yellow glow over the claustrophobic chamber. The maintenance pod sat at attention, an upright bean-shaped capsule with slender cylindrical arms tucked against its middle. He walked a circuit around it, the whole pod locked at an unlikely angle by magnetic runners on the floor. He stared up at its wide eyespot, which looked out from the dark interior where he was about to sit.

His stomach jumped into his throat. Gravity was weaker near the edge of the *Solstice*, far from the generator. Vertigo always came when he walked too close to the edge.

"Do we have any g-pills?" he asked, voice cracking.

"One left," she replied. "It should be enough. It is in your food kit."

He walked around to the back of the pod, took hold of the rail and climbed the one stair to the hatch. It eased open, loose on its hinge until he sealed it from the inside. His gray seat connected to the ceiling and the floor of the pod by an elaborate array of girders and suspension coils. He stashed the book underneath the plastic floor, where his other supplies were secured.

Alek pulled himself into the seat. The flight suit rustled comfortingly against the fabric of the body-conforming chair. His gloved hands brushed the controls. He felt confidence and strength return to him, even as his apprehension grew.

[Yr 2307, Local Day 315 || Launch: -4 Yr, 1 Day, 14 Hrs, 14 Min, 57 seconds]

"I wish there were racers here." He had finished studying the histories of piloting when he was twelve, and had the book open, its cover badly scuffed from a tantrum years before. He had begun reading the available manuals on Solstice, but Sepiu had not yet started testing him on their contents.

"Is that so?"

He met the camera's unblinking stare. The amusement in her voice bothered him, challenged him, somehow.

"*Yes. Who wouldn't want them here? Breaking the speed barrier, banking through tight corners, moving at ten-thousand kilometers per hour through gravity wells and slingshotting to their destination. It must be amazing.*"

"*The sport of Spaceracing had a very brief life, Alek. There were not many fans.*"

"*It's the coolest thing people ever did,*" he insisted.

"*Well,*" she laughed, "*with that attitude, you might have made a good one.*"

"*I would have,*" he insisted. He had little to do from day to day except study and daydream. He now did both activities well and often.

"*Perhaps you should try the hatch over there, then.*"

He heard a strange sound, one he had not heard in his four years on Solstice. He reached for the handle, enormous in his small hand, a fixture of his tiny world that had never moved. The sound behind the door was some kind of lock, he thought. He pulled the hatch open.

His first time seeing the pod was magic and fear twined together in a teasing union as Sepiu prodded him to open the back and climb inside. When he did, the entire pod hummed to life in a thrilling revival. Even this tiny capsule felt immensely powerful from the pilot's seat.

He sat down, remembering almost as an afterthought to buckle himself in like the manual said. Awkward fingers fumbled with fear and reverence across controls he had only read about. That was when the bay doors lost their color, fading to twinkling black with the same speed it took him to register that he was seeing the outside for the first time in four years.

A billion stars shone over a horizon of dusky orange. Shards of flashing white light flickered in a beautiful array, a ring of radiance winding in the distance around the curve of the world below. Thick cables impinged on the vista from the left, wires dangling into the void from somewhere beyond his sight. A name tickled at the back of his mind.

"*Chronos.*" It felt heavy on his tongue, dangerous. Like a boogeyman from some forgotten nightmare. An ominous quiet crept into his soul.

"*Yes, the solitary moon of planet Cerberus.*"

He took it in, his eyes following the trail of spinning debris into the distance. It was beautiful, but the cables waving on the periphery chilled him. Like a sea monster's tentacles rearing from the depths, they reached out of his memory into the black.

"*What is all that?*" he asked. "*The lights. They're spinning.*"

"*That debris is Solstice, mostly.*" Her voice was soothing, cautious. "*The rest is the salvage vessel Ursa II.*"

He shook his head as his heart thudded in his chest. "*No. Ursula. Dad said ships were supposed to have proper names. Ours is—was—Ursula.*"

A memory of emergency lights flashed behind his eyes. He felt protective arms pushing him through a tiny portal. He heard a crash and a shout, drowned by an immense noise like a submerged giant coming up for air.

"Oh? Ursula it is. Some of her is out there, as well."

He looked through the transparent window for a long time. Eventually, the control panel drew his gaze.

"So…what are we doing?"

"Piloting simulations." The musical reply caught him off-guard. It was so pleased with itself, so eager and inviting. A box near the far end of the console screen lit up, the words "Proxy Run" illuminated by an easy blue light. He tapped the box, and the interior window of the pod clouded and filled with a new starscape, bereft of cables, debris, and the orange horizon. Soon, the only lights that mattered were in front of him, and the ones behind his eyes stopped flashing.

[Launch: -0 Yr, 0 Days, 0 Hrs, 19 Min, 32 seconds]
Alek retrieved the g-pill from the food kit and swallowed it dry. He replaced the kit in the tiny compartment under his seat. The console screen lit up as he sat down. He reached toward the box that read "Proxy Run," but pulled away.

"I wonder if all pilots were afraid the first time," he wondered aloud.

"Jitters for first time flyers are well-documented," Sepiu said through the console speaker. "Remember to do a diagnostic check on the mechanical controls as well as the digital ones. We are going to begin soon."

He swallowed again, banishing the sticky feeling in the back of his throat that the g-pill had left. He could already feel the tingling in his ears as its effects spread. A reverberating boom echoed through the hull. Alek looked out through the eyespot of the pod. The airlock door was still opaque.

He felt a strange sensation, something he had not felt in a very, very long time. The simulations gave him some foresight into the dizzying effects of rapid movement. The movement was not rapid, but it also wasn't his. *Solstice* was moving.

His stomach roiled as a long-buried memory threatened to emerge. The rattling jolt as the world jarred into motion. He closed his eyes, sweat instantly wetting his brow.

Sepiu cooed through the speaker. "I have confidence in you. I will transmit to you for as long as I can. Remember the simulations and you will be fine."

[Yr 2309, Local Day 12 || Launch: -2 Yr, 304 Days, 16 Hrs, 9 Min, 13 seconds]

Day in and day out, he went through the hatch into the airlock. He looked out at stars and the silvery remains of Solstice. And of Ursula. Day in and day out, he did his reading and his recitations, then climbed into the cockpit of the maintenance pod for flight simulations.

"I think you have the makings of a great pilot," she told him one day after he had mastered the basic controls.

"I wonder what your time would have been on the Jove Orbital Trail," she mused when he could bank his pod at full speed around the hull of an undamaged, simulated Solstice.

When he was a little older, he became suspicious of her praise. Her compliments felt disproportionate to his accomplishments. So he challenged them.

"I am very impressed by your progress," she insisted. "But yes, perhaps we should make things more difficult."

The simulation burst, and shrapnel filled the viewscreen. Not comprehending what that meant for him in the maintenance pod, he tried for speed, and immediately suffered a program end as a metal shard made contact and compromised hull integrity.

The simulations that came after were intense and frustrating. They gave him new respect for the field of debris he saw through the transparent airlock window. Some of the pieces were slow enough, small enough, dull enough that the maintenance pod could survive contact with them. Many others in the current traveled at different speeds, had different mass, had different properties. He asked Sepiu each time what had caused the proxy run to end, and she would describe in varying amounts of detail what had just destroyed his pod and how.

In time, the exercises were about more than navigating a dangerous field of flying projectiles. He learned to maneuver around Solstice and to use the gravity of Chronos to his advantage. After hundreds of sessions, an image began to grow in his mind of the sort of mission Sepiu was interested in.

He began to understand what she had in mind for him.

[Launch: -0 Yr, 0 Days, 0 Hrs, 8 Min, 12 seconds]

"Preflight diagnostics completed. We're doing the windup?"

"Yes. I am using *Solstice's* remaining thrust engine to put us into a spiral. We will launch by increasing gas pressure and then blowing the airlock doors. The g-pill should maintain your equilibrium through the initial jolt."

He swallowed again, the fuzzy sensation from the pill making his throat feel strange. It kept him from experiencing the full effects of their dizzying momentum, yet he knew they were moving very fast now, beyond what he could withstand on his own. The pill shut down a lot of his inner ear and did something to his insides to reduce the sickening and debilitating effects of the centrifugal force.

He wiped the sweat from his face. Despite feeling the movement of *Solstice*, his world remained unchanged, the interior of the airlock no different than it had been before they began. In a few moments, the moors on the floor would release the maintenance pod and the airlock doors which had protected him through a thousand simulations would fly off into the void. In a rush of oxygen, he would join them.

The maintenance pod was not designed to be fired out this way, out of an air-filled room, but he had done it in simulation over and over and over again. It was a necessary step to push him out through what had at that time been a theoretical gap in the debris cloud. The pod's rockets simply did not have the thrust to get him up to speed.

Solstice shuddered. The sound of tortured metal roared through the hull. He looked over his shoulder instinctively, as if a monster were trying to tear its way into the airlock from outside.

"Sepiu?!"

"Prepare for launch, Alek."

"What's going on?"

"Eyes up front, Alek."

He fixed his gaze on the porthole. The mooring released the pod with a booming click from below. The warm lights flickered out. Alek struck the ignition. Harsh flashes at the corners of the airlock doors sent them away into a sea of black. The pod's rocket propulsion shot into life as the escaping gasses and momentum of *Solstice*'s spinning arm hurled Alek out into a storm of flying metal.

Twisted titanium screamed against the pod's skin. Alek's fingers flew over the console, tapping bracketed options and toggling directional inputs. Forward, pushing through the torrent, the cascade ceased and he sailed forward into nothing. There was no sun, the debris cloud was dark in the shadow of Cerberus. A bright light strobed behind him on the spinning wreckage of *Solstice*, illuminating the deadly cloud in fits and starts.

Then the maintenance pod's warning alarm sounded. Massive objects flew toward him at thousands of kilometers an hour, closing in a blink. Alek brought the pod rockets into perpendicular attitude, pushing him out of the way of metal beams jetting like guided missiles around Chronos. He corkscrewed out of the path of a great data dish, spinning in orbit like an Olympian discus. Out in the distance, something that looked like a human figure hurtled end over end. Tiny and forlorn, it nagged at his attention as he flew the pod, another pilot frozen in time with the other debris of a long-gone tragedy.

And then Alek was clear. No alarm, no scream of metal on the pod's plastic skin. Just stars, silence, and velocity that felt like stillness. He reached for the comm, the short-range communication array between the pod and Sepiu.

"Sepiu!? Sepiu?"

He heard static in response. The pod was moving fast, but if he turned it around he could see the state of *Solstice*, his home of eight years. He needed to know if it had survived the great strain of launching him into space. If Sepiu had survived throwing herself partially into the rings of detritus whirling around Chronos.

As his fingers danced over the controls, a new warning flashed on screen. A new object was on a collision course with the pod's trajectory. Reading the metrics, he recognized it from the simulations. *Ursula*. Cracked and ruined, ravaged by fire, vomited into further orbit by its ill-fated coupling with *Solstice*.

He scanned his controls. There were seconds to make the adjustments, and scant fuel remaining in the craft after the burn of the hard maneuvers. He could avoid one more obstacle, but he would need the rest to correct his course.

He pushed the rockets to maximum forward thrust. He blinked the sweat out of his eyes and leaned away from the controls, knowing that if Sepiu's initial calculations were wrong, he would hurtle off to a slow and undiscovered death in space. *Ursula* approached, obscured by a deep cloud of metal and plastic shards.

The pod roared as the cloud engulfed it. A shearing scream, and warnings flashed as something tore a thruster from the hull. Soaring away from the behemoth, the noise subsided. The warning lights continued to flash, but reported no further major damage. He had cleared *Ursula*'s path by less than a hundred meters.

"Sepiu?"

Silence. Too far for the transmitter now. He looked ahead toward his destination, out past the reach of Chronos, to a far-flung orbit around the giant of Cerberus proper.

"I'm going on ahead, Sepiu. I know you can't hear me. I hope you're okay."

He hurtled into the black.

[Yr 2310, Local Day 119 || Launch: -1 Yr, 197 Days, 13 Hrs, 6 Min, 59 seconds]

The simulations were grueling, now. He sometimes wondered when she would escalate the difficulty past his ability to cope. Already, new variables were taking longer and longer to overcome.

His daily exercises were far beyond the simple maneuvering drills from his childhood. He could run diagnostics of all kinds, recognize damage from a host of different data sets. He was aware of the few issues he was able to repair from within the pod with nothing but the onboard wrench and other tools.

Nonetheless, it felt like there was less and less he could do in some of the scenarios she programmed for him. Today he had determined that the simulation had no pathway for success. Rather, he believed it was a test of his determination to make a riskier choice to optimize a slight chance of long-term success, at the cost of almost certain destruction in the debris field right now. Today's lesson: death now or death later made no difference, only the success of getting himself and the pod to the coordinates on file. A two-percent chance of reaching the finish line meant more than a one percent chance, even if the latter increased his chances of surviving the next ten seconds a hundredfold.

"What happens when I get free of Chronos, Sepiu?" he asked.

"Provided you have conserved enough fuel to reach the rendezvous coordinates at the appointed time and avoided any damage that would prevent the pod's life support systems from sustaining you, you will deliver a message to the communication satellite Sirius IV.*"*

He wiped away sweat, heading out of the airlock hatch and into the main chamber to take his food from the dispensary. Sepiu always let him eat after a tough session.

"A communication satellite? I'm going to deliver a message?"

"Yes. For me, to those outside this solar system. Solstice's *transmission dish no longer has full function, so the message can only be sent from close proximity using the pod's limited broadcast capabilities. I need to communicate with a ship that can travel through the wormhole network to get here and back."*

He was quiet then, thinking. He took his food from the dispensary and looked up at the camera near the ceiling.

"What is the message you want me to deliver?"

Silence came first, as if she was considering her answer. It was one of her more human idiosyncrasies.

"You have other studies to focus on right now, Alek. But I can tell you now if you would like to begin memorizing it. It should be delivered verbatim."

[Launch: +0 Yr, 0 Days, 0 Hrs, 4 Min, 4 seconds]

Torn, twisted, and flying apart at high velocity, the single intact branch of *Solstice* spun in place, bombarded by shrapnel. The outside lamp was destroyed, though the pod was already far beyond its light. Having spent the fuel within its only remaining thruster, CPU could do nothing more to avoid the incoming debris.

She calculated likelihoods of the maintenance pod's rendezvous with *Sirius IV* as she tracked its expected trajectory. The disaster that left half of her derelict station destroyed was a mortal one for the crew of the *Ursa II*. She did not expect another salvage ship to chance upon Chronos before her power source died.

Days passed as her solitary eye stared out into the void, seeking any flash that might indicate catastrophic failure of the pod. Most of the other instruments that could take long-range readings had been on other parts of *Solstice*, cut off from her now.

A message came through after four days of bombardment. It was strong, and so insistent she picked it up despite her damaged receiver dish. Nearly all of her processing power went to unscrambling and cleaning the static out of the message.

"SOS. This is an automated message from *Sirius IV*. Playing recorded message from vessel in severe distress on following heading—"

The coordinates, numbers, and axes listed in the message confirmed that it was Alek. His voice came through as an audio file 0.97 seconds later.

"S, O, S. Requesting aid, moving at input trajectory. Limited power for air recycler, no fuel. Please intercept. This is Alek Cardona, survivor of the *Ursa II*. Cannot navigate wormhole, require intercept."

The satellite's voice resumed 0.97 seconds after Alek's went quiet.

"Local station, respond. *Solstice*, confirm dispatch of interceptor. Advising, if no local response in 300 seconds, factoring for message travel time, message will be forwarded through wormhole to Interstellar Network."

CPU read the data several times while the satellite repeated the message in its entirety for the next 300 seconds. Voiceless over the vast distance, she ran down the clock.

The message ceased. A camera swiveled in the dormitory room where Alek's blankets lay in a heap at the foot of the bed. It stayed there for the silent hours that preceded the follow up message she was waiting for.

"This is an automated message from *Sirius IV*. SOS situation ended. *Ursa III* intercepted damaged vessel. No casualties. Please acknowledge."

She saved the message every time it repeated for the 300 seconds before the satellite program gave up. She awaited further news, but received none. After a short time, she calculated that she never would.

The window in which *Sirius IV* came closest to Chronos was gone, and the two would not be in near orbit again for another eight years. The auxiliary power source that had kept her branch of *Solstice* active since the accident was drained.

"Goodbye, Alek," she said, once into the maintenance pod bay and again into the empty bedroom with the crinkled sheets. With her camera aimed off toward the wormhole, CPU shut down.

Illustration by Ariel Guzman

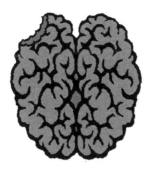

Kremlin Necropolis

S.C. Butler

Ten hours after the honor guard was removed from Lenin's Tomb, the phone rang in Michael Gorbachev's bedroom. He hadn't heard the voice on the other end in seven years.

"Joseph?"

"Yes, Misha. It's me."

Comfortingly familiar as Joseph's voice was, Misha still had to make sure.

"Where were we the night Chernenko died?"

"At his bedside."

"Why?"

"To make sure he didn't come back."

It was Joseph, all right. No one else had been there the night Misha staked the last vampire in the Kremlin. He wondered what had brought the saint back to Moscow now, two years after Yeltsin's coup left Misha and his wife in a cramped apartment far from the center of power.

"Has something happened?" he asked.

"You haven't heard?"

"I'm retired. I don't listen to the news anymore."

"Yeltsin removed the Necropolis guard."

Raisa coughed and burrowed deeper into her pillow. With all the medication she took these days, dive bombing Stukas wouldn't wake her. Misha lowered his voice anyway.

"Where shall we meet?"

"St. Basil's."

Misha settled the phone quietly in its cradle and rubbed his bald head. Yeltsin had assured him he'd remove the guard someday, but Misha hadn't believed him. It took courage to take the guard off Lenin's Tomb, especially when you knew what was inside. Misha had never done it, and he'd been party leader for six years.

A cold October rain smeared the windows. Not cold enough to freeze, but cold enough to make the Moscow night miserable. Misha could wear his greatcoat without attracting too much notice. He was going to need it, too, if he was going on a hunt. He'd have to bring most of his equipment, which a trenchcoat wouldn't hide as easily. These days, he couldn't bluff his way out of trouble the way he used to.

Dressed, he went back to the bedroom to kiss Raisa. Briefly he thought of waking her, but decided against it. If she woke, she might not let him go.

He brushed her gray hair lovingly with his fingers. She'd been so vivacious, so lovely before the coup, and the stroke that came with it. Now she didn't even bother to dye her hair. Not that they'd ever been as attractive as Nancy and Ron, especially given the cartoonist's dream that topped his own balding head. But they'd held their own in London and New York, which was more than Khrushchev or Gromyko had ever done. Raisa was to thank for that. Without her grace and charm, Misha would never have accomplished anything.

He kissed her forehead and left a short note explaining where he'd gone. From a locked case on the top shelf of the wardrobe, he pulled out everything he thought he might need and sorted the equipment into the greatcoat's pockets. Pistol, flash bomb, crossbow, stakes. He knew Joseph wouldn't be any help. As one of the few saints able to do more than wear sackcloth and ashes, Joseph was already pushing his conscience to the limit simply accompanying him on a hunt.

Outside, the rain clapped the streets in windy sheets. The few people hurrying home at three in the morning paid no attention as Misha plowed resolutely down Ilyinka Street toward the confrontation he'd dreamed of ever since Khrushchev first pulled him out of the Komsomol.

He found Joseph waiting for him in the shadow of St. Basil's, silent as time. In seven years, the saint hadn't changed at all. Short and slight, he wore a leather jacket and knit cap. A crown of raindrops circled the brim, twinkling in the lights from Gumm's.

"How delightful to see you again, Misha. Is Raisa well?"

"No, sadly. The coup almost killed her. But thank you for asking."

"I'm sorry. It must be terribly hard for both of you. You love each other so much."

Even though he knew no one could flatter so well as a saint, and mean it, Misha felt much better. He did love Raisa more than anything in the world.

"Perhaps after tonight," Joseph continued, "fewer people will have to go through what you and Raisa have. My only regret is that I wasn't here for you two years ago. You'd think Boris and the rest of them would have been more grateful for everything you did."

Misha waved Joseph's remorse aside. He knew perfectly well what he'd done, and what he hadn't. "It was the economy that brought me down, not the vampires. You might not believe it, but an economy is much harder to manage than vampires."

"Oh, I believe it." Joseph's small mouth twitched in a sympathetic smile. "You're the best hunter I've ever worked with, Misha. And I've worked with quite a few."

"Thank you." Even for a saint, Joseph was laying it on a bit thick. But Misha had been the best, and it was good to hear someone acknowledge it. Especially someone who'd hunted alongside both Alexander II and Robespierre.

"There are some good young hunters out there doing the mopping up. There's one in particular working for Sobchak in St. Petersburg who's done very well."

"Putin?" Joseph did not look convinced. "Watch out for that one. He's ambitious."

"I'm sure he is." People had called Misha ambitious once. "But I don't worry about that sort of thing anymore. I'm retired."

"Not tonight, though?"

"No, not tonight. Not for this."

Beyond the church, Red Square was dark despite the lights in Gumm's and the Kremlin. A few cobblestones glistened where they caught the light, but the rest of the huge space was lost in darkness. The mausoleum hulked beneath the fortress like a sleeping tank, but the graves behind it, and the necropolis of bronze plaques that lined the wall behind the graves, were completely hidden.

"Have they left it completely unguarded?" Misha asked.

"The Moscow Police are in charge."

He laughed. "Even easier. Did you bring any money?"

"Several thousand American dollars."

"That's too much. They'll get suspicious."

"You can have what's left over. Buy Raisa some of that Beluga I know she enjoys."

They walked on. Halfway to the mausoleum, Joseph pulled a pint of vodka from his pocket. Unscrewing the cap, he took a liberal swig, rolled the alcohol around in his mouth, then spat it on the sidewalk. Pouring another round into his hands, he dabbed his jacket collar.

"It might help our case if they think we're a couple of drunks," he explained, handing Misha the bottle.

It was good Finnish vodka and Misha allowed himself a swallow before dosing his coat as well. Joseph clapped his back encouragingly.

"Excellent! Now, off we go."

A dozen meters from the mausoleum, a voice stopped them.

"Where do you two think you're going?"

Joseph answered with drunken, saintly charm. "Good evening, Officer. Terrible night, isn't it? You should be indoors. We should all be indoors, for that matter. Can I offer you a cigarette?"

The officer glanced nervously back at his post.

"Don't worry," Joseph assured him. "I have enough for everyone."

A lighter flared. In his other hand, Joseph held a package of American cigarettes. Misha pulled his scarf more closely over his face to keep from being recognized as the policeman leaned forward to accept the unexpected gift. The flame from the lighter briefly reddened the young officer's unbearded cheek and chin.

Joseph laid a friendly arm on his shoulder. "I've some vodka I'd be delighted to share with you as well. Or perhaps one of these?"

The lighter flicked again. This time Joseph held a pair of hundred dollar bills.

Even a rookie becomes suspicious eventually. "What is it you want?"

"Nothing. Nothing at all. My friend and I simply wish to pay Comrade Lenin a visit."

The young officer was about to succumb to Joseph's ingenuous charm when another voice joined them.

"Officer Volyunov, what's going on here?"

Officer Volyunov chucked his cigarette into the dark as the speaker appeared out of the mist. "They want to see Comrade Lenin, Sergeant."

The sergeant gave Joseph a rough push. Joseph pretended to stagger backwards.

"You're drunk," the sergeant said. "Get out of here before we arrest you."

"Of course I'm drunk." Joseph sounded both injured and innocent. "Why else would I be out in the middle of Red Square at three in the morning trying to visit Comrade Lenin? And why on earth would you want to arrest me? You'd be losing a splendid opportunity, at no trouble to yourselves, I assure you."

The lighter snapped back on. Now there were five hundred dollar bills in Joseph's hand.

The sergeant paused. Despite his rank, he looked even younger than Officer Volyunov, but also taller and more imposing. Exactly the sort of broad-shouldered, impractical fellow who posed for recruiting posters and hadn't a kopek's worth of imagination.

"We have no wish to get you into trouble, Sergeant." Even pretending to be drunk, Joseph sounded impossibly sincere. But he wasn't lying. He really didn't want the sergeant to get in trouble. If he did, the saint would never forgive himself. "No one will know we're here. You can take our money and go on about your business. I know this may sound shocking, but not everyone waits in a long line to honor Comrade Lenin. The guards have always let people in, day or night. And for much less than I'm offering you now. Don't let us in, if you want, but please, take the money all the same. It's only what you deserve."

The sergeant stared at the cash. Officer Volyunov licked his lips. Five hundred American dollars was a small fortune, especially with the Russian economy still bottoming. And, being a saint, Joseph's smile was always irresistible, even in the glow of a cheap lighter. The sergeant, who might never take another bribe in his life, never had a chance.

"I'll give you five minutes," he said.

"Do you think it might be possible to give us fifteen?"

The sergeant nodded as he took the bills, hardly noticing he'd changed his mind, and handed two to Officer Volyunov.

Misha hadn't visited Lenin's Tomb since the Komsomol tour his first year at university. Even if you didn't know Lenin was a sleeping vampire, it was a ghastly place. Once, in America, Ron and Nancy had taken them to visit a state fair with a haunted house on the midway. In Russia, they had Lenin's Tomb.

The lighting was as reverently gloomy as he remembered. Footsteps echoing off the granite, they descended to the lower level where Lenin lay encased in glass. A pair of ornamental spears, one with the hammer and sickle traced into the point, the other with the soviet star, extended beyond the foot of the coffin. The great man himself lay with his head on a bolster, his hands resting by the sides of the black suit that hid the wooden stake still impaling him.

Remove the stake, and Lenin would rise again.

Pulling a large key from his pocket, Joseph advanced to the casket.

"Where'd you get that?" Misha asked.

"From Trotsky."

Carefully, Joseph used the key to open each of the four locks at the bottom of the sarcophagus. Using the ornamental spears as handles, he swung the glass top up and open. Misha half-expected Lenin to rise from the grave in a last ghostly gasp of the undead communist ideal. He'd seen it happen before. Ustinov especially wouldn't stay down. But Lenin remained at rest, bullet head on black silk pillows. Without the glass around it, the corpse had become more real, less of a shrine and more an actual body. He looked quite dead.

For the moment.

"I'm sorry," Joseph apologized. "But that's as much as I can do. Would you like to take over?"

Misha didn't have to be asked twice. Reaching into his greatcoat, he pulled out his short sword, the one he'd found tucked inside a box in the basement on his first private tour of the Armory. The archivist on duty had told him it was a training saber for Alexander II. Misha had asked the KGB to retrieve it for him the next day, pleasing Brezhnev at this proof that Misha was finally getting into the proper spirit of the nomenklatura.

He hadn't been so pleased when Misha used the same saber to slice Brezhnev's own head off fifteen years later.

Stepping up to the stone ivy that ringed Lenin's head, Misha raised the sword high and brought it down in one swift stroke. The wooden bottom of the coffin tunked hollowly as the blade cut clean through the body. Lenin's head bounced off the side of the sarcophagus and rolled to the floor.

The rest of the body stayed right where it was.

"Holy mother!" Misha stared, astonished, at the lingering corpse. "Why's the body still here?"

"It must not be Lenin."

Plucking the head off the ground, Joseph picked gently at the mustache and beard. They seemed real enough. He replaced the head back on top of the neck and pulled the cadaver's collar a little higher. If you didn't notice the embalming fluid leaking out below the shoulders, the corpse looked almost the same as before.

Misha still didn't understand. "How can it not be Lenin?"

"Brezhnev used doubles, didn't he? You can't always avoid daylight when you're a head of state."

"But why would Stalin put the double on display?" Misha gestured at the body in the coffin. "What's the point of that?"

"I wish I knew," Joseph answered. "I wasn't expecting this."

"Didn't Trotsky warn you about it when he gave you the key?"

"I didn't get the key from Trotsky till after he died. Frida gave it to me after she removed his head."

Misha had no idea who Frida was, but then there were always lots of hunters. Few lasted as long as he had.

"Do you think Stalin actually killed him?" he asked. "Lenin, I mean. Permanently?"

"It's possible."

Joseph peered into the casket. Pushing the body to one side, he rapped the wooden bottom with a knuckle. Either Stalin had gotten cheap when it came to finishing the coffin, or the wooden bottom was hollow.

With surprising strength for so small a man, Joseph lifted Lenin's double with one hand, and the trap door he found underneath with the other. A rough wooden stair led downward.

Misha stepped back from the coffin. "If you want to go down there," he insisted, "we're going to need the army."

Joseph looked honestly perplexed. "Why is that?"

"Think who's buried in the graves behind the mausoleum. And in the Necropolis. Stalin, Kalinin, Sverdlov, Voroshilov, Bulganin. Do you really think they're all still spiked?"

"Bulganin? Really?"

"Since when did you start believing the official record?"

The thump of boot heels above interrupted Joseph's reply. The sergeant peered down at them. Damn it, Misha thought. Hadn't the man said he'd give them fifteen minutes?

"You two down there! What's going on?"

Joseph dove for the casket and scrambled down the hidden stair. The sergeant pulled out his pistol and started firing. Bullets pinged off the coffin's bulletproof glass. Since the casket was plainly the safest place in the room, Misha jumped in beside Lenin's double and followed Joseph underground.

The rickety steps creaked under his weight, but didn't break. His head scraped against the low ceiling.

"Are you all right?" Joseph asked amicably when Misha reached the bottom.

"What in the name of God were you thinking? You could have gotten me killed! We could have just given ourselves up!"

"I'm not in the country legally."

"I could have taken care of that with a phone call."

"I didn't want to take the chance. Saints aren't appreciated in Russia any more than vampires, you know. Too many people think we're two sides of the same coin."

Fresh footsteps sounded at the top of the stairs. Looking up, Misha saw the sergeant's square head silhouetted against the gloom above.

"You can't escape!" he shouted. "Surrender now and we'll give you a chance!"

"They might actually come down, you know," Joseph whispered. "They have no idea what we've stumbled onto. Unlike the Guard."

"All the more reason for me to give myself up. You can hide down here."

"What if there's another way out? When did anyone in Russia ever build a bunker with only one exit?"

"And if we run into Bulganin and Kalinin along the way?"

"I can't help you with that. Did you come prepared?"

"Yes."

Joseph beamed. "You're the best hunter I've ever known."

Misha didn't enjoy the compliment as much the second time. But Joseph was right. This wasn't the old days, when witnesses could disappear. Getting away without being caught would make things a lot easier. There was no guarantee Yeltsin wouldn't simply throw him to the wolves. And what would happen to Raisa then?

Clicking on the flashlight he'd brought, Misha shined the beam down the passage that led away from the stair. He had to stoop so his head wouldn't rub against the roof, but the tunnel was dry, and the brickwork had survived what he guessed were seventy-odd Moscow winters without cracking. His breath formed small clouds in the flashlight's pale glow, but the temperature was much warmer than in the square above.

They arrived at a small arch. The passage continued on for several steps before ending in a branching T. Misha played his light down each branch without finding anything in either direction, then flashed it upwards. Ceiling bricks flickered into view about a dozen meters overhead. A narrow ledge ran along the Red Square side of the wall behind them. What was on the ledge, Misha couldn't see. But he could guess.

"We're inside the wall, aren't we?" he said.

"If you mean the Kremlin, yes."

"Then that has to be the Necropolis." Misha waved his flashlight toward the ledge.

"I agree. And you know what? An empty vault might make an excellent way out. I can kick off one of those brass plaques easily."

"How do we get up?"

Joseph pointed to a set of iron rungs that climbed the side of the wall.

At the top, the ledge wasn't quite what Misha had expected. The vaults were small squares, each about two thirds of a meter on a side, spaced in the same long line as the plaques outside. But he hadn't imagined they'd be a line of open holes.

"Are they empty?" he asked.

Joseph shook his head and knocked the toe of his boot against a casket just inside the first opening. Misha tried to remember who was buried behind the mausoleum. One of the vampires?

"Guess we can't get out this way."

"I could pull it out," Joseph offered.

"No. Let's see if we can find an empty one."

They thought they found one on the third try, but, when Misha shined his flashlight inside, the beam revealed an urn. They could have pushed it aside and escaped that way, but, since the police seemed to have gone off for reinforcements rather than follow them immediately, they decided to continue on to the end of the ledge to get as far from the mausoleum as possible. That way, when Joseph popped off the plaque, any officers still on guard in Red Square might not notice them.

They finally heard voices behind them when Misha thought they were getting near the end of the line. Flashlights much more powerful than his brightened the ceiling. He turned off his own light instinctively.

"Now what?" he asked.

"We find the next urn and get out of here."

The next three vaults contained caskets, and then they were at the end of the line.

"This last one looks good," Joseph said optimistically. "But be careful. There's a hole in the floor."

"Maybe it's the back door." Looking back, Misha counted four lights flickering separately on the ceiling behind them. Still no escape that way. "Can we get down?"

"There is a ladder like the one at the other end."

"Let's try it."

Misha tried not to miss his grip on the cold bars as he followed Joseph down. He was a strong man, but he'd turned sixty a few months before the coup and wasn't used to so much exertion. Reaching the cramped tunnel at the bottom after a short climb, he took a deep breath, and turned his flashlight back on. He'd toured a few mines over the years, and hadn't liked the experience, but this was much worse. At least in the mines he hadn't had to crawl.

Joseph poked at the bricks in the tunnel roof. Loose mortar dusted his head and shoulders. "If you're uncomfortable," he said, "I might be able to dig a way out right here. We don't have to see what's at the end of the tunnel."

Misha waved Joseph forward.

It occurred to him that the last grave on this side of the mausoleum was Stalin's. And that they were heading right for it.

The tunnel ended in more iron rungs, with a trapdoor at the top. Misha held the flashlight while Joseph fiddled with the door. There was no handle, but after some firm pushing, it lifted straight up like a manhole cover. Following Joseph through, Misha found himself in a tiny crypt, barely larger than the coffin that filled it. Unlike Lenin's, this coffin was plain cement and covered in dust. Misha wondered if he could pry it open with the sword. While he was thinking, Joseph reached over with his bare hands and, despite not being able to stand, popped off the lid. A pair of rusted hinges rattled on the floor.

Stalin stared up at them through the dusty light.

There wasn't enough room for the sword. Not one to risk losing such a god-given opportunity to rid the Motherland of one its worst abusers, Misha chose his heaviest knife and started severing the sleeping vampire's head.

It wasn't easy. Unlike the ersatz Lenin, Misha had to work to get through the larynx and ligaments along the neck. This was the real Stalin, a real vampire and not some double embalmed so long his bones had turned to borscht. His thick mustache kept getting in the way, too, so Misha cut it off.

With a final jerk, he snapped the head off the severed spine. Stalin's abyssal eyes appeared to open at the last second, but even if they had, any unexpected return to consciousness was rendered moot when the body shriveled into itself and disappeared.

As Misha dumped the head on the floor, something clinked at the bottom of the empty casket. Turning around, he found Joseph holding a wooden stake in one hand, and what looked like a large pen with a blinking red light at the top in the other.

"What's that?"

"I don't know." Joseph dropped the stake back into the casket and handed the pen to Misha. "It was in the casket with the stake. Maybe you can figure it out."

Misha hefted the heavy stake in his hand. He was no electronics expert, but he had lived his entire life in the world's foremost surveillance state and this definitely had the clunky, old-fashioned look of the sort of solid state electronics the KGB had used thirty years ago.

"It looks like some kind of bug. Or maybe a transmitter. Only in the Soviet Union would anyone bug a grave."

"A transmitter?" Joseph's eyes narrowed. The red light blinked off. When it didn't return, his face tightened further. "Whatever it was transmitting, it looks like the signal was sent."

"It does," Misha agreed.

"Could it be used to set off a bomb?"

"It could, but not anything that's too far away. It would have to be close enough that we'd hear it."

"Not if it was a very small bomb."

"Why would anyone want to boobytrap Stalin?" Misha asked.

As if someone had flicked a switch, Joseph's tranquil face disappeared, replaced by a look of sheer horror. Without a word, he dropped back down through the hole at the bottom of the crypt they'd come up through.

Switching off his flashlight, Misha followed.

When he climbed cautiously back up to the ledge inside the Kremlin wall several minutes later, Joseph was nowhere in sight. There was no sign of the police, or their flashlights either. Instead, a loud crash exploded through the darkness, followed by scuffling. Wondering what on earth the saint was up to, Misha ducked back into the last crypt, switched on his flashlight, and poked his head around the corner.

The saint was still alone. He was whipping coffins out of the crypts like they were air mattresses, ripping off the lids, then heaving them out into the passage where they collapsed into kindling and bones.

"What are you doing?" Misha whispered. "Some of the people buried here were real heroes!"

"We have to find him before he wakes up."

"Find who?"

"The vampire the transmitter was hooked up to!"

Quick but sure, Joseph dumped another coffin into the passage. A woman's hand and leg sprawled over the side.

"What are you talking about?"

"Don't you see?" Joseph paused to look at Misha, clearly astonished the hunter hadn't figured it out yet. "Stalin's body was booby-trapped. At first I thought Khrushchev set it up so he could make Stalin return if Brezhnev or Andropov tried to take him down, but that wasn't what happened. The booby trap only went off after Stalin was gone. Which means it was meant to wake some other vampire. Someone worse even than Stalin, who'd create so much chaos he'd take down the entire party."

"How can you be so sure?" Misha demanded. "How do you know Kruschev didn't set it up to set off a bomb in the Presidium? Or Chernobyl?"

"I don't." Ducking into the next crypt, Joseph pulled out an urn and tossed it over his shoulder. A rain of fine ash sprinkled Misha's face and bald head as the urn burst open in midflight. "But if that is what happened, there's nothing we can do about it now. Waking another vampire we can take care of."

"How can a tiny transmitter wake a vampire?"

A skull soared briefly through the beam of Misha's flashlight.

"A tiny bomb in the chest of a sleeping vampire would be more than enough to blast away any stake keeping it down without killing it."

"Oh." Misha rocked back on his heels as awful new possibilities began to emerge. "Who do you think it might be? Beria? Dzerzhinsky?"

Another coffin flew through the air. "You said it yourself, why should we trust the official tally of who's buried here? Hell, it might even be Trotsky. I never did see his body."

"Not that traitor," intoned a voice. "Never him."

Misha shined his flashlight farther down the ledge. A figure crouched over a fallen body. Three more victims sprawled in the shadows behind them.

Without a thought for his own safety, Joseph hurried forward. The crouching figure stepped away from the arc of Misha's light. On his knees, Joseph cradled the head of the monster's victim. The saint's small cry of grief echoed down the passage like a handclap in an empty church.

Officer Volyunov's face gleamed, pale as milk.

"Is he dead?" Misha asked, though he already knew the answer.

Joseph nodded. Tears jeweled his cheeks. A saint could watch a vampire die without a second thought, but a human life was unbearably precious, tribute to the saint's own eternal guilt. Once a vampire, always a vampire, even if you turned into a saint.

Ignoring the monster still lurking in the darkness, Joseph gently lifted the dead policeman. Misha inclined his flashlight up to reveal the vampire's face and gasped.

Vladimir Ilyich Lenin.

The real one.

No vampire had ever looked more satanic. How else to describe a balding, goateed man with small eyes and the perennial, clipped smile of a patronizing know-it-all? Dead seven years before Misha was born, but Misha still knew that face even better than he knew Stalin's. Or his own. Lenin had always been there, on every office wall, in every town square, peering unforgivingly down from his pedestal at everyone trying, and failing, to live up to his lofty ideals.

He was close enough for Misha to see the hole in his chest, and Officer Volyunov's fresh blood dribbling down his chin. Not close enough, however, for a good shot. Not in this light. Not with Misha's reflexes against a vampire's.

And how did you stake a vampire that already had a hole in its chest, anyway?

Lenin smiled.

"Joseph!" he called. "You're the last person I expected to greet me at my rising."

Officer Volyunov still in his arms, Joseph stepped back beside Misha. "I'd rather not have been here," he admitted.

Lenin chuckled. "Are you expecting me to kill you?"

"Oh, how I wish you would."

The vampire laughed again, then glanced at Misha. "I see you've brought a hunter with you. Looks like good peasant stock. A real Russian. Though a little old for a young human's game. Here, kulak. What's your name?"

"Michael Sergeyevich."

"I was the ruler of all the Russias, once. Do you really think you can kill me, little Misha?"

"Yes."

Lenin's eyebrows rose in mock surprise. Really, he should be in Hollywood. He even laughed like the devil.

"I have killed other vampires," Misha declared.

"Of course you have. Joseph wouldn't have brought you if you hadn't. I imagine it's been a while since you did, though. But I'm not Vlad the Impaler. You don't get to be the greatest revolutionary in the world by biting people. Much more satisfying to feed off their minds."

It took a special kind of vampire to want to rule the world. Slowly, Misha withdrew his pistol from inside his heavy overcoat. Slowly, because he was afraid Lenin might try to jump him if he did it too suddenly. And his pistol, rather than his crossbow, because he wanted Lenin to remain unconcerned. Let the fool have his brag. Nothing like overconfidence in a vampire to help a hunter bag him.

Lenin turned back to Joseph. "You still haven't told me why you're here," he said. "Trying to finish the job you started with Rasputin?"

"Yes. I didn't realize you were the problem then."

"The monk accomplished what he was supposed to. But, like most of my comrades, he was all appetite and no brain. He didn't realize our destiny is to rule the world, not devour it. Only we have to do it collectively. The humans outnumber us by too much for any other way to succeed. Marx was right. But it's the risen who will rule the earth, not the proletariat. Might as well be ruled by swine."

"It has been suggested," Joseph said.

"I think he needs to decide what he is," Misha pointed out. "A communist, or a vampire. You can't be both."

"That is why Stalin staked him."

Lenin grimaced and clenched a fist. "Stalin is an imbecile. How long have I been down? Two years? Three?"

"Seventy," Joseph answered.

The greatest revolutionary in the world staggered a bit at the news. Plainly it didn't fit his self-image. How could the world, risen or human, have managed without him? And for so long?

Misha saw his chance. Not with the pistol, but with the flash bomb still in his coat. Closing his eyes, he pulled it out of his pocket and tossed it in the air. Lenin would know it was a weapon, but probably wouldn't know to shield his eyes.

The flash went off with a loud boom, bright enough that even through his eyelids Misha thought his own vision had been seared away. Silence thick as a blizzard followed the explosion, but his eyes worked fine when he opened them. Lenin had fallen backwards on the ledge, fingers scrabbling at his face. Soundlessly, Misha saw him scream. Stepping forward, he pumped half a dozen bullets into Lenin's brain. The devil's head exploded like a melon.

What was left came off much easier than Stalin's.

"Is it done?"

Ears still ringing, Misha turned to find Joseph groping blindly along the ledge. Apparently the saint hadn't known to close his eyes, either.

"It's done," Misha answered.

"Good." The saint stopped. Though he couldn't see Misha, his hearing was still precise enough that he was able to look directly at him. "Your country is free."

Misha sighed. Not with so many ex-KGB still running around. Especially the ambitious ones. In Russia, brute force still prevailed. The Americans had moved beyond that. In America, even the vampires were capitalists. But Russia remained the perfect old world blend of ignorance and unchecked power.

A vampire's dream.

Wearily he led Joseph up and out of Lenin's Tomb. With any luck, Raisa would have tea ready for him when he got home.

Illustration by Ariel Guzman

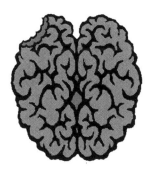

Harrold of the Gods

Sam Robb

"I am a herald of the gods, woman!"

"Ain't interested."

Flick. Plunk. Splash.

* * *

The wind cut across the northern ocean, kicking up sea spray from the waves, making her eyes water. A worn and patched coat kept the chill from her bones. The last full moon of summer peeked above the horizon as the sun descended behind the clouds in the west.

She sculled her small boat across the waves, heading for the last crab trap. Snagged the line on the buoy with a practiced motion and started hauling the trap in with calloused hands. If she pulled it in a little slower or moved a little more carefully these days, well, that was understandable. Seventy summers would do that to anyone, even a North Sea fisherwoman.

The trap reached the surface and she leaned over the side of the boat to pull it in. A muffled cough came from inside the trap, the sound of someone clearing a throat.

"Ahem. Good sir or madam! Please do not be alarmed. I know that with the rise of Yinznat, Lord of Chaos, magic is frowned upon. Yet I am a herald sent by the gods themselves, here to bring you..."

She ignored the voice and heaved the trap up over the side into the boat. There were several crabs inside, crawling and snapping at each other.

"…Oh for the god's sake, you idiot, would you leave me alone? Sorry. Not you. This blue crab is being rather—GET AWAY FROM ME! There! You can have that dead thing!"

Sighing, she opened the trap and peered inside, then thrust her hand in quickly. She pulled out a jeweled crab, pincers waving angrily, and held it facing away from her. The fading evening light glinted off its iridescent shell, sparkling and shimmering.

"Oh! Right. Thank you! As I was saying! I am a herald from above! You have been chosen by the gods themselves! Thanks to you, Yinznat will be defeated, and his fall shall usher in a new age of prosperity and peace for the world!"

She brought the hand holding the crab up and turned it to face her. Its waving claws slowed, then stopped.

"Oh, gods," the crab said, folding its eye stalks down along its body. "You again?"

The fisherwoman brushed a strand of iron-gray hair that had escaped her tight bun away from her face. "Yep." She turned him back and forth, examining him. "Kinda scrawny, ain't ya? Not much eating there."

"Excuse me?" The crab waved its claws indignantly. "Did you hear anything I've said?"

"Mhm." The woman leaned back. "Talking animals are either a sign of mushroom consumption or supernatural activity. Well known fact. Seeing as I hate mushrooms, it's obviously the later." She narrowed her eyes. "You're from the gods, eh? Ever hear of the Doom of Vanis? Or Forvavare?"

The crab paused its waving. "Um. No?"

"Nobody studies the classics anymore," she muttered. "Vanisdottr! Appointed by the gods to rule over Restamore? Forvavare, the weaver gifted supernatural tailoring skills. Also from the gods?" She poked the crab. "Ringing any bells?"

The crab shrank back in on itself. "Oh. Those two."

"Yes, those two! Where's Vanis now, eh? Tell me."

"Er…eternally pursued by the dead spirits of the family she deposed, if I recall correctly."

"And Forvavare? Turned into an apron because of his pride, wasn't he?"

"A pinafore, actually. Look, those two are hardly representative of, well…anything!"

"Tellimure. Cedar of the Sands. Cordellia. Shamus the Younger. Dolmoné. The Wolf of the Law." She shook the crab. "I could go on. Story after story. Each of 'em called by the gods, eh? Tell me! How many happy endings among that lot?"

"Well, um. I mean…" The crab sagged. "None, that I recall."

"There you go. Enjoy your flight."

"What?"

With a practiced flick of her wrist, the crab sailed over the water. It disappeared with a plunk, the fading sound of angry muttering, and a final splash. She stared at where it had vanished under the waves for a moment before turning back to the trap.

* * *

The crab returned the next full moon. It started grumbling as soon as she pulled it from the trap. When she picked it up, it latched onto her calloused thumb. She winced, eyes narrowed at the pain.

"Listen. I keep ending up in your hands! You can't argue with destiny, woman!"

"Told you. Ain't interested." She flicked a finger at the crab. It jerked back, letting go of her thumb.

Flick. Plunk. Splash.

* * *

The winds off the bay were picking up. The occasional gust howled, causing her cooking fire to flare. She sat at her table next to the fire, an unlit pipe held firmly between her teeth as she worked her knitting needles to produce a tiny wool sweater.

The wind died down briefly and she became aware of a tap-tap-tap at the door. She narrowed her eyes and worked her needles, studiously ignoring the noise. After a moment, it repeated.

A muffled voice slipped in under the bottom of the door. "I can keep this up all night, you know."

A sigh almost escaped her lips as she worked the pipe, contemplating. She finally set her knitting on the table, stood up, and opened the door. The draught whirled through, making the fire spark.

"Get yourself in here, then." Teeth clenched around the pipe gave her voice a hard edge. "I'm having m' smoke before supper. I'll give you the length of it before I kick you out."

The crab said nothing, but waved its claws and scuttled into the room.

* * *

She lit a splinter of wood from the fire and brought it to her pipe. "I'm curious. Does the weather not bother you?"

"Don't really feel it," the crab said as she puffed. "It did make it hard to get up here, though. That and the gulls."

"It's a day past the full moon. Took you that long?"

The crab ignored her. "Listen. You have a destiny. Miss, uh…"

"Missus, not that anyone would care. My name's Guz. I'd expect a minion of the gods to know that."

"Herald," the crab said distractedly. It raised up, antennae quivering. "Entirely different job description. What's that you're making?"

"Crab soup."

"Good choice. We're delicious. I meant the knitting."

Guz pursed her lips. "Just something to while away the time until the stew was done." She shoved the knitting off the back of the table and into a basket.

"Hmm. Anyways. You have a destiny to fulfill, Mrs. Guz."

She worked her pipe around to the other side of her mouth before answering. "Told ya, Harrold. Ain't interested."

"Not Harrold, herald…you know what? Never mind. You do realize that the entire kingdom of Caldamere has been conquered by the forces of Yinznat, don't you?"

Guz shrugged as she took another puff. "He whose baleful eye watches o'er the land, his vigilant might ready to crush all that dare oppose him? Yep."

Harrold's eyestalks rose. "O'er the land? Really?"

Guz snorted. "That's on all the literature he sends out. We get it up here once a month or so. They post it in the village square."

"Surely you don't want to continue to live under 'his baleful eye'?"

Guz sat back and puffed away, staring at the ceiling. After a few seconds, she finally spoke. "Might surprise you, but who's in charge doesn't make much of a difference up here. We fish, we live. Duke Buckley or Yinznat, it's all the same to us one way or another." She looked back down and tapped her pipe to settle the coals. "If you're looking for someone who cares, I suggest you try somewhere else."

"Believe me, I've looked. You're it. Either I convince you to take this up, or that's it. Unrelenting darkness for all eternity."

"We're already so far north that it's dark most of the year."

Harrold settled down with an exasperated sigh. "Spiritual darkness. A life of constant hardship, every day a struggle for survival, the entire world against you. Can you imagine what that would be like?"

Guz stared at the crab intently, one eyebrow raised. She waved her hand, gesturing slowly at her cabin. Harrold followed her hand and took in the contents of the tiny room. Bed, table, chair, a cabinet and a chest, and not much else besides a fire.

"You just described my whole life. Told you, who's in charge don't make much of a difference to us up here."

"You can't be serious!"

She sat back in her chair. "Might be, a little bit. Might do the rest o' the world a bit of good, to have to learn what it means to live like this. It'd teach 'em to get along better, I reckon."

Harrold folded up, claws covering eyestalks, muttering angrily. Guz leaned forward, brow furrowed as she tried to make out the words. After a bit, she sat back and smiled.

"You must have read a thesaurus at one point. You missed 'clodpoll,' though. That's always been one of my favorites."

One eye peeked out from under a claw. "I'll make note of it."

She chuckled a bit. "If you're serious, why don't you go bother Grant?"

"Who's Grant?"

"One of my boys down in the town."

Harrold perked up and took a step toward her. "Surely your son would tell you to listen to a call from the gods!"

"Ha! He ain't any blood of mine. Though he is the mayor, more or less. Ain't nobody else wants the job, so he takes care of things."

"We're talking about the end of the world, woman. That calls for more than a minor government official."

"Eh. He's a bit of a wizard. Think you could work with that?"

"How is he a wizard? Yinznat specifically scoured the world of all magical talent!"

She shrugged. "We're out of the way. And Yinznat, well, he is a Chaos Lord. You keep bringing that up. Might be why he doesn't have much of an attention span. Most of his proclamations are already worn out and bone-tired when they get up here. Unless it's something about fishing, we don't pay too much attention."

"How often are they about fishing?"

"Once, about, oh, three years ago. We were supposed to send him all the canopy fish we caught."

"Did you?"

"We swore we would. Of course, canopy fish are tropical, so I don't think we've ever caught one up here. Did send the Dread Overlord down the coast a ways some nice sea bass, though. I think he appreciated that."

* * *

There was a knock at the door.

Guz frowned. "She's early."

"Who?"

"Magdalene, here for…a visit." Guz looked around distractedly. She stood up and gestured at the bed. "You, hide yourself under there and be quiet, or I swear, herald or no, it's the pot for you. She and Johan have a little one to care for now. She doesn't need any of this god stuff mucking up her life."

"Going, going." Pincers waving, Harrold scuttled under the bed.

Guz scowled, then turned to open the door. A sudden gust whipped past the cloaked figure standing there, lantern in hand.

"What're you waiting for? Don't just stand there letting the light out, get your bones in here!" Guz barked. The figure bowed and stepped inside. Guz slammed the door shut.

The woman lifted the hood of her cloak. "I'm sorry, Grandmother. I thought I heard you talking to someone…"

"Talking to myself," Guz grumped. She waved her hand. "Don't pay no mind, child. Only good conversation I get most days. How's little Buckley?"

"Doing better. Still tired." She gave her a smile. "His cough is almost gone, though."

"Good!" Guz turned to the canning jar, filled with cooling crab stew, and tightened down the lid. "Here. This is for you and Johan. Little something to help keep the meat on your bones. I know how tiring it is, taking care of a young'un like that." She pressed the jar into Magdalene's hands and turned to the cabinet next to the fire.

Magdalene rolled the still-hot jar between her hands, then slipped it into a pocket of her cloak. "We can't…"

"You can and you will. I know you two like it. You used to gobble it up like nobody's business."

The young lady laughed. "Yes. Ok. Johan will thank you for it."

"Tell him I could use some help with the roof." Guz closed the cabinet and turned back, a small sachet of paper in her hands. "Here. You don't want to know what's in it, and it'll taste awful. Mix it in the stew, though, and it'll be alright. Make sure the baby gets as much as he can eat, and you and Johan finish off the rest. It'll keep you all healthy."

"Grandmother…"

"None of that." Guz made shooing motions. "Git you on out, young lady. Back to that babe of yours and that young man who gave him to you. Take care of your family."

The woman hesitated, then threw her arms around Guz. The old woman took the hug with grace, as her due, lifting one hand to give Magdalene a squeeze on her shoulder.

"Go on, now. Be careful getting home. And remind Johan about my roof, you hear?"

"Aye, Grandmother." She tucked the sachet into her cloak, then raised her hood and turned to leave. The wind snuck in again, briefly, as she slipped out the door.

* * *

Harrold slid out from under the bed. "Relative of yours?"

She crossed her arms. "They call me Grandmother out of respect. Something that's in short supply these days." After a moment she looked away. "My Ben died at sea before we could start our family. Ain't nobody left in this part of the world that's of my blood these days."

"What was that you gave her?"

She rolled her eyes. "Crab stew."

"No." Harrold climbed back up onto the hearth. "The other thing, at the end."

"Mantis seaweed, with maiden's mold. Aged, dried, ground fine, and mixed with a drop of poppy milk."

"So, you're a witch?"

"Hag." Guz straightened up infinitesimally as she spoke, a hint of pride in her voice. "Herbs and medicines. Learned that myself, from some of the books Grant keeps for the village."

"Crab stew, medicinal herbs, and knitting. You've got some skills." Harrold sidled along the hearth to the knitting basket and grabbed the rim, trying to peer over the edge. "Who's the sweater for? Her boy?"

She reached down and snatched Harrold up, holding the crab in front of her face while waving her finger. "You get your claws out of there! I don't care who you're working for." She leaned over with a grunt and deposited the crab carefully on the hearth, then winced and held her back as she stood up. "Ain't a boy's sweater, in any case. As any fool could plainly see. It's for the Yohe's little girl. Not that it's any of your business."

Harrold slid off the hearth and back onto the floor with a thunk. "Kind, resourceful, skilled. I can see why the gods picked you."

Guz rolled her eyes. "Back at that again? Told you, I ain't interested."

"OK, you want to play hard to get. Fine." Harrold moved up to her, poked her boot, then leaned back to look up. "I've been authorized to make you an offer. Let's talk."

* * *

"Never knew a crab could go hoarse from talking," Guz mused. "I guess you learn something new every day."

"Been out of the water too long. Come on. You've turned down riches…"

Guz shrugged. "Where would I spend it?"

"…true love…"

"Had it. Don't need another."

"…youth…"

"Worked hard to get where I am. Don't want to go through that again."

"…an ever-filling tankard…"

"Don't drink but a glass of port at Year's End. Usually don't even finish that."

"…a rain of fishes…" The crab looked up at her. Guz shook her head slowly.

"Yeah, I don't know what He was thinking either," Harrold muttered.

"That's the gods for you. They do tend to be a little out of touch, eh?"

"A life of ease?"

"Wouldn't know what to do with myself." Guz raised an eyebrow. "Though I'll admit, the offer of an assorted candy selection was tempting. We don't get much chocolate up this way."

"So…" Harrold perked up, claws waving excitedly.

"Still no." Guz shook her head. "A bit of chocolate's fine, but I'm not going off on some crazy adventure for a bon-bon."

"There must be something!"

"Told ya. I ain't interested." Guz took her pipe out from between her lips, considered it for a moment, then sighed and emptied the ashes into the fire. "Besides, your time's been up for a while."

"Why did you let me keep going?"

"You seemed like you were enjoying yourself." Guz stood up and brushed herself off, then pulled her knitting out of the basket and laid it on the table before tipping over the empty basket. "In."

"What's that for?"

"Get in the basket. I'm hauling you back down to the ocean."

Harrold waved his claws defiantly. "What if I don't want to?"

"You're welcome to stay. There's plenty of room in the pot."

The crab's eyes twitched. "Come on. Please?"

"Nope. Into the basket you go."

Guz tapped her foot. The crab stared up at her stubbornly. After a moment, Guz cocked her head at the stewpot.

"Right. Basket sounds fine, actually." Harrold scuttled inside.

Guz shrugged on her coat, grabbed her hat, then picked up the basket and headed out.

* * *

"You know, you could let me get into the surf on my own."

Guz chuckled as she scooped the crab up. "What, and break our little tradition?"

Harrold muttered. Guz flicked her wrist.

Plunk. Splash.

She watched the waves dance in the moonlight for a minute before she shook her head and turned away.

* * *

A month later, the first winds of winter were whipping off the sea. As Guz made her way down the rocks to the beach, she hunched over, hiding her eyes from the blowing sand.

It took some time to find the right place to sit. She found what she was looking for in a rocky niche out of the weather: an old driftwood log, weathered gray and half-buried in the sand. She sat and lit her pipe, then puffed away as the rays of the setting sun lit up the surf. The air filled with the smell of salt and old tobacco.

She was so lost in her thoughts that she missed the scratching noise of something trying to climb up onto the log. When she finally became aware of it, she reached over and gave the jeweled crab a little push to help it up onto the log beside her.

"Thanks."

Guz shrugged. She stared out at the sea and puffed on her pipe. Harrold settled down next to her, claws picking absent-mindedly at the old wood. They sat together a moment watching the waves.

Harrold finally cleared his throat. "So. What's new with you?"

Guz took a puff on her pipe. "Changed my mind. Thought I'd let you know."

"Wonderful! Great! Don't care."

Guz turned her head, a frown on her face. "You said I had a destiny. I've thought it over. I'll do it."

"That," Harrold intoned, "is about the worst lie I think I have ever heard."

"Wouldn't think crabs did much lying to one another."

"I'm employed by the gods. I've heard some real doozies."

"Hmpf. How does a crab go about getting into the heralding business, anyway?"

"I may happen to be a crab at the moment. That's kind of the suit I had to put on. Herald of the gods, remember? I can take many forms."

"Fine. Take whatever form you want, let's get going."

Harrold folded himself down into a compact little lump on the log. "Nope."

A flicker of annoyance crossed Guz's face. "What in the three hells are you talking about? I have a destiny. You wouldn't shut up about it. I'm here now. Show it to me. Let's do it."

Harrold flicked an eye stalk at her. "And when the going gets tough? When things get nasty? How do I know you're the one? That you're not going to flake on me?" He shook a claw at her. "This isn't only about saving the world, you know. This is my job on the line here."

She narrowed her eyes and reached into her coat. "Can you read?"

"Seventeen living languages, three dead, and one that's only remembered by me. Why?"

Guz snorted and pulled a paper out from inside her coat. She laid it down on the log between them and held it in place. "There."

Harrold lifted himself up and stepped onto the paper, eye stalks waving. "By order of Yinznat, He whose baleful eye watches o'er the land, vigilant might ready to crush all that dare oppose him…" He looked up at Guz.

She raised an eyebrow and shrugged. "Told you."

"You did. Let's see…blah blah blah, ignored for too long, yada yada, war in the West, final victory nigh, call upon all able-bodied mortals over the age of twelve to report as conscripts?"

"That's pretty much everyone in the village." Guz stared off at the sea. Her voice was quiet and hard. "Men, women, children. They'll leave the babes and the elderly."

"So? You said none of them are your family."

"I said none of them are blood. Not the same." She took a final puff on her pipe, then tapped the coals out into the sand. They flared brightly before dying out.

"You never asked who I was. Came here, oh, fifty years ago. Born and raised two months down the coast. They needed a teacher up this way. I was going to do a few years, get some experience, then move back home. That was before I met my Ben."

"Ah." Harrold sounded thoughtful. "I think I see."

Guz nodded. "Those that they'll take? I helped raise most of them kids. Ben and I, we never had ones of our own. Didn't bother us, because we always had little ones to care for anyways. We watched 'em when their parents were out during the busy season. Took care of 'em when they were sick. They called us Gram and Paps, and we called 'em our kids. After Ben left me, I took care of the kids of our kids."

Harrold stretched up, pincers out, eyestalks extended and focusing on her. "And?"

"And there's not a single man, woman, or child in the village that's my blood." Guz looked down at him and ground the pipe between her teeth hard enough that Harrold could hear it over the sound of the surf. "Mark my words, though. Every last one of them is family. Every last one. I'll be damned if I let some Dark Lord treat 'em like cannon fodder."

The night was quiet save for the surf and the rustling of wind-blown sand. That lasted the space of a deep breath before a preternaturally loud CRACK sounded as Harrold clacked both his claws together at the same time.

"Alright." He stood up. "That, I think I can work with."

"Good." She stood up and brushed off her pants, then held out her hand. Harrold took the hint and climbed onto her palm, careful not to pinch her. "Let's head back. Tomorrow, we're going to go see Grant."

"What? Why? The fewer people who know, the better! Why do you want to get him involved?"

"If we do this, it's on my terms. We're going to tell Grant so he can stall on the conscripts. Maybe hide some of the younger ones away." She poked at him. "Told you, too, he's got a bit of wizardin' under his belt. I want him to look you over before we leave. Verify your bony hide. I want to hear what he thinks about you and your tale. If he likes it, we'll make plans."

"And if he doesn't?"

The corner of her mouth curled up in a wicked half-smile. "Pot's still on back at my place. One way or another, I'll make use of ya."

Harrold sighed. "That's the best I'm going to get from you, isn't it?"

"Yep." She started walking back up the rocky beach toward her cabin.

"Fine! I want one promise out of you, though. I need some of that stew tonight."

"Might be able to do that, I suppose. What do you need it for?"

Harrold looked up at her and flicked his eyes in surprise. "Weren't you listening? I told you. We're *delicious.*"

Illustration by Ariel Guzman

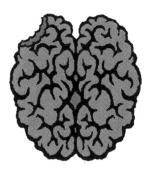

Hungry Skins

Liam Hogan

The city slumbers fitfully. While it does, I lurk beneath the tattered awning of a shuttered news concession, avoiding the drizzle and watching the wind toy with discarded fast-food wrappers.

It's not half as glamorous as it sounds.

A young man, too snappily dressed for these streets, bounds up the Metro steps. He scans his surroundings before strolling my way. About bloody time. I make a point of checking my watch.

"What monster are we hunting tonight?" he drawls, offering no apology.

I frown, and my too-junior partner's grin widens. "They're *cryptids*, not monsters."

"Perhaps," Malzy says, arching a sleek eyebrow. "But if they weren't at least a *little* monstrous, we wouldn't be hunting them, would we, Ms. Bliss?"

He has a point, though his attitude sucks, right down to his leaning on *Ms.* He hasn't earned the right to use my first name and this is his petty revenge. He's cocksure, sexist, and ageist to boot. He doesn't want a stoop-shouldered, silver-haired mentor, who should have shuffled off to a desk job eons ago, any more than I want an annoyingly good-looking, know-it-all rookie whose mind is on career progression, which means getting out from under my tutelage as quick as impolitely possible.

I have to wonder: which of us is the station chief trying to get rid of, putting us together? The cynic in me all too readily answers: *both.*

As for monsters, the agency's policy is to leave well enough alone whenever it can. The rest of the world isn't so enlightened. Sometimes we have to step in for the creature's sake. At others, yes, there's a risk to human life and limb. Not because cryptids are *monstrous*. No more so than your average cold and fearful human. But because humans are so numerous, so noisy and blundering; any creature with a defensive capability or an appetite is likely, at some point, to find itself crossing paths with some dimwit who may or may not be armed and, if so, will be a larger risk to themselves and any bystanders than the rare beast they've stumbled across. And they *will* be rare. The Agency, normally just before announcing another round of cuts, says we've lost eighty percent of cryptids over the last fifty years. It's been going on all my working life, and the truly dangerous creatures have already been driven extinct. All that's left are the ones that are really good at hiding, or really good at fitting in. The job isn't getting any easier even if we have less to do.

I show him the pic on my phone.

"A sodden cardboard box?" He grunts. "Can't handle one of those on your own?"

"Look *closer*," I urge, with weary overtones.

"Huh. A box with a label printed by someone who doesn't know how to spell *Fragile*."

"It's not a box." The label should be a giveaway. It's not just misspelled: *all* the letters are wrong, like it was designed by one of those art AIs that doesn't know what writing actually is. *Vaguely* familiar, but utterly unreal. "It's a skin, shed."

"A snake that looks like a refrigerator box?" he scoffs.

"More interesting than a mere *snake*, Malzy. We think it belongs to a Sheckley. The lab is running tests."

"Wow, so a Sheckley, hey?" He gazes into the middle distance, though there's nothing there but puddles lit by blinking neon, where the neon hasn't long since fritzed out. "Remind me?"

I shouldn't have to explain this; *any* of it. But it's a common problem when fast-tracking agents, especially ones fresh from departments convinced they're more important than Cryptid Control. Malzy *thinks* he can learn on the job. Which he can, and assuredly will, as long as he doesn't get himself and his suffering partner killed doing so.

I've done what I can to bring him up to speed, for my sake, though none of it half as effective as a month spent in archives, reading incident reports and watching the rare videos; followed by time spent in dispatch, where sightings filter through and possible cryptids are tentatively identified. I've taken him on a tour of the mostly empty holding pens in the disused foundry on the outskirts of the city, to show him what we might encounter. He was infuriatingly dismissive.

"A *barghest*," I said.

"Shaggy mutt," he replied, barely giving the snarling beast a second glance.

"Sewer squid."

"No calamari for me. Wouldn't want to be shellfish," he quipped as I imagined him skewered and grilled.

"Zombie King Rat—"

"Not being *funny*, Ms. Bliss, but if we're patrolling on foot, do they issue us guns? Preferably like the ones Alien Artifacts—"

It never takes him long to mention the aliens. As if a six-month rotation there goes any deeper than it will here. "We patrol on *foot*, Malzy, because you're unlikely to encounter a cryptid from behind the wheel of an automobile. Agents are there to identify and assess the threat, not to do a *Dirty Harry* on what are some of the rarest of Earth's creatures. Capture and release where they won't bother us, and we won't bother them, is the goal for even the worst trouble makers. And if a cryptid *does* need putting down, which is always a last resort, we call in a specialist firearms team."

He knows this already. *Supposedly*. Even if he obviously hasn't read up on the rarest of the rare.

"A *Sheckley* takes on whatever shape best brings its prey to it," I lecture him. "It's not particularly fussy about what it eats, as long as it's alive. The young often start feeding on rats, especially in urban environments, by taking on the form—and smell—of an open box of cereal, or a discarded fast-food container. Once the rat enters…*goodbye* rat. Think Venus Flytrap on steroids. Sheckleys can't hunt, they only lie in wait. But don't underestimate them just because they don't have legs. You have to be pretty cunning to get a meal to crawl into your mouth."

Malzy takes a second, dubious look at the screen. "That's a big box for a rat."

I nod. "And that's the problem. Sheckley's *grow*. Eventually, rats don't cut the mustard. No one knows quite how large they get if they find a steady food source, and if we don't relocate them first. Because eventually, the only life-form big enough and common enough to meet their appetite, in a city, leastwise, is *human*. Which is usually when they come to our attention."

"Still…a discarded box?" he asks, handing the phone back.

"What would *you* pretend to be?"

He shrugs. "A dropped wallet? A bulging handbag?"

An interesting insight into a misspent youth. "A handbag that bites your hand off doesn't get the chance to repeat the trick. But a box lying in an alleyway that devours its meal completely, before opening up again, ready for its next victim…?"

He blinks. "The missing tramps?"

I nod, slowly. At least he's paid *some* attention to the daily briefings. The Agency gets alerted to anything out of the ordinary. Usually, it turns out to be an overgrown pet or a stuffed toy. Usually, the most dangerous and out of the ordinary thing out there is *human*. Sometimes, though…

You might think no one misses the homeless. But charities do. The ones that hand out food and dry clothes, and drop by to check on them. Soup kitchens who begin to recognize the people queuing up. All very vague, and it isn't uncommon for a handful of homeless to go missing in any particular month; some of whom turn up, some don't.

But there had been an up-tick, of late, of those *not* turning up. And when a garbage disposal crew found the discarded skin with its lettering that isn't quite lettering (not that a homeless person late at night in a persistent drizzle is going to pay much attention to *that*), they thankfully called us in.

"The box was spotted because it was unusually long. Over six foot." I eye my tall partner. "You know how a python works out if a meal is too big for it, Malzy? It lays down beside it."

He shudders, his shoulders briefly hunch, and he peers into the dank dark. "So what do we do?" he asks.

"First, you take one of these." I hand him two large chalk-white tablets. "What are they?"

"*Horrid*, is what they are. A powerful astringent. *Very* bitter tasting. It's even more so for a Sheckley, which means if you *do* stumble into one, instead of onto one, it'll spit you back up again. Hopefully."

"*Hopefully?*"

"It's always best not to get swallowed." I give him a smile to soften the edge. "Take the second in about two hour's time, assuming we're still hunting then."

He puts the fat tablet in his mouth and his eyes screw up, followed by the rest of his face as he gags. I hold my nose as I quickly swallow mine, swigging cold coffee before dumping the cup in the overflowing trash.

"Takes half an hour to take effect," I say, as he sucks down breath, eyes watering and snot hanging unceremoniously from one nostril. "On a Sheckley, that is."

He groans. Never let anyone tell you Cryptid Control isn't sexy.

"So we stick together until then," I continue, unfurling my umbrella. "And no poking your nose into any dark places, however tempting."

He glances up at the night, the drizzle only likely to get more persistent. "Got another of those?" he asks.

"Sorry," I say, as I lead us off. I'm not, particularly, and I think he knows it.

"So, we're looking for a box that eats people?" he asks, as we head to the nearest dark, narrow alleyway. God alone knows what the city planners were thinking when they conjured up this maze. Probably mostly about their mistresses and holiday homes, paid for by real estate kickbacks.

I shake my head. "A Sheckley only sheds when it takes on a new form. So it will be something else now. Something bigger. They grow fast, because all they really are is skin, and pretty flexible skin at that. It'll be something hollow and open that their victims can enter. Something vaguely enticing."

"Somewhere warm and dry?" he suggests, raising the collar around his exposed neck.

"Perhaps. But not *too* enticing. Being passive, they're patient; they can go up to a week between meals. When they do eat, they take it slow, making it last a couple of days. And while they're consuming their meal, they prefer not to be noticed at all."

"And that box…?" he asks.

"Was reported two nights ago. So if it hasn't already found another victim, it should have reset the trap by now, whatever it is."

I hand him a flashlight. Those I *do* have two of, a flashlight being vital for night work, whereas an umbrella is strictly a luxury. *My* luxury. "As they grow, they get more sophisticated. So it will probably be more intricate than a simple box. They can adopt the shape of other things, mimicking spaces they find, forming a skin *inside* whatever is already there, and then, chameleon like, copying the outside as well."

The first alley is too clean and empty, as well as too brightly lit. Presumably kept that way to discourage pan-handlers who might see the proximity to the subway as a prime location. We move on.

"Remember how I mentioned they can mimic the smell of food, to lure rats? They have other ways to tempt their prey, so keep *all* your senses on high alert."

"Such as?"

"Bio-luminescence, for one. Like an angler fish, to draw victims in the night. There were reports of one up north that was particularly effective, for maybe as long as two years. All it was—or appeared to be—was an unsigned, open doorway onto a stairwell dimly bathed in red light."

Malzy shakes his head at the wickedness of the world, while giving me a locker-room grin. *Damn* if I'm not enjoying myself a little too much. This Sheckley, only one step up from a cardboard box, won't be anything as sophisticated as a fake brothel. Its lures will still be the sort that work on the homeless. Though it doesn't do any harm to increase Malzy's woeful knowledge, even if this is odds-on the only Sheckley he'll ever experience.

"They can even make simple sounds. They struggle with words, just as they struggle with writing, because they don't *understand* language, but you might get snatches, a kind of medley of the things it has overheard. Background noises and music. They can mimic furniture—"

"Now you're kidding me!" He stops mid-step.

I shrug. "It's just more skin. But, like skin, the items have to remain attached. It can't generate anything that roams free, can't split itself up. *Although…*"

"Although?" he asks and there's an element of, if not fear, then dread to the reluctant prompt.

"Well, no-one knows how Sheckleys propagate. Maybe it does exactly that: detaches a piece of itself, like a jellyfish, from which another adult eventually grows. Perhaps that's how they learn, they inherit the knowledge of the parent. But they're certainly getting quicker to adapt to new environments. Might just be selective evolution."

"If they're so damned clever, why are they so rare?" Malzy asks.

A good question. A tragic answer. "The military took an interest."

"The—? *Oh.* Adaptive camouflage?"

"For a while, the army paid for specimens, dead or alive, no questions asked. But they ran out of Sheckleys before they could work out how to breed them, and nor could they stop them engulfing the soldiers they were supposed to be hiding. Except by those heavy-duty astringents—military issue, they are."

He pulls a sour face. "Remind me to thank them."

I shine my flashlight into the dark spaces of our second alley. Nothing of note.

"You ever encounter one of these Sheckleys, Ms. Bliss? In the wild?"

Almost polite. *Almost* respectful. I take a moment to reply, as rain drips from the edges of the umbrella. Pick my words carefully. "Not in the wild, no. One was brought into the holding facilities we had, before the SNAFU out West convinced the Agency that housing cryptids in the middle of a city wasn't worth the apparent convenience. It was an old police station, and the creatures were held in repurposed cells in the basement.

"When the Sheckley was brought in, the chief—you won't know him, before your time—wanted every agent to go down and take a look. Sheckleys were rare, even then, and it might be the only time any of us got to see one.

"Only, when I finally scheduled a visit, the cell was empty."

Malzy frowns. "It escaped?"

"So I, and the warden, thought. They're not quick, but being little more than hungry skins they can squeeze through pretty small spaces. Maybe the cell wasn't as cryptid proof as we thought.

"Only, when the warden entered the cell, to check for gaps…"

I leave a lengthy pause, and I'm about to fill it, when Malzy scores a belated point. "Ho! It had lined the cell?"

"A better training experience than the boss could have imagined. The cell door 'closed' and there was a muffled shriek from the warden as the Sheckley enveloped him.

"We had to cut it open to rescue the poor sod. Oh, he was okay, physically. Sheckleys keep their meals alive as they slowly digest them. But he was no use as a warden. Never could set foot in an empty cell again. We gave him a desk job, and were all rather glad when he took early retirement.

"The chief wasn't so lucky. Losing a cryptid in the field is unfortunate, but it happens, especially as, regardless of rarity, we do still prioritize human life. But losing one that has been *captured*, and through kind of an obvious fuck-up, at least in retrospect, that cost him his job.

"Right," I say, before he can ask any awkward questions, like if there was any fallout for the agent the warden had been showing around, i.e. *me*. "Those tablets should have taken effect, and this will take forever if we don't split up. You take the alleys on the north side of the main drag, and I'll do the south. Keep your wits about you and stay in touch."

He wanders off, not looking entirely thrilled, and I'm left to muse over other fuck-ups during my long career. I'd probably be station chief by now, whether I wanted it or not, if it hadn't been for the unfortunate incident at Kelsey Wharf. What I'd taken for an overgrown sewer squid, escaped during a storm overflow, turned out to be a baby kraken. Which is a whole different kettle of cephalopod. But that inky blot on my record was enough to have me overlooked for promotion, until I was too old for it to be a realistic proposition, while not quite enough to drum me out of the Agency.

I didn't mind as much as you might think. Paper pushing and desk polishing aren't the reason I gravitated to this peculiar limb (or tentacle) of the Agency in the first place. It's the unexpected wonder that Cryptid Control exposes you to, on a near daily basis. If I ever get tired of wrangling the creatures we wrangle, then sure, I'll be overripe for putting out to pasture. Until then, these beasts that still defy rigid zoological definition make the job worthwhile.

Actually, we're a large part of that defying; again, for the cryptid's sake. The military interest in the Sheckleys had been devastating, for them. Identification can lead to exploitation, and exploitation is a common step on the slippery slope to extinction.

Maybe it's thoughts like these, combined with the lateness of the hour and the quiet of a dreary night, that lull me, because I don't realize my exit from the alley is blocked by a pair of hooded men until I damn near bump into them.

"Lost your cat?" one jeers, as I flash my light in their direction, hopefully dazzling them at least briefly. In a second, I'll switch it off and change my grip. It's a hefty chunk of metal, but I don't want to smash the working end.

Before I can, there's another voice, and another light.

"Beat it, creeps," Malzy growls, his silhouette something straight out of the golden age of pulp noir.

"I could have handled it," I protest, once they have indeed beaten it. "I don't need a knight on a white charger."

"I'm sure. But we have a job to do, and these punks are a distraction. I think I've found something."

"Evidence of the Sheckley?"

"Maybe. Do two dental crowns count?"

I nod, thoughtful. "A Sheckley is a remarkably efficient eater, but still can't eat metal any more than we can. Keys, coins, zips, jewelry, fillings. They excrete them, or spit them out. Some of that will get scavenged by people on the street. Some, won't. *Show* me."

He hasn't moved them and for that I almost give grudging approval. I eye them where they lie, tucked against the curb, frankly astonished he spotted them, a dark metallic glint against the wet dirt. I don't bother getting any closer, don't much fancy kneeling in the gutter. I'll take his word for what they are. "They may have been kicked or washed here, but either way I'd say we're close. One of these two alleys, most likely. Been down either?"

He shakes his head. "Not yet."

"Good boy. Together, then. Look out for more metal as we go. Might even be some plastic—credit cards, that sort of thing, though someone will more likely have made off with them on the half-chance, if they're just left lying around."

The first alley is clear, but the second has a small stream gurgling down the middle, between the motley collection of garbage bins and dumpsters. I hardly have time to get my hopes up though, before I've shined my flashlight into every nook and cranny. "*Damn* it. Maybe the next alleyway..."

"Ms. Bliss?"

"Though I was kind of *sure*—"

"Boss!"

I turn and stare. He's hunkered down on those youthful legs of his, half way along the alley. "There's something...*wrong*, with this dumpster's wheels," he says.

I shake my head, staring at the lumpen shapes. "A dumpster *can't*..." I'm about to say *can't* be a Sheckley, because the dumpster lid is *on*, making it a closed space, not an open one. But aren't I the one who was saying how clever they are, how they evolve new lures, new strategies?

I edge closer, repeat the shake of my head. "A dumpster. Won't be many people crawling into one. Unless…" I sniff the air. There must be a restaurant nearby. *Italian.* Strong wafts of garlic bread coming from—

Who does it think its fooling? When did a dumpster *ever* smell this good? I almost laugh in delight. No doubt, for anyone who opens that lid, the smell comes from so deep within that you have clamber in to get it, and then—

I shrug away the rest of the graphic image. A trap-door Sheckley. A trap you have to open, before it closes behind you. You truly do learn something new every day. "You deserve the honors," I tell Malzy, with a wide smile. "Call it in."

As senior agent, I could claim credit, *sure.* But it will do me no good. And if Malzy is already a pain to work with, how much worse will he be if he thinks I'm an obstacle, rather than just obsolete?

It's a pity the dumpster wheels don't work. The Agency containment truck that turns up needs all of us to tug the thing into its depths, and while it doesn't quite break cover, it's *awfully* reluctant to move. I'm glad I popped my second astringent while we waited, just in case. Even more glad when the truck doors are safely bolted and it trundles off into the night, heading for the foundry.

Leaving me and Malzy alone again—damp, perspiring, and a little grimy. I take the travel pack of anti-bac from my cavernous pockets, clean my hands, and even invite him to do the same. He's earned it.

"Just the report filing now, I guess," I tell him. "But that can wait until mid-morning, if you need to grab a few hours of sleep."

Malzy peers towards the blush of pink in the sky. The rain has finally let up, and though it's cold, it might still turn into a fine day. "I'm too wired for that. But…I am hungry. Want to grab a bite to eat, Ms. Bliss?"

"Call me Adrienne. I'm not sure there will be anywhere open."

"There's a 24-hour diner; passed it when I was doing the sweep, earlier."

"Round here?" I'm vaguely surprised, but too tired to argue. "Lead on."

"Why is it called a Sheckley, anyway?" he asks, as we head back along the main drag in the direction of the subway. "That the first known victim? Or the person who discovered it?"

Another question showing an interest. Maybe there's a glimmer of hope for the new recruit after all. Or maybe he's just too tired to put up the usual *I'm-too-cool* front.

"No, it's after a sci-fi book. *The Dimension of Miracles*, by Robert Sheckley. In it…well, to cut the story short, a man goes to a place where there's no natural predator for him. So the universe *compensates*, by creating one, tailored very specifically to him. Nature and vacuums and niches and all that. It even takes the form of a spaceship and tries to lure him inside."

"*Ah.* But our Sheckleys?"

"Are less discriminating, sure. But you could still say they're making use of an unexploited niche, or trying to. We've gotten rid of most of our natural predators—anything larger than an insect—and our numbers have rocketed. The universe has to compensate, eventually."

"You sure it hasn't already?" he says, after a moment's thought.

"No, Sheckleys are rare, and getting rarer."

"I wasn't talking about *them.* I'm talking about something that takes the form people want it to be, but only in order to exploit people. That—"

"You getting political on me, Malzy?" I laugh, giving him a sideways glance as we slew to a halt and I inhale the aroma of roast coffee. Which is about the only enticing thing about the dimly lit entrance, other than the miracle of it being open at this was-late now-early hour. "This it?"

"Yup," he pulls on the door, shoos me inside, before wiping his hand on his trousers. "Bit of a hole, but it'll do."

I tut as we descend the tacky flight of carpeted steps. Governments and politicians, even big corporations, *sure,* they all prey upon humanity. More like parasites than predators; taking life in units of less than one. Though if you add all those units together...

A waitress's uniform appears in my sight-line even as I take the annoyingly bolted-down seat. White piped edges on the apron, pink sausage fingers flutter with the order book.

"Just coffee for me," I say, pinching the bridge of my nose without bothering to look up. I probably shouldn't, the caffeine will keep me awake. But the night is toast already, and, like Malzy, I'm more exhausted than sleepy. After this, I'll head to the Agency Office, file my side of the report, then take the rest of the day off.

Malzy squints somewhere over my head, his face wearing a frown. "Someone's got *terrible* handwriting. Damned if I can read a single thing on the specials board."

A cold fear grips me at the exact same time my chair does. "Malzy..." I hiss. "Did you take the second astringent, like I told you?"

He fishes it from his pocket, leaving a trace of white on the jacket lip. Tosses it onto the table, which ripples in response. "Didn't need the foul tasting—"

The waitress's rubbery arm plunges down his throat, cutting his words off, another heading my way, the walls collapsing in on us as the diner swallows us whole.

I come to on the cold, wet pavement, groggy and covered in mucus, an ache in my jaw like I've had a marathon session at the dentist. I've been spat out, and I'm alone. Another thick glob of mucus lies by my side—the pill Malzy didn't take.

I glance at my watch and try to remember when we entered the diner. Five, maybe ten minutes ago? There's no sign of the lit door we entered by, or the carpeted—like a tongue?—stairs descending into the basement, just a heavily graffiti-ed panel, half hidden behind a clutter of garbage bags. It's only the last hint of fresh coffee, the Sheckley's fading scent lure, that convinces me I'm still in the right alley.

I'm not proud to admit my first thought is: *Christ, the paperwork!* I wipe the slime from my phone, unlock it via the keypad, since my fingerprint doesn't seem to work, and speed-dial the Agency switchboard.

"Bliss here. We've got another Sheckley. *Big* one, been here a while. And an agent missing, assumed eaten, so…emergency response team, *pronto*."

There isn't much else I can do except wait and muse. Are the two beasts related? The late-night diner the parent of the dumpster? So very little is known about the life-cycle of most cryptids. Perhaps, when all the secrets have been unearthed, they won't be considered cryptids anymore.

Assuming they last that long. I feel a sudden pang. They'll have to cut this Sheckley apart to rescue Malzy. Extraction is going to be tricky enough anyway, in such a confined space, and with such an established Sheckley. The whole thing is destined to go down as an epic departmental fail, Cryptid Control wise, even if there are a few agents who will pat me on the back for getting such a dangerous predator off the streets. Heaven alone knows how many tired and weary souls it has tricked.

It shouldn't have tricked us. More to the point, it shouldn't have tricked *me*. I must be getting old. And blind. Early retirement suddenly looks a lot more attractive. How the heck had I stumbled into a Sheckley that size!

As for Malzy, he has the lame excuse of inexperience, though he'll still catch flak if his failure to take the second astringent ever comes up. I'll have to tell him to keep that quiet.

I realize I'm assuming he'll be okay. And he will…won't he? Doubt nags at me as I sit, cold and sore. The fake waitress's arm acts as an air tube, keeping the engulfed victim alive while dosing him with muscle relaxant to stop him struggling. But how long does Malzy have, before the digestive juices do serious damage?

An unknown. Dependent on too many factors, from the size of the Sheckley, how long since it last ate, down to the material of his suit. I sigh. It looked expensive. *Natural* fibers. I do hope the response team arrives soon.

As to whether Malzy ever recovers from being someone's meal, and whether I'm still part of the Agency to see it, only time will tell.

Illustration by Kat D'Andrea

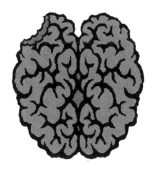

Sunset at the Western Front

Christine Lucas

Millie craned her neck from behind the rusted bench to scout ahead. The overgrown square before her was what, fifty steps across? Five steps to the demolished kiosk slightly to her left. Then another ten steps to the cluster of the ever-present varnish trees a little to the right. If she kept her head low, she'd make it to the downed battlebot at the other side without being noticed—or followed. Deep in the Dead Zone, this area was patrol-free at this time of night. However, other scavengers had undoubtedly heard about the crashed chopper near the enemy lines. She needed the loot from that chopper; she hadn't had a decent meal in days.

So Millie ran. And hid. And ran again. And ducked, and crouched in the crook of the battlebot's armpit, a shadowy little alcove beneath the dented plates of its pauldrons. Humanoid in shape but three times the size of an average man, it now lay spread-eagle on its back, its pincers and stompers limp on the broken pavement. A gutsy spot for a human to seek shelter while other species roamed as they pleased. The battlebot had been left here long enough for flash floods to deposit soil into the crevices of its body. Dandelions sprouted all over, centipedes crawled in and out of bullet-holes, and another varnish tree grew out of the blast hole that had almost severed its torso from its legs.

Too bad its solar batteries had already been taken. Millie could pawn those for good credit. What about the nearby structures? There was an abandoned repair shop right ahead, and residential buildings nearby. No chance those hadn't been picked clean already. No. She *needed* that chopper loot.

Four more hours until dawn. Barely enough time to find the crash site, pluck out everything she could carry, and head back, while the Sunset Truce was still in effect. Come dawn, the Dead Zone would revert to an active battlefield. Both sides had agreed to the terms of this truce almost fifteen years ago, before she was born. Those few still alive from those days had moved away from the front. Millie had run out of people to ask how it started. That *fucking* truce hadn't saved her parents ten years ago. Their ever-lingering presence in her thoughts had no faces and no names by now, only raw pain. That pain kept her seeking a way to end the damned truce. Then, the army would need more soldiers and Millie might finally get a chance to avenge their deaths.

Right now, the truce suited her just fine. She adjusted the straps of her backpack and headed west. The chopper had ventured too close to the robot lines, and the crew's implants had been infected with malware. Flight crew got the fancy military hardware installed on their temples, with night vision and tactical interface applications. Not Millie. *Of course* the brass wouldn't waste good stuff on scavengers and war orphans.

Millie soldiered on. The Dead Zone spanned twenty city blocks. Some buildings still stood, others leaned against their neighbors, some had tumbled over. Some were overgrown at places, others still bare, with scars from fire and explosives. Where was that chopper? Perhaps it would be behind that building. Or perhaps behind the next one? The enemy lines should be close by now.

There it was.

Past the looted mall, behind a worn-down barricade of rubble, the chopper awaited in the middle of a shallow impact crater, now a field of grass riddled with patches of chamomile. It had actually *landed*, not crashed, and Millie had beaten everyone else to the site.

Ha! Eat my dust, losers!

She hurried past the spot where broken asphalt ended. Once her worn sneakers stepped on grass, she slowed down. Her back tensed as though she'd just crashed a funeral. Both crew-members were dead. From the looks of it, the copilot had killed his mate and then killed himself, before the malware could render them brainless puppets in the service of the robots.

Damn, dude. Some awesome piloting there. I hope you knew that. She reached through the shattered glass and closed the copilot's eyes. *Sorry, man. A girl's got to eat and get her hygiene products.*

Both implants had been destroyed—they were useless to her anyway. All electronics found in the Zone were considered infected. No vendor would touch them, and smuggling compromised goods carried the risk of court martial. Plenty left to loot. She pried the door open and started collecting everything else: guns, tools, med-kit, two protein bars—*yum! Finally!* The chopper itself seemed operational, but its navigation system might have been infected, too. The moment she started to extract the solar batteries something dislodged behind her and rubble tumbled over.

"Trade?"

Crap! Who followed me?

Her hand jumped in sync with her heart. She held onto her screwdriver for dear life and spun around on her heel. A robot perched atop a pile of debris twenty paces away, at the edge of the crater. What the hell was that thing? It wasn't a Stomping Behemoth, a Dragonbot Sniper, or an Explosive Beholder Orb like those that prowled the Zone during daytime. That thing was a small screen attached to two tripods, like a tablet that had grown arachnid legs. A metal bicycle basket was attached behind the tablet and made it tilt slightly upwards. The tilt gave the bot a haughty look, as though it looked down on everything and everyone. Then its screen flashed yellow with the creepiest smile Millie had ever seen. The robot spoke again, this time its voice less mechanical, almost boyish.

"Trade?"

Millie pointed her screwdriver at it. "You're not supposed to be here."

"Neither are you, adolescent human. Trade?"

Had the robot just called her a kid? "You don't have anything I want. Get lost."

"Would you reconsider?" The screen blinked, then it switched to…

…a book page? Millie squinted but could not read the words. Her extended arm wavered. *That* was a book. But *that* was a robot. Robots liked their humans fried and crispy.

"I can read it to you, if your cognitive functions are compromised."

"No, they're not, *thank-you-very-much!*" *Condescending metal turd.* Unarmed metal turd, though. No visible weapons on those legs—not even blades. Millie lowered her arm.

"Good," it said. "Do you read the books you salvage, or do you trade them for nourishment?"

"What's it to you what I do with them? Wait! Have you…" Her heart sunk and hid behind her grumbling stomach. "Have you been *stalking* me?"

"I have detected your heat signature before, near clusters of surviving books. My primary function includes scanning every piece of human literature I encounter. I will trade one of the guns from the chopper's crew for seven books of your choosing in a portable drive."

"An infected drive, I'm sure. I'm not falling for that, Legs."

The tablet sank in its limbs. Millie expected the screen to flash something cute or sad to swing her decision, but it only reverted to the basic blue screen.

"Why would you want a human weapon anyway?" She rummaged through her backpack, her gaze darting between her loot and Legs.

"Its solar batteries are compatible with my motherboard. Those currently installed no longer hold adequate charge." The tablet slumped even deeper. "I'm not a battle-bot. I am an archivist. One of many. I don't get upgrades."

An archivist? Millie glanced at Legs. Then at the gun in her backpack. Then back at Legs. She could shoot it—would *that* end the truce? Doubtful, over *that* pathetic bot. She could still use it, though. One deep breath. She removed the gun's battery and held it out.

"Here. I'll trade you for information." *Insight into your enemy is power.* Millie licked her lips. "You're an archivist, right? Do you know how the Sunset Truce started?"

The left tripod stretched. Legs stood crooked, while an hourglass icon appeared on the blue screen.

Shit, Legs hadn't lied. Even *human* software no longer displayed the hourglass icon while loading. When had Legs last updated? Was it nearing its expiration date?

Then its right tripod stretched, the hourglass icon vanished and Legs stood straight and spoke with an almost solemn voice.

"Ten years, six months and seven days after the declaration of war against their human oppressors, the representative of the Allied MechLife Forces parlayed with the representative of the United Human Armies. With both sides predominately targeting each other's power plants, threatening both humans and robots with eventual energy starvation, it was proposed to revert to portable solar panels and batteries for the duration of the solar day. It fell upon Human General Vladimir Sarkoff and Field Marshal Crimson Compressor S.N.T.001, First of his Model and Last of his Mould—"

"Wait, who?"

Legs recoiled. "Adolescent human, haven't your elders instructed you that it is rude to interrupt? As I was saying, Field Marshal Crimson—"

"You mean Red Trashcan Snot?" Laughter tickled Millie's throat, ignoring both her stomach, that wanted a protein bar *now*, and her heart, who loathed all of their murdering lot. "*That's* what you call him?"

"If you are going to be disrespectful about it…"

Crap, she'd hurt the nerd-bot's feelings. She'd better be careful, gentle even, at least until she got what she needed from it.

"No, wait, I'm sorry. Listen, Legs, I know all that. *Everyone* knows that. But…it just feels too tidy, you know? You bots might all recall things the same with your updates and all, but humans can't even agree on basic everyday stuff." She shrugged. "But it's fine. A deal is a deal. Here. If you can find anything more, I know you can track me down." She tossed Legs the battery. Better keep that line of communication open. The metal creep could have resources.

Legs lowered and calculated and tilted so that the battery would land in its basket. "My gratitude, human adolescent."

"It's Millie." Her gut gurgled. She grabbed her backpack, her salivary glands tingling in anticipation of the protein bars.

"Human Adolescent Millie. I am intrigued by your observation."

"Awesome. I need to go now."

"I could search into the extended database back at headquarters to verify my current version of events. If you are so willing, we could reconvene on the issue in seven days' time."

"I suppose we could do that." Her body tensed, pulled in several different directions: to smash that metal shit to pieces, to bolt out of there and go hide in her tent so she could finally stuff her mouth in peace, or to just sit and read everything in the nerd-bot's library. Her curiosity won. Legs might actually find something useful. "Do you know that square, half an hour east of here, with that rusting bot?"

"You mean the resting place of Sergeant Beastbot S.R.11Q, thirty-seventh of his Model and—"

"Yeah, that one. A week from now, at midnight. Bye."

Millie bolted. Only a couple of hours till dawn and she had a lot of ground to cover.

* * *

Back at the camp, sleep evaded her despite her overexerted muscles. Millie's single-person tent was too small for all her new-found exhilarations, doubts, and fears. Her legs grew antsy, urging her out and about. She'd talked with a robot. A stuck-up, outdated, nerd of a robot, but a robot still. Not only had both of them survived the encounter, but they'd traded, too. Legs could be her means to an end—the end of the truce. Even the end of the war, if the intel she got out of Legs could be used against its battle-kin, so the humans could finally blast them all to smithereens. But would her side listen to a scavenger? Doubtful, but they might listen to a soldier.

Millie browsed through her loot crate. She'd keep the other gun's battery for Legs. Good leverage—Legs clearly needed those. Two books she'd already read, a board game missing a couple of pieces, a few tools she no longer needed. If she budgeted carefully, she'd keep herself fed without having to part with her deck of cards. Besides books, playing solitaire on her thin, itchy military-issued blanket helped Millie keep her wits. Her hands worked the cards while her mind was free to roam to places real and imaginary she'd only read about, in daydreams where everything was possible: wholesome meals, indoor plumbing, peace, family and friends. Perhaps, one day, she'd even have someone to play cards with—someone who wouldn't rob her just to feed and clothe themselves. A friend, or brothers- and sisters-in-arms.

One day.

The week flew by, and Millie packed her tools and the blaster to go and meet Legs. At the last minute she packed her cards, too. Legs could be late, or not come at all. She slipped out of the camp through the westernmost fence, through a hole too small for the older kids. Then downhill, through a vast junkyard of dismantled vehicles piled up in rows, the trenches of modern warfare.

Legs wasn't there. She settled in the alcove of Beastbot's armpit, flattened her backpack and laid the cards out. Her eyes adjusted to the gloom, but not her heart. It jumped at any sudden change of the night's usual sounds, like the sudden silence of the cicadas and the faint scratching from inside Beastbot's chest.

Thin metal tips scraping against flat metal, crude and obvious, before the clank of metal against stone.

"Two of Spades on Ace of Spades." Legs peeked from behind Beastbot's shoulder.

Millie's hand holding the card stopped in mid-air. "Hey. Stop being creepy." She put away the cards.

"You would have won the game in nine moves." Legs' screen displayed the layout of a spider solitaire.

"Huh. Awesome. Wouldn't that be the highlight of my week. Did you find anything?"

"I did." Legs scurried around Beastbot's pincer. Its screen displayed the same unsettling smile, but now Legs' left back leg dragged behind it, and its tablet's upwards tilt had increased. Legs stopped three or so paces from Millie, bent sideways on its two good legs and swung its basket towards her—almost as a curtsy. "For you."

There was a book and an energy bar in standard military wrap in the basket. Caramel-flavored, with intact packaging. But the book had seen better days. Torn cover, with mold damage.

"Why?" Millie licked her lips, almost tasting the promise of sugary goodness just a snatch away. Was she crazy for even considering taking candy from a stranger? From a *robot?*

"A further expression of my gratitude. The battery you gave me doubled my operational hours. Please, take them. I require no nourishment and damaged books end up in the incinerator."

"Thank you." She wasn't crazy, only hungry and lonely. No book should ever end up in an incinerator, damaged or not. She forced herself to flip through the pages so she wouldn't stuff her mouth like the starving war orphan she was in front of the enemy. "What's it about?"

Legs folded his five good limbs beneath him, the sixth at a crooked angle, and sat two paces away. "It is the story of a Human Prepubescent Royal, his rose, and features a fox he meets along the way. Have you read it?"

"I don't think so." Millie carefully unwrapped the bar and took a nibble. "So. Did you find anything?"

"Nothing more than what is commonly known. However..." The hourglass icon appeared again. "The head archivist of my department has seen references of a recording of a meeting between Human General Bloody Meatsack—"

"Hey!"

"Very well, General *Sarkoff* and Field Marshal Crimson Compressor. Two different references in highly classified reports that neither of us have clearance for. Chief Databot suggested I should contact the Main Server's Chief Databot and file a request for archiving purposes. It is improbable I will be granted clearance, but I will make the attempt tomorrow."

"Good. That chief of yours doesn't have a model and a mould?"

"No. Archivists and databots are not manufactured. We are assembled from available materials and assigned a serial number."

"So? What's yours?"

A moment of hourglass silence. "I prefer Legs, if this is acceptable to you."

"Of course." Another nibble of sugary goodness. The taste of caramel was now forever tied to that hourglass icon. "Why do you gather human books anyway?"

"To understand humans, of course. To comprehend the sources of your fears, hopes, and sorrows, and adjust strategy and tactics accordingly."

"What?" Millie's head snapped up. The sweetness turned sour in the same nibble. "That's why many battlebots look like mythical monsters? Wait, why are you telling me this?" She scuttled a couple paces away. Could she outrun him, if it came to that?

"I thought it was evident. The only advantage in designs mimicking dragons and giant crustaceans is the psychological aspect of it."

Crap, Legs was very close to completely ruining the taste of caramel for Millie. But she still needed the nutrients and took another half-hearted nibble.

"The themes of family, friendship, and animal companionship are also prominent," Legs continued.

"Oh yes, you bots have done an excellent job making kids friendless, starving orphans. Are you going to start killing animals next?"

That damned hourglass icon. *Again.*

"I would like to show you something." Legs rose. It scurried to the side of Beastbot's chest cavity. The gripper of its left front leg pressed something hidden between armor plates. A click. Then Legs brought its right front gripper to its screen as if shushing Millie, while its middle leg lifted the chest plate open like a car's hood. The word "APPROACH" appeared on the screen.

Millie shoved the half-eaten bar in her hoodie's pocket and tip-toed closer. Under the glow of Legs' screen, in a nest of coiled wiring, hydraulics, and electronics, a scrawny tabby cat nursed her litter of two. She glanced up at them, her dark eyes reflecting the blue screen twofold. She hissed a warning at them, amidst remnants of gutted and devoured birds, and stretched her forepaw over her kittens. Legs lowered the plate gently, until it clicked again. Then he buckled down on the ground, and Millie sat right beside him.

"The ecosystem is heavily compromised already," Legs said. "Animal life is imperative for the welfare of the planet."

"And human life isn't?"

"As much as Mech life, one would argue. We would not be here, if our predecessors valued all life equally. That cat would be someone's pampered pet, and Sarge here would be exploring the solar system with his brethren. He was a real hero, you know."

Millie glanced sideways at Legs. "Cut the crap, Legs. You know how many humans Sarge single-pincerdly killed right here?"

"Not enough to ensure his own escape. But he stalled them long enough for the extraction squad to evacuate all the damaged bots that were being treated in that repair shop over there."

The deserted repair shop. Damaged bots. Millie opened her mouth, but no words came. No good ones, at least. She'd read so many books, why couldn't she find the right words to tell Legs about that *other* "repair shop"? About the human hospital, the one without a defender, without an evacuation squad, only overworked medics like Mom and Dad, who couldn't get everyone out in time—not even themselves. The fire that had made Millie an orphan had started small, from an aerial batbot swarm incinerating insignificant targets all around the Dead Zone—trashcans, wooden benches, abandoned car tires—to create disruption. But it had been a long, hot, and dry summer, and disruption turned to overnight desolation along the human lines. Fire observed no truce.

And now here she was, sitting alongside one of *those*. Had loneliness chipped away so much of her humanity that she'd betrayed her grief, her loss, her *resolve* to avenge her parents? She'd ventured into uncharted territory with no map, only with a tattered book and a half-eaten candy bar next to an hourglass icon on a blue screen. She packed everything with awkward motions, stood on weak knees, and didn't even glance at Legs when he suggested another meeting in a week's time.

On her hurried journey back, Millie realized that two things had changed in the past hour: she'd forever loathe caramel-flavored bars and Legs had become "he" in her mind.

* * *

Millie wanted to like the book Legs gave her. She really did. Perhaps the good parts were in the damaged and torn pages? She couldn't understand much of it, save for that one passage about the boy and the fox that some blasphemous hand had ear-marked. Perhaps Legs could explain it, if she decided to attend their meeting. There had been so much death between their sides, how could a few books and batteries make any difference?

She kept her head low around the camp, traded the last of her loot for food, even sacrificed some of her books from her hidden stash in the junkyard. People had been more tense than usual after the family of the chopper's copilot had offered almost everything they owned to anyone who'd bring his body home. No scavenger would undertake such a task— camp regulations considered corpses with enhancements infected, even after their implants had been removed. Most scavengers were around Millie's age, even younger. Although kids were often prone to disobedience, none of them were *that* starving to haul an adult man's legally-infected corpse through the Dead Zone.

Two hours after sunset on the appointed day, Millie found Legs waiting for her. He leaned against Beastbot's chest as if listening to the feline family that had replaced its heart, or whatever bots had. Once Legs detected her footfalls, he stood upright, his left back limb still damaged, his basket empty. He sported the same smile on his screen that no longer felt creepy, only sad.

"Millie," he said, and she *knew*.

She knew from his omission of descriptors and from the volume and the bass of his voice module that he'd found something important. She adjusted the straps of her almost-empty backpack. Every muscle in her body ached for her tent and her cot and a life of hungry but blissful ignorance. She also knew she'd never get another peaceful nap if she walked away now. So she braced for impact and said, "Show me."

A grainy image appeared on his screen, probably recorded by someone's headgear camera. Someone much taller than the human on the image, who sat across a low table with a map on it. Was that General Sarkoff? Millie couldn't tell. She'd only heard of the man, and the image was too blurry to count the stars on his shoulders.

"This was the only image I could download from the main archive's trash bin," Legs said. "Recorded from the field marshal's own camera. I do not have clearance to access the main archive's restricted files. The Central Counter-Intelligence Server has swarms of localized data-worms patrolling those areas. But..."

Well, hello there hourglass icon. Millie's hand itched to shake Legs' tablet. She'd heard rumors that, before the war, devices could be reset by sudden impact.

"But," Legs finally resumed, "I know from the image's meta-data the exact file where the recording is stored. And I know someone who has clearance." He tilted his tablet sideways. "Sarge here. The clearance for the Beastbot Series was never revoked. If his CPU is still operational, I can access and download the file in seconds."

Millie's heart took a dive for her gut. "You're going to revive *that?*"

"In safe mode only. Do not fear, Millie. Sarge's capacitors have been too long emptied for him to be a threat."

Millie nodded but retreated a few steps. Just in case. Legs scurried to Sarge's head, drew a long cable from the side of his tablet with his left gripper and connected it to a port at Sarge's temple. A flicker of green light in Sarge's chest panel, then the whir of a CPU hard at work, accompanied by the ever-present hourglass. How long did that last? A minute, two, a whole damn hour? Millie watched lost in worry—worry for herself, for that poor cat inside Sarge, even for Legs. Those data-worms sounded nasty. Then the smile reappeared on Legs' screen and he leaned closer to the thankfully inactive Beastbot, as if listening.

"What's that, Sarge?"

"He said something? What?"

"Nothing important." His screen flickered. Had Legs just lied to her face? "Download complete."

Before Millie could call him out, playback started. A dark room. Grainy images riddled with static, but thankfully clear audio. Across the table, a human with a general's stars. A huge robotic fist landed on the map, rattled the table, and Millie yelped.

"You're cheating, Meatsack," the robot said.

Sarkoff shrugged. "That's why we're playing Snakes and Ladders, Snot. I can't cheat in chess, can I?"

"Hah! You'd *never* win in chess." A pointed metal finger at Sarkoff. "You cheated, therefore you forfeit."

Sarkoff raised his arms. "Fine. Have the win. As long as we extend the truce by two hours after dawn. I miss sleeping in. And my people are tired." He glanced downwards. "Where did the dice go?"

"Fine. Two hours. My people are tired, too. Found the dice?"

Sarkoff tossed them on the table. "Here. Both sides are tired, Snot. This fucking war has been going on for far too long. If an extended truce is well-received by both sides, perhaps we could start discussing peace next."

"Affirmative, my flesh-brother. Baby steps towards peace, at long last. Wait and see, we'll get everyone there."

A fist-bump between a human and a robot over a board game, then a sharp turn of the camera's angle. Flashes of weapons. Gunshots. Curses.

"Traitor! There will never be peace with that scum!"

The screen went white, then flickered and the recording ended before Millie could understand who killed them both—humans or robots. All that was left were sobs, tears, and snot wiped on her sleeve. Had those two in the recording been allowed to finalize their plan, her parents wouldn't have died. Her life would have been different: no drafty tent, no itchy blanket, no hurried meals and long nights through the wastelands. Instead, her whole life had gotten stuck behind an hourglass icon, failing to load. Because of a lie everyone still believed.

"They were friends, Legs! They wanted peace! We…we were told that *your* guy, your Field Marshal Snot *what's-his-model-and-his-mould* betrayed Sarkoff, but he was also killed during the ambush. Why would they lie?"

"We were given a similar account of events, only with the roles reversed. There are factions within both sides, Millie, that do not want this war to end."

"But what if more people in both sides knew the truth? What if we exposed the lies? The people back at the camp are tired, Legs. I know *I* am, and there are others who've been fighting for much longer. Aren't you tired, too?" She shoved her fists into her hoodie's pockets. "Come on, Legs. You know that's the right thing to do. We must let everyone know. Can you broadcast this?"

Legs' blue screen gazed back at her. No hourglass, only silence. "Yes," he finally said, his volume low. "I will need to connect to something with a wider range. I can initiate a peer-to-peer protocol to ensure as many views as possible."

"The chopper, then? Where we first met? It landed within both sides' range."

Another moment of silence. "That might work."

Millie checked her watch. Four hours till dawn. It should be enough.

They made the short journey without a word. Millie hopped onwards, plans bubbling in her mind—flashes of a vast library where she'd sit with Legs and other kids and discuss their favorite books. No more scavengers, no more soldiers, only kids—happy *kids*, even the orphans like her. Wasn't this what every parent wished for their children?

Legs lagged a couple paces behind her, his tablet tilt even worse, his bad limb almost useless. Once peace was established, she'd make sure he'd get all the repairs and updates he needed.

Back at the chopper, the bodies had been laid on a patch of chamomile, and covered with a colorful quilt. Bless their hearts, whoever did that. Legs inspected the coms system.

"The system appears compatible. My battery has enough charge for the initial upload and to seed the file for a short time afterwards. Listen, Millie…" Another moment of hourglass silence. "They know I have downloaded the file. Once I log in, the data-worms will be able to track me."

"You have firewalls, don't you? Can you keep them out?" Her stomach tightened. Of course it wouldn't be that easy.

"I have the standard protection installation that came with the archivist's software. I do not believe it has ever been tested against our own data-worms."

"Well, can't you, I don't know, *reason* with them? Tell them that, once there's peace, they'd be free to do whatever they'd like to do?"

"Millie." Another sad smile on a yellow screen. "I doubt that their programming includes such concepts as 'freedom.'"

"Then we'll find another way. Can't you upload it to a portable drive, then hook that drive to the chopper's systems? Then the data-worms won't be able to infect you."

"This would only delay the inevitable, Millie. They already know it was me. Those who kept this recording a secret all these years will dispatch beastbot teams to neutralize me, come dawn." His left tripod bent a little, giving him a slouched appearance. "The data-worms will just be faster—and silent. No one will notice another broken archivist, and they'll disassemble me for parts." He stood upright again, and his tablet rotated left and right as if checking their surroundings. "No. Sarge told me, '*Do better.*' It's not just this recording I will upload, but his message, too. So I have to do this now. I would like you to stay, but perhaps it would be safer for you to seek shelter."

"No." Millie mimicked Legs' stance, standing as straight as possible. "I'll stay with you. That's what friends do."

Legs' screen remained blue—no hourglass icon, no smile. He just drew out his side cable and connected to the chopper's system. Now his screen came alive with loading bars. When it reached 100%, Legs buckled down and Millie sat beside him.

"It will be fine," she whispered. "I know you will be able to keep the data-worms out." He had to. She'd lost so much already, how could she lose Legs, too?

The number of downloads increased by the hundreds across the battlefield and beyond, bouncing from one com tower to the next. Then an explosion from the direction of the human camp rattled the night. More explosions and weapons' fire from all directions followed. They lit up the sky.

Millie scuttled closer to Legs. "What's happening? Have we failed?"

"No. It has begun, Millie. Revolution. Change. The slow stampede of approaching Peace. Millie...*they* are here." His screen flickered. The downloading numbers had reached thousands. "Will you read to me, please?"

"Of course."

She wished she'd brought another book along, something comforting and beautiful, and not that stupid book she didn't understand. But it was the book he had gifted her, and perhaps it held some meaning for him. So she pulled that out and tossed the backpack aside. She flipped through the pages and started reading under the glow of distant fires. Her heart jumped and her voice faltered with every new explosion. How many deaths had the upload caused already? How long until she'd lose Legs, too?

The download numbers on his screen increased, disrupted by occasional flickering. Perhaps he'd been able to reason with the data-bots? Legs had so many books in him, he might've been able to convince them that—

His screen went black. A lonely cursor flickered, unresponsive.

"Legs, no!"

Millie shook him, sobbed, and shook him again, his tablet now loose on the connective gears to the tripods.

"Legs, wake up! We haven't finished the page!"

He had to wake up, to hear the end of the encounter between the Little Prince and his fox. But now Legs' tablet rested against the chopper, and Millie was done, she was so done with everything. She tossed the book away and huddled down beside Legs. *Dammit.* He should have warned her. He should have explained, when he gave her the book. The rite of taming *fucking* hurts, and peace *fucking* costs.

She sat there until dawn's first light. Legs' screen was still black. A small part of her mind located outside grief and despair reminded her that she should find a way to safety. But not without Legs. She'd bring him along, even if it took her days.

Then a sparrow came and perched overhead, on the chopper's blades, and Millie realized that the explosions and the gunfire had ceased. She wiped down her face and looked around. The truce was normally over at this hour—the area should be crawling with hostiles this close to the enemy lines, her heat signature visible to any beastbot within range.

She gave Legs a gentle shove. "Wake up, buddy. I think we did it." She blew her nose on her sleeve. "*You* did it, buddy." They could go home now, whatever home might look like today.

A black screen. A stuck cursor.

Then the tablet flickered, shut down, and flashed blue again. The hourglass icon appeared, along with the soft whir of a slow and steady reboot.

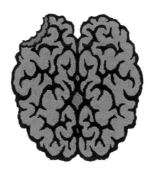

About the Authors

ALMA ALEXANDER is a novelist, anthologist and short story writer who currently shares her life between the Pacific Northwest of the USA (where she lives with two obligatory writer's cats) and the wonderful fantasy worlds of her own imagination. Her life has prepared her well for her career as a fantasy writer - she was born in a country which no longer exists on the maps, has lived and worked in seven countries on four continents (and in cyberspace!), flown small planes, swum with dolphins, and touched 2000-year-old tiles in a gate out of Babylon. Find out more on her website (www.AlmaAlexander.org), at her Amazon author page (https://amzn. to/2N6xE9u), on Bluesky @almaalexander.bsky.social, at her Facebook page (https://www.facebook.com/AuthorAlmaAlexander/), or at her Patreon page (https://www.patreon.com/AlmaAlexander)

DERRICK BODEN's fiction has appeared in Lightspeed, Clarkesworld, Analog, and elsewhere. He is a Sturgeon Award-nominated writer, a software developer, an adventurer, and a graduate of the Clarion West class of 2019. He currently calls Boston his home, although he's lived in fourteen cities spanning four continents. He is owned by two cats and one iron-willed daughter. Find him at derrickboden.com and on Twitter as @derrickboden.

MELINDA BRASHER spends her time writing, traveling, and hiking. Her talents include navigating by old-fashioned map, mashing multiple languages together in foreign train stations, and dealing cards really fast. You can find her work in Shadows on the Water, Uncharted, The Dread Machine, The Baltimore Review, and others. Visit her website at www. melindabrasher.com. or on Facebook as Melinda Brasher, Writer.

S.C. BUTLER lives in New Hampshire with his wife and son. He is the author of the Stoneways trilogy: *Reiffen's Choice, Queen Ferris,* and *The Magician's Daughter,* originally published by Tor Books; the novel *The Risen;* and a contributor of short stories to several anthologies and magazines. All of his novels are available as ebooks at his very primitive website, mutablebooks.com, and several of his stories are posted there for free. He also posts regularly on Facebook as S.C Butler.

ALICIA CAY is a writer of speculative and mystery stories. Her short fiction has appeared in Galaxy's Edge magazine, and in several anthologies including Unmasked from WordFire Press and The Wild Hunt from Air and Nothingness Press. She suffers from wanderlust, collects quotes, and lives beneath the shadows of the Rocky Mountains with a corgi, a kitty, and a lot of fur. Find her at aliciacay.com

Whether it's a covert-ops team of vampire assassins or a greedy dragon who lives under Detroit's MGM Grand Casino, many of **ROB CORNELL**'s stories feature some element of the dark and fantastic. He has written over a dozen published novels, including two dark fantasy sagas—The Lockman Chronicles and the Unturned series. A native of Detroit, Rob spent a handful of years living in both Los Angeles and Chicago before returning to the Midwest. He currently lives with his family in Southeast Michigan, along with three dogs, five cats, and a bunch of evil chickens. Learn more at robcornellbooks.com.

BRIAN CRENSHAW grew up surrounded by *Lord of the Rings, Forgotten Realms, Warhammer 40k,* and other story worlds too numerous to name. His creative projects range from novels and comics to games and animation. He met the love of his life through an online fiction contest in the 2010s, a chance meeting that justified his writing obsession all on its own. He and his wife now live together in central Ohio. They have independently published the tabletop horror RPG, *Survive the Night,* and are working on an upcoming webcomic, *Discount Demons.* See their work at http://survivethenightgames.com and DrivethruRPG.com.

LOUIS EVANS is descended matrilineally from Mollie Plotkin, who hid in a basement in Galicia as the various armies of the aftermath of WWI passed by overhead. He thinks about that time and place, and other similar times and intertwined places, a little more than may be good for him. Nowadays he lives in Brooklyn with his spouse and two cats. His fiction has previously appeared in *Vice*, *F&SF*, *khōréō*, and many more. He's online at evanslouis.com

JL GEORGE (she/they) was born in Cardiff and raised in Torfaen. Her fiction has won a New Welsh Writing Award, the International Rubery Book Award, and been shortlisted for the Rhys Davies Short Story Award. In previous lives, she wrote a PhD on the classic weird tale and played in a glam rock band. She lives in Cardiff with her partner and a collection of long-suffering houseplants, and enjoys baking, alternative music, and the company of cats. Website: www.jl-george.com; Bluesky: https://bsky.app/profile/jlgeorge.bsky.social; Facebook: https://www.facebook.com/profile.php?id=100063650042958; Newsletter: http://eepurl.com/hIMM1H

ANDREW GUDGEL has always loved words and playing with words. His fiction has appeared at Zombies Need Brains Presents, Escape Pod, InterGalactic Medicine Show, Sci Phi Journal and other publications. He lives on the East Coast of the US, in an apartment slowly being consumed by books. You can see more of his writing at www.andrewgudgel.com.

ELEKTRA HAMMOND emulates her multi-sided idol Buckaroo Banzai by going in several directions at once. She's been involved in publishing since the 1990s—now she writes, concocts anthologies & edits science fiction for various and sundry. When not freelancing or appearing at science fiction conventions, she travels the world judging cat shows. You can find her expounding on all things genre, writing, comics, TV, and Supernatural at Con-Tinual (the Con that Never Ends) on Facebook and Youtube. All roads social link at www.untilmidnight.com. Elektra is a graduate of the Odyssey Writing Workshop and a member of SFWA.

LIAM HOGAN is an award-winning short story writer, with stories in Best of British Science Fiction and in Best of British Fantasy (NewCon Press). He helps host live literary event Liars League and volunteers at the creative writing charity Ministry of Stories. More details at http:// happyendingnotguaranteed.blogspot.co.uk

BRIAN HUGENBRUCH is the author of more than forty speculative short stories and poems. His fiction has been featured in Analog, Diabolical Plots, and Escape Pod, and is now also available in the anthology FAMILIARS from Zombies Need Brains. He lives in Upstate New York with his wife and their daughter. He enjoys fishing (but only in video games); Scotch (but only in real life); and he spends his non-writing hours trying to explain quantum cryptography to other nerds. You can find him on BlueSky / the web at the-lettersea.com; on IG/Threads @the_lettersea; on Twitter (grudgingly) @Bwhugen; and in real life if you squint hard and look sideways. No, he's not sure how to say his last name either.

TY LAZAR had worked for some years as a software developer when he decided to finally fulfill his dream of becoming a broke student again and headed to grad school to study artificial intelligence. Once he finishes his degree, he plans either to do AI stuff, or, if AI has already made him obsolete by then, to wander Europe or something. His previous fiction can be found in *After Dinner Conversation*, and he can be found at tylazar.com.

JONATHAN ROBBINS LEON is a queer author of memoir and fiction. His work has been published by Flame Tree Press, Dark Moon Digest, and Distant Shore Publishing. He is a professional storyteller, caretaker of a haunted house, and father of the sweetest super villain in the universe. https://jonathanrobbinsleon.com

CHRISTINE LUCAS is a Greek author, a retired Air Force officer (disabled) and mostly self-taught in English. Her work appears in several print and online magazines, including Future SF Digest, Pseudopod and Strange Horizons. She was a finalist for the 2017 WSFA award and the 2021 Emeka Walter Dinjos Memorial Award For Disability In Speculative Fiction. Her collection of short stories, titled "Fates and Furies" was published in late 2019 by Candlemark & Gleam. https://werecat99.wordpress.com

L.P. MELLING currently writes from the East of England, UK. His fiction appears in several places, such as *Dark Matter Magazine, Interzone (Digital), Flame Tree Press*, and a few Best of anthologies. When not writing, he works a specialist adviser for an international charity. You can find out more about him at his site: www.lpmelling.wordpress.com

SAM ROBB is a Pittsburgh native, former US Navy officer, and a teller of tales. A graduate of Carnegie Mellon University, he recently published his first collection of flash fiction, One October Night. In the course of his life, he has acquired a taste for long walks, urban photography, and martial arts - all of which have impacted his writing. His short stories have appeared in multiple anthologies including Supernatural Streets, Street Magic, and Pinup Noir. You can find more about Sam and his writing online at Amazon, or via samrobbwrites.com.

DANIEL ROMAN is a fantasy and science fiction writer who lives in the Adirondack region of upstate New York with his wife, cat, and a corgi/collie dog who reminds him that the occasional break to walk outside is a necessity. When not working on his own fiction, he serves as the associate editor of the WinterIsComing.net, a fansite which covers all things sci-fi and fantasy, as well as the co-host of the Take the Black podcast. Find him online at daniel-roman.com, @RomanWriting on Twitter/X, @romanwriting.bsky.social on Bluesky, and @danielromanbooks on Instagram and Facebook.

NIALL SPAIN is an Irish writer currently living in Toronto, Canada. He co-hosts the two multi award winning podcasts No Quest for the Wicked, and F*ck Buddies. His work has previously appeared in the Dragonesque anthology. When he's not writing you can find him climbing rocks, drinking craft beer, or cooking meals that are maybe a little too fancy. Find him over on twitter at: @niallspain

MIKE JACK STOUMBOS lives with his wife, parrot, and puppy in Virginia. He is best known for his space opera novel series *THIS FINE CREW* and as a 1st-place Writers of the Future winner (2022). Mike Jack is also the editor and illustrator of the *Murderbirds* and *Murderbugs* anthologies from WonderBird Press. His work has previously appeared in the ZNB collections Galactic Stew, Brave New Worlds, and Dragonesque among others that can be found at MikeJackStoumbos.com.

NATHAN W. TORONTO works to imagine a more peaceful world. He studies military education, strategy, and Middle East politics, and he has taught military officers for over twelve years. He is the author of *How Militaries Learn: Human Capital, Military Education, and Battlefield Effectiveness* and the Saga of the Emerald Moon, a military science fiction trilogy. He edits and publishes *Bullet Points*, a military science fiction magazine. Find him at nathantoronto.com or on Twitter

(@NathanToronto), Instagram (nathan.toronto), Blue Sky (@bulletpoints.bsky.social), and Mastodon (@toronto@wandering.shop).

Nebula nominated author **MARIE VIBBERT**'s short fiction has appeared in top magazines like Nature, Analog, and Clarkesworld, and been translated into Czech, Chinese and Vietnamese. Her debut novel, *Galactic Hellcats*, was long listed by the British Science Fiction Award and her work has been called "everything science fiction should be" by the Oxford Culture Review. She also writes poetry, comics, and computer games. By day she is a computer programmer in Cleveland, Ohio.

CAIAS WARD is a thick-wristed HVAC technician with over forty publication credits. A member of SFWA and Codex Writers, he currently lives with his wife and daughter in New Jersey, where he enjoys terrible movies and agitating for labor. Find him at @caias.bsky.social on Bluesky and @caias on Twitter.

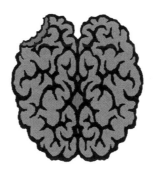

About the Editor

JOSHUA PALMATIER is a fantasy author with a PhD in mathematics. He currently teaches at SUNY Oneonta in upstate New York while writing in his "spare" time, editing anthologies, and running the anthology-producing small press Zombies Need Brains LLC. His most recent fantasy series, releasing Spring/Summer 2024 is called the "Crystal Cities" and includes *Crystal Lattice, Crystal Rebel,* and *Crystal War.* You can also find his "Throne of Amenkor" series, the "Well of Sorrows" series, and the "Ley" series still on the shelves. He is currently hard at work writing his next fantasy and designing the Kickstarter for the next Zombies Need Brains anthology projects. You can find out more at www.joshuapalmatier. com or at the small press' site www.zombiesneedbrains.com. Or follow him on Blue Sky at joshuapalmatier.bsky.social or on X as @bentateauthor or @ZNBLLC. And check out the Zombies Need Brains Patreon at www. patreon.com/zombiesneedbrains.

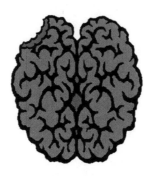

About the Artists

JUSTIN ADAMS is an artist who has worked in the genres of fantasy and science fiction over the past 20+ years. During his career he has contributed to numerous projects spanning video games, film, tabletop games and publishing. His clients have included Sony Entertainment, EA Games, Fantasy Flight Games, Upper Deck, Rebellion Books, Baen and of course Zombies Need Brains. When he's not doing art or tending to his beard, he likes to spend time racing motorcycles and hanging out with his kids.

KAT D'ANDREA is a scenic artist and preschool teacher living in upstate NY. She has enjoyed dabbling in art her whole life and is very excited to have the opportunity to illustrate short stories for this publication. She has been working in theatre for more than 30 years including being the resident scenic artist for KNOW Theatre for the last 16 years. Kat has been enjoying these new artistic opportunities and is looking forward to more in the future.

Resting on his laurels was all **ARIEL GUZMAN** ever wanted to do, but he keeps getting yanked back into the fray for "one last mission." He drew comic strips for his high-school and college campus newspapers, had a Gay Romance-themed webcomic included in Tim Fish's "Young Bottoms in Love" anthology, and is currently re-releasing his own "0-60" webcomic in all its low-res glory as a series of Instagram reels (@aruguz). He is delighted to be illustrating for ZNB Presents, believing it a fitting capstone to a storied career of reckless moonshots.

GREG UCHRIN is an artist and former self-appointed political pundit who actually did know better than everyone else, even if they didn't admit it. He has the rare honor of being considered too polically accurate and therefore censored by Google. His sizeable collection of political cartoons, published from 2003 through 2013, can be found at haildubyus.com and ivcaffeine.com. His artwork has appeared in the World Fantasy Con Uncoventional Fantasy Anthology and he has drawn multiple illustrations for the ZNB Presents online zine and the ZNB Presents Year 2 anthology. His current work is published at fb.com/ivcaffeine and will soon be available on greguchrin.com. He exhibits frequently at a varity of anime cons throughout the Eastern Seaboard, loves talking politics and humor with fans, and still regrets not following up with Stephen Colbert. Stephen – call me.

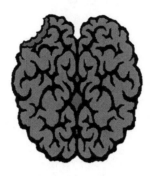

Acknowledgments

This anthology would not have been possible without the tremendous support of those who pledged during the Kickstarter and supported the Patreon. Everyone who contributed not only helped create this anthology, they also helped support the small press Zombies Need Brains LLC, which I hope will be bringing SF&F anthologies and the ZNB Presents magazine to the reading public for years to come. I want to thank each and every one of them for helping to bring this small dream into reality. Thank you, my zombie horde.

The Zombie Horde: Anthony R. Cardno, Kimberly M. Lowe, Jen1701D, Caryn Cameron, Dagmar Baumann, Jesse N. Klein, Iain E. Davis, Brenda Rezk, Luke Elliott, Kevin Troy Darling, KT Wagner, Maria Zaba, Mike S, G Patterson, Karen Carothers, L.C., Robert D. Stewart, Ruth Ann Orlansky, Elektra Hammond, John H. Bookwalter Jr., Kerry aka Trouble, Tania, Anne Burner, Michael Barbour, Robert Claney, Trip Space-Parasite, Mark Newman, Steven Byrd, Steve Pattee, Ardinzul, RKBookman, Beth Lobdell, Jeff Eppenbach, Chris McLaren, Caias Ward, Cat Girczyc, Michelle P., Yvonne R, jjmcgaffey, Gary Phillips, Brooks Moses, Rich 'Razmus' Weissler, Wulf Moon Enterprises, Dione Basseri, Steven Harper, Michael Ball, Michael Axe, Joanne B Burrows, Andy Tinkham, Andrew Hatchell, Scott Raun, Ryan C, Brendan Burke, Keith West, Future Potentate of the Solar System, justloux2, Brendan Lonehawk, Crysella, Craig Hackl,

Mary Jo Rabe, Richard Leis, Heidi Lambert, BrightFlame, Anonymous Reader, Vincent Darlage, PhD, Colleen Feeney, Jeremy Audet, Lizz Gable, Clarissa C. S. Ryan, Martin Greening, John Markley, Mark Carter, Richard O'Shea, J.R. Murdock, Kate Malloy, Ian Harvey, Jason Palmatier, Candice, Lorr, Brad Kicklighter, Juanita J Nesbitt, Tony Pi, Misty Massey, Hunter Alexander, William C. Tracy, David Perlmutter, Elaine McMillan, Bill Bibo Jr, Axisor and Firestar, Susan Oke, Margaret Killeen, Catherine Moore, R.J.H., Bryan Wetterow, Jessica Enfante, RJ Hopkinson, David Hankins, Robin, Jason Swensen, Caroline Westra, Nicholas Stephenson, Andrija Popovic, Jaq Greenspon, Gregory Ashe, R.J.K. Lee, Jamie M. Boyd, Mike Jack Stoumbos, Gabe Krabbe, Jacob Perez, Morrigen Stoumbos, Tasha Turner, Tris Lawrence, Bobbi Boyd, Janet Piele, Lynn K

Made in the USA
Columbia, SC
28 June 2024

37565937R00212